I0632863

Investigations
of the Future

also translated and introduced by Brian Stableford:

Anonymous: Sâr Dubnotal vs. Jack the Ripper; *Anthologies*: News from the Moon; The Germans on Venus; The Supreme Progress; The World Above the World; Nemoville; Investigations of the Future; *Allorge*: The Great Cataclysm; *Asselineau*: The Double Life; *Bérard*: The Vampire Lord Ruthwen; *Bessière*: The Gardens of the Apocalypse; *Bleunard*: Ever Smaller; *Bodin*: The Novel of the Future; *Brown*: City of Glass; *Caroff*: The Terror of Madame Atomos; *Champsaur*: The Human Arrow; *Derennes*: The People of the Pole; *Driou*: The Adventures of a Parisian Aeronaut; *Dunan*: Baal; *Duvernois*: The Man Who Found Himself; *Eyraud*: Voyage to Venus; *Falk*: The Age of Lead; *Féval*: Anne of the Isles; The Black Coats ('Salem Street; The Invisible Weapon; The Parisian Jungle; The Companions of the Treasure; Heart of Steel; The Cadet Gang; The Sword-Swallower); John Devil; Knightshade; Revenants; Vampire City; The Vampire Countess; The Wandering Jew's Daughter; *Féval, fils*: Felifax, the Tiger-Man; *Haraucourt*: Illusions of Immortality; *Kahn*: The Tale of Gold and Silence; *La Hire*: The Nyctalope vs. Lucifer; The Nyctalope on Mars; Enter the Nyctalope; *Lamothe-Langon*: The Virgin Vampire; *de Lautrec*: The Vengeance of the Oval Portrait; *Le Faure & de Graffigny*: The Extraordinary Adventures of a Russian Scientist Across the Solar System; *Le Rouge*: The Vampires of Mars; The Dominion of the World (w/*Guitton*); *Lermina*: Panic in Paris; Mysteryville; The Secret of Zippelius; *Méry*: The Tower of Destiny; *Mettais*: The Year 5865; *Moselli*: Illa's End; *Nizet*: Captain Vampire; *de Parville*: An Inhabitant of the Planet Mars; *de Pawlowski*: Journey to the Land of the 4th Dimension; *Pellerin*: The World in 2000 Years; *Ponson du Terrail*: The Vampire and the Devil's Son; *de Régnier*: A Surfeit of Mirrors; *Renard*: The Blue Peril; Doctor Lerne; The Doctored Man; A Man Among the Microbes; The Master of Light; *Richepin*: The Wing; *Robida*: The Clock of the Centuries; The Adventures of Saturnin Farandoul; Chalet in the Sky; *Rosny Aîné*: The Givreuse Enigma; The Mysterious Force; The Navigators of Space; Vamireh; The World of the Variants; The Young Vampire; *Rouff*: Journey to the Inverted World; *Ryner*: The Superhumans; *Spitz:* The Eye of Purgatory; *Steiner*: Ortog; *Tiphaigne de la Roche*: Amilec; *Varlet*: The Xenobiotic Invasion; Timeslip Troopers (w/*Blandin*); The Martian Epic (w/*Joncquel*); *Vibert*: The Mysterious Fluid; *Villiers de l'Isle-Adam*: The Scaffold; The Vampire Soul; *Ward & Miller*: The Song of Montségur.

Investigations
of the Future

translated, annotated and introduced by
Brian Stableford

A Black Coat Press Book

English adaptation and introduction Copyright © 2012 by
Brian Stableford.
Cover illustration Copyright © 2012 by Mandy.

Visit our website at www.blackcoatpress.com

ISBN 978-1-61227-106-4. First Printing. August 2012. Published by Black Coat Press, an imprint of Hollywood Com-
ics.com, LLC, P.O. Box 17270, Encino, CA 91416. All rights
reserved. Except for review purposes, no part of this book may
be reproduced or transmitted in any form or by any means,
electronic or mechanical, including photocopying, recording,
or by any information storage and retrieval system, without
permission in writing from the publisher. The stories and
characters depicted in this novel are entirely fictional. Printed
in the United States of America.

TABLE OF CONTENTS

Introduction

In his prospectus for *Le Roman de l'avenir* (1834)[1] Félix Bodin argued that early futuristic fiction had consisted exclusively of utopias or apocalypses: designs for hypothetical ideal societies that used the future as a convenient imaginative frame or religiously-inspired visions of the end of the world. He suggested that it was both inevitable and desirable that a different kind of futuristic fiction would eventually develop, in which the future would be described in a manner more akin to the way that Walter Scott had set fiction in various eras of the past, thus producing a kind of fiction that might seem to *belong* to the future, as if it were contemporary fiction written at a future date.

When he wrote that prescription, Bodin was probably only vaguely aware of the difficult of the task he was proposing, but he must have been much more sharply aware of it by the time he had attempted, as any brave man would, to practice what he preached; the bulk of *Le Roman de l'avenir* consists of a fragment of exactly such a novel, which was eventually abandoned, at least in part because it was failing miserably to live up to his manifesto, being drastically corrupted by utopianism, shaping up as if its denouement were going to be an apocalypse of sorts, and quite unable to achieve any trace of apparent narrative realism.

Almost three generations later, Anatole France, in *Sur la pierre blanche* (1905; tr. as *The White Stone*), observed that, with only one conspicuous exception, writers of futuristic fiction had used the future merely as a canvas on which to paint their hopes and fears, and that it was only very recently that anyone had set out to explore its possibilities with an open

---

[1] tr. in a Black Coat Press edition as *The Novel of the Future*, ISBN 978-1-934543-44-3.

and curious mind. The exception he cited was H. G. Wells—rather ironically, as Wells, after a brief exploratory period, had already stopped doing that and had begun to focus as narrowly on his hopes and fears as anyone else. France was, however, correct; by 1905, it was possible for writers of imaginative fiction to examine future possibilities in a distinctly different way, viewing them as a fan-like spectrum generated by ongoing developments in science and society and making judgments of desirability secondary to questions of rational plausibility. Fiction of the kind envisaged by Bodin was at last becoming feasible.

It was, in fact, possible by 1905 for a writer tacitly to adopt the stance of an investigative reporter, interrogating the future in terms of endeavors that people might attempt to undertake with more or less success, according to the degree to which science and technology could support their projects. That was, in fact, what the playwright and dramatic theorist Jean Jullien pretended to do explicitly in *Enquête sur le monde futur* (1909) and here translated as "An Investigation of the World of the Future," in which the author poses as a reporter dispatched to America to interview the men whose projects and discoveries are in the process of laying the foundations for the future development and transformation of human society. If Anatole France read the book in question, he would probably have dismissed it as a relatively insignificant text because it does not take its quest very seriously, offering a series of sarcastic fantasies that eventually takes care to undermine its own dubious authority comprehensively, but if one looks at it in the contexts of previous attempts to explore the future with attitudes that have something in common Bodin's proposal, it can easily be seen that it reproduces and extrapolates features typical of many, if not all of them—most particularly its convoluted rhetorical strategy—and is more significant than a casual glance at its frothy surface might suggest.

Classic rhetorical analysis divides strategies of persuasion into three: *ethos*, *pathos* and *logos* (which one might be tempted to describe as the three musketeers of oratory had

Alexandre Dumas not broken the apparent pattern in naming Aramis). *Logos* refers to the logical and factual substance of an argument, while *pathos* refers to appeals to emotion— attempts to "push the buttons" of the hearers or readers, thus exciting indignation, compassion etc. *Ethos* refers to the manner in which speakers or writers attempt to establish their own credentials entitling them to the trust of hearers or readers, including the establishment of their own moral and political stance. Any argument inevitably involves all three components, but they vary considerably in the manner of their deployment.

Logos—the heart and soul of any argument, although its routine mistreatment and occasional cunning clouding by *ethos* and *pathos* is what got rhetoric a bad name in post-Socratic philosophy—is awkwardly problematic in any exploration of the future, because we have no way of knowing what the future might actually bring, and can only base our speculations of hypothetical arguments of an essentially dodgy nature. Given that attempts to calculate future possibilities and then to alter the balance of apparent probabilities are the basis of all rational behavior, however, the difficulty of weighing up such possibilities ought not to be construed as a prohibition—which is the principal reason why utopias and apocalypses seem attractive as imaginative projects. If, however, one attempts an investigation of investigations of the future, especially those undertaken with something of the spirit of Bodin's prospectus, what is most striking about them, and arguably most interesting, is not the inevitable dubiousness of their *logos*, but the extraordinary contortion of their *ethos*.

As Jean Jullien was obviously aware in planning *Enquête sur le monde futur*, there was something of a tradition, imported to France from America, of newspaper "hoaxes," in which fictitious reportage would present series of fanciful inventions. The most famous of all was the "moon hoax" perpetrated by the *New York Sun* in 1835, which offered a series of supposed telescopic discoveries made by the astronomer John Herschel about life on the moon, which became gradually more extravagant as the series progressed, ultimately extending into the realm of the absurd. Reproduction of the moon hoax stories in European newspapers caused a sensation, and gave rise to numerous parodies, including four by Joseph Méry (tr. as "The Lunarians" in *The Tower of Destiny*).[2] The most notable French example was a series of articles in *Le Pays* in 1864 reporting on the alleged discovery of a Martian mummy enclosed in a meteorite buried in the rocks of Colorado and the proceedings of the scientific commission appointed to examine it, which turned out to have been written by Henri de Parville and was reprinted in book form as *Un Habitant de la planète Mars* (1865)[3].

These two endeavors not only helped to establish that the press was the ideal medium for the continuation of the great tradition of "tall stories" that had always been inherent in oral discourse and had taken advantage of the apparent authority of the written word to insert some of its most outrageous examples into scripture and history, but also demonstrated that fake reportage was a useful medium for speculative fiction. Parville, in particular, wanted to exploit the possibility of a "double bluff" in practicing a kind of reverse psychology. His serial was a hoax in the sense that it was a lie pretending to be true, but the lie was a convenient vehicle for raising and exploring serious questions of possibility relating to the nature of the universe, the distribution of life within it and the relationships between Earth and other worlds. There is, of course, a popular saying which holds that "there's many a true word spoken in jest," and that refers not merely to accidental instances but to a deliberate rhetorical strategy by means of which serious allegations are disguised as jokes, often in order to give the speaker or hearer "potential deniability" if accused of insult, slander, dishonesty or insanity.

---

[2] available from Black Coat Press, ISBN 978-1-61227-101-9.
[3] tr. in a Black Coat Press edition as *An Inhabitant of the Planet Mars,* ISBN 978-1-934543-45-0.

The relevance of these observations to Bodin's prospectus for a new literature of the future is that—as he discovered himself—one cannot simply sit down and launch such a tradition from scratch. While the very idea of setting the future seemed so unusual as to be absurd in itself, the rhetoric of such fictions was problematic, and the fact that there was an existing tradition of apocalyptic visions, which saw the future in terms of a fixed, divinely determined destiny was not a help but a hindrance. The futuristic utopias to which Bodin also called attention were a relatively recent development in 1834, having been pioneered by Louis-Sébastien Mercier in *L'An deux mille quatre cent quarante* (1771; tr. as *Memoirs of the Year Two Thousand Five Hundred*) only half a century before—previous utopian designs having been located for narrative purposes in remote locations of the globe—but they too were no help, especially in France, whether the trivial noun *utopie* was widely used to mean something inherently impossible and hopelessly naïve.

The simple fact was that, in the beginning, exploratory fiction about the future required some kind of apologetic strategy, and the most attractive one available was the kind of double bluff inherent in newspaper hoaxes, which loudly proclaimed their non-seriousness in order to create the imaginative space necessary to raise questions and examine ideas that could, in fact, be as serious as the author cared to make them. Because newspaper hoaxes posed as contemporary reportage, however, they could not be straightforwardly adapted to futuristic fiction. The most fundamental problem of narrative strategy involved in constructing hypothetical futures was, in fact, the problem of narrative access, which was initially limited to visionary experience—a means of access that carried an inevitably stigma of implausibility.

This problem of access not only compelled a strategy of apologetic non-seriousness in the *ethos* component of futuristic fiction explicitly represented as visions, but those which attempted to by-pass that artifice. Bodin must have written the bulk of *Le Roman de l'avenir* some time before its publication date or else he would certainly have called attention to the fact that his friend Charles Nodier, perhaps partly under his influence, had published two futuristic stories in the *Revue de Paris* in 1833 that disposed of any such frame—"Hurlubleu" and "Leviathan Long" (combined in translation as "Perfectibility")[4]—but the consequence of that highly unusual innovation was that Nodier had to strive even harder to establish that he was joking.

Over time, the necessity of that apologetic strategy diminished, partly because the more it was practiced, the more familiar and less bizarre the idea of narratives set in the future became. A crucial literary watershed was reached in the late 1880s, when H. G. Wells, in order to facilitate the endeavors of his brief exploratory phase, invented a time machine for the use of "The Chronic Argonauts" (1889; revised as *The Time Machine*, 1895): a facilitating device that could shift a narrative viewpoint into the future "bodily," in such a way as seemingly to evade the inherent unreliability of visionary experience. Relatively few subsequent narrative excursions into the future employed an explicit time machine, but the device itself became unnecessary almost as soon as it was invented, having done the essential work of establishing that the future could be regarded as a habitable narrative space, into which a writer could stop without having to issue a preliminary potential defense of sanity, effectively denying ridiculousness by admitting it. On the way to that watershed, however, and in the years that followed it, there was unsteady process of evolution, illustrated by the sequence of stories reproduced in this anthology.

Théophile Gautier's "Paris futur," first published in *Le Pays* in December 1851 and reprinted in 1852 in *Caprices et zigzags*, here translated as "Future Paris," was not the first essay-cum-fiction to bear that title, as Gautier's friend Joseph Méry had published one several years earlier, but Méry's was

---

[4] included in the Black Coat Press edition of T*he Germans on Venus*, ISBN 978-1-934543-56-6

far less interesting, and is best seen as a tentative preliminary to two far more extravagant adventures in futuristic fiction, "Ce qu'on verra" and "Les Ruines de Paris" (tr. as "What We Shall See" and "The Ruins of Paris" in *The Tower of Destiny*), both dating from the mid-1840s. Gautier's piece was, however, the direct inspiration of Arsène Houssaye's "Paris futur" (1856; revised 1889 as "En 3789"), with appeared in a collection of essays to which Gautier was also a contributor, and probably of Victor Fournel's "Paris futur" (1865), although the latter also had the more proximal inspiration of Baron Haussmann's remodeling of the city of Paris during the latter days of the Second Empire. The side-branch of the sequence begun by Méry's "Les Ruines de Paris" eventually became prolific in its own right, provoking Alfred Bonnardot's "Archaeopolis" (1857; tr. in *Nemoville*),[5] which in turn provoked Alfred Franklin's *Les Ruines de Paris en 4875* (1875), here translated as "The Ruins of Paris in 4875").

The rhetorical strategies of the earlier items in this group of stories is relatively straightforward, although Gautier's shows the relative sophistication one would expect of a writer of his genius, but Franklin's, extrapolating and capitalizing on the extra twists introduced by Méry and Bonnardot, is noticeably more convoluted in its exploitation of the moral and political stance adopted by the various signatories of the letters sent by the explorers of ruined Paris to their base in New Caledonia. The essence of the joke is that those notional narrators are in earnest, although the true narrator, Franklin, is a committed satirist who expects his readers to see the unstated truth shadowing their errors. The story deliberately opens up a considerable "distance of stance" between the actual and notional narrators, and it is the reader's appreciation of the width and depth of the gap in question that gives the work its particular appeal. The strategy is in some ways demanding, requiring the reader to keep in mind two distinct narrative threads—that of

---

[5] available in a Black Coat press edition, ISBN 978-1-61227-070-8.

the story's surface and that of its buried core—as well as to draw inferences from hints of varying delicacy, but it is correspondingly rewarding, augmenting the conventional double bluff of the humoristic contemplation of the future in such a way that it become, in effect, a triple bluff.

It would be overstating the case to say that such triple bluffs eventually became routine; they remained an exception rather than the rule—but Maurice Spronck's *L'An 330 de la République*, first published in 1894, deserves special attention as a work that makes particularly clever and telling use of that kind of "ethical distance," carefully and seductively varying its width and depth to considerable effect. The variance in this case makes the story's underlying rhetorical strategy even more convoluted than Franklin's or Jullien's; the latter attempts a similar effect, but suffers slightly from its fragmentary nature, thus being unable to contrive the kind of crescendo effect that Spronck develops so forcefully. It is Spronck rather than Franklin or Jullien who contrives most effectively to manipulate *ethos* into *pathos*, producing a truly remarkable work. H. G. Wells probably did not read it, but must surely have heard a report of its crucial arguments, because the Utopian design set out in *A Modern Utopia* (1905) seems specifically designed to counter and neutralize the deadliest of Spronck's sly but devastating criticisms of socialist utopianism.

In presenting this sequence as an example of the slow progress made by literary attempts to follow the broad philosophical lines of Bodin's prospectus, it must not be forgotten that the literary endeavors that such attempts were supposed to supersede did not and could not disappear, and were not entirely absorbed into it. Utopianism and apocalyptic writing survived in their pure forms as well as becoming components of a more generalized futuristic literature. I thought it worthwhile, in presenting this "evolutionary sequence" to illustrate by contrast the very different rhetorical strategy associated with one of those other literary strands, so I have added as an appendix *La Vision d'Hébal* (1834; here translated as "Hebal's

Vision") by the philosophical historian and Academician Pierre-Simon Ballanche, who spent his entire life laboring on a comprehensive account of human history as an alleged reflection of cosmic history, embodying the principle of "palingenesis." He never finished it, of course, and hardly started, because the task was simply too large, but he did publish this summary vision of it—supposedly extracted from the incomplete third volume of the project, *La Ville des expiations* [The City of Expiation]—which remains a pure apocalypse in spite of its infection by scientific ideas and the author's attempts to adopt Catholic dogma to a philosophical frame that cannot logically accommodate it.

"Palingenesis," which, in its most general sense, means regeneration, is a term that eventually came to have a more specific relevance in the context of 19th century French speculative fiction when the notion of "cosmic palingenesis"—serial reincarnation on different planets scattered throughout the universe—was popularized by Camille Flammarion, but the devout Ballanche would have been far more familiar with its appropriation by theologians to dignify Christian baptism, and it was from that starting point that he developed his own eccentric notion of the history of the human race as a series of regenerative ordeals imposed by virtue of the Fall, in which the vicissitudes of individual life not only mirror the iterative emergence and collapse of civilizations and cultures but the entire story of Creation.

The merest glance at *La Vision d'Hébal* is sufficient to illustrate the differences of its rhetorical strategy from those of the other authors featured in the anthology, which are even more obvious in its *ethos* than it *logos*, but it is worth noting that it is driven by the same perceived need for apology, which Ballanche feels far more keenly than Gautier *et al.* simply because the very last thing he wants to be taken for is a joker. He is ardently desirous of importing the whole force of revelation into his arguments, and must therefore employ a very different argument to support his employment of the visionary method, and there is a certain irony in the fact that the rhetorical weapons he takes up in order to do that are, if one looks through the *ethos* and the *pathos*, logically fatal to his case. One suspects, considering the excess of his protestations, that he knew that only too well. There is no doubt, however, that he got carried away by the surge of his own rhetoric, to the point of becoming the only devout apocalypse-monger in history who almost contrived to forget that, when the Day of Judgment comes, it is us, not God, who are supposed to be in the dock.

There is a certain unfairness in comparing Ballanche's futuristic fiction with the other works included here, the distinction between them being greater than that between chalk and cheese, let alone apples and pears, but it is, nevertheless, worth raising the question of which one of them is most perspicacious, not in the relatively trivial matter of anticipating future developments in the human condition, but in analyzing that condition fruitfully and accurately. Ballanche's assessment of our ordeals is in deadly earnest, while his rivals' are flippantly farcical (and, in Jullien's case, a trifle risqué), but in the quest to represent existential experience and recommend an appropriate ethical stance in respect of it, Ballanche is not merely an also ran but finishes last by a distance. That is the whole point of attempting to follow Bodin's prospectus, no matter what difficulties are involved in doing so.

The following translation of Théophile Gautier's "Paris futur" was taken from the Google Books version of the third edition of the collection *Caprices et Zigzags* published by Hachette in 1865. The translation of Arsène Houssaye's "Paris futur" was taken from the Google Books version of the anthology *Paris et les parisiens au XIXe siècle* by Alexandre Dumas, Théophile Gautier, Arsène Houssaye et al. published by Morizot in 1856 and the *gallica* version of the 25 août 1889 issue of *La Grande Revue. Paris et Saint-Pétersbourg*. The translation of Victor Fournel's "Paris futur" was taken from the Google Books version of *Paris nouveau et Paris futur* published by Jacques Lecoffre in 1865. The translation of

Alfred Franklin's *Les Ruines de Paris en 4875* was taken from the *gallica* version of the book published by Léon Willem in 1875. The translation of Maurice Spronck's *L'An 330 de la République* was taken from the *gallica* version of the book published by Léon Chailley in 1894. The translation of Jean Jullien's *Enquête sur le monde futur* was taken from the *gallica* version of the book published by Bibliothèque Charpentier in 1909. The translation of *La Vision d'Hébal, chef d'un clan écosssais, tiré de La Ville des expiations* was taken from the Google Books version of the book published by Jules Didot aîné in 1834.

Brian Stableford

Théophile Gautier: *Future Paris*
(1851)

Paris is infinitely self-obsessed; it regards itself, with the greatest naivety, as the center, the eye and the navel of the universe. It scarcely admits that anything exists outside of itself. It knows, vaguely, that there is a little dot on maps, which the English call London, on the edge of a thin twisted thread that the English call the Thames, but it does not worry about that, and calmly awards itself the crown of civilization. Give a pure-blooded Parisian a square of vellum, a pen and colors, and say to him: "Make me a sketch of the map of the world!" and he will do it like a citizen of the Celestial Empire; Paris will take up almost all the available space, and the other kingdoms, drowned in semi-darkness, will only figure as memoranda, like those unknown or unexplored countries that geographers indicate by dotted lines.

That comes from one thing: that Paris, like the good bourgeois it is, never goes out of the house, or, if it does go out, hardly ever goes beyond the fortifications. Versailles is its Timbuktu. To which you will reply that if Paris never goes out, it is because it is perfectly comfortable at home. The objection is specious, although it is not unjustified. Paris, intoxicated with itself, always has its nose pressed up against a mirror, like a myopic person shaving, with the idea of making his portrait more attractive. How many publications in prose, verse, engraving and lithography has Paris not produced, in order that no feature of its precious physiognomy should be lost?

It is a pity that paradox—the green fruit that, ripened by time, can become the truth!—has gone out of fashion; we shall develop one that, although seeming strange at first glance, is no less veracious. It is that Paris does not exist.

We know full well that by searching, one will find on the banks of the Seine a few small heaps of plaster that, strictly speaking, form alleyways of a sort, whose aggregation might, if necessary, constitute what ne generally has the habit of calling a city. Piganiol, Sainte-Foix, Dulaure and many others have compiled the history of that pretentious rubble in approximately-quarto volumes,[6] but histories do not prove anything; only fairy tales are true.

What impure candles, what hunchbacked, gummed-up, surly, unhealthy, counterfeit houses covered in leprosies and warts, devoid of air, devoid of light and devoid of sunshine, unworthy of being inhabited by rabbits or pigs! The kraals of Hottentots, which one enters on all fours, the caves of Troglodytes, and the huts of Laplanders and Greenlanders, half buried in the snow, jaundiced by a perpetual smoke of half-rotten fish, are pleasant places by comparison! Three out of four streets are no more than gutters of black mud, as in the times of the frankest barbarity. No trace of art, no elegance, no sense of alignment; plaster boxes pierces by square holes, surmounted by frightful metal chimneys—those is what are known as nineteenth-century houses, in a city that claims to be the modern Athens, the queen of civilization! Truly, one is tempted to desire that some Nero might take it into his head to offer himself a representation of the burning of Troy by setting fire to the city, which is made of bricks and ought to be made of marble!

Talk to me about Nineveh and Babylon! They deserve to be called cities; they raise a commendable profile on the horizon for you. But in those days, constitutional government had not been invented; gunpowder, printing and steam were unknown; no one held forth on the subject of progress.

---

[6] Jean-Aymar Piganiol de La Force (1673-1753), Germain-François Poullain de Saint-Foix (1698-1776) and Jacques-Antoine Dulaure (1755-1835) all wrote classic works on the history of Paris.

Often, when I stroll in some somber plain at dusk, and the livid horizon is cluttered by great banks of cloud, heaped on top of one another like the blocks of an immense aerial city fallen into ruins, Babylonian dreams come to me, and phantasmagorias in the style of Martin[7] pass before my eyes.

I begin by carving gigantic trenches out of the flanks of distant hills for the foundations of edifices; soon, the angles of frontons are sketched in the vapor; pyramids cut out their marble faces; obelisks rise up in a single jet, like granite exclamation marks; immeasurable palaces are elevated in superimpositions of retreating terraces like a colossal staircase, which only giants of the pre-Adamite world could climb.

I see stout columns extending, as strong as towers, fluted with spiral grooves in which six men could hide, friezes made of sections of mountains and covered with monstrous zodiacs and menacing hieroglyphs; the arches of bridges curving over a river that gleams throughout the city it traverses like a Damascene sword in a half-cut pass; lakes of salt water in which domesticated leviathans leap, shining in a radiant light, and the great golden circle of Ozymandias sparkling like a wheel detached from the chariot of the sun.

Bathed at its base in the ardent russet mist thrown up by the restless activity of the city, seething with work of pleasure, the temple of Belus[8] invades the sky, where it will challenges

---

[7] The reference is to John Martin (1789-1854) who became famous for vast paintings of Biblical and mythological scenes unparalleled in their mystic grandeur, such as the *The Fall of Babylon* (1818). Gautier spells the name Martinn, by virtue of a minor stylistic quirk that also affects a handful of other names cited in the story. Although it is arguable that I ought to have retained the quirk by reproducing the names as the author gives them, I have usually substituted the more familiar spellings in order to facilitate the reader's understanding.

[8] Belus is one of many possible renderings of the name of the Babylonian god Bel or Baal, to whom classical and scriptural references are numerous, but Gautier is undoubtedly thinking

---

the lightning, by means of eight convulsive efforts, each of which produces an enormous tower taller than the steeple of Strasbourg or the pyramid of Giza; the cloud cut its sides with their stripes and the entablatures of the final stage are blanched by threads of eternal snow.

Other temples are also inscribe their severe and magnificent forms on the horizon, whose grandeur only serves to make the enormity of the temple of Belus stand out more sharply; and in the background, in the incandescent redness of the sunset, one divines the dismantled silhouette of Lylac,[9] the colossus of pride, the walls of which the Ancient of Days has caused to crack by setting his hand on its summit as on an excessively weak staff. The flames of the evening filter through the cracks, through which behemoths and mastodons pass without brushing their carapaces, and create the most bizarre plays of light; one might think that a conflagration were trying to devour the formidable ruin that the wrath of God has not entirely cast down, and whose summit still rises above the waters of a new Deluge.

Here and there, the black chaos of buildings lights up; basalt sphinxes display their hindquarters and stretch out their claws on granite pedestals, forming an avenue a league long at the door of some palace. Above the rooftops, in the midst of the crowns of palm trees and baobabs, surges the trunk of a bronze elephant, blowing a jet of water into the air, which the

---

of a legend said by secondary sources to have been recorded in a book by Artabanus, in which Belus was a member of a race of Titans who escaped their destruction by the gods and built a tower in which to reside in the city that became Babylon.

[9] Gautier also refers to a place called Lylac in a book about travels in Spain, where he couples it with the tower of Babel, but I cannot find any such reference outside his work; I suspect that it is his own humorous invention; several species of the shrub lilac (*Syringa*) have common names including the word "pride" (e.g. Pride of Moscow), thus licensing his symbolic association.

wind scatters into fine pearls and silvery mist. Ramps go up and down, tracing angles on the flanks of terraces; the prows of ships, the tips of masts and antennae betray the presence of canals; staircase-streets bring daylight into the crowd of edifices, and in the distance, according to the hazards of perspective, the girdling walls appear, creating a roadway three hundred meters from the ground, in with six or eight teams of four might gallop abreast.

That, at least, bears some resemblance to a city, and stands out jaggedly against the background of the sky. Cause the shadows of passing clouds to soar over it, in order that the scene might be complete, like prodigious black eagles; strike with unexpected gleams the formicary of the multitudes that crowd the squares, the crossroads and the external doorways; cause caravans to unfurl in the plains of sand, like the coils of infinite serpents, laden with the treasures of all the worlds, and enthrone, in the center of the grandiose city, a king as powerful as a God, as feared as a God, and invisible as a God, by the name of Tiglath-Pileser, Merodach-Baladan or Belshazzar,[10] who, by his enormities, will force the Eternal to write on his walls!

A city like that plunges as far into the ground as it rises into the air; its roots go in search of the nucleus of the world and only stop when they arrive at the surfaces of interior lakes or the furnace of the central fire. Beneath the living city extends the dead city, the black city of motionless inhabitants. Broad ventilation-shafts, gaping like the mouths of Hell, lead to the region of crypts and syringes.[11] Funereal tribes labor in the vomitory cities, tribes of gravediggers, the slaves of death;

---

[10] I have altered all three of these names to correspond with the usual names of the kings of Assyria and Babylon to whom they obviously refer, although the fact that Gautier renders the third as Balthazar, more usually attached to one of the Biblical Magi, my be an intentional double meaning.

[11] The term syrinx, of which syringes is the plural, refers in this context to a kind of Egyptian tomb hollowed out of rock.

those who melt the natrum and the bitumen in boilers; those who weave the mortuary bandages; the coffin-makers, the painters, the gilders and the sculptors of tombs—all those whose works will never see the light of day, and who trace inscriptions by the yellow light of a lamp that lacks air that are immediately covered by shadow and will only ever be read by sightless eyes.

That crepuscular population, which has no communication with the upper city except for the corpses that it receives, could fill a city larger than Rome; they are born, they marry and they die in that obscurity. There are vanquished nations there, forced to re-enter the earth and cede their place in the sun to the victorious people; the necropolis whose threshold they inhabit is the work of vanished races, and its immensity frightens even the most audacious Babylonian architects.

There are interminable corridors, all lined with panels of hieroglyphs and cosmogonic bas-reliefs, leading to pits as black as the abyss and as profound, into which one descends by means of bronze crampons. There are chambers hollowed out of the living rock, the center of which is occupied by enormous sarcophagi of basalt and porphyry, without anyone being able to comprehend how they were brought here; rooms in which torches cannot illuminate the depths, where entire cycles of generations, complete reigns with their princes, their mages, their poets, their soldiers, their horses and their war-elephants sleep, with their backs to columns sustaining ceilings that one cannot see, so high are they.

The further one descends, the more the mummies take on gigantic proportions and strange physiognomies. Under the pale brown of balm unknown profiles are designed, with features as if carved with blows of a hatchet in blocks of stone; faces reminiscent of the muzzles of primitive animals; foreheads in which the wrinkles seem to be streaks of lightning or the beds of torrents; unvanquished limbs that corruption dares not attack, and the muscles of which are tangled like the beams of a scaffold. One can see there the companions of Nimrod, primitive hunters who drew bows made from the

24

jawbones of whales, and fought hand-to-hand with mastodons, the paleotherium, the dinotherium and all those colossal and monstrous beasts produced by an earth intoxicated by strength and youth, which, if they had lived, would have ended up devouring the world.

The contemporaries of Chronos and Xixuthros[12] repose in the inferior circles into which no one ever descends, because it requires lungs more powerful than those of present generations to tolerate the air, impregnated with the bitter perfumes of the sepulcher. The secrets that envelop those mysterious tombs are lost, or only known to the old men of the subterranean people, so laden down with years that no one any longer understands heir archaic language. Below them are couched the kings who lived before Adam, but the crust of the earth has thickened so much since their death that they lie at an incalculable depth, and it is as if they had become the bones of the world.

Is that not a necropolis superior to Père-Lachaise, the cemetery of Montmartre, etc., etc?—where we cannot leave our dead to sleep peacefully for more than seven years, where the phrase *concession à perpetuité* is a true derision and signifies no more than the "always" of lovers;[13] where the tombs

---

[12] Chronos is a common misrendering of Cronus, the name of the leader of the Titans who rebelled against his father Uranus but was eventually overthrown by his own son Zeus. Classical descriptions typically show him carrying the scythe or sickle that he used to castrate Uranus—an image transferred to that of "Father Time" by virtue of the phonetic misunderstanding that linked his name with *chronos*, [time]. Xixuthros is a Hellenization of the name of the Sumerian king Zuisudra, who was said to have ruled immediately before the Deluge and to have survived it, much as Noah did in Hebrew mythology.

[13] Paris developed an acute shortage of graveyard space in the 18th century, which eventually led to the remains they contained being dug up and removed to ossuaries in the catacombs in order to make way for new graves. Famous people

are veritable playthings devoid of sadness, dignity and grandeur, and which give rise to the belief that a population of dwarfs is interred there, so meager are their proportions and so miserly the space allotted to them. But we have no greater understanding of death than of life, and, under the pretext of progress, we shall soon have gone back four or five thousand years. The imprint of Adam's foot, which can still be seen in the rock of the isle of Serendip, is nine handbreadths long! We have degenerated somewhat since.

Enormous as the ancient world was, however, and no matter to what depth we have lowered what we call civilization, there will be the means—and the future will doubtless make use of them—to build a greater city, more beautiful and more exotic than Babylon, Nineveh and Persepolis: to surpass, in reality, the most frenzied audacities and the most extravagant deliria of Piranesi and Martin; and, if you will permit, we shall try to sketch it out for you.

For an initial assumption, permit us to pass a steam-roller over present-day Paris, which will crush its houses and its monuments and make it a perfectly uniform plateau; then we shall broaden the Seine, hollow out its bed and bring the Ocean to our threshold. Any city that cannot take a foot-bath in the sea is unworthy of the name. Ships impregnated with the perfumes of India and Java will come, like weary horses that nonchalantly lean their necks on the necks of their companions in harness, to support their bowsprits and sculpted prows on the granite quays of future Paris, From the present location of the Pont Royal one will see a host of masts, rigging and crossbeams more complex than a virgin forest in America; one will see entire fleets arriving and departing with sails unfurled or towed by steamboats: all the movement of the most active seaport.

---

sometimes obtained a "concession of perpetuity" for their tombs, but prestige is fleeting in a society continually overturned by revolutions, so many such concessions were subsequently overturned.

There will only be a single church, which will occupy the location of the Panthéon. It will be consecrated to the Divinity. That unique church will have immeasurable proportions; the entire Latin mountain, carved into steps, will serve as its staircase. Its towers and cupolas will make such a profound dent in the border of the sky that the stars will bloom like golden acanthus flowers on the capitals of the upper floor. Notre-Dame would be able to enter throughout the giant porch without ducking her head.

In that hybrid temple, all the architectures of the past, present and future will be concentrated: one will find there, in the most knowledgeable forms, the granitic vertigos of Ellora and Karnak, the desperate aspirations of the ogives of the cathedral of Seville; the Gothic spire, the Byzantine cupola and the Oriental minaret will form harmonious chords in that symphony of stone, sung to God by an entire people. The myths of Genesis, the allegories of the fall and the redemption, the remuneration of good and the punishment of sins, the symbols of the celestial powers, executed in mosaic, will cover the walls in warm and rich hues. Gold will scintillate on the interior walls with a profusion worthy of the Incas; a population of statues will animate the friezes, the niches, the inter-columnar intervals and the scroll-work of doorways.

Instead of bells, whose bronze capsules only produce a lugubrious and monotonous psalmody, towers of immense organs will be established, with pipes as long as the column in the Place Vendôme, whose bellows will be activated by eight-hundred-horse-power steam engines. Religious music, expressly composed, will be played at different hours of the day, and whirlwinds of harmony will pass over the city, dominating all its rumors and reminding the distracted crowd of the idea of God. Inside the temple, vaults disposed according to the laws of acoustics will give a marvelous sonority to the sacred canticles; the preacher, from the height of his giant pulpit, aided by telephone, will exhale the divine breath like one of those great angels with clarions whom painters depict in Last Judgments, as if from the edge of a cloud.

Although Gothic cathedrals are beautiful, it is permissible to believe that an edifice summarizing the three hundred churches of Paris in one would offer the eyes a silhouette even bolder and more surprising. The unity of God will be more clearly manifest in the unity of the temple, and his omnipotence in the formidable mass of the ensemble. You might raise the objection of the distance that many of the faithful would find themselves living from the house of the Lord, but future means of locomotion will be improved to such a degree that what seems to us to be a long distance today will be devoured with a rapidity scarcely appreciable by thought!

Now that God is comfortably lodged, let us occupy ourselves with the nation's elected leader. We will establish on the Butte Montmartre, which will be broken up under enormous pressure and which, heaped up for that purpose, will serve admirably as filling-material for terraces and supportive structures. Glasshouses, orangeries, stables and other outbuildings will occupy the first step that pyramid of constructions, whose bottom layer will begin at the present location of the church of Notre-Dame-de-Lorette. Terraces linked to one another by gentle slopes will support palaces and colonnades, from the center of which will spring other palaces, less vast, until one arrives at the summit of the edifice, at the mysterious and splendid sanctuary of the leader's tower, a unique chamber lined with sheets of gold constellated with gems and ornamented—more expensively still—with the most beautiful paintings of the great masters.

On the four faces of that tower, as many balconies will open, in the direction of the four cardinal points, from which the leader, clad in gold, diamonds and carbuncles, will be seen by the people in a wave of velvet and a beam of light. That leader, chosen by the nation, will be the most handsome, most intelligent and strongest man in the realm; so that, being superior to everyone else in all respects, hey will be obeyed passionately. Those wounded by his genius will be subjugated by his beauty; his height cannot be measured at less than eight feet. That Titanic stature he will combine with a form worthy of Antinous, Meleager and the most delicate conceptions of Greek art. A rational diet and transcendent hygiene will maintain him in an admirably youthful and healthy condition, and such an equilibrium of humors that his decisions cannot be other than impartial and judicious. His words will be collected and engraved in marble like oracles, and by night, scribes will keep vigil beside his bed in order to look out for the words that escape him in his sleep; for it is imperative that none of the leader's thoughts are lost, every one of them being a benefit for the people and for humankind.

When the leader descends into the city, it will be a splendid sight to see the ranks of the procession unfurling, from the summit of the palace to the base. The ecstatic population will watch that realization of its dreams of magnificence from rooftops and balconies; leaders must give the people they govern, under penalty of disaffection, the spectacle of the plastic forms of power. There is in the depths of every human being, no matter how poor or humble, a secret aspiration toward the enchantments of opulence. The love of gold, purple and marble torments all souls to a greater or lesser extent. It is, therefore, a sacred duty for the powerful and the rich to give the multitude the alms that do not impoverish in any way: the alms of the vision of their luxury.

A thousand tympanists mounted on five hundred elephants—elephants will by then be perfectly adapted to the French climate—will open the procession, accentuating the rhythm of symphonies of brass instruments much more powerful than the bugle and the saxophone, executed by four thousand black men dressed in scarlet cloaks striped with gold or of blue striped with silver. Lines of magistrates, priests, scientists, poets and artists, dressed in severe or shiny costumes, will come next. Then the leader, in a sparkling chariot pulled by domesticated lions and tigers, horses of particular breeds that do not resemble any of ours, or by some animal of new invention, in copper, steel or some other substance; for minerals will then have been raised to the level of life by the efforts of science. Machines will be made that will reproduce themselves.

The leader's staff will follow thereafter: cup-bearers, pantlers, chamberlains, grooms, etc. If one is astonished not to see military men in the procession, it is because there will no longer have been any for a long time. War will be suppressed, with the vestiges of ancient barbarism; engines of destruction will have been found of such power that resistance would be impossible on either side. There has to be a certain correlation between offensive arms and the human body: some equilibrium beyond which courage no longer exists. Achilles, and Mars himself, would flee before an improved cannon firing sixty cannonballs a minute, each of two or three hundred pounds.

The city will be possessed of an architectural magnificence of which no idea can be formed: without falling into the ennui of a stupid uniformity, the streets, conceived according to a rational plan, will each present a physiognomy and an ensemble; one street will affect the Byzantine style, another the Gothic style, a third the Moorish style, yet another that of the Renaissance. Greek and Roman architectures will also display their specimens. These curiosities will serve to vary the character of quarters built, in general, in a new style that we cannot yet design, but which, in all probability, will be akin to what the Spaniards call *plateresco*.[14]

The architects of that time, instead of trying to dissimulate the parts of their constructions, will give them a great deal of relief and emphasis; they will draw ornamental motifs full of character and novelty from clearly-delineated roofs, windows, doors and beams. The façades will no longer be flat, like those of today; the cornices, the balconies and the main

---

[14] The literal meaning of *plateresco* is "in the style of a silver-smith"; the style flourished in Spain in the late 15th and early 16th centuries, providing an intermediary between Gothic and Renaissance styles, leavened with Moorish influences.

body of the building will permit reliefs prohibited now by a misguided administration.

Large slabs of white marble or lava enameled in various colors, in such a way as to form mosaics, which will replace our horrible modern paving-stones. Streams of crystal-clear water will run in the gutters on either side; as for household wastes, they will run into two parallel sewers excavated beneath the houses, perpetually swept away by forceful currents.

Double railway lines will run along the middle of the road, for barrows, carts, drays, fiacres, carriages and all such barbaric forms of transport will have been suppressed by the force of circumstance. Immense and numerous squares full of trees, flowers and fountains will absorb vapors, cleaning the air and distilling carbon dioxide; at every step, children, women, old people and dreamers will find places there to rest and stroll, and the least of the works of nature will take their place in the midst of the constructions of human genius, and will provide a reminder that there is a God—something that can easily be forgotten in the cities of the present day.

In summer, canvas awnings striped with bright colors and sprinkled with scented water, will shelter passers-by from the sun; and in winter, vast panes of glass, posed between cornices, will protect them from the vicissitudes of the season. Streets that are too wide to be covered in this way will have arcades than can be closed by glass partitions.

Every house will have an exterior outlet to its heating-system, in order that people can enjoy the mildest temperatures in closed passages, and head-colds and pneumonias can be avoided. In the opulent quarters, these corridors or cloisters—whatever one cares to call them—will be decorated with tapestries, orange-trees, magnolias, laurels, camellias and other flowering shrubs. This disposition will bring about significant modifications in costumes; the bright and pale colors, and the gold and silver embroideries that mud and rain deter will not take long to reappear. Our descendants will finally take off the mourning that all of Europe has long worn.

There will only be four theaters—one for song and lyrical declamation; one for dance and picturesque spectacles; one for drama and tragedy; and one for comedy, pantomimes and exhilarating farces—but of an unprecedented beauty and magnificence, worthy of a people that claims to be the most intelligent in the world, but which presently goes to take its pleasure in pestilential hovels to which it would not send its convicts. They will all be large, airy and comfortable; the boxes will offer the comforts of the most refined apartments; one will be able to take perfumed baths in the bathrooms, while watching the performance through golden grilles; one will be able to eat there, pay visits and receive them in the forestage drawing-rooms, and one will enjoy those composite pleasures, so unfamiliar to us poor civilized folk, who can only proceed in enormous sessions.

The stage will be lighted from above and not from below, as is stupidly contrived today; that amelioration will permit to achievement of optical effects of complete authenticity, and will modify the system of decoration in which so much talent is completely wasted. The machinery will be so simple and so perfect that a single engineer, stationed at a small keyboard, will be able to change the theater from top to bottom by pressing a copper button or flicking a switch. The staff will be innumerable; there will be a hundred lead singers, the worst of whom will be as good as Rubini,[15] as many leading dancers, and so on. The chorus would, if necessary, be able to form an army.

Stock exchanges, chambers of commerce, conversation halls, porticos for philosophical chitchat while strolling and Élysées for little children will all be disposed with an understanding of hygiene and wellbeing of which we have no idea, and which only poets could glimpse with the interior eye that they use to gaze upon the future.

---

[15] Giovanni Battista Rubini (1794-1854), the most famous Italian tenor of his era.

Thanks to studies in climate management, Paris will enjoy a temperature quite similar to Naples. A large zone of forests will encircle the city like a green girdle, to block winds and hold back fogs, which their foliage would absorb to return them to the earth, to be converted into springs and streams. When the weather threatens to be rainy, the detonations of monstrous artillery pieces, by means of the commotion caused in the atmosphere, will break up and disperse the banks of cloud; if that is not sufficient, aeronauts will go up into the region of the clouds in metallic balloons and, dragging the vapors into the turbulence of their wake, will tow them away to area of countryside that need water. The sky will be swept every morning as the streets of Paris are now swept.

There will no longer be night; over every square will rise lighthouses, minarets of Moorish architecture whose summits will emit discharges of electric light so intensely bright that gaslight would be silhouetted in black against its flame. These lighthouses will project over the city a white and blue light ten times as bright as the brightest Oriental moonlight. One will be able to read the most microscopic print thereby five or six leagues away in the countryside. The only way that people will be able to recognize night is that they will be able to see more clearly then than by day. Gas lighting, today so noxious, will exhale the most delightful perfumes and the sweetest aromas.

The people of that time will sleep very little; they will have no need to forget life in that intermittent death we call sleep; their existence will be so well-organized that they will never experience fatigue, the resistance of matter will be vanquished, and alimentation detached from all its grossness.

If we wanted to, we could take our hypothesis much further and describe he mores of future Paris with as many details as a novelist of the intimate school of Monsieur Balzac would supply, but this is enough to prove to Parisians who flatter themselves that they have a capital how profound their error is. It will take them another thousand years merely to equal London, and God knows that we are not an anglomaniac!

Arsène Houssaye: *Future Paris*
(1856)

One evening, I was one of ten skeptics gathered in the Café de Paris by one of our number, a miracle seeker—a modern Cazotte-Swedenborg—who wanted to tell us about one of his apocalypses.

"Do you know," he said to us, "where the transformations of Paris will end? Listen to me. I spent the night in the Place de la Concorde in the company of that eloquent sibyl, the moon. She told me a great deal about the future, while discreetly spreading her white light over the completed Louvre, on the Rue de Rivoli, which was approaching completion, and on the Champs-Élysées, which was just starting out. You won't believe it, because you have the weakness of being strong minds. I read on the Obelisk an issue of a newspaper printed on Indian silk, *textilis aër*; it was the *Moniteur de l'Empire universel* for the first of May 3855."

The skeptics started to laugh, but the lunatic continued, in a firm tone: "Messieurs, I'm going to recite the Paris news to you, just as I read it."

And, as if he were reading the exceedingly universal *Moniteur*, he read:

"The moment has come! The ordeal that the inhabitants of all the planets have been enduring has ended victoriously. Paris was yesterday, and will be for six years, the inn of all the living, the central nucleus of all the arts. On the seventh day of our Genesis we have the right to pause in confrontation with the monument of six days and to judge that it is good. On disembarking here the guests that come to us from Saturn and Mars will forget the horizons of their maternal planets. Paris is henceforth the metropolis of Creation!

"Oh, if Monsieur Arago, the discoverer of two thousand years ago had witnessed yesterday's celebrations, he would have been in danger of succumbing to his delirium. He would have shed his blood on the ground to convince himself that he was alive! The sea is pressing its enclosed and outdated waves in their most impetuous flow through bridges with immeasurable spans: the sea that is sad not to be licking with its thousand green-tinted tongues the palaces of the masters of matter; the sea whose first waves cradled the Herculean stranglers of monsters. The city is thirty leagues around; Versailles and Fontainebleau quarters lost among so many others, projecting over less peaceful arrondissements the refreshing scents of their twenty-centuries-old trees.

"A few kilometers from the Rue de Rivoli, Sèvres, which has become the permanent market of the Chinese, our nationals since the war of 2850, displays its pagodas with their tinkling bells, in the midst of which the reconstructed ancient manufacture of *porcelaine à la reine* still exists.[16]

"Where are you, once over-celebrated shade of Fontenay and Saint-Maur, Ville-d'Avray and Bellevue? Now, it is in the faubourgs that noisy industry agitates; it is there that the factories are where founders harden their submarine rails, and the delicate networks of steel that are the wings on which excursionists venture into all the currents of the atmosphere?

"Where are you, Champs-Élysées, favorite theme of the novelists of the year 1855? Urban villas, circuses, sanctuaries of Polichinelle, where are you? In that alleyway, paved in concave iron, covered with roofs of crystal, the bees and hornets of finance are buzzing! The capitalists of the Great Bear are debating with the speculators of Mercury. Shares are being issued this very day in the debris of Venus, half-consumed by

---

[16] Sèvres was once the center of porcelain production in the vicinity of Paris, but the techniques in use there were overtaken in the late 18th century by those of André-Marie Leboeuf, whose superior product, manufactured in the Rue Thiroux, was favored by Marie-Antoinette and became known, in consequence, as *porcelaine à la reine.*

her own flames! What a conflict of Pactoluses,[17] what a rattle of billions!

"Where, then, was the so-called Palais Mazarin, the Institut, now in ruins, in which one of our fashionable hair-dressers has established a wing-shop at the sign of the United World? Our Institut occupies all the space that extends from the Champ-de-Mars, that magnificent restaurant for our schoolchildren, to the Jardin des Plantes, prolonged as far as Sceaux. In that sacred path of our Académies, the Greek porti-cos lead to schools build on the models of Heidelberg, Flor-ence, Benares and Peking! A cascade has sprung from the ground in the same place where the attempts was made to raise the heavy dome of the Panthéon, and the channeled waters of the cascade bear amorous students through perfumed squares where the mud of the Faubourg Saint-Marceau once asphyxi-ated rag-pickers and frightened philosophers.

"When the emperor returns to the capital after a few weeks' vacation in Australia, at the gallop of his fifty-horsepower carriage, from the city gate to his Louvre, he pauses under two thousand triumphant arches; he passes fifty colossi built in his image; ships with eighteen decks fire all their artillery on all the shores of our Ocean; the mirages of electricity eclipse the sun at midday, and that idolatry of the subjects for their sovereign consternates the last devotees, who remember that their idols never received such homage.

"And now that the sky bathes with its perpetual radiance the city in which the great work is concluded, now that human beings, reconciled with God by virtue of the indefinite effort of their labor, can rest alongside the furrows that have borne all their fruits, and incessantly repeat a triumphant canticle of delight; now that within those walls of marble and gold, all the sensible scourges—disease, poverty and even death—have been vanquished by the indefatigable fighters; now that people scarcely remember the mythological epochs in which the

---

[17] The waters of the River Pactolus, like King Midas, were reputed to be able to turn objects to gold.

world lived in hate; now that the discord of mind is tamed like the waves of the Ocean; now that women, mistresses of their own destiny, have forgotten the lie that once made them slaves and practice with a resolute sincerity the immutable law of storm-free love; now that the energy of the living has obliged the dead to frequent the eternal fatherland of intelligence and surrender their secrets, too long buried; now that for Paris, capital of the universe, all is serenity, light and joy, who will dare to say "No!" to progress? Who will not mourn our ancestors in the nineteenth century, so deplorably deprived, so estranged from all the advantages that we enjoy by right of conquest, we the Parisians of the year 4000?

"Who will dare to emit a doubt when, like the Pistheterne[18] of the poet of the earliest times, humankind has espoused the handsome genius of sovereignty in front of dispossessed Jupiter? Who? Perhaps a few rhymers of fossil elegies, who no longer find in a place in that city, whose vulgar speech is a hymn, for their songs without echo. Who? A few amorous oldsters who, indifferent to the magnificent expansion of liberated hearts, blind to the multiplication of suns, regret pleurisies beneath balconies, the intoxication of supposedly-sweet tears and the rare joys of obscure sacrifice. But they are the buffoons of Paris metamorphosed! The exhibitors of yesterday have nothing to debate with its phantoms."

The prophet had finished. We went away silent and tormented—but after a few minutes, the least credulous of the group cried:

"Messieurs, I demand to consult the *Moniteur* of the year six thousand!"

And we began to laugh again.

---

[18] This name might be an eccentric or mistaken rendering of Pisistratus, the name of a rebel against the Athenian aristocracy who subsequently seized power; while ruling the city he instituted a festival associated with the first attempt to produce a definitive version of the Homeric epics.

Note:

The bulk of the supposed quotation from the future newspaper was reprinted by Houssaye in his *Grand Revue. Paris et Saint-Pétersbourg* in 1889, in connection with the centenary of the Revolution. The text of the first few paragraphs is identical, except that the date 1855 is changed to 1889, but after the paragraph ending with the word "homage" two new paragraphs were inserted. They read:

"Out of the tomb of a poet named Victor Hugo, a little less well-known than Homer, his ancestor, an altar has been made for present and future poets, but there is doubt that the poet ever existed, just as Homer's existence is doubted. A few pages have been found of *La Légende des siècles*, sublime pages that have escaped the fury of wars and revolutions. Critics argue as to whether it was Hugo who wrote the *Méditations* attributed to someone named Lamartine and the *Nuits* attributed to someone named Musset.

"What supports the supposition that Hugo existed is that, not far from his tomb one finds a few ruined monuments of the Carnot dynasty."[19]

In the subsequent text, the word "gold" is substituted by "porphyry" and the last two paragraphs (which are retained even though the narrative frame has not been introduced) are modified as follows:

"'Messieurs, I demand to consult the *Moniteur* of the year six thousand, to see whether the world will continue its march to the point of vertigo.'

"One skeptic, who had not said anything thus far, asked permission to point out that, after all, love, that beautiful invention of the ancients for the moderns; poetry, that supreme link between the finite and the infinite; the sky, constellated

---

[19] The descendants of the mathematician and member of the Convention Lazare Carnot (1753-1823) included four more noted scientists and politicians, including Sadi Carnot, elected President of the Republic in 1887. (Houssaye was not to know that he would be assassinated in 1894.)

with stars that had been more beautiful to our wonderstruck eyes before science; and art, which reveals the gods among human beings—all those enchantments of vanished worlds—had not been rendered obsolete by what is proudly known as progress."

Victor Fournel: *Future Paris*
(1865)

"I have only to begin."
(Words attributed to M. Haussmann.)[20]

*"What remains to be done is at least
as considerable as what has been
accomplished."*
(Speech made by the Prefect of the Seine
to the Municipal Commission,
29 November 1864.)

At that time, I had a vision.

It seemed to me that have slept profoundly for a long time, I suddenly woke up as the first hour of the year 1965 was chiming—and the angel sent by God to protect Paris lifted me up by the hair, and transported me to the top of a monument, from which he showed me the great city extended at my feet.

This is what I saw.

I saw a marvel that would have excited the admiration of Barrême and caused Monge and Legendre to fall down in ecstasy.[21]

---

[20] Baron Haussmann was appointed Prefect of the Seine in 1853 because his predecessor was reluctant to bear the vast expense of the planned reconstruction of Paris sanctioned by Napoléon III, whose chief architect and author Haussmann became; he still held that position when Fournel published this story, and probably read it; we can only speculate as to the extent and tenor of his amusement.

[21] François Barrême (1638-1703) gave his name to a "ready reckoner" intended to assist accountants, lawyers and the like,

During my slumber, Paris had successively broken through its new boundary and overflowed in all directions into its surroundings, swallowing them up into its bosom. It was now more than a hundred kilometers around, and filled the entire département of the Seine by itself. Versailles was its royal vestibule; Pontoise was proud to form one of its suburbs. Every day the citizens of Meaux climbed the towers of their cathedral to see whether the Parisian wave had finally reached them. Step by step, the stumps of its boulevards, departing from the plain of Monceaux, came to expire on the edge of the forest of Chantilly, neatly remolded into an English park. The Boulevard de Sebastopol had driven its tip, as a scout, to the gates of Senlis, and islets of grandiose houses, scattered here and there across the bare and arid plain, in a disorder wisely regulated by the compasses of engineers, like as many surveyors' poles and guide-stones, were helping Paris to flow rapidly along the road to Fontainebleau.

The time was long gone when a timid and backward audacity had wanted to make the Arc de Triomphe the center of the city of which it had originally been the advance sentinel; overtaken by the rising tide which it thought it served as a lighthouse and rallying-point, Chalgrin's monument was no longer anything but a wreck still afloat in the remotest distance of the bloated capital, and that entrance-gate, which had wanted to change its role, now punished for its ambition, resembled an exit-door to Old Paris. The city had made half its journey toward the Ocean, and the Ocean had advanced to meet it, to the extent that the old legend of Seaport Paris was finally a verity. The monstrous cancer, still spreading, had eaten into all the living flesh surrounding it, and, from one annexation to the next, all of France had become its suburb.

---

also used in France in the teaching of arithmetic. Gaspard Monge (1746-1818) published a standard textbook on geometry. Legendre was the publisher and notional author of the guide-book produced for the cab-drivers of Paris in the era in which Fournel write his story.

By dint of transforming itself and embellishing itself, the great city had finished up donning a new skin from head to toe. No vestige any longer remained of the tenebrous past that still dishonored its splendor in 1865. A century of assiduous works, directed by half a dozen prefects who handed on as a sacred heritage the furious monomania of building and the *delirium tremens* of demolition, had made it the archetypal capital of modern civilization.

In the center extended a vast square, a league in circumference, around which radiated in all directions, like the corridors of the Mazas[22] around its chapel, fifty boulevards, not more beautiful than but just as beautiful as one another.

Each of these fifty boulevards was fifty meter wide and, in compliance with regulations, was bordered by houses fifty meters high with fifty windows on the façade. All these houses, whose width was equal to their elevation, formed a long series of gigantic cubes, regularly aligned. Sage laws had determined, along with the uniform base, the mode of exterior decoration and interior distribution; each of them enclosed an equal number of apartments of equal dimensions. The same sage laws had similarly determined the location and form of shops of every sort. There were, for example, as with prefects, first class, second class and third class cafés, and for every category the number of rooms, tables, billiard-tables, mirrors, ornaments and decorations was regulated with care and foresight.

Only first class cafés, of course, were admitted to the line of the boulevards. Thus, the eye was not wounded by the shocking disparities that the indiscipline of individual initiative produced, left to its own devices. The centralizing level, that instrument of complete civilization, had passed everywhere. Manufacturing industries, workshops and petty commerce were located in the intermediary quarters; there were

---

[22] The Mazas was one of the prisons of Paris, reckoned ultramodern in 1865, having been opened in 1841.

main streets and service streets, just as there are main stair-ways and service stairways in well-organized houses.

From that square one could, with a single glance, by piv-oting around oneself, embrace the whole of Paris, perceiving all its gates. The middle was occupied by a huge monumental barracks, circular in form, surmounted by a lighthouse—an immense and vigilant eye from which, every night, a powerful beam of electric light launched forth over all points of the city—pierced, facing the fifty boulevards, by fifty embrasures, through each of which the muzzle of a cannon projected, and flanked by elegant rotundas, which were police stations.

On the fronton of the barracks, a bas-relief (*utile dulci*)[23]—the work of a professor at the École des Beaux-Arts, regenerated by the salutary intervention of the administrative element—represented the Glory of Public Order, in the uni-form of an infantryman of the line, with an aureole around his head, slaying the hundred-headed Hydra of Decentralization. A frieze distributed around the edifice the most gripping epi-sodes of that great battle, finally terminated.

Fifty sentinels, posed in the barracks' fifty sentry-boxes facing the fifty boulevards, were able, by means of telescopes to see the fifty sentinels of the barrière twenty kilometers away. A vast system of electric wires, radiating from the cen-ter to the perimeter, put all of those hundred posts in commu-nication, and sent each member the necessary signals from headquarters within a single second.

A first circular boulevard, a hundred meters broad, bor-dered with arcades, made a circuit of the square. The last, of identical breadth, made a circuit of the city, following the enclosure of the new ramparts on the inside. The old fortifica-tions, destroyed and filled in, were no more than a subject of dissertation or archeologists, like Philippe Auguste's walls.[24]

---

[23] The useful [in combination with] the agreeable.

[24] The *enceinte* constructed in the reign Philippe II (1165-1223) in 1190 or thereabouts—the first of five (not counting

In the interval, arranged at one-kilometer intervals, ten boulevards half as wide were concentrically arranged, for Paris in the year 1965, ideal in its symmetry, and in which, by a prodigious effort of the municipal imagination, a means has even been found of subjecting curved lines to the principles of straight lines, offered the inestimable advantage of being rigorously founded on the decimal system. One could go through it and study it like a problem in mathematics.

At each intersection of the ten circular boulevards with the fifty boulevards forming the spokes of the vast wheel, a square was situated, in accordance with the purest geometrical theories, the perimeter of which was exclusively composed of monuments—for monuments were not permitted to be scattered everywhere, without order and method. They were centralized.

Provincials and foreigners had no need of any guides to visit Paris; it was sufficient for them to follow the boulevard directly in front of them on leaving their hotel; by nightfall, they found themselves back at their point of departure, having seen all the curiosities of the first circle, without having had to go into lateral streets, abandoned to the necessities of ongoing life. The next day they began again for the next circle. They knew in advance where to find all the town halls, barracks or theaters, which alternated like the rhymes in an epic poem, and they could determine by a mere glance at a map of the city in which direction it was necessary to seek the various categories of edifices, just as mathematicians determine the fourth term of a proportion. No Englishman ever felt the need to venture beyond the boulevards, and no Parisian remembered having encountered a single one of them in the street. The monuments had their lines, just like the omnibuses; monuments with domes here, monuments without domes there; antique style to the right, modern style to the right.

---

two minor expansions), the last one being constructed by Louis XVIII in 1818.

The city's chief engineer had invented a powerful machine for transporting the ancient edifices that had been preserved into the alignment. By that means the Hôtel de Ville had been moved five hundred meters, and the Hôtel des Invalides had been obliged to rotate on its axis in order to take its place in the new city. The Buttes de Saint-Roch, Saint-Geneviève and others had come to take their places meekly in the Bois de Boulogne, the Bois de Vincennes and the Parc de Monceaux, where they figured among the natural curiosities, hollowed out with caves and fitted with waterfalls. Mont Valérien had been carved into the Colossus of Rhodes, each of whose hands held a gigantic torch over the city, while each of its feet accommodated a hydraulic machine, which fed the waters of the Seine into countless channels. Montmartre was topped by a dome ornamented with an immense electric clock-face that as visible two leagues away, extending to four, which served to regulate all the clocks in the city.

The great goal pursued for such a long time had finally been fulfilled—that of making Paris an object of luxury and curiosity rather than usage, an *exhibition city*, placed under glass, a universal hostelry, a object of admiration and envy for foreigners, impossible for its inhabitants but unique for the comfort and enjoyments of every sort that it offered the sons of Albion. When a Parisian had the pettiness to complain, the reply was that only contemptible individuals would not sacrifice their personal comforts to the masculine joys of patriotic pride.

The monumental system followed in the Paris of 1965 had produced certain consequences that I remembered having seen appearing elsewhere. As the construction of buildings and their architectural genre were determined *a priori* by the general plan of the city, instead of being adapted prosaically to needs and functions, it resulted that edifices were sometimes employed for unforeseen purposes. Primary schools and fire-stations were accommodated under domes. There were palaces that were only occupied by their concierges, and others that only lodged fountains. Once a palace was built, no one knew what to do with it, and hastened put in statue or a garden, or to have a fresco painted, or even to make it available, in order to utilize it, to a senior civil servant with nothing to do. Furthermore, every palace, even the ones that only lodged a fountain, had its sentry, its guards, its governor and its administration.

The principal roads invariably reproduced the same disposition: along the houses ran a sidewalk divided into two sections by the two streams of pedestrians walking in opposite directions; along the sidewalks ran a causeway for vehicles, which, according to their direction, took one side of the street; in the middle, separated from the roadway by a parapet, there were four sets of railway tracks for the trains that furrowed Paris in every direction. At intervals, footbridges connected the two sides of the embankment, and even in the streets into which they trains did not go, at all the crossroads and all the most crowded locations, overpasses like the one I once saw on the Canal Saint-Martin aided pedestrians to cross the ocean of omnibuses and fiacres swirling beneath his feet without any risk of being splashed with mud or crushed.

Every night, at two o'clock in the morning, after the theaters had closed and when the entire city was plunged in the arms of Morpheus, steam engines passed through the streets, removing the day's mud and driving filth into the sewers. Five or six regiments of sweepers, followed by an army of floor-polishers, spread out along the sidewalks and maintained the bitumen like the parquet of a drawing-room.

The fifty boulevards that radiated from the center to the circumference bore the names of the principal cities of France, and the fifty corresponding gates those of the départements of which each of the cities was the principal place. The names of the capitals of Europe had been reserved for the concentric boulevards. The most important squares and bridges were baptized with the names of the empire's victories; the secondary squares and crossroads with the victories of royalty. The names of generals, ministers, industrialists, and even a few writers, had been distributed, in a logical and maturely studied order, to the intermediary streets, with the result that a knowledge of history and geography helped one find one's way around Paris, just as a walk through Paris was a lesson in history and geography. Merely by guiding heir horses, coachmen had become the most knowledgeable men in France, and they were thinking of presenting themselves *en masse* to the Institut. Every Thursday and Sunday, one saw schoolteachers and parents walking groups of children through the city methodically, carefully pointing out the names and the directions of streets. Paris had become a huge mnemonic display, both synchronic and chronological, and the map of the capital was one of the elementary texts adopted by the Imperial Council of Public Education for the mutual schools and the inferior classes of the lycée.

Needless to say, the vile labels that once inscribed tenebrous stories of the mores and customs of old Paris at every street-corner, were nowhere to be seen. No more Rue des Juifs, de la Truanderie, du Grand-Hurleur, des Mauvais-Garçons, du Fouarre, des Francs-Bourgeois, de Tire-Chape and de Vide-Gousset. Away with all that! It reeked of the Middle Ages and bad company.

The eye was no longer saddened by those great black and somber monuments in the Gothic—which is to say, barbaric—style that had been spared by a residue of superstition. By virtue of restorations, Notre-Dame finally looked presentable. Saint-Germain-l'Auxerrois had been razed in order to augment the Place du Louvre, and, while regretting the belfry of the Mairie, the inhabitants had applauded that sage determination. The three clock-faces and the carillon of the belfry had been transported to the Tour Saint-Jacques, whose ground floor had become a National Guard post, in order that it should at least serve some purpose.

I searched for the Faubourg Saint-Germain, but it had disappeared; the Faubourg Saint-Marceau, but there was no trace of it; the Faubourg Saint-Antoine had been thrown into the dustbin The fifty-meter boulevards were enthroned everywhere, with the equality of their splendor. On the sites of the large houses in the Rue Saint-Dominique and the Rue de

47

Varennes, those obsolete refuges of aristocratic idleness, and the locations where the colleges and cloisters of the old University—the debris of feudalism and scholasticism—had opened, long rows of sparkling department stores and gilded cafés extended as far as the eye could see.

From whatever angle one looked at the new city, it was always the same Paris, the majestic and splendid Paris, as befit the capital of the world. It no longer had any head or tail, any beginning or end; one thought that one was at its heart everywhere, which furnished poets—a few of them remained, alas; the administration even tolerated those madmen benevolently, nourishing them at its own expense in a prytaneum in order that they might write cantatas for feast-days—with a ready-made opportunity to compare the great city to the vault of heaven.

On looking at the houses more closely, I observed two details that had initially escaped me, and which singularly intrigued my curiosity. To the façade of each one, a small instrument was fitted, similar to a meter, the purpose of which I could not understand. My guide explained to me that it was an aerometer, serving to measure the number of cubic meters of respirable air strictly necessary to each apartment and to verify that each tenant enjoyed the share of oxygen to which he was entitled. On all the roofs series of little outbuildings were aligned, which, I soon learned, were designed for supplementary tenants; the houses had their imperials, just like trains and omnibuses. While the ground-floor shops cost fifty to a hundred thousand francs to let, and the smallest apartment was about ten thousand, the price of these outbuildings was not above a thousand écus. They were the usual abode of government employees and unmarried journalists. As for workers, relegated to beyond the city wall, they traveled five or six leagues every day by rail to go to work, but they were allowed to go into palaces in their smocks and caps, and candidates for election to parliament occasionally reminded them that they were "the sovereign people."

Every twenty meters, along all the boulevards, there were charming public urinals, each with three compartments, in the form of Gothic towers—for the administration, in order to respond to the calumnies of certain pamphleteers lodged in roof-kiosks, had set out to prove that it understood all styles.

Newspaper-sellers had stalls at every street-corner. Thanks to the pressure of public opinion, enlightened by long experience, and the salutary measures taken by a paternal administration, undiscouraged by persistent ingratitude, the number of responsibly-edited papers had multiplied in a fashion reassuring with regard to public order. Service at these stalls was provided by a special corps of uniformed agents, to whom other agents in the service of public security brought bundles of papers every morning and evening containing the free appreciations of superior agents, without uniforms, regarding the government, which paid them very well in order to keep stricter control of them.

I had descended to the ground and was walking at hazard through the streets of old Paris—I mean the Paris of 1865—in company with my guide. The boulevards stretched away one after another, squares were succeeded by other squares, domes by colonnades and colonnades by domes. But for a painful aching in the soles of my feet, it would have seemed to me that I remained motionless in the midst of a vast stage-set that unfolded around me, perpetually repeating itself.

After walking for a few hours, I suddenly emerged in front of the Palais-Royal, and saw with satisfaction that it had been combined with the Louvre, along with the Tuileries. I went around the latter palace, looking for the garden, but did not find it; except for the part reserved to the château, it had become invisible. The tennis court, the municipal post office, the Café de la Terrasse and the Orangery had extended their stone ramifications in all directions. A modest branch of the Marly machine[25] was lounging over the great fountain, linked

---

[25] *La Machine de Marly* was a masterpiece of 17th century engineering built to supply all the water features in the palace

by a subterranean canal to the Seine, and the Avenue des Champs-Élysées extended its border of houses as far as the Place de la Concorde.

On the other side of the river, two boulevards intersected on the location of the Luxembourg Gardens, which had long abused municipal tolerance by leaving sixty or sixty thousand square meters of excellent terrain unused and removing considerable capital from circulation. The Rue Soufflot had been connected to the Rue de Fleurus through the garden and the Rue Bonaparte to the Rue de l'Ouest, for the greater convenience of carters and to put Bobino in communication with the Panthéon. The Avenue de l'Observatoire shone proudly in its polished asphalt sidewalks. A cab-stand covered the lawn of the Orangery; in the place where the Nursery had been, the odor of lilacs had been replaced the odor of troopers; improved absinthe was being sold in the Medici Grotto, and water-carriers came to refill their buckets at the Jacques de Brosse fountain.

By way of compensation for the Romantic soul, however, the authorities of the year 1965 had put flower-beds in the Place Saint-Sulpice, around the Obelisk and the Arc de Triomphe at the Étoile, thus according nature its right to sunlight, but without permitting it to infringe that of the boutiques. Besides which, an ingenious improvement had been introduced into the fabrication of gardens. The administration bought them ready-made, to order. Trees made of painted cardboard, and flowers of taffeta, played a leading role in those oases, where precaution as taken as far as hiding artificial birds in the foliage, which sang all day long. Thus, what was agreeable in nature had been conserved, while avoid everything about it that was inappropriate or irregular.

---

of Versailles, involving fourteen giant water-wheels and 221 pumps. It required a permanent staff of sixty to maintain it, but kept breaking down, thus eventually becoming something of a joke. It was not actually situated in the commune of Marly.

Suddenly, near the middle of the former gardens of the Tuileries, I emerged into an immense square, the cupola of which had been glazed, as a precautionary measure against the insults of sun and rain. Its perimeter was entirely formed by four monuments, which summarized marvelously he principal interests and essential needs of a great capital: a Mairie, a barracks, a theater and a branch of the Bourse. By virtue of a glorious and well-deserved exception, the square, instead of bearing the name of a victory, bore the name of a victor—the man who had vanquished the darkness and resistance of old Paris, the promoter of that great monument of transformation that had only been followed in being surpassed. In the middle of the square, on a tall bronze pedestal, stood a colossal statue of the second founder of the city, in the costume of a Great Aedile, clad in a toga and laticlave. Half-risen from his curule chair, he was extending a finger toward a map of Paris spread out before him, with an imperious and serene gesture, and in his other hand he was holding an open pair of compasses, gleaming like a sword-blade. Little genii were at his feet, playing with spirit-levels, pickaxes and trowels.

As I drew nearer, I perceived that the statue also served as a heater and a stand-pipe. It had the nozzle of a pump in its breast and the flue of a stove in its back; it emitted fire at the top and water at the bottom. In addition, it played the role of a candelabrum by night. In the dark, the interior flame lent fantastic gleams to the bronze, and the heat outlets, located between the lips, the eyelids and the nostrils, were transformed into sources of light, reflected infinitely by the vault of crystal. That fashion of utilizing the useless and regenerating art by means of a salutary injection of industry struck me as a brilliant revelation of progress in relation to the new capital.

The four faces of the pedestal were filled with as many expressive and ingeniously-selected bas-reliefs. On the front one saw the City of Paris coiffed by her towers, directing a procession of suburban communes, and coming at its head to prostrate herself at the feet of the Great Aedile, who was lifting her up while kissing her hand.

To the right, the Great Aedile was sitting at his work-desk, plunged in profound meditation, with his eyes glued to a map; to either side of him, Art and Civilization were raising their torches to give him light, and the municipal committee, were ranged in a circle in religious silence, like the sheaves in Joseph's dream.

To the left, the Great Aedile was stamping his foot on the ground, causing a forest of domes, campaniles and colonnades to spring forth, which came to arrange themselves in front of him to the enchanting sounds of a concerto of lyres played by the Amphions of the municipal committee.[26] In one corner, I vaguely made out an episode in which the City of Paris was playing a role that I could not quite make out; I could not determine exactly whether she was putting her hand on her heart in a gesture of eternal gratitude or on her purse, in order to pay for the municipality's violins.

The posterior face of the pedestal was divided into two sections; one represented the Assumption of the City of Paris, borne up toward the clouds in the arms of a legion of architects and engineers, as naked as Amours, by virtue of the requirements of style. France, hand extended, was contemplating it in an attitude of ecstatic admiration, and London, Vienna, St. Petersburg, Berlin, Rome and Constantinople, symmetrically arranged in the foreground, were burning incense in cassolettes.

The other half represented the apotheosis of the Great Aedile, and I only have a confused memory of it. I only remember that, in one lower corner, Posterity, as serene and

---

[26] Amphion, the son of Antiope, allegedly by Zeus, became legendary for organizing the fortifications of Thebes by playing his lyre, thus compelling huge blocks of stone to organize themselves magically—a key scene in Euripides' *Antiope*, which presumably presented difficulties in staging.

grandiose as the angel that appeared to Heliodorus,[27] was driving the hideous monsters of Envy and Denigration into a pit with strokes of a whip.

I heard a blow resound. Ah! How hard Posterity was striking! A second stroke. I stirred feebly, thinking that I could already feel Posterity's lash upon my own head. It seemed to me that someone was marching toward me, and I recoiled instinctively, stammering a few badly-articulated words. A vigorous arm shook me.

I sat up straight. Through the partly-open window beams of sunlight and torrents of dust were extending as far as my bed. The noise of spades and pickaxes, the song of saws, the axles of heavily-laden carts and Berthelet wheelbarrows grating on the stone, filled my ears like a whirlwind. My concierge was beside me; he resembled the Civilization of the right-hand bas-relief.

"A nightmare, Monsieur?" he said, clutching his cap respectfully in his hand.

"No, no—a dream, a beautiful dream! But if it was only a dream, why did you wake me up?

With a sad and gentle smile he handed me a piece of paper that he was holding. It was an order from the City of Paris—the third in six years—to clear the locale within two months, in order to make way for the extension of the Boulevard Saint-Germain.

"Oh!" I cried. "It wasn't a dream, as you can see!"

---

[27] Fournel presumably has Eugène Delacroix's fresco *Heliodorus Driven from the Temple* (completed in 1861) in mind; it can still be seen—a trifle dimly—on the wall of Saint-Sulpice.

Alfred Franklin: *The Ruins of Paris in 4875*
(1875)

I

To His Excellency the Minister of the Navy and Colonies, at Noumea (Caledonia)[28]
Within sight of Paris, 20 May 4875

Monsieur le Ministre,

The exploration fleet of which Your Excellency placed me in command has completed the first part of its task.

If, as tradition says, Noumea owes its origin to a Parisian colony, I have found the cradle of our ancestors. I have found the most beautiful, wealthiest, most famous and most sumptuous city of the old world, for it is within sight of the ruins of Paris that I am writing this dispatch. It will be delivered to Your Excellency by Lieutenant Inveniès, who had the glory of being the first to set foot on the land for which we were searching.

On 10 May, the winds had suddenly turned from south-south-east to south-south-west, the sea became very heavy, the

---

[28] Noumea was, and still is, the capital of the French territory of New Caledonia in the south-west Pacific. Between 1860 and 1897, New Caledonia was a penal colony, to which many of the Communards of 1870 were transported; Franklin could not know when he wrote the story that most of its political prisoners would be allowed to return to France in 1879, when they were granted amnesty. Nor could he know that there would be a native rebellion on the island in 1878, which commenced a long guerrilla war.

barometer dropped below eighty millimeters and a furious tempest dispersed the ships of the squadron. My fears were all the greater because the region in which I was sailing is unknown, and my frigate was being driven the wind with a speed of twenty-five knots. Soon, the water penetrated below decks, broke through the wall of the engine-room and threatened to put out the fire.

At midday, our position being 34° 3747″ north latitude and 42° 24′ 40″ east longitude, the wind suddenly dropped and a rapid current carried me eastwards, where we perceived land. Two of my ships, the *Répertrix* and the *Eruo*, were then able to rejoin me, and we advanced with extreme caution. Sounding only indicated a depth of six fathoms, and we were surrounded by a prodigious quantity of rats, which it was necessary to disperse with rifle fire.

Finally, at about two o'clock, we dropped anchor on a good bed of fine sand, in an immense and safe harbor. A large river was slowly emptying its waters there, and on the coast, as far as the eye could see, a dense curtain of trees concealed the horizon from us. I gave orders to gather the flotilla, and decided to spend a little time there. My crew needed rest; we had not had any fresh meat for a fortnight, and the corvette *Eureka*, which I am sending you, required urgent repairs.

I admit that at that moment we had no idea that we were so close to the objective of our search. Kortambert, in fact, in the geographical fragments so expertly restored by Monsieur Dartieu, says in a positive manner that Paris is situated about two hundred kilometers from the sea.[29] It is necessary to rec-

---

[29] The notional author inserts a reference: "Kortambert, *Fragments*, Dartieu edition, liv. I, ch. 7, p.5.—Conf. Meissas et Michelot, IV, 9, 11; Expilly, IX, 5, 3, and Malte-Vran, VI, 4, 7." Franklin probably had Eugène Cortambert's *Leçons de géographie* [Lessons in Geography] (1846) in mind when improvising this reference. The confirmatory references are presumably to Achille Meissas and Auguste Michelot's *Nouvelle géographie méthodique* [New Methodical Geography]

ognize, however, that our scholars and geologists, even in their most boldest hypotheses, are far from having exaggerated the incredible violence of the cataclysm that wrecked the entire old world, and which only our little island had the privilege of escaping.

At about five o'clock, while the crew was at table, our eyes were attracted landwards by flames and clouds of smoke, which were rising a short distance away behind the trees. I immediately sent out a launch with a dozen men, commanded by Lieutenant Inveniès, to investigate.

They came back in the evening, at nine eighteen, bringing news that caused hope to leap in our hearts.

Three or four kilometers from the coast, our men had found a town of rather wretched appearance, the inhabitants of which, numbering approximately two thousand, appeared to be prey to a great agitation. The flames that we had seen from afar were completing their work, and three or four dwellings had been reduced to a pile of rubble. It was easy to see that the conflagration had selected the least constricted and the least poor, and, as they were not adjacent to one another, it was easy to deduce that criminal intent had designated them for the ravages in question.

The natives ran to our sailors and pressed around them, all speaking and shouting at the same time, fighting to get closer to them and studying them with a child-like avidity. Five minutes after its arrival, the little troop was surrounded by a compact crowd, whose curious gazes and frankly indiscreet attitude was not at all threatening. A few words pronounced by Lieutenant Inveniès were immediately understood, and they replied to him in a language that has, like ours, striking analogies with French.

The mores of this population, with which we have since been able to familiarize ourselves, offer strange contrasts. In

---

(1827), Jean-Joseph Expilly's *Manuel de Géographie* [Handbook of Geography] (1757) and Conrad Malte-Brun's *Géographie universelle* [World Geography] (1870).

the bosom of this savage tribe, which seems to have sprung from the ground in these uninhabited regions, among these barbarians clad in animal skins, one observes virtues, vices, tastes, defects and aspirations that are usually the product of refined civilizations.

Their great preoccupation is the quest for pleasure. Everything is an occasion for celebration; on the slightest pretext, they assemble outside or gather in one another's homes to sing, eat, drink, dance and talk. Any event occupies and amuses them, any spectacle delights them. Noisy, talkative, restless and impressionable, they become enthusiastic without reflection, and become weary just as rapidly. Self-regard is the most obvious of their faults. Everything that glitters and everything that gleams attracts and impassions them: the sight of plumes and braid excites them madly. They are also good, frank, hospitable, generous, brave, intelligent, delicate, even full common sense, so long as it is not a matter of governing their little city.

Unfortunately, that is the habitual subject of their conversations, and the only one on which they permit no mockery; they are, however, wont to assure themselves, by the periodic overthrow of their leaders, of distractions that are dear to them and the pretext for glorious anniversaries. Sacrificing everything to form, they are more preoccupied with the title that their leader will bear than the manner in which he will rule them.

There are, in any case, many other difficulties to resolve in organizing authority in a population in which everyone yearns to command and no one consents to obey. The most modest individuals dream of a public function that will give them at least a few subalterns to govern, but all of them, even the poorest and most ignorant, believe themselves to be perfectly capable of ruling the tribe; they talk incoherently about the city's affairs, emitting ideas, theories and principles as insensate as they are disparate, and, when they do not see them adopted, experience an imperious desire to revolt. The clever lie in wait for a opportunity, seizing it when the moment comes, and in a trice, the leader is overthrown. Then there are cries of triumph, public rejoicing and endless parades through the town; they congratulate one another, compliment on another and embrace one another.

When our men arrived, it was the evening of one of these great days, and the flames we had observed came from a few huts that had been set on fire in the riot. In consequence, the dethroned chief and his two principal ministers found themselves homeless.

The lieutenant also learned that these improvised revolutions took place twice or three times a year. However, he was told that this one would certainly be the last, and that an indefinite era of calm and concord was about to commence for the population. It had, in fact, just adopted a form of government that limited the exercise of power to thirty days, and determined that a new leader had to be chosen every month; every citizen would thus have his turn, and would live in peace, nurtured by that sweet hope.

That ingenious expedient, which might seem bound to content everyone, is not, it seems, as sure a remedy as one might be led to believe, and it has already been tried more than once without success. Everything goes smoothly for a month, apparently, but the head of state often refuses to stand down to the end of his term of office, and it always requires a revolution to reclaim the throne from him.

Women greatly envy men the privilege of governing and making revolutions; for want of anything better they strive to dominate in the hut, and often find a latent but incontestable despotism there. Impressionable, passionate and nervous, they alternate between behavior that is good, gentle, affectionate, sharp, nagging or cruel, according to atmospheric conditions. They are witty and refined, but thoughtless, futile, frivolous and frenetically flirtatious. Gracious, frail and delicate, but avid for pleasure, they support fatigue with an inconceivable energy. Pleasure has an instinctive attraction for all of them, which the most reasonable are sometimes impotent to combat, and they express irresistible needs corollary to the state of mind in question by means of a term that does not exist in our language, the reflexive verb "to amuse oneself." When a woman speaks of "amusing herself," wise husbands lower their heads and wait for the fit to pass.

The population is strongly attached to the territory that it has occupied since time immemorial, and very proud of its petty city. They fought for the honor of showing our sailors around, who were obliged to visit every part of it, and received the most cordial welcome everywhere. People also boasted to them about the beauty of the surroundings, and above all, the imposing spectacle presented by the ruins of an immense city situated half a league away. The day was too far advanced, however, to permit an immediate excursion, so the lieutenant brought his men back to the ship, where their stories filled us with surprise and joy.

The next day, I sent word that I would pay my compliments to the new leader that the natives had chosen. I reached land at about three o'clock, accompanied by my senior officers. Indigenes sent to meet me cleared a passage for us through the tightly-packed crowd and led us to the leader's hut, where everything had been arranged for a solemn reception. Guards with a stern appearance defended the vicinity, and the ephemeral sovereign awaited us there surrounded by his ministers.

He was clad in an ample wolf-skin constellated with variously colored seashells, glass trinkets and small objects in polished metal: buckles, rings, nails, paper-clips, collar-studs, buttons and bells. His head-dress, composed of feathers of various sorts, was augmented by an oyster-shell, whose nacreous surface gleamed in the sunlight. I strove to seem dazzled by so much wealth, which pleased the leader greatly without surprising him. His manners, however, were not lacking in dignity or grace and he responded without the slightest embarrassment to the compliment that I addressed to him.

We set out on foot, followed—or, rather, escorted—by the entire town, men, women and children alike. No one had wanted to miss the party, and the ill and infirm were seated in crude carts. The chief noticed my surprise, doubtless mistook it for fear, and sought to reassure me, confessing to me, besides, that no human power was capable of retaining his subjects in their homes on such an occasion. By way of reply I took off my sword, and ordered my officers to do the same. Our gesture was immediately understood and saluted with enthusiastic cheers by the joyful crowd, whose members, breathless with curiosity, admired the gilded ornaments of our uniforms, commented on our slightest gestures and pressed around us, competing for our glances.

For about half an hour we followed the verdant banks of the river, whose breadth appeared to be at least double what it had been in the times of the French, if one can rely on the estimations of Du Laure and Joanne.[30] Finally, we climbed a small hill and arrived at the summit, and an exclamation escaped all our throats.

In front of us unfolded the most impressive scene that can ever have been offered to human contemplation. It was really Paris, none of us had any doubt about it; those grandiose

---

[30] The notional author adds another reference: "Du Laure, Fragments, I, 3, 26; Joanne, Extracts, VI, 9, 12.—Conf. Varbertet et Magin, IX, 2, 16; Mentelle, III, 7, 21; Max du Camp, II, 27, 9." The primary references must be to Jacques-Antoine Dulaure's *Histoire physique, civil et morale de Paris* [The Physical, Social and Moral History of Paris] (1839) and to the regularly updated guide to Paris compiled by Adolphe Laurent Joanne and Paul Joanne, which was current when Franklin wrote the story. The confirmatory references are presumably to Charles Barberet and Alfred Magin's *Précis de géographie historique universelle* [A Historical Summary of World Geography] (1841), Edmé Mentelle's *Choix de lecturers géographiques et historiques* [Selected Lectures on Geography and History] (1783) and Maxime du Camp's *Paris: ses organs, sees functions et sa vie* [Paris: its anatomy, its functioning and its life] (1870).

ruins really were the tomb of the queen of the Old World. Her proud head still floats above those desolate spaces.

In a valley whose extent our eyes could scarcely embrace, domes, columns, porticos, slender steeples, immense heaps of rubble, frontons, statues, capitals, entablatures, ridges and cornices projected pell-mell. To our left we could see, boldly and proudly outlined against the dark sky, the crown of the triumphal arch elevated by one of the last Poleons of France to the glory of her armies. No earthquake had, therefore, obliterated the great city, and it ought to be possible to rediscover today what it was three thousand years ago, when the gigantic avalanche of earth, ash and sand under which it is buried descended upon it.

We stood there pensively for some time, absorbed in mute contemplation. Silence had fallen around us, as if, habituated as they were to the view, its grandeur still induced and indefinable effect of terror and vertigo in them. They did not know, however, what riches, marvels and memories lay beneath those heaps of sand, beneath that arid plain, where only a few sickly and jaundiced grasses grew. They say that it never rains there, and that the sky is always veiled; a superstitious dread prevents them from bringing their flocks to graze there, and even the bravest dare not venture there by night.

People recount that on certain stormy nights, life seems to reveal itself within those abysses. Myriads of phosphorescent glimmers skim the ground, and confused sounds resound in the bowels of the earth. Hammers fall on anvils, machines hiss, workmen shout, horses whinny, carriages roll heavily over paved roads. Outbursts of laughter mingle with stifled sobs, dolorous plaints with mocking sniggers, blasphemies with chaste prayers. One can hear the clamor of orgies and the sighs of virgins, imprecations and sacred canticles, the gnashing of teeth and joyful songs, dull groans, desperate cries and the murmur of amorous voices, the rattle of chains and the sound of kisses, the collapse of stacks of gold coins and the croaks of hunger. Then, suddenly, the strident call of the clarion resounds, and, over the tumult, causing all heads to bow, the grave voice of thousands of organs rises up, launching funereal symphonies into space, which seem to be announcing the funeral of an entire world. Then, gradually, the fires go out, silence is reborn, and death resumes possession of its empire.

It depends on you, Monsieur le Ministre, whether a part of these dreams will become realities. You understand, however, and the great intelligence of the Emperor cannot fail to agree with you, that in order for a rapid and complete result to be obtained, it will be necessary for the means at my disposal to correspond to the importance of the objective prescribed for us.

I have the honor of being, with respect to Your Excellency, Monsieur le Ministre, your very humble, very devoted and very obedient servant,

Admiral Baron Quésitor.

II

To Admiral Baron Quésitor, Commandant of the Caledonian Naval forces in the French Seas
Noumea, 30 June 1875
Minister of the Navy and the Colonies
Office of the Minister
No. 8717
(n.b. Note this number in the margin of the reply)

Monsieur l'Amiral
I have had the honor of communicating to the Emperor the dispatch from Paris that you addressed to me on 20 May last.

His Majesty has instructed me to transmit his congratulations to you, and deigned to sign yesterday a decree that, on my suggestion, confers upon you the Grand Cross of the Imperial Order of the Green Falcon.

His majesty desires that the clearance of the ruins of Paris be commenced without delay and be carried out with all possible rapidity. With that intention, He is placing under your command two infantry regiments and three regiments of military engineers, forming a total of 5,122 men, who will be embarked in the early days of next month.

The administration is putting at your disposal, in addition: 10,321 pickaxes, 9,814 spades, 2,503 sets of pincers, 1,001 mattocks, 6,062 birch brooms, 3,603 heather brooms, 1,025 horsehair brooms, 6,206 wheelbarrows, 1,409 tumbrils, 807 watchmen's cabins, 1,206 skips, 301,837 kilos of rails, 12,004 sleepers, 203,128 rail-chairs, 711,902 rivets, 127 spirit levels, 142 surveyor's poles, 59 rotating plates, 24 steam-cranes, 19 mechanical sweepers, 201 portable engines, 99 locomotives, 3,001 horses, 603 mules and 13 photographers.

It has been decided that a scientific commission will be attached to the expedition. It is composed of three members of the Académie des Beaux-Arts, three members of the Académie des Inscriptions et Belle-Lettres and three members of the Académie des Sciences. You will, I have no doubt, treat these venerable scholars with all the respect that is their due, and you will obtain inspiration from their experience and advice.

Receive, Monsieur l'Amiral, the assurance of my most distinguished consideration.

Minister of the Navy and the Colonies.
Comte A. Statarie

III

To His Excellency the Minister of Public Education in Religion and the Fine Arts in Noumea (Caledonia)
Paris, 30 November 4875

Monsieur le Ministre,
The scientific commission charged by Your Excellency with exploring the ruins of Paris has remained silent for some time, leaving it to Admiral Quésitor to keep the ministry up to date with all the details of the expedition. We did not want to

send out our first report until the results obtained would not only be of a nature to satisfy public curiosity but also to focus the attention of archeologists.

The moment has now come, and it is to me that the honor of representing the commission with regard to Your Excellency has fallen.

No incident troubled our crossing, which was too rapid to allow us to make many significant observations en route. On 21 August we came into harbor, and less than three weeks thereafter, a double railway line having linked the ruins to the sea, all the equipment was disembarked, an immense camp extended around Paris, and the clearance commenced.

The geological agglomeration that covers Paris is far from presenting a uniform surface; soundings carried out at intervals have permitted us to establish that although, at certain points, it rises thirty-six meters above the original ground level, it is sometimes only thirteen or fourteen meters deep. It is formed by successive layers, which were certainly superimposed on one another with prodigious rapidity. The origin and nature of the upheaval will remain, according all appearances, permanently insoluble problems; however, the form that the debris of organized bodies has assumed and the direction that the mineralogical deposits have affected reveal to the most inexperienced eye a great irruption that arrived from the southeast.

The entire mass can be divided into two quite distinct parts.

The upper stratum, which nowhere exceeds five meters, is composed of earth, ash and sand, forming three beds of various thickness.

The second stratum reveals the most varied elements. On proceeding from top to bottom, one first encounters two thick banks, one of quartz and the other of marl; they rest on a thin deposit of chalk, which is succeeded by two considerable foundations of oysterous schist and lobsterous clay. The latter system is characterized by the presence of an immeasurable quantity of oyster-shells and fossil fish, all of which are known to our ichthyologists. We have found, among other debris, the remains of *Anguilla tartarea, Astacus burdigalensis* and *Goujo friturius*.[31]

The flora is equally rich, and offers us, especially in the inferior layers, a few interesting subjects of observation. The most abundant species are the laurel (*Laurus militaria*) and the camellia (*Camellia feminea*), very often accompanied by petrifactions, among which one can make our leaves of tobacco (*Nicotiana cigaretica*) and absinthe (*Ductaria charantonia*).

The fauna has not furnished us with the opportunity for any important discovery. However, the bones of *Canis canichus* and those of *Felis gouttierius* are numerous, and we have discovered a complete head of *Lepus civeticus*—but these animals are already described in our treatises of paleontology.

I am limiting myself to listing here the most salient facts that have emerged from our observations; this brief summary will shortly be completed by a detailed memoir that my colleague Monsieur E. de Beaupré intends to address to the Académie des Sciences. The conclusions are explicit; they undermine a few historical data admitted previously, and provide a definitive solution to the chronological quarrel that has divided archeologists for such a long time. In fact, M. de Beaupré has demonstrated, with evidence, that the great geological revolution in which France was destroyed occurred toward the middle of the seventeenth century, no later than the year 1700 of the Christian Era. One must therefore, unhesitatingly, regard as falsified or interpolated in the surviving fragments of French authors, al the passages that seem to accord Paris a longer existence.

The Emperor's orders instructed us to clear, before anything else, the triumphal arch erected on the right bank of the

---

[31] All the Latin names in this passage and subsequent ones are jokes, mostly easily penetrable; *Anguilla* is a genus of eels and *Astacus* a genus off crayfish but *Goujo* is an improvisation based on "goujons" [of fried fish].

Seine. Three days sufficed for that work, and the glorious monument emerged intact from the shroud that had enveloped it for thirty centuries. It was then permitted to us to admire at our leisure that masterpiece of ancient architecture, to which, without any doubt, these beautiful lines from the *Anthologie Française* are addressed:

Rise up toward the skies, [gate of][32] victory
So that the giant of our glory
Might pass through without bending down!

All the faces of the monument are covered with perfect-ly-preserved sculptures. Beneath the arch, twenty meters high, a multitude of names engraved in the stone were designed to conserve the memory of the principal victories won by the French, and on thirty shields placed around the attic one can read the names of their most illustrious generals. We have established that important distinction without difficulty. A fragment of Duruy includes a list, unfortunately incomplete, of the principal French leaders,[33] and in that number feature the Ducs de Valmy, Montebello and Castiglione, whose three names we have found inscribed on the shields. The effects of time have, however, rendered the majority of these inscrip-

---

[32] The notional author inserts a footnote: "These words are missing from the original and have been thus restored by Monsieur Walken. One recalls the long debate that he sustained with Monsieur Laignes, who preferred "portico of victory." On this issue, consult: *Lettre de M. Walken à M. Laignes, au subjet d'une épigramme attribué à Victorugo et insérée dans le troisième volume de l'Anthologie française*, Noumea, 3860, octavo." At the end of the verse he adds a second footnote giving the reference: "*Anthologie française*, t. iii, ch. Ix, p.281." The quotation is from Victor Hugo's "À l'Arc de Triomphe de l'Étoile" in *Odes et ballades* (1837).
[33] The notional author includes a reference: "Recueil général des historiens français t. VIII, p. 117."

tions illegible, and we are far from having succeeded in deciphering all of them. We can, however, cite among the battles
those of Kellermann, Lannes, Augereau, Ney, Masséna, Lafa-
yette, Kléber, Dumouriez and Murat. We have similarly
gleaned the names of generals Valmy, Montebello, Castiglione, Elchingen, Austerlitz,[34] Marengo, Wagram and Aboukir.

This triumphal arch and the immense avenue that precedes it comprise the most grandiose entrance to a capital of
which the imagination has ever been able to dream; reality
here exceeds the fantastic tales in which the marvels of Babylon and Nineveh are celebrated.

Twenty meters wide, ornamented with flower-beds and
fountains, shaded by centuries-old trees whose roots we have
found transformed into lignite, the avenue extends as far as the
eye can see, bordered along its entire length by constructions
lavished with marble and gold.

Here, however, a difficulty arises. How can such a considerable number of princely dwelling gathered in the same
place be explained? We have contrived to resolve this question
triumphantly.

Garnier and Cassignac relate, in fact, that one of the last
sovereigns of France, having been obliged to reconquer his
throne by force of arms, rewarded the zeal of the leaders who
had helped him in that struggle with the gift of sumptuous
habitations.[35] Is it not natural to presume that they were built
in the vicinity of the monument consecrated to the glory of
French warriors, and that they became a kind of addendum to
it? We hesitated to admit this hypothesis, however, in spite of

---

[34] The notional author notes: "Joanne (*Extraits*, V, IV, 109)
informs us that the name of this general was given to one of
the bridges of Paris."

[35] The notional author gives the reference: "*Fragments de
l'histoire dite du 2 decembre*, in the *Recueil general des historiens françaises*, t. IX, p. 314." The mangled reference is to
Adolphe Granier de Cassagnac's *Histoire du directoire* (1851-
55).

its plausibility, until an interesting epigraphic discovery dispelled all our doubts.

In the course of the excavations at the extremity of the avenue, an engineer discovered an indicative plaque similar to those placed at the corners of our streets. It bore the words:

AVENUE DES CH... ...ES.

Enlightenment was there, and did not take long to illuminate our eyes. A brief discussion sufficed for us to restore the letters erased by time and complete the inscription, which must obviously have been:

AVENUE DES CHEFS-ILLUSTRES.

The Avenue des Chefs-Illustres terminated in a vast square, once magnificently decorated, but only one of its ornaments survives intact: an immense needle formed by a single stone, twenty-five meters high and entirely covered by characters that we have been unable to decipher. We think that it ought to be recognized as an *ex-voto*, probably a religious monument erected to the memory of the ancient sailors who inaugurated river commerce, always so active on the Seine. In fact, the situation of the square on the bank of the river, a fragment of an inscription—ERE DE LA MARINE—and the debris of numerous rostral columns all concur in demonstrating that the interests and services of river navigation were centralized in that location.

A precious discovery results from these observations and the impossibility of comprehending a single word of the symbolic writing with which the monument is covered. We see there the proof that among the French, as among many other peoples of antiquity, the priests had a special language, known only to initiates and unintelligible to laymen. I will add—a fact whose great importance will not escape Your Excellency—that Monsieur Nairan believes that he recognizes in these mysterious characters a vague resemblance to the hieratic script of the primitive Egyptians.

I have the honor of being, with respect to Your Excellency, Monsieur le Ministre, your most humble, most devoted and most obedient servant,

L. Le Rouge,
Membre de l'Institut,
Académie des Inscriptions et Belles-Lettres.

IV

To His Excellency the Minister of Public Education in Religion and the Fine Arts in Noumea (Caledonia)
Paris, 28 December 4875

Monsieur le Ministre,

Since the date of its last report, the scientific commission to the ruins of Paris has continued its work actively, but the ice and snow have recently created a fairly serious obstacle for us, and ten days have been spent installing our workers—previously lodged in tents—in the cleared buildings, as best we could.

However, in spite of the relative slowness with which we are now advancing, the progress made in the month of December has yielded precious secrets, and also embarrassing problems.

On leaving the Place de la Navigation one encounters an important road to the right, bordered on one side by houses preceded by covered arcades and on the other by a very extensive garden, the extremity of which we have not yet reached.

We know from Max du Camp[36] that gardens were very rare within the perimeter of Paris. Our first thought was, therefore, that the immense space must have served as a cemetery,

---

[36] The notional author adds a reference: "*Fragments*, I, 19, 37."

and partial excavations carried out a trifle haphazardly at various points have confirmed this supposition.

Several tombs still exist. In those that we have opened all traces of organic matter have disappeared under the effects of the centuries, but the group and the statue that surmounted two of them were still in a perfect state of conservation.

The group is composed of three individuals: a vigorous man and two young people, doubtless his sons; all three are engaged in a desperate struggle with snakes that have them in their coils. We have no information about the terrible accident that cost the family members their lives, and the geographical location of Paris scarcely permits the supposition that snakes of those dimensions can ever have lived wild there; these must therefore have escaped from a menagerie, and only been recaptured after immolating three innocent victims.[37]

The statue, similarly sculpted in marble, represents a knife-grinder busy sharpening a blade on a stone. The head is beautiful ad expressive, but we have no way of knowing by virtue of what exceptional circumstance a tomb of white marble was build for a man of such humble status, and who seems to have hardly possessed enough to enable him to buy clothes. Perhaps it is necessary to see him as the hero of one of the popular insurrections so dear to Parisians.[38]

On the other side of the street, the clearing of the buildings has only furnished us with one discovery worthy of inclusion in this report.

In the middle of a small quadrangular square lay a fallen equestrian statue in bronze. The horse, massive in form, sup-

[37] The statue presumably depicts the myth of Lacöon; Napoléon I had looted the original of the most famous Classical statue representing the story but it had been returned to the Vatican after his fall; numerous copies and castings can still be found in Paris and elsewhere.

[38] The original of this statue is similarly antique; again, numerous copies exist, including one by Fognini designed for the gardens at Versailles.

ports a thin young woman, frail, delicate, dressed in iron armor and wearing a crown of laurels. She is standing upright in her stirrups and her right hand is waving a flag. On the front of the granite pedestal, a very brief inscription has become illegible.

This singular monument constitutes an enigma, of which we have given up attempting to penetrate the meaning.

In order to study the woman more closely, we have separated her from the horse, and in the cavity thus opened, we have found the following words traced in chalk: *République française. Pucelle d'Orléans*: an inexplicable phrase, which complicates the problem instead of clarifying it.

We have had several discussions on this subject. Many hypotheses, sometimes very ingenious, were proposed, discussed and set aside, then taken up again re-examined, modified, and finally rejected. Despairing of arriving at a satisfactory solution, we have taken the decision to pack the statue up and send it to Noumea, in the desire that it be submitted to the examination of our colleagues at the Institut.

I have the honor of being, with respect to Your Excellency, Monsieur le Ministre, your most humble, most devoted and most obedient servant,

J. Lepère
Membre de l'Institut, Académie des Beaux-Arts

V

Imperial Institute of Caledonia (Fine Arts Section)
Account of the Session of 17 March 4786, M. Duparc Presiding

The President. The floor is given to the reporter of the committee charged with examining the equestrian statue found in the ruins of Paris.

M. Legendre, reporter. Before making known to you the conclusions that the committee has reached, I think I ought to summarize briefly for you the three hypotheses that remained standing at the time the closure of the debate was declared.

According to some of our colleagues, the statue that you have before your eyes represents one of those warrior women known in antiquity by the name of Amazons. The adversaries of that opinion, however, respond that the statue is armored in iron, while the costume of the Amazons consisted solely of a short breastplate. In another respect too, the statue is too complete, for everyone knows that the Amazons had their right breast excised because it hampered the use of a bow. Finally, none of the words inscribed inside the monument are able to lend any support to it.

That inscription, they add, ought to be our principal guide, and, in fact, includes everything that we seek. If one brings together three passages contained in the fragments of Thiers, Michelet and L. Blanc,[39] one cannot doubt that the French were governed for some years by a woman named République. Is it not quite natural that a statue of her was erected, and that she should be represented on horseback, clad in armor and crowned with laurels?

That second opinion rallied more partisans than the first—without, however, yet being able to satisfy the majority.

Even admitting the reality of the historical fact, it was objected, perhaps the first part of the inscription only indicates that the statue was erected under the reign of that République,

---

[39] The notion author gives the reference: "Recueil general des historiens français, IV, 9, 11; V, 7. 8; VII, 12, 3." Jules Michelet devoted an entire volume of his mammoth *Histoire de France* (vol. 7, 1835) to Jeanne d'Arc, effectively formulating the now-familiar mythical version of her exploits. Adolphe Thiers produced an *Histoire de la revolution française* (1824-27) in his early days, before becoming President of the Third Republic in 1871. The fervent radical socialist Louis Blanc, long a thorn in Thiers' side was one of the leading participants of the Revolution of 1848.

in which case it is the second part that ought to furnish the solution o the problem.

Minerva, the goddess of war, is more often represented fully armored, with a shield on one arm and a spear in the other. The helmet is undoubtedly lacking, but let us not forget that Minerva disputed the golden apple with Juno and Venus on Mount Ida; the French, whose gallantry became proverbial, did not want to hide that charming face under a helmet; they left uncovered the only beauty that was ever shown to humans by the chaste goddess who punished the indiscreet gaze of Tiresias by depriving him of sight, and who always conserved her virginity.

This third hypothesis, based on a literal translation of the two lines doubtless traced by the artist himself, is also in accordance with the most incontestable scientific, historical and artistic data; it is the one that has prevailed in the bosom of the committee.

The committee thinks, therefore, that the statue sent from Paris represents Minerva, and that it was founded in the city of Orléans under the government of Queen République. In consequence, it expresses the desire that a request be addressed to His Excellency the Minister of Public Education, soliciting the gift of this ancient Minerva, to replace the modern bust that ornaments our meeting hall.

.These conclusions were adopted unanimously.

VII

To His Excellency the Minister of Public Education in Religion and the Fine Arts in Noumea (Caledonia)
Paris, 2 March 4876

Monsieur le Ministre,

We began the year rather sadly, awaiting the arrival of the *Scrutatrix*, which did not dock until 8 January, but the day after, our venerable senior member told us in solemn session about the distinctions accorded to us. It is, therefore, with the expression of our very sincere thanks that our report will commence on this occasion, and we beg Your Excellency to transmit to the Emperor the homage of our respectful gratitude.

The decorations accorded to the army have been distributed to it by Admiral Quésitor, after a grand review during which the name of His Majesty was cheered enthusiastically several times. The tribe established on the banks of the Seine made haste to enjoy the spectacle, and those last representatives of the Old World mingled their cries loudly with those of our soldiers.

The intelligence of these still-half-savage people cannot be praised too much. Incessantly in contact with us, they are trying to discover the secrets of our civilization, and are appropriating them, one by one, with a prodigious rapidity. Several of our methods have already been improved by them, and our country is in their debt for numerous inventions that we have hastened to adopt.

They now know about our political institutions in the smallest detail, and criticize them loudly. Strangely enough, as soon as they broach the subject, passion carries them away and reason seems to abandon them. These barbarians, totally unfamiliar a few months ago with our social organization, gladly propose improvements to us in this matter too. They have already offered us two or three complete systems, each more unreasonable than the last, which overturn all received ideas on the subjects of taxation, public education, religion, municipal elections, etc., etc. They would be particularly delighted to see us adopt the fundamental principal of their government, which consists of changing their leader as often as possible.

In spite of these aberrations and the scant success they obtain with our soldiers, the little tribe still manifests a very real sympathy toward us, and seems to be following the progress of our endeavors with keen interest.

The latter are continuing actively, and we have discovered the imposing necropolis in which, since the origin of the monarchy, the mortal remains of French sovereigns were deposited. It is an immense palace situated at the extremity of the cemetery described in our last report. The upper floors have collapsed, but the ground floor had supported their weight almost everywhere without weakening, and its vas halls have conserved incomparable historical treasures for us.

Two of them enclose stone coffins, large, massive and charged with inscriptions in hieratic characters. We observe there that the sacerdotal language of the French varied through the centuries, for several inscriptions differ from the kind employed on the monolith in the Place de la Navigation. The script is heavy regular, literal rather than symbolic, but just as indecipherable.

The connecting rooms are full of statues and busts representing the kings and queens of France, whose bodies doubtless rest in the subterranean pats of the edifice. There are also groups representing the principal events of their reigns.

Some of these sovereigns wear the costume of Roman emperors, but it is not necessary to conclude therefrom that the French sometimes adopted it. Only four or five kings, H. Martin[40] tells us, had the innocent mania of having themselves represented thus. Others are almost nude; the latter preferred to imitate certain gods of primitive religions. Even the queens did no escape this defect. We already knew by way of Jehan de Sismondi[41] that one of them, named Diana, had posed more than once for status of that goddess, and we have discovered here the marbles to which the veridical history makes allusion.

Venuses are equally numerous, and there is one among them that surpasses all the rest by the boldness and delicacy of its execution. She is nude to the waist, and her left knee,

---

[40] The notional author's reference: "*Recueil général des historiens français*. XII, 17, 12." The reference is presumably to H.-Marie Martin's *L'Empire et la Révolution* (1861)

[41] The notional author's reference: "Fragments de l'histoire de Henri II." The reference is to J.-C.-L. Simonde de Sismondi's *Histoire des français* (1821-44)

slightly raised, seems to be retaining unaided the thousand pleats of a garment ready to fall. The torso is supple and lively. The breast recalls those pretty lines from the *Anthologie*:

> Do you see those azure veins,
> Light, delicate and polished
> Running over those rounded breasts,
> In the whiteness of pure marble?[42]

The head, noble and proud, expresses a power conscious of itself and always sure of victory. The two arms are missing, unfortunately, and we have searched for them in vain. Monsieur Chevalier thinks that the masterpiece in question ought to be attributed to the sculptor Karpeau,[43] who flourished toward the end of the sixteenth century.

While our photographers took possession of the necropolis, we pursued the course of our research, and we found ourselves in the presence of two churches constructed in the same plan and inked together by an octagonal tower. We have only cleared the façades, which are very elegant, and we have learned therefrom that one of these temples was consecrated to Saint Marie du Louvre. Indeed, an inscription engraved in the stone, and doubtless incomplete, includes the words MAIRIE DU LOUVRE and all philologists are aware that in old French, the etymologic A that bore an accent was reinforced and became the diphthong AL; thus Bretagne was written

---

[42] The notional author's reference and note: "A. de Musset, Anthologie française, II, 4, 9. These lines demonstrate the gross error into which those scholars have fallen who claim that the French poets always alternated masculine and feminine rhymes." The original, which uses an ABBA rhyme-scheme, contains three adjectives accompanying feminine nouns and one a masculine noun (ironically, *sein* [breast]). The poem cited is "Sur trois marches de marbre rose."

[43] The garbled reference is presumably to Jean-Baptiste Carpeaux (1827-1875).

Bretaigne, Champagne Champaigne and Marie Mairie, etc., etc. Your Excellency is not unaware that philology has become, in our day, an exact science of the same kind as algebra.

The combination of all the data, the text of this inscription having confirmed the data furnished by architectural examination, has demonstrated with mathematical rigor that the monument in question was built before the sixteenth century of the Christian Era.

While digging in the ground in front of this church, an engineer discovered two bottles of white glass, taller than they are broad, cut at right angles, whose purpose we do not know. Nearby was found a small lead medallion, which seems to us to merit profound study.

Approximately twelve millimeters across, it has the form of a regular hexagon and is traversed in the direction of its thickness by a fairly strong wire. On one of its faces three interlinked capital letters are depicted, which we believe to be a J, a V and a B. The other face presents the mutilated inscription:

VIN ???
??
B LL

The two letters making up the second line are illegible and there is only room for a single letter at the end of the third line.

I can make a firm declaration on this issue. In the discussions held to search for the meaning of this numismatic enigma, Monsieur Pinson made the initial suggestion that perhaps we had in our hands a specimen of the military medal instituted by one of the last Poleons of France.[44] I recalled in my turn

---

[44] The notional author's footnote: "Voy. Les Pharaons, les Sésostris et les Poléons, rapprochements historiques. p.209." i.e., See *The Pharaohs: Historical parallels between the Sesostrises and the Poleons.*

that Latin was frequently employed at that time in inscriptions. That was a flash of enlightenment, and Monsieur de Lonpont immediately proclaimed that it must have read: VINCIT IN BELLO. No more doubt was permissible.[45]

This medal must therefore have shone on the breast of a soldier, a French warrior to whom the fatherland rendered this solemn testimony: *Brave in War!*

I am gripped by emotion as I write these lines, and it is with them that I wish to terminate. Our next report will tell you about the new direction we adopted several days ago, and all the hopes that it promises us for the future.

I have the honor of being, with respect to Your Excellency, Monsieur le Ministre, your most humble, most devoted and most obedient servant,

L. Valfleury
Membre de l'Institut,
Académie des Inscriptions et Belles-Lettres.

VIII

To His Excellency the Minister of the Navy and Colonies, at Noumea (Caledonia)
Paris, 6 April 4876

Monsieur le Ministre,

It is with despair in my heart that I take up my pen to write this report, doubtless the last that Your Excellency will receive from Paris. I do not wish, however, to attempt any justification of my conduct here, and I do not wish to devote myself to any recrimination against the men you have given me as auxiliaries and have betrayed the Caledonian flag in such a cowardly fashion; I owe Your Excellency a sincere and impartial account of the facts, and here it is.

---

[45] One hesitates to disagree with such a brilliant deduction, but is it possible that the three letters were actually SVP and the half-erased name Vincent de Paul?

Since the beginning of the month of April, I had noticed certain mutinous tendencies among our soldiers; the repression was prompt and energetic, but ineffective. Soon, murmurs, and even threats, reached my ears. I interrogated the officers but their embarrassed, evasive replies told me nothing. Resolved to put an end to it, I announced that I would review the troops the following day.

I slept on board, and toward midday I arrived in the Avenue des Chefs-Illustres, where all the troops were in battle formation.

A sickening spectacle met my eyes. Most of the men had refused to put on their dress uniforms and were wearing their working clothes. Mingling with the indigenes, they were laughing, sinking, smoking their pipes and passing bottles from hand to hand, which, once emptied, they threw away. When I arrived, the officers took up their positions but they remained mute and impassive. As soon as I set foot in the avenue I was greeted by hurrahs, acclamations and confused cries whose meaning I could not make out. It seemed that the wretches had been suddenly afflicted with vertigo. I tried to speak, but the cries redoubled, and I was able to make out the following phrases: *Long live the Republic! Freedom of the Press! Right of Association! Down with Capital! Organized labor! No more exploitation of human by humans!*

I understood everything.

I understood the error I had made I allowing my troops to associate with the indigenes—but the political fantasies of those barbarians were so irrational that the contagion of such follies seemed impossible. Alas, I am now convinced that the scholars who affirm that Noumea was once a French colony are not mistaken; the voice of the blood has made itself heard; it only required a spark to awaken instincts dormant for nearly thirty centuries!

I did not know what decision to make, when a man emerged from the ranks and came straight toward me.

By his insignia and the nacreous seashell resplendent in his head-dress, I recognized the present leader of the indigenes.

"Monsieur l'Amiral," he said to me cheerfully, "you can see that all resistance is futile. We have eight thousand well-armed men, and no foreigner can any longer set foot on this territory, which belongs to us; bow down to the inevitable and join us. The reign of tyranny is over; you can read on our flag the three words: *Liberty, Equality, Fraternity*; they will go with us around the world." He smiled, and added: "For that, one admiral is not too many; accept my offer, therefore, and you can retain your title, your functions and your brilliant uniform."

Indignant at this proposition, I turned to the venerable scholars that Your Excellency gave me as advisers, and interrogated them with my gaze.

They all bowed their heads.

The chief went over to them. "Monsieur Syssel," he said to one of them, extending his hand to him, the position you have solicited in the new government is granted to you. By a decree signed ten minute ago, you are appointed the curator of the monolith of the Place de la Navigation..."

7 April.

Yesterday's dispatch was interrupted by a visit from our new leader. He explained to me the political ideas that will serve as a basis for his government, and the social reforms he is considering. Some of them seem to me, in reality, very sensible, even urgent, for in many respects, the foundations on which modern society rests are barbaric, unjust and fortunately decrepit. I therefore decided that I ought not to refuse him my collaboration and the support of my long experience.

At any rate, unless I can swim all the way back to Noumea, I am compelled to remain here, since all my mariners have abandoned me and my fleet has been confiscated. I shall, in consequence, enclose this dispatch in a securely-sealed bottle, and will then throw it into the sea, and hazard will deliver it to you, Citizen Minister, when it wishes.

Farewell and Fraternity,
Admiral Quésitor.

Vanitas vanitatum, vanitas vanitarum et omnia vanitas. Non est priorum memoria; sed nec eorum quidam quae postea future sunt erit recorrdinato apud eos qui future sunt in novissimo. Vidi cuncta quae fiunt sub sole, and ece unversa vanitas.

(Ecclesiastes)[46]

---

[46] Vanity of vanities, vanity of vanities; all is vanity. There is no remembrance of former things; neither shall there be any remembrance of things that are to come with those that shall come after. I have seen all the works that are done under the sun; and behold, all is vanity and vexation of spirit. *Ecclesiastes* [1: 1, 11 & 14]

Maurice Spronck: *Year 330 of the Republic*
(1894)

> *Future Time! Vision Sublime!*
> Victor Hugo[47]

The Celebrations in Orléans

On the sixteenth of Messidor in the year 313 of the Republic (2105 of the Christian Era) the Commune of Orléans
was to celebrate the centenary of its liberation.

Great public celebrations were authorized and organized
by the municipal council; invitations were sent by telephone to
the four corners of the civilized world, summoning the representatives of other communes to the peaceful solemnity. Many
cities, having accepted, sent deputations; others, more luke-
warm, simply sent phonographs loaded in advance with sympathetic speeches. Yet others, either indifferent or enclosed in
their local egotism, or even driven by paltry jealousies, invented vague excuses of found means to stay away. The feast was,
nevertheless, everything that could be expected, and left a
durable impression on everyone.

The Orléanais had attached an extreme importance to it.
For them, the date of 16 Messidor 313 was not only the anni-
versary of their liberation; it also marked the end of a political
conflict that went back for some forty years, whose bitterness
time did not seem to have soothed. The existence of a simple

---

[47] The first line of the poem "Lux" from *Les Châtiments*
(1853), an anticipatory hymn to the universal republic, written
shortly after the *coup d'état* that ushered in the Second Empire
and sent Hugo into exile.

equestrian statue, a statue of Jeanne d'Arc, had sufficed to foment and maintain that long internal dissent.

The Progressivist party demanded imperiously that Jeanne d'Arc and her mount should be taken down and returned to the foundry; the Conservative party, weakened from day to day by the diffusion of liberal ideas, pleaded extenuating circumstances, and demanded that the monument of vanished barbaric epochs be kept as a curiosity. The adversaries were always slandering one another over the affair, with the venomous acrimony appropriate to free men, and as it is in the nature of certain individuals never to shut up, it was rare for two weeks[48] to pass without a polemic reopening the issue, always sustained by an incessantly renewed interest.

The Progressivists wanted to make the most of everything that was outdated, and even immoral and dangerous, in honoring a bronze image of a woman in whom the majority of the oldest and most stupid abolished superstitions were incarnate. Jeanne symbolized respect for governmental authority, belief in God and the immortality of the soul, patriotic idolatry, the cult of military legend and the exaltation of virginity. Was she not one of the most complete type-specimens of ignorance and ancient savagery in History?

The Conservatives did not deny these undeniable arguments, but, imperfectly emancipated from the religion of their ancestors, they could not shake off all attachment to the things of the past. They alleged, with specious logic, that the protectress of Orléans could scarcely be declared responsible for a philosophical and moral faith which was that of her era, and that her visions could, in any case, be explained by hysterical disturbances. To which the radical faction replied that it was quite disposed to grant plenary indulgence to an irresponsible individual, but that, on the other hand, hysteria had never

---

[48] Although the future communards have restored the months of the Revolutionary calendar they obviously have not followed its example in abolishing the week and replacing it with periods of ten days.

constituted an entitlement to any kind of commemorative monument.

In the state of peaceful tranquility and perfect happiness at which humankind had arrived, quarrels of that magnitude did not often arise. The public—who, deep down, regarded Jeanne d'Arc as a joke—was amused by the debate and followed its ups and downs attentively, commenting scrupulously on even item of the attacks and ripostes, marking the hits and observing the parries as if in a fencing match. Enormous sums had been wagered on one side or the other by the time the affair was cut short by a communal plebiscite. The electorate, which had been tempted to take an interest in the heroine's fate, did not want to seem to be siding with reaction, and voted unanimously for the removal of the statue.

The measure was, in any case, necessary. Since Europe had entered into its Golden Age, the number of benefactors of humanity had increased in such proportions that no one knew where to place the most modest bust; the external façades of houses were plastered with them from top to bottom. The streets, squares and crossroads were cluttered with a host of celebrities sculpted in marble or cast in metal. When the day came that the Commune of Orléans decided to erect a monument to the illustrious chemist Claude Moullard, no vacant surface worth of him any longer remained. The partisans of Jeanne d'Arc sensed that their resistance was futile; all those who were able to do so settled their bets honestly.

In spite of the annoyance of settling these accounts, no one dared protest against the honor rendered to Claude Mouillard. There was unanimous recognition of his immense worth as a philanthropist and scientist; no one was unaware of his admirable work in relation to the fabrication of artificial comestibles, and were in accord regarding the expansion that the science of alimentary chemistry—still in limbo in the first century of the republic—had undergone thanks to him. When he died, his industrial methods had brought within the range of everyone—and in profusion—fake nourishment as tasty and almost as healthy as the genuine article.

Such entitlements certainly merited a monument like the one in which the glory and the features of the great man would be immortalized. Upright, in a meditative attitude, he dominated from the height of his marble pedestal several majestic groups of allegorical sculptures, from which a figure of Abundance stood out, cornucopia in hand. The artist had been able to imitate the fabric of garments with an incomparable perfection.

In a truly civilized and happy country, the organization of a celebration is never without grave difficulties. Without extreme ingenuity, in fact, it becomes almost impossible to distract people whose life is a perpetual distraction. One does not distribute food to people who are overflowing with nourishment. One does not offer concerts, scenic representations or nocturnal illuminations to a city in which every inhabitant possesses a theatrophone and which is illuminated by electric light from dusk to dawn. If horse racing still retained some attraction in 313, it was only because the Society for the Protection of Animals had succeeded in rendering racecourses very rare. As for the inauguration of a statue, the charm of the unfamiliar had been missing from that king of spectacle for a long time.

It was, however, necessary to invent something in honor of Claude Mouillard and the centenary of Orléans. After infinite hesitation, the chief magistrate of the city, the Supreme Companion had an idea. That idea consisted of a complete archeological reconstruction of the barbaric life of the first century of the Republican Era.

Improvements in technology, made it quite easy to give certain quarters of the modern city something of their former wretched and unhealthy appearance. The electricity could be turned off for twenty-four hours: no more electric light, but lighting by gas; no more aerial locomotion, but carriages drawn by genuine horses, circulating through the streets and transporting the celebrants to different centers of the festival. In the suburbs, vast halls would be constructed in which the old industrial crafts would be practiced. Scenes of war and torture, such as hanging or the guillotine, would be staged in an immense hippodrome. Restaurants would furnish their clients with natural aliments, prepared and seasoned in the ancient style.

Two of these proposals, unfortunately, drew violent protests from the indefatigable Society for the Protection of Animals. Its members declared unanimously that to harness any living being to any sort of vehicle whatsoever was to take humanity back to the bleakest times of its history. In addition, the phrase "natural aliments" had made them anxious. Were sheep to be killed and their flesh eaten? When they learned that the planners of the program really did intend to do that, their exasperation knew no bounds. They threatened to leave the sacrilegious city *en masse*, and would certainly have done so if they had been more confident that anyone would try to stop them.

The solemn date finally arrived. At dawn, the municipality had artificial clouds launched, which dampened the ardor of the sun and spread a little moist coolness through the atmosphere. At the same time, the refrigerating machines maintained the temperature at exactly twenty-one degrees Centigrade. Vaporizers of rare perfumes were installed in several districts. On the route that the official procession was to follow and in the boulevards in the vicinity of Claude Mouillard's statue, the marble of the streets was covered with precious carpet and the houses were decorated with bright fabrics, without any manifestation of bad taste.

At eight o'clock in the morning, the guests arrived; they were immediately received at the municipal palace, while the various engines of aerial locomotion that had brought them returned to park outside the city without there being any need for police. At eleven o'clock, the last belated delegations were introduced; the last consignments of phonographs had reached their destination and were only waiting to be placed on the speech stage to recite their compliments. The procession formed up in good order, and began to file away.

Each of the important individuals who composed it was seated in a mobile armchair, powered by electricity, somewhat analogous to ancient tricycles and easily steerable. It would, in fact, have been impossible to impose the obligation of a twenty-minute walk on men and women exclusively devoted to intellectual labor, long unaccustomed to physical exercise. The mobile armchair was, in any case, in common use among the people of the fourth century, for the last twenty-five or thirty years everyone had been making use of them, hardly quitting them except to go to bed.

At the head of eleven hundred and twenty representatives of foreign communes, the Supreme Companion of Orléans, Citizeness Paule Bonin, rolled in her tricycle. Although she was not surrounded by any of the theatrical paraphernalia dear to barbaric epochs and races, having no particular escort, no fancy uniform or multicolored decorations, the moral prestige with which she was clad was sufficient indication of her high status. The members of the crowd bared their heads as she passed by with respectful sympathy.

Citizeness Paul Bonin had once been pretty, but at the age of thirty-four she no longer was. Like the majority of her contemporaries, male or female, she had been afflicted by morbid obesity at a young age and had not taken long to reach an amplitude that would have rendered life impossible for her in a less perfect civilization. An ingenious system of corsetry armored her from her knees to her shoulders, compressed her thighs, held in her belly, clutched her waist, pulled in her torso and supported her arms, while her blotchy cheeks and chin descended over that amorphous ensemble in several stages. Only her eyes and forehead retained a forceful and, so to speak, intellectual beauty: the eyes were profound and brilliant between the heavy eyelids; the forehead was thoughtful, denuded and polished by long nights over the entire surface of the cranium, scarcely garnished now by a few tufts of graying hair.

No one had devoted herself more fully, body and soul, to disinterested and incessant labor for progress, science and the public good than Paule Bonin. Equipped with the solid and varied education that the commune gave to everyone, exempted by a superior social organization from the slightest material cares, she had been able to develop without hindrance and make the most of the marvelous resources of her genius.

At fifteen or thereabouts, like the majority of young people to whom the state of their health permitted it, she had dissipated in disorder time that would have been better spent in study, but even that time had not been wasted in her case, for it had taught her the vanity of love and pleasure; free of the moral prejudices that had once imposed duties on women different from those of men, she had tried the subtlest sensualities one by one; at twenty, having sampled everything and got past everything, in the great appeasement of her fatigued senses, she had renounced vulgar pleasures in order to devote herself to more nobly intellectual tasks and cultivate higher ambitions. In her voluntary solitude she had savored the joys of knowledge and understanding, and her heart beat then for humanity. Several significant discoveries had assured her the gratitude of her fellow citizens during her life and a statue after her death.

When all the delegations were ranged in their armchairs around Claude Mouillard's monument, the master of the municipal fanfare pressed the lever of his music-box, and a triumphal march sprang forth from the immense crate mounted on six wheels, executed by a mechanical orchestra with impeccable precision. A murmur of admiration greeted the last notes of the piece.

After that, Citizeness Bonin's tricycle climbed the inclined plane that led to the stage of honor; with a painful effort she lifted up her corpulence and made her speech in a standing position A further approving murmur underlined the peroration, and it was the same after each speech or phonographic audition. Two and a quarter hours later, the ceremony was concluded; the pedestal of the statue disappeared beneath wreaths and foliage. The audience dissolved, its members departing at hazard through the city in quest of diversion.

They amused themselves like civilized folk, with a correct reserve, devoid of the feverish excitement that savages put into their pleasures. The archeological reconstructions were sampled; the natural meals, judged to be a trifle repulsive, were less than successful, and only a few unfeeling individuals decided, for reasons of dilettantism, to bite into foodstuffs that had once been alive. The horse-drawn carriages attracted the curious. The various spectacles reproducing ancient wars and tortures interested the crowd by virtue of the perfection of the staging and the exactitude of the details. The triumph of the theatrical machinery even caused an incident that might have had grave consequences.

The program of tortures included an execution by guillotine. When an admirably constructed automaton was seen to emerge from the prison door, sustained by the executioner's aides and accompanied by the priest, with a bloodless face and eyes rolled back in fear, a tremulous lower jaw and a shortness of breath that caused the shoulders to shake, a frisson of horror ran through the crowd. At the moment when a flood of red liquid spurted on to the ground from the mannequin lying on the platform, it was too much for the impressionable nerves of the audience; cries of protest and anguish burst forth; men and women fainted; a few attempted to race toward the exits, knocking down the old and the disabled; a general bustle was produced, in the midst of which the strident howls of epileptics abruptly seized by fits were heard. It was fortunate that there was no fatal accident to be deplored, but the following day the press fulminated, with good reason, against bloody exhibitions worthy of another era.

With the exception of that hitch, however, nothing troubled the joy of the celebrations. The inconvenience of gas lighting, the slowness with which the street-lights had to be lighted one by one and the yellow light that the spread around them, and that entire display of obsolescence, offered the

Orléanais an entirely new spectacle, and made them smile. Those who were not completely worn out by the fatigues of the day stayed up quite late wandering in their tricycles through the archaic décor of the city, philosophizing among themselves on the beauty of science, the progress of human-kind and the good fortune of living in the fourth century of the Republican Era.

A Retrospective Glance

Like every other commune in the world, the Commune of Orléans had not arrived at that condition of miraculous prosperity without effort. Indeed, it had only been achieved by noble struggle against inequality, poverty and injustice. An expense of inexhaustible devotion, relentless labor and, too often, abundant bloodshed made up the melancholy and glorious balance-sheet of the supreme crisis in which civilization was obliged to fight for several centuries against the inertia and ignorance of ancient barbarity.

The French Revolution had prepared everything but, in reality, had founded nothing. For a hereditary nobility it substituted an aristocracy of money, for one oppression another no less heavy. It had never contrived to understand that a society remains infallibly reduced to impotence so long as it has not shaken off such shackles as religion, patriotism, property and the family. The Convention marks a date in history; it did not advance the earthly well-being of the species by an inch.

The various regimes, monarchic or Caesarian, that were imposed thereafter lacked the capacity to cut through the problem of popular claims. For nearly eighty years, save for the brief clarity of the Second Republic, Europe seemed to hesitate. Illustrious thinkers designed admirable systems; a few apostles, more inspired, excited a multitude of bloody riots that maintained the crowd's consciousness of its rights and obtained advantageous situations for the majority of their leaders. Nevertheless, the general march of progress was extremely slow; it required a simple dynastic and national question to emerge by chance to provoke a cataclysm and give the legitimate aspirations of humankind a further recrudescence.

The Franco-Prussian war provoked by the personal ambitions of King Wilhelm and Emperor Napoléon III was the evil from which circumstances were to bring forth good. Only the proclamation of the Paris Commune would have sufficed to pay for the thousand of cadavers strewn on the battlefields; it was the first material realization of the idea that was later to dominate the world; it would create a symbol for future social reformers.

By igniting a civil war before those who were then called foreigners of enemies, the Parisian insurrectional government denied the fatherland and affirmed universal fraternity; by shooting the priests, magistrates and officers that it detained as hostages, it put to death religion, the magistrature and the army—all the agents of ignorance and servitude; by burning houses and palaces, it cast down the idols of property and capital. Later, it had its martyrs. And then, as right always remains right, and ends up triumphant in spite of everything, a time came when a frightened bourgeois parliament no longer dared keep the heroes of the communalist revolution in its prisons; with regard to its victims it played the game of pardon; with a derisory generosity it offered forgetfulness of its own crimes to those it had robbed, exiled, imprisoned and massacred. The wretches submitted in silence to that supreme insult, and did not forget anything. The propaganda resumed.

The seed of future happiness was sown and had germinated; it only remained to blossom. The political and moral condition of Europe did not furnish it with an unfavorable terrain toward the end of the first century of the Republican Era. In those societies which claimed to be more or less democratic, and which were more or less strongly hierarchical, the so-called ruling classes did not possess any guiding principle and scarcely knew anything other than their immediate and egotistical interest. On the other hand, with the diffusion of education, the ruled classes were gradually emancipated from the old tutelage by means of which they were formerly controlled. With every passing year, they demanded more imperiously their share of wellbeing and enjoyment; they threatened recourse to force to obtain justice; in spite of their poverty and the legal shackles that enchained them, they syndicated their disseminated aspirations and contrived to organize for the struggle.

Everyone felt the imminent and probably implacable necessity of that struggle; in reality, however, it remained impossible as long as the powerful military administrations that resulted from the Franco-Prussian War had not been dissolved.

The system of the armed nation might have served the cause of socialism as well as aggravating the burden of taxation by making the barracks a meeting place between agricultural workers and factory workers. Nevertheless, it maintained nationalist sentiments in the masses, and constituted an almost unbreakable guarantee of immunity to the rulers. There, too, right ended up victorious; when militarism had reached the full measure of the ridiculousness, shame and horror implicit in its essence, it crumbled, to the unanimous applause of populations.

A long time before, philosophers had already demonstrated the monstrosities of war. They accused it of not settling anything; on the other hand, they proved, figures in hand, that every battle cost a considerable number of human lives, and created an obstacle to the development of agriculture, industry and commerce; they established, furthermore, that a bullet or a cannonball could kill a man of genius as easily as an imbecile, and an honest man as easily as a rogue—by virtue of which, they concluded the immorality of the international duels in which primitive races invested their most cherished glory.

Some of those memorable philanthropists had devoted themselves to working for peace with an apostolic passion; slowly, by dint of hard work and patience, they obtained appreciable results. A time came when they were able to bring followers of the same doctrine together in conference, once a year, and exchange opinions on all the questions on which they were confident of agreement. As for the others, they distanced themselves pitilessly from the order of the day in fear of stirring up conflicts, and experience proved many times over that this precaution was wise, for if the peacemakers were admirably in agreement about the advantages that peoples would obtain from not fighting, they often quarreled violently about the practical means of obtaining that ideal.

No plausible reason seemed to exist that prevented these anti-war organizations from prospering. They pleaded in favor of disarmament, preached the theory of arbitration and enjoyed general esteem. It required a series of misfortunes to turn their intentions to evil and give them a role in European affairs that they had not sought.

Shortly before the meeting that was to take place in Lausanne in the Spring of year 112 (1904 C.E.) it appeared that a new party was about to emerge at the conference, in opposition to the old one, which it charge with weakness, negligence and lack of intelligence. The party in question claimed to be unwilling to persist eternally in the platonic eloquence that was fundamental to the various societies in favor of peace, and wanted to attempt to regulate amicably the multiple litigious points that maintained Europe in arms. That breach of entrenched custom seemed full of peril to many sound minds; naturally, they did not say anything, for fear of seeming timid, but they thought it nevertheless, and events proved them right.

All the newspapers of all nations immediately went on campaign as soon as there was a vague suspicion of the plans being hatched by a fraction of the conference-members; they engaged in polemics and immediately afterwards sent reporters to gather information in haste; the latter came back furnished with a mass of confused or contradictory items if information, which provoked denials, on to which further affirmations were grafted, followed by replies, slanderous accusations, personal insults, provocations and duels.

After three weeks, European governments began to get anxious about the public excitement that they sensed increasing around them, which might overflow at any moment; they thought about agreeing among themselves to forbid the threatening manifestation that was in preparation, but none dared take the initiative of a first move for fear of seeming fearful.

The Conference therefore took place, and had no difficulty in unmasking its intentions from the outset. When the committee had been appointed, one of the French delegates mounted the platform and demanded that, in accordance with human rights, the Alsace-Lorraine question should be settled by arbitration and a plebiscite. An immense racket composed of cheers and boos interrupted the orator's speech. He was obliged to sit down, while the president's hand-bell rang desperately, without being able to subdue the tumult.

The members of the audience were shouting at one another from their eats, refusing to listen to their rare colleagues who had maintained a measure of self-control. Words extremely insulting to the two nations involved were liberally exchanged by Frenchmen and Germans, supported by their respective friends.

From the armchair to which he was confined by an attack of gout, old Octave Thomas waved his senile hands in vain, moaning in an unctuous voice: "Don't talk like that, my friends! My dear friends, don't talk like that!"

No one took any notice of his advice. The din only died down when fatigue and dust had almost worn out the vocal cords of the adversaries

Unfortunately, in response to the outcry of German public opinion, the government of the Empire could not avoid demanding explanations from the French Republic. The latter replied courteously that it had nothing to do with the crusade preached by its nationals; that it deplored their excesses and disavowed their actions. Immediately, however—fearing that it might be accuse the press of pusillanimity and platitude—it added dryly that it was not abandoning and never would abandon the territorial claims formulated by the victims of the Treaty of Frankfurt.

For three days, bittersweet dispatches inundated the two chancelleries; the respective Parliaments of the two States posed questions, read manifestos, improvised speeches and protested their profound love or peace, while declaring vehemently that they would be massacred to their last infantryman rather than submit to the slightest humiliation. The newspapers, for their part, printed kilometers of patriotic prose. On the fourth day, in the evening, the German general staff gave the order to mobilize a division of the army, as a comminatory measure—upon which, on the morning of the fifth day, France mobilized two.

At the news of this double event, a frisson passed through Europe. Everyone understood that the moment had come for the great liquidation so long delayed, and without vain protests, in silence, they made preparations for the inevitable conflict. Only one power made a final effort to intervene between the belligerents: England protested in the name of humanity and offered its good offices to sort things out, on condition that it was allowed to occupy Egypt and Morocco. It was too late; there was not even time to examine the proposal.

The Conference in favor of arbitration and disarmament continued its work nevertheless with the punctuality that true faith generates. Frightened by its own excesses, it had not taken long to take precautions against itself and to remove from the agenda the numerous burning subjects of contemporary politics. Then, relieved of any awkward concern, it had joyfully plunged back into its habitual speeches on the murderous horror of battles and the immorality of cannonballs. The members had already voted the seventh paragraph of the accustomed motion for the suppression of war when they learned that a cavalry battle between dragoons and uhlans had jut bloodied the Franco-German frontier. For the first time it was necessary to change the wording of the statement with which the conference terminated its sessions. There were no longer any grounds to give one another the annual felicitations.

There is no need to say any more about the frightful drama of the year 112. No one is unaware of its dark vicissitudes, its long-uncertain outcome and its abrupt and unexpected denouement. In five weeks, fifteen million bayonets had been attached between the confines of the Urals and the straits of Gibraltar; there had been furious fighting in Lorraine and Poland, the contending forces incessantly obliged to change tactics by the improvement of engines of war, the victors of one day vanquished the next, the domestic lives of peoples suspended and ruined, their national existence always at the mercy of a supreme catastrophe, which was nevertheless not produced anywhere. In five months, the billions swallowed up could no longer be counted; four million men had perished. There was a moment of instinctive stupor in the souls of the combatants; the hostilities stopped of their own accord, and propositions of settlement were timidly emitted.

The members of the Peace Conference, recovered from their recent disillusionment, thought it an opportune moment to return to the stage. They held a private meeting and began composing a memoir full of fraternal maxims, which almost reignited the conflict. Except that, as Europe was in a state of siege and subject to military rule, the governor of Paris took it upon himself to dissolve the Society in Favor of International Arbitration, and, with soldierly brutality, threatened to throw its members into prison it they would not be quiet.

Negotiations between diplomats resumed; France and Russia, less exhausted than their powerful rivals, demanded disarmament, the restitution of Alsace-Loraine and a rearrangement of the Balkan states. A treaty was finally signed and the world was able to breathe again.

Never in any epoch, it must be admitted, has progress moved as rapidly as in the half-century that followed the upheaval of year 112. The monarchic powers fell, one after another, almost without revolutions; emancipated from royal and aristocratic oppression, freed from anxiety about foreign invasions and relieved of a considerable part of the tax burden, nations were able to devote themselves to the development of civilization, science and general wellbeing. The earthly reign of humanity was beginning.

The organization of labor and the abolition of capital could obviously not be organized for the day after tomorrow without many unfortunate attempts being made, and blood sometimes being shed. Violence was rare, though, and limited to places where the spirit of reaction resisted the flow. There were almost none of the scenes of massacre, burning and pillage that the prophets of the barbaric past had raised as a scarecrow before the eyes of crowds.

Experiments were made, successively and honestly, with the various panaceas of the old schools of socialism: fixation of salary scales by the State; the intervention by the central authority in relationships between owners and workers; the limitation of the working day to eight hours; the takeover and exploitation by the collectivity of all individual wealth; the abolition of inheritance...

These significant reforms not only ruined the great financial feudality but also many more moderate capitalists; nor were they carried out, it is true, without a very considerable and rather disquieting diminution of the public purse. They were accepted, however, out of love of justice; then again, it is always a great amelioration of misery to think that one is not alone in being subject to it and that others are suffering as much as we are.

The malaise was, in any case, only transitory; happiness does not emerge from social transformations, although they contributed to it when the discoveries of science had resolved the problem of economic production. From the second half of the second century onwards, the employment of the motive force of electricity gave industry an unprecedented impetus; the ebb and flow of the tides, waterfalls, rivers, and hills and mountains exposed to the wind were equipped with cumulative apparatus from which the fluid radiated to hundreds of factories; machines thus activated at a derisory cost, incessantly improved by engineers, where able to produce the objects of manufacture that had previously been the most costly by the billion.

At the same time, the only major revolution in chemistry since the work of Lavoisier permitted the infinite transmutation of the vulgar vegetable matter that nature produces in inexhaustible quantities; cultivation of the land became almost unnecessary; the harvest of raw materials, marine or terrestrial, was accomplished effortlessly by means of mechanical methods; human genius gradually transformed the external world into a prodigious and well-equipped laboratory only requiring perfunctory surveillance.

In the face of the abundance and the superabundance of riches, the eight-hour day did not take long to be reduced by the force of circumstances to six, to four and then to two hours. Soon, even the slightest daily assiduity became superfluous; the technology of manufacture assumed responsibility for supplying the needs of consumption amply, provided that every citizen devoted a few minutes of his week thereto. In the end, it was deemed simplest, for those duties, to hire a certain number of Chinese workers collectively; and as it was to be feared that the presence of these foreigners might constitute a danger, each commune prudently assembled a militia of Muslim mercenaries, camped outside the city, submitted to very strict discipline and always available in the improbable case of any internal or external disturbance. Henceforth, there was no one in the civilized societies who could not abandon themselves entirely to noble occupations: to the intellectual research that is the true purpose of life.

One supreme progress remained to be accomplished, however, before humankind had taken the final step of its absolute development. In spite of the successive ameliorations induced by time and mores, Statist tyranny still weighed heavily on individual liberty at the end of the second century. To be sure, the ancient national denominations were little more than geographical expressions; the sentiment of patriotism had vanished from the most credulous souls, along with supernatural and religious beliefs. First the provinces and then the communes had gradually acquired an almost complete autonomy. Nevertheless, simply by the fact of creating, maintaining and exploiting the major means of transport and communication—roads, canals and railways—a central administration persisted, extending its ramifications from one end of a territory to the other, mistress of a police force and an army of functionaries, invested with the exorbitant privilege of levying taxes. People resigned themselves to the ineluctable necessity, but not without secret resentment.

As always, it was science that abolished that vestige of ancient slavery. About the year 185, aerial navigation, hampered until them by a series of checks and uncertain results, entered abruptly, and with complete success, into the domain of everyday practice. In less than twenty years, it supplanted all the other means of long-distance locomotion, in such a way as to annihilate the vast more or less governmental organization that dominated European societies and maintained a vague memory of former centralization. Less than twenty years thereafter, the various communal agglomerations found themselves definitively liberated; each one had its own budget, its own laws, its own political constitution and administrative personnel, recruited internally, without any other control than that of its own will, and was not paralyzed by any tutelage in the expansion of its civilizing activity.

The proclamation of the independence of the commune of Orléans had been issued on 16 Messidor 213, to the cheers of the crowd. Humankind had reached the Promised Land and entered into it.

A Few Shadows on the Picture

Resentful minds still exist who deny the possibility of further progress and contest the value of the progress thus far obtained. Thus, in the present epoch—the most prosperous ever—a few hypochondriacs contrive to draw subjects for complaint from the very prosperity they enjoy, and devote themselves to the darkest prognostications on the future of the European races. They claim to be suffering from ennui, as if ennui were plausible when one possesses a profusion of the

99

superfluous as well as the necessary, and one can devote one's life to research into scientific laws.

Psychologists and physicians, consulted about these anomalies, have concluded that they are due to psychopathological lesions, whose location some place in the bone marrow and others incline to situate in the anterior lobes of the brain. Neither party, in any case, is able to indicate effective treatments—but their studies have not been a waste of time and have put them on the path to important discoveries; one day, they will acquire certainty and prove experimentally to anyone who will listen that degenerations of the nervous system are congenital, hereditary and incurable.

The incessantly increasing suicide rate seems to justify their thesis; suicide is beginning to become a normal kind of death, if one judges by the official statistics; it does not spare children any more than adults; since the middle of the third century it is admitted by mores and does not astonish anyone.

Pessimists reconcile themselves to that state of affairs by affirming that the evil is incurable; optimists contest the supposition that the phenomenon is an evil, seeing it as a simple manifestation of individual liberty. Economists, being more conciliatory, are willing to concede that the phenomenon is not evil in itself, but contend that its generalization would bring about harmful consequences and threaten future societies with non-existence.

The problem of the continuation of the species was, in fact, one of those that modern civilization had not completely resolved. As the world advanced on the path to human perfection, the excess of deaths over births had increased with disconcerting regularity; people appeared to be reproducing less as material wellbeing grew. Was there a contradiction between the two terms? Some said so boldly, but the more reasonable refused to believe it, for it would have been too painful to see the effort of so many centuries only serving the happiness of two or three generations and then concluding in universal annihilation.

The truth, sad to say and yet incontestable, is that the prodigious blossoming of medicine and surgery had favored that disquieting sterility to some extent. It was all very well to suppress the pains of childbirth by means of anesthetics; women scarcely cared to subject themselves to the annoying months of a pregnancy, which was all the more difficult because their bodies were more delicate. Ovariotomy advantageously replaced the perilous and repulsive abortive operations of old; for a long time the operation had not presented any danger; it only demanded a few days of care and rest; the practice had gradually spread among young women and the majority declared themselves satisfied by it.

Public opinion, it is true did not accept the custom right away; in several communes, in fact, it was never freely accepted. In 237 a very curious discussion on the subject had occupied for nearly five weeks the meetings of the Municipal Council of Orléans; and although the liberals ended up triumphant, it was not without having endured the most virulent attacks on the part of their opponents.

The latter, in the name of the higher interests of the race, wanted to oblige women to retain their ovaries, and would not have hesitated to sanction that exorbitant obligation with the harshest penalties. The liberal fraction made the virtuous decision to oppose that retrograde system; it replied that in a society where criminal responsibility was not longer admitted and lapses from the law were assimilated to simple cases of morbidity, it seemed illogical to want to punish infertility, even voluntary. What would that resurrection of rights of the State in opposition to the inalienable rights of the individual signify? What would become of the primordial principle of the liberty of each, solely limited by the liberty of others? How could the amputation of an organ harm the independence of anyone?

Confronted by these arguments, the Conservative fraction remained mute, or persisted stubbornly in invoking the brutal evidence of the diminution of the number of births.

In spite of the continual emigration of country-dwellers to the cities, the population was, in fact, thinning out everywhere. No one thought of denying the phenomenon. Did it, however, imply catastrophes as imminent in reality as in appearance? Did it constitute, in sum, a commencement of peril? The prosperity and intellectual development of a country might perhaps be inversely related to the number of its inhabitants. A few young women were, in any case, to be found who clung to the instinct of maternity, and were helping to fill in these voids. Although turned away from nobler endeavors in consequence, they were doing useful work and merited encouragement.

Then again, medicine, impotent against suicides and responsible to some extent for the sterility of women, also offered manifest compensations. The epidemics that had previously killed children, the elderly, the infirm and the debilitated—all the wretches to whom nature had refused resistant health—in droves had disappeared. The rickety, the blind from birth, deaf-mutes, epileptics, idiots and monsters survived as well and for as long as anyone else. Tubercular and cancerous infections, without being cured completely, had been attenuated sufficiently to permit sufferers often to carry their diseases into old age. Civilization rightly saw this as one of its finest conquests in the victorious struggle against death, and the teratological sciences found advantages therein; the pullulation of civilized insanity and deformity furnished them with an experimental field such as they had never known before.

It was possible to admire for a long time, in the commune of Marseilles, an acephalous little girl that the savant academy of the city had succeeded in keeping alive by fabricating an artificial trachea and esophagus. It was concluded from this abnormal instance that the absence of the head reduced sensibility to simple reflexes and only left a human being with a very rudimentary vegetative mode of existence, akin to that of a mollusk. For eleven years, daily observations were carried out of the interesting subject; unfortunately, she decided to die one day, without the autopsy being able to determine clearly why. The Marseillais were slightly saddened to lose one of the most attractive curiosities in the country, but they poked fun at the ultra-scientific debates that took place around the unfortunate cadaver. One questionable joker even insinuated that the young monster might have died of a cerebral congestion.

Even better than the finest arguments, this anecdote at least demonstrates the prodigious virtuosity to which medical artistry was becoming incessantly more susceptible. It is only just to say that this virtuosity was also becoming incessantly more indispensable in confrontation with the new necessities created by therapeutics.

For several centuries, in the midst of the general inactivity, the employment of artificial stimulants, usually based on alcohol or opium, had expended singularly. Attempts had been made at first, in various regions and repeatedly, to prohibit their commerce and impose rather heavy punishments on the delinquents. Apart from the fact that the repression in question was offensive in principle, people were soon obliged to observe once again that any legal measure contrary to rights remains fatally inapplicable. The toxic compounds continued to flow; when one could not procure them outside, chemistry permitted them to be easily manufactured at home. The laws, which only ended up multiplying products that were less pure and more dangerous, ended up being repealed.

There was, in any case, no proof of the hypothesis of social decadence occasioned by the use of intellectual poisons. Great works have been accomplished in all eras by alcoholics and morphinomaniacs; if, in a variable lapse of time, each of them is doomed to almost certain physical and mental degeneration, the overstimulation of their genius has always given its contribution to the progress of humankind in advance. Why demand more of epochs in which strength and muscular activity no longer have any reason for being? Does not the nobility of human being consist in bringing life to the brain, even at risk to the body?

Medicine intervened usefully to attenuate the most dangerous cases. Antidotes had been discovered that slowed down the principal effects of intoxication and often avoided fatal accidents. The case was cited of a woman who, declared doomed at the age of thirty-eight, recovered without any serious infirmity other than a complete paralysis of the arms and legs, and did not die until her eighty-third year. Until the last moment, her intelligence remained lucid; every day she drank a liter of laudanum, having her biscuits dunked into it, and dictating works to her phonograph that some people considered to be remarkable.

Science, however, obtained much less obvious results when it had to treat patients afflicted with congenital lesions, and the quantity of those patients increased every year, all the more surely as the other scourges were no longer carrying out their murderous but salutary selection within the species. With regard to those unfortunates, there were no illusions with regard to the chances of success; doctors were content to employ a few preventive measures essential to general security.

For instance, in spite of all remedies, criminals conserved a stubborn propensity for crime, and the fourth century is still waiting for the alienist who can cure theft or murder. All attempts thus far have failed.

As it had previously been perceived that the ensemble of the condemned scarcely surpassed the level of intellectual culture inculcated by primary education, it was concluded that the diffusion of further education would diminish, if it did not reduce to zero, the number of crimes against property and persons. With time it was necessary to recant on that issue; murderers provided with all their diplomas committed no fewer murders.

The law, as transformed by physiology, did not permit them to be declared responsible, but was still forced to isolate them to safeguard their fellow citizens; no task demanded more tact and knowledge of how to distinguish between externally similar individuals. Not a week went by without errors or abuses coming to light. Public opinion, when it had nothing better to distract itself, commented with pleasure on the stupidity of the committee delegated to the service of criminology and demanded its abolition—but the following week, it demanded that its powers be increased if a series of bloody incidents suddenly awakened the instinct of personal security in everyone.

All in all, apart from a few faults and a few annoying incoherencies, nothing was more admirably in conformity with the religion of human pity than the administration devoted to the surveillance and maintenance of criminomaniacs. Setting out from the dogma that every so-called guilty party is unfortunate and ill, it treated him more carefully and gently as he manifested more malevolent dispositions. That evidently did not alter his natural antisocial tendencies—in spite of all the benefits that had once been hopefully anticipated from such medication—but it saved morality and furnished an inexhaustible pasture to the sensitivity of philanthropists.

Vast establishments installed with the latest refinements of comfort, so as not to be reminiscent of a prison, received individuals reputed to be dangerous. There they were served and cared for by a numerous body of nurses responsible for furnishing their domicile with all possible distractions, and, if they had a whim to go out, to accompany them outside. Never, in fact, was complete sequestration ordered, except in cases of furious delirium—and then advantage was taken of intervals between crises to allow the unfortunates certain appearances of liberty. They sometimes took advantage of that to yield to their unhealthy tendencies and commit some murder; their guardians were then reprimanded severely, even threatened with destitution. Fortunately, these events, although too frequent, were nevertheless rarer than one might think.

In conclusion, there are not and never will be societies as absolutely perfect as those imagined by poets and the constructors of utopias. In spite of certain grave defects, the European civilization of the fourth century approaches the ideal more closely than any other has ever done in any epoch of the world's history. Freed from the servitudes that laws of nature or aristocratic tyrannies once imposed, emancipated from ignorance and superstitions regarding an afterlife, liberated from great calamities such as epidemics and wars, provided from birth with a material wellbeing that would have eclipsed the most sumptuous of old, humans, happy and free, know for the first time the reign of justice, fraternity and progress. If a few reforms still remain for them to accomplish, science is extending its conquests every day, and offers the hope of an unlimited development on the victorious road on which they now march with a sure tread.

Events in Andalusia

If it is always painful for a trusting and sensitive soul to see its hopes and legitimate convictions belied by the brutal intervention of events, how much sharper the disillusionment seems in the heart of a writer whose entire life has been con-secrated to a vocation revealed as chimerical! He does not have the resource of fooling himself by forgetting his former opinions, denying them, or, at least, accommodating them to the new situation imposed by the facts. His prose, molded in printed characters, remains as an irrefutable witness to his error and establishes bitterly, for him more than anyone else, the depths of the abyss between the dream of yesterday and the reality of today—not to mention that human malevolence will never spare him the humiliation of hearing himself unan-imously taken for an imbecile by his readers and his col-leagues.

In the present case, however, who could have foreseen, while the festival in Orléans was being celebrated in 313, that, less than sixteen years after that date, such frightful catastro-phes would have changed the face of the world? Is it, there-fore, necessary to doubt that comfortable and peaceful civili-zation, which was so sweet and which one enjoyed so much? Such a doubt would be very serious. In addition, it would imply the corollary of an extravagant mysticism, that humans are not here to resolve the question of general wellbeing, and that they have, on the contrary, a goal beyond their own happiness and that of their fellows. It is better, in spite of the appearances furnished by history, to persist in humanitarian and social faith. An intransigent attitude is in conformity with the spirit of progress. Besides which, it is more dignified.

Errors have certainly been made. If those who were trivial could not possibly do anything against the menacing perils, it is certain that the municipal administrators, to whom the care of public interests and safety had been delegated, gave proof of a lamentable negligence. Some of them, since subjected to the just execration of posterity, have tried to defend themselves by claiming that they did not govern because their fellow citizens were ungovernable: a pitiful excuse, for, although the right of a free people consists of not being subject to any kind of authority, it does not follow that it is duty bound to take responsibility for its own misfortunes.

Moreover, whoever the real guilty parties might be, an impartial study demonstrates, with evidence, that in the universal disaster, the radical party is perhaps the only one that has nothing for which to reproach itself. The proof is that it has never ceased to preach the march forward, to issue loud cries for reform and to maintain a pitiless opposition to everyone in a position of responsibility.

Contrary to long-standing opinion, while Europe, from the beginning of the Republican Era, was accomplishing its admirable political, intellectual and moral evolution, Islam was expanding alongside it, invading the whole of Africa on the one hand, and absorbing Asia all the way to India and the Far East on the other. Ignorant, poor, fanatical and barbaric, it nevertheless constituted a force, and one would have been wrong not to foresee that it might one day become a danger to world peace.

Even before abandoning their powerful centralizations of earlier days to the profit of autonomous communes, the European nationalities had gradually let go of their distant domains, whose conquest and conservation were costing too much money and blood. The shameful protesters who, in the beginning, criticized the expeditions and colonial annexations, without daring frankly to demand the withdrawal of expeditionary troops and the evacuation of the annexed territories, were eventually emboldened. Supported by a public sentiment that was no longer blinded by the vainglory of militarism, and became more disgusted every day by those laborious and costly enterprises, they had inveighed vigorously against the inhumanity and injustice of every armed occupation.

Humanity and justice are words that are never invoked in vain before honest men, when one makes us of them to flatter resentments or the desires of personal egotism. A day came when the barbaric States, by means of a few articles of vague vassalage, reacquired power over their former Arab possessions. Everyone congratulated themselves on an event that liberated France from continual occasions for expense, trouble and annoyance, and did not prevent her living tranquilly within her own boundaries.

It was the epoch of the great mechanical and chemical discoveries that had transformed the conditions of existence so marvelously. The decrease of the population and the increase of wealth constituted a guarantee for the Muslims that no one would seek to disturb them in their empire. They were even offered the means of improving themselves by contact with civilization. By subsequently invading Europe, scorning the most elementary human right, they therefore gave proof of an indescribable brutality and demonstrated once again the pernicious influence of religious fanaticism.

At first, things seemed to be working out quite well. Although continually stirred up by marabouts preaching holy war, agitated incessantly by the last representatives of a few great families hypnotized by the memory of the Spanish Caliphates, who had been piously handing down from father to son, for centuries, the keys to their houses in Grenada or Cordova, and bellicose by nature and education, the Arabs did not attempt any irruption on the far side of the Mediterranean. Satisfied to feel that they were masters of Africa, they made no attempt to emerge therefrom, and merely authorized themselves to abduct a few women occasionally, or risk a few raids on the European coast. These acts of piracy injured the communes that were exposed to them profoundly, but they were too circumspect to worry the cities situated inland.

Some alarmists claimed, it is true, that the questions of armament neglected by the superior races since the establishment of the definitive peace, were of great interest to the Mohammedan potentates; they made the most of the fact that the dislocation of nations had led to the almost complete suppression of all navies and serious artillery, and that if any conflict ever broke out in such conditions, unexpected resistance might be encountered, and bitter disappointments experienced.

In spite of these disturbing prognostications, public opinion remained unmoved. Everyone knew that if the barbaric states were organizing powerful armies, it was to defend themselves against their Sudanese or Saharan rivals, or to fight one another, not with the objective of preparing an aggression against Europe for which no one could see any reasonable motive. In any case, one could count, in the last resort, on the terrible explosives or other engines of destruction that science had at its disposal, and on the moral force that the prestige of intelligence always provides against half-savage hordes. In that they were mistaken, for intellectual prestige is revealed by the notoriously unequal consequences of the prestige of several million bayonets; as for the explosives, on the day when it became desirable to make use of them, it was realized that the licensed mercenaries had communicated the formula to their fellow citizens a long time before.

Unfortunately, everyone was unaware of these details. So, it was with much astonishment that in Floreal 300 the news arrived of a disembarkation of Moors in Andalusia.

Sharp disagreements had existed for several years between the communes of Almeria, Motril and Malaga on the one hand and the Sultan of Morocco on the other. The peren-

109

nial brigandage committed by the latter's subjects had ended up exhausting the patience of the coastal cities. Weary of feeling that their protests were futile, of seeing their ambassadors tricked or even grossly misled by Moroccan functionaries, they decided to threaten reprisals. Less than two weeks later, four young Malagan women were abducted by pirates and their family massacred. Action was decided; a boat belonging to fishermen from Ceuta was seized, and its crew hidden from view.

This manifestation of energy certainly caused more emotion on the Spanish coast than the African. The Andalusians, frightened by their own audacity and terrified by the thought of its possible consequences, lived in the worst apprehension, expecting the Sultan's vengeance at any moment. In order at least to assuage his fury, they treated their prisoners with respect, surrounded them with concern and lavished all the joys of the most refined luxury upon them—so effectively that after a week of detention, six of the eleven savages fell ill by virtue of over-indulgence at table. One of them, in spite of the physicians, even went so far as to die within forty-eight hours of hastily ingesting twenty seven raspberry ice-creams.

The announcement of that accident did nothing to calm the general anxiety of the population. The inhabitants of Malaga trembled in feeling the suspicion weigh upon them of poisoning their hostages. They could already hear their neighbors accusing them of compromising, by imprudence and incompetence, the good reputation of the entire Iberia peninsula. At this juncture, their attitude was firm and calm; they courageously threw out the municipal council in office and appointed a new one.

The latter immediately went into session, and after five hours of stormy debate, voted on a motion whose import was that the situation was grave, although not desperate, but nevertheless capable of becoming so. The next day, it decided to elect a committee charged with investigating the best course to follow in order to enter into negotiations with His Majesty the Sharif. The report of this committee was unanimously approved, when it was seen to conclude with the release of the ten prisoners from Ceuta. For one thing, they were beginning to seem an embarrassment; for another, it was thought that the move would be appreciated by their government as a mark of courtesy and a proof of peaceful intentions.

These wise efforts were, however, to remain in vain. While the Andalusian communes were preparing to make all the concessions not incompatible with their dignity, the Sultan, supported by the Deys of Algiers and Oran, mobilized his troops, gathered them at various favorable embarkation points, and requisitioned all available commercial vessels for their transport. This suspect activity was materially impossible to hide from the other side of the Straits of Gibraltar; those against whom it was directed were not unaware of it. They were obliged to see nothing and say nothing in order not to frighten themselves; then, passing abruptly from their feigned security to a very sincere alarm, they resolved not to prolong an intolerable state of affairs any longer.

Public meetings were convened; new committees were set up; an initial political program was drafted that was poorly welcomed, and immediately replaced by a second that was much better received; the municipalities declared themselves permanent and fell into accord in order to concentrate on the appropriate measures to be taken—except that they nearly fell into dispute in studying the best voting system and exchanged bitter words while dividing up their various tasks. Nevertheless, quickly getting a grip on themselves, they recognized unanimously that it was a worse moment than ever to sever their formerly amicable relations and give rise to internal disputes. A tribunal of arbitration was instituted with the aim of cutting through litigious matters. Finally, the Grand Council of the Federation of Communes was able to open the session and begin its work.

Things proceeded there with a promptitude to which one cannot pay too much homage. After having established, not without supportive evidence and testimony, the rectitude of the Andalusian cities and the bad faith of the Moroccan gov-

ernment, it listed minutely the conciliatory measures attempted in the interests of peace; it did not try to conceal that these
measures had remained sterile; it showed the Sultan rejecting
all the advances of diplomacy, refusing any explanation of his
military preparations, making alliances alarming to general
tranquility—in a word, organizing all the elements of an offensive war. In those conditions, the Grand Council judged
that a conflict was becoming more likely by the day, and concluded that force would probably have to be met, before long,
with force.

In order not to be found wanting, it voted three resolutions: firstly, to send to His Majesty the Sharif an official letter
designed to make an impression on his mind by signaling the
gravity of the events that were about to occur and for which he
would bear the responsibility before history; secondly, to
appeal to the sentiments of solidarity of Europe entire, and to
ask for help in the form of men, arms and equipment; and
thirdly, to verify the number of condition of the mercenary
contingents and reinforce them by supplementing them with
all the free citizens that the physicians declared approximately
sound and fit for service.

The second part of the last article was not passed without
difficulty, but it passed. The embarrassment was renewed,
however, when serious discussion began as to how it was to be
executed. The young people proposed as recruits were devoid
of any enthusiasm. The beauty of the task confronting them
was represented to them in a celebratory fashion; the necessity
of communal salvation was alleged; they were even proclaimed in advance as "heroic defenders of the great humanitarian fatherland"—but these various means of persuasion left
them cold. They replied with the celebrated line that one of the
first apostles of social emancipation—a député in the Parliament of the Third French Republic—had written: "The fatherland is wherever one feels at ease."[49] And they affirmed that

---

[49] The quotation, with slight variations, goes back to Classical
times, where it was employed by Euripides and Cicero; it

they felt very ill at ease in a country where people were at risk of getting killed. Frequently desertions soon emphasized the disfavor attached to the idea of enrolling free citizens, and the project was abandoned.

The appeal to European brotherhood similarly had only limited success. Ordinarily, the Andalusians were not well-liked; the mildness of their climate, the richness of their soil and the eternal clarity of their blue sky, beneath which life was spontaneously joyful and carefree, had spared them much effort in the conquest of happiness; they were seen as possessors of privileges that were due solely to chance; without anyone daring to admit it, a vague sentiment of envy was mingled with the apparent cordiality of habitual relationships; no one was displeased to witness, for once, their distress. To be sure, these deplorable jealousies were not unanimous, and some exceptions merited praise. The city of Orléans, among others, only listened to its generous inspirations; to each of the ten most seriously threatened communes it sent two special delegates, who lavished fine words on the inhabitants and congratulated them warmly for devoting themselves thus to the cause of civilization.

It is sad, even today, to think that all that feverish activity was a complete waste of effort. No appeal to humanity or justice could prevail against the brutal fanaticism of the Sultan. He wanted war regardless; he had been anticipating and preparing for it for a long time; as soon as the moment seemed opportune, he unleashed it without scruple.

To tell the truth, it was less a war than a simple takeover. As soon as the first movements of the enemy fleets had been advertised by the semaphores of the European coasts, the municipalities went to the invaders to surrender to their discretion and beg for mercy. Only one city, Cadiz, thought it was in

---

popularity seems to have been renewed in France by Voltaire. Spronck was a député himself, and might have heard the citation from the radical benches on more than one occasion; his specific reference is probably to Louis Blanc.

any shape to resist. Confident in the energy of its militia and a corps of volunteers recruited to the last minute, it refused access to its harbor to the ships arriving there, sank three of them that tried to force access, and obliged the rest to retreat to the open sea. That act of temerity earned it a few days respite. A paltry advantage! Especially when one thinks of what that ephemeral independence was going to cost.

Two days later, a double assault, by land and by sea, ended with a check to the Muslim troops. The Moors retreated again, but the besieged had suffered as much as the assailants; sixty per cent of their mercenaries, the only resource on which they could seriously count, were killed or injured; the rest, exhausted by fatigue, were killed at their posts the following morning when the second attack was launched—and the way was open for the frightful reprisals that the victors exacted.

As much out of vengeance as to issue a warning to other adversaries of the futility of any attempt at self-defense, Emir Ali-el-Hadji, the commander of the Muslim forces at Cadiz, resolved to destroy the unfortunate city. Before the battle, he had promised his soldiers ten hours of pillage; until sunset he unleashed them into the houses and the streets, with no restraint or control; only at dusk did he order his officers to sound the rally and reorganize their troops. The remaining men, women and children were sent to Africa and sold in the slave market—and the Emir withdrew, leaving behind, as a monument to his wrath, a heap of deserted ruins from which the smoke of recent fires rose up.

That atrocious example had not even the excuse of political necessity; it was gratuitous cruelty. For, if such a crime terrified populations, it could not distress them any more than they already had been since the disembarkation of the first enemy launch. The Arab leaders knew, and did not doubt, that their campaign would be reduced to a simple military stroll. With a little patience and mildness, they would have ended up, without spilling a single drop of blood, by triumphing over a paltry band of fanatics.

114

Fortunately, that monstrous violence was not renewed. Impressed by the noble moral resignation of his victims, His Majesty the Sharif consented to formulate in advance the law that would be imposed upon them; everyone knew thereafter what to expect. So harsh were the conqueror's conditions that they were even worse than the capricious exigencies of soldiery.

In exchange for immediate submission, the communes would be respected; given a solemn promise to convert to the region of the Prophet, the citizens would retain their lives and the liberty, and keep all their property; in case of refusal, they would be obliged, three hours after an announcement by the public criers, to have evacuated the cities in order to withdraw northwards, beyond the mountains of the Sierra Morena; any attempt at rebellion, any infraction of the regulations or even any delay in carrying them out, would be punished by death or slavery.

Thanks to the self-control of the vanquished, these excessive penalties rarely had occasion to be employed; out of dignity and prudence, the Andalusians did not expose themselves to them. Not much inclined to try out the political and social advantages of the Moroccan regime, they emigrated *en masse*, without waiting to be obliged to do so, hastily carrying away a few remains of their past splendor.

In the confusion of that immense exodus, however, which retreated before the impatient march of Berber cavalry, who would ever be able to count the number of unfortunates who died of fatigue, fright or distress? The survivors of the lugubrious tragedy were dispersed throughout the continent according to the hazards of exile. Those who, at the price of a sorry abdication, were able to remain in their homes rapidly succumbed to a mode of existence to which they were ill-adapted. In less than two months, the last vestiges of a great human family had been swept from the surface of the world. And if the invasion stopped, it was because that was what the invaders wanted.

Europe, initially more surprised that frightened by that bold display of force, did not take long to feel grave anxiety. Conscious of the splendors of its civilization, it had only ever envisaged with disdain the hypothesis of foreign aggression. This one struck it with amazement, then fear. Suddenly, it thought itself doomed. Calm returned on the day when it acquired the assurance of not seeing the Moors extend their conquests beyond Andalusia—but the memory of the alarm was not completely effaced as soon as the crisis was over, and for a long time it furnished material for interesting discussions between the various schools of political theorists.

The theoreticians, a few of whom still existed in each commune, could be divided in a general fashion into two principal groups: those who had been frightened and had been reassured, and those who had also been frightened, but were not reassured. The former enjoyed a reputation for wisdom and clear-sightedness that was refused to the latter, and achieved much greater success with their contemporaries. People were grateful to them for having confidence in the future, appreciative of the subtle scientific, philosophical and strategic considerations by means of which they proved that further offensive action by the Muslim armies was implausible and impossible. People like to hear them talk, if only to reassure themselves.

As for the others, there would be no need to mention the sinister prophecies they repeated incessantly if events had not justified their apprehensions in a most untoward fashion. Then again, it is not widely known that it was by virtue of their efforts and with their support that the famous Anti-Peace League was organized, the vogue for which occupied idle public opinion for a while.

The founder of that society with the bellicose title was the famous Frédéric Ledoux, already well-known for his works on *Methods of Intense Reproduction for the Human Species*. He set out, in the heart of civilization, to resuscitate the military spirit and organize a movement for the creation of permanent armies. He only contrived interminable purely oratory polemics, from which nothing emerged and nothing could emerge. When people wearied of hearing the same arguments indefinitely repeated with regard to a single question, they moved on to something else; the Anti-Peace League ceased to attract lovers of casuistry and eloquence; it died for want of adherents.

Nevertheless, it had succeeded in maintaining a few vague dreads in the strongest minds. On the other hand, several communes in Spain, predisposed to circumspection by the proximity of the Moors, issued complaints in all directions, demanding protection against the peril of an eventual Arab irruption. As much to give them satisfaction as a measure of general security, three hundred and thirty-two cities formed a syndicate with the aim of founding a new society called *The Modern Missions*, which took responsibility for civilizing the Islamic populations and proving to them that all humans are siblings, free and equal.

This vast project, whose history will not be forgotten by philanthropy, would certainly have exerted the most salutary influence if its impetus had not been interrupted at the outset by the ill will of the Mohammedan functionaries. Not only did they welcome the delegates of the Modern Missions unsympathetically, but when they discovered the objective of their voyage they expelled them brutally. The majority took that as read and did not persist; the most devoted reacted audaciously by commencing lecture tours.

They came to grief; at the first meeting, they were nearly stoned to death by the audience as sacrilegious blasphemers; the police showed up in time to disperse the crowd with truncheon-blows and rescue the injured orators. The justice of the cadis, however, to which they were immediately deferred, did not think the punishment sufficient. Accused of propagating perverse doctrines and provoking disturbances, they were condemned to various punishments. Some were beaten on the soles of their feet; others had their ears or noses cut off; the most severely compromised were subjected to an amputation that, in raising their voices by an octave, deprived them of any

117

future criminal conversation with women. They were then invited once again to return to their native land, not without having been warned that in case of recidivism, their heads would simply be cut off.

These signs of malevolence immediately discouraged the apostolate; after a few months of popularity, the Modern Missions suffered the same fate as the Anti-Peace League and other similar societies; they no longer served as anything but motives for periodic banquets, accompanied by speeches and toasts. In any case, their discredit was explicable by the remoteness of the catastrophes that had determined their birth; four years had gone by since the inauspicious events of 300. The emotion provoked by the sack of Cadiz had had time to die down; the conquerors were not thinking of advancing the limits of their conquests, and nothing authorized the anticipation that they would ever think of it. Europe was weary of the artificial agitation maintained around that already-ancient history; it demanded to be left in peace and that no one should any longer talk about Andalusia, Andalusians, Allah or his prophet.

The Invasion

Circumstances then seemed to conform with this desire for appeasement. In 302, the author responsible for the war, the Sultan of Morocco, died, abandoning a burdensome succession to his twenty-five year old heir, his son Ibrahim III—who was later to become Ibrahim-el-Kebir.

That terrible manipulator of men had only vaguely revealed, in his childhood and youth, the characteristic predispositions by which superior destinies are announced. Taciturn and melancholy, he had the reputation of possessing an average intelligence. A few close acquaintances were however, astonished by the harshness of the gaze that sometimes pierced his ordinarily veiled pupils, and those who also knew about his cold determination, carefully dissimulated, his physical and moral strength of resistance and his secret religious mysticism divined that, beneath his superficial and insignificant personality, another was immersing itself, doubtless unknown to everyone else, in mysterious and redoubtable dreams.

For a long time, no one in Europe knew about the part he had played in Andalusian affairs, the organizational genius he had deployed in preparing for the expedition, and the political activity with which he improvised the government of the annexed territories. His future subjects were unaware of it themselves, and, in the simplicity of their souls, attributed all the glory to his father, the Sultan. A dominator purely for the love of domination, certainly convinced of his divine right, Ibrahim cared little for the favor of crowds. He was a model of the veritable Oriental autocrat, enclosed in his superhuman majesty, almost invisible, exercising his unlimited power from the depths of his palace and only appearing at solemn moments to take command of the believers and lead them in holy war.

It is only now, on looking back at the totality of his actions, that the implacable unity of his thought and the patient energy he employed in pursuit of its execution, becomes obvious. The vast projects accomplished on the threshold of his old age were incubating in his solitary mind from the days of his most distance adolescence. Before coming to the throne, he sketched out their first lines with the invasion of Spain. As soon as his rule began, he set to work with the stubborn tenacity of a monomaniac, and did not want to be distracted from them until he saw them completed.

Indifferent to the means, by violence or by cunning, by cruelty or persuasion, for twenty-seven years he stirred up Islam until he had centralized its scattered strength in his hands. He had begun with his own empire, overhauling the old public services whose weakness he sensed from top to bottom. He had renewed his armaments according to the givens of modern science; he had ensured the resources of his treasury thanks to regular increases in taxation. A few attempts at more or less open resistance were drowned in blood, only contributing to the confirmation of his power and the increase of his prestige by means of terror. When he judged that he was the

119

master of a solid instrument, he turned it against neighboring States; then began the series of murderous campaigns and the formidable assembly of political alliances that as to conclude in a sort of confederation of the African peoples, under the supremacy of Morocco.

Not content with that uncontrolled temporal authority, the Sharif was able to combine it with the mirage of a pretended religious mission. A descendant of Mohammed, he claimed to receive inspiration directly from the prophet, and he made himself believed. At the same time as he demolished and reconstituted an immense continent according to his desire, he dared to retouch the Quranic texts, and his reform, instead of dooming him, elevated his renown to the level of sanctity and extended his moral influence to the ultimate bounds of the Asiatic world. A day came when he realized in his person the most prodigious dream of absolute despotism that had ever been able to haunt a human brain. He was both the infallible pope and the victorious Caesar of five hundred million fanatical and bellicose human beings.

For whomever has penetrated the march of history, and knows that every seed tends in a fatal manner to develop until the full blossoming of its latent strength, the appearance of Ibrahim-el-Kebir in not an inexplicable phenomenon. The conqueror should have been anticipated long before the conquest; he was, in sum, the supreme conclusion, the finished incarnation of the genius of Islam in its various aspects. The struggle between the Orient and the Occident had only been intermittent since the Crusades. Europe believed that it had been terminated by victorious skirmishes distributed throughout centuries of truce. It was mistaken, and paid for its error with its ruination.

The writer who will one day study the great Muslim invasion—if there is such a writer and anything is studied henceforth—will not be able to take any account of the distant origins to which the events of the year 329 are connected. Now, in the disarray of the frightful crisis, scarcely dormant, before a future veiled in black, who can think of a work of science and thought? The documents and the witnesses no longer exist. About the tragedy in which civilized society foundered, everyone only knows sparse fragments and particular details. The totality remains obscure, almost inconceivable, resistant for the moment to any kind of serious commentary.

All that is known is that, on the vastest terrain, hostilities were engaged in conditions almost identical to those that gave rise in 300 to the Andalusian-Moroccan conflict. Misunderstandings generated by the bad faith of the Sultan gradually determined an acute overexcitement on both sides. Europe, without admitting the possibility of its definitive annihilation, was nevertheless not unaware of Ibrahim's military resources; it feared a new strike on another portion of its territory. Its fault—a most honorable one—was in believing once again in justice, right and reason, and wasting its time in diplomatic negotiations with an adversary decided on the worst violence. Some have suggested, it is true, that such manifest forbearance can be explained simply be a natural reluctance to fight, but such hypotheses are tantamount to nothing less than an accusation of cowardice.

In the spring of 329, the Sharif revealed his intentions brutally with the invasion of Spain, a disembarkation in southern Italy and the pillage of several inoffensive localities on the coast of the former French Provence. At the same time, two Asiatic emigrations began, one toward the Balkan peninsula, the other toward Russia by way of the northern coast of the Caspian, picking up along their route the innumerable hordes every-ready for adventures, and dragging in their wake a population of women and children. It was not a war; barbaric Asia and Africa were overflowing simultaneously into Europe.

As soon as the first impact, the latter folded up. It possessed no navy, no armies, no defensive works, nor any administration save for a few hundred thousand disparate petty municipal organizations, in no condition to agree on any communal action in two or three weeks. Certain of its scientific superiority, it had been living for generations in the blind faith that the discoveries of its chemists and engineers would guarantee an eternal security. It simply forgot that, in the midst of the general pacification, it had totally neglected the maintenance of its destructive machinery; it forgot, above all, that in the first and second centuries of the Republican Era, while it was spreading its civilization among neighboring races, it had taught them the existence, the manufacture and the use of the engines that were now being turned against it.

Confronted with the simultaneous attack on five points of the frontier, there was chaos on a gigantic scale: an enormous and abrupt flow of populations toward the center and the north. The wave of invaders rolled through dead cities; it slowed down to disperse through the deserted territories—but only the winter, one of the most precocious and rigorous mentioned in history, arrested its surge. Islam had already reached the banks of the Dnieper in the east; in the south it occupied the Danube valley, Lombardy, the Mediterranean coast from the Alps to the Pyrenees, the southern slope of the Garonne basin and the whole of Spain. It was only waiting for the favorable season to resume its march.

That respite, which seemed to leave room for residue of hope, was perhaps, in contrast, the most atrocious episode of the drama. An immediate denouement would have been preferable to the prolonged agony of the five months of feverish terror. The last illusions crumbled rapidly; the vision of the inevitable imposed itself; it only remained, from one day to the next, to await the arrival of the final catastrophe.

One is obliged to recognize, however, that no supreme effort was neglected for the salvation of Europe. All were in vain. The Muslim militias, probably bought by their co-religionists, scarcely took the trouble, in the presence of public misfortunes, to hide their sentiments. From the start, partial mutinies occurred; discipline relaxed; it became impossible to place any trust in troops whose loyalty as suspect. At the slightest attempt at repression, rebellions burst forth; in several communes, the civil authorities were attacked by the soldiers, people were massacred and houses sacked. An internal war was evidently imminent. People congratulated themselves on being able, almost everywhere, to pay off the mercenaries that had not already deserted, taking their weapons with them.

In spite of the gravity of the situation, the energy of the vanquished did not give way yet. It was necessary to reconstitute effective militias in haste. Ancient administrative rules were exhumed from libraries, which attempts were made to apply as best anyone could. Virtual conscription was introduced. Dictatorships had emerged in several places, without anyone wanting to ask why or how; they were, at least, able to pursue and constrain the refractory, improvise different services, provide the most urgent measures and put a vague cohesion into the chaos of individual initiatives. Their work would have been entirely worthy of praise if it had not been due to an authority whose legal origin for which one sought in vain.

In the spring of 330, without counting three further armies in Poland, Bohemia and western France, a hundred and twenty-five thousand men found themselves concentrated south of the Loire, entrenched behind the Cévennes, ready for action in the Rhône valley. In the absence of superior officers, they had been put under the orders of a Council of General Command made up of twenty members and charged with guiding the movements of the ensemble. Among them, the biographer of Charlemagne and Napoléon, the celebrated Adolphe Thibaudier enjoyed a reputation for competence merited by previous endeavors. In the meeting where the commencement of operations was discussed, he reminded his colleagues that all illustrious strategists always commended offensive tactics; he quoted examples, and his opinion—coldly received at first—ended up rallying the majority vote.

The army of the center started marching, already demoralized by the fatigues of the new life to which it had been subject for four months. Divided into five corps, it was to head for Lyon by five different roads in order to take up the most favorable position from which to fight thereafter.

It will one day be a very interesting subject of study to discover how the dislocation—one might say the vanishing—

123

of that mass of men occurred. Many doubtless died of disease and privation; many probably also allowed themselves to be overtaken by discouragement and abandoned the posts confided to them. The rout must have been completed in a continuous fashion by a multitude of individual desertions, for no one ever advertised any insubordination on the part of any substantial group refusing to obey their leaders' orders collectively. As for soldiers killed in pitched battle, they cannot enter the calculation; the number of those who fell under the sabers of Moorish cavalrymen in the vicinity of Roanne has been establish incontrovertibly; it amounts to exactly eighty-two.

That unique encounter with a handful of Muslim scouts was, however, sufficient to determine the final disaster. Ibrahim had calculated well in distributing far ahead of him, sometimes sixty, eighty or a hundred leagues from his first line, a few isolated squadrons whose mere passage frightened the populations and paralyzed all resistance. On 18 Prairial 330, three leagues from Roane, when the enemy forces were still moving through the Dauphiné and had not yet passed Valence, one of the parts of this extreme advance guard ran into a European column. The most frightful stampede immediately broke out, spreading with astounding rapidity, even to those whom distance sheltered from an immediate attack. Fortunately, the Arabs, sensing their mounts were tired, only demanded one effort from them and did not repeat the charge. They had lost five men, one of whom broke his back falling off his horse and four others being killed by the explosion of an ammunition-wagon.

The moral effect of this unfortunate engagement was no less immense for that. It reverberated in two or three days to the limits of what remained of the civilized world. The ruination of an entire army was nothing compared to the devastation of the last surviving energy. Terror and despair hallucinated imaginations; the refinements of cruel atrocities were attributed to the Muslims; people had nightmarish dreams of torture while awake.

To cap it all, epidemics that had vanished centuries ago—typhus, smallpox and the plague—arrived along with the Asiatic hordes. Abruptly extracted from the distant receptacles in which they were eternally dormant, whipped up by the coming-and-going of enormous human agglomerations, the horrible scourges traveled the entire extent of the immense battlefield in less than a month. Victors and vanquished, equally afflicted, succumbed in hundreds of thousands. Cadavers rotted in the open air, on the roads or in abandoned houses, thus incessantly creating nuclei of contagious infection. While the voids in the ranks of the invaders were incessantly filled by the flood of new immigrants, however, some invaded regions, and those on the brink of invasion, were depopulated in a matter of days, without anyone, in the universal disarray, thinking of helping the victims.

Then, confronted by that sudden accumulation of misfortune and suffering, a wind of furious madness seemed to have passed through Europe. Men, woman and even children refused to await their imminent destiny and killed themselves. That communal suicide was the last macabre elegance of that great society's death-throes. Rendezvous were arranged for a particular time; after indescribable orgies in which blood was shed more often than not, in the midst of the fumes of intoxication, the guests cut one another's throats or burned one another alive in their homes. The crowd watched these lugubrious spectacles dazedly, or applauded them with cries of incoherent joy, their eyes already shining with a similar dementia.

Soon, the nervous frenzy of the wretches reached its paroxysm. A kind of homicidal delirium shook their deranged brains. Instances of cannibalism were cited in several cities, some of which were accompanied by dreadful circumstances. All the inmates of all the madhouses appeared to have poured out simultaneously into society. Bands of lunatics descended into the streets, uttering hysterical howls at random, massacring passer-by, whose cadavers they tore apart with their fingernails, and bringing down building with explosive charges. Sometimes, battles were fought between two troops of these madmen. Entire communes were seen annihilating themselves in this manner with their own hands, in a sudden and general crisis of destructive fury.

When the Muslim armies filed into Orléans, the city had been nothing more than a heap of smoking ashes for nine days.

On 28 Vendemiaire 331 Ibrahim-el-Kebir arrived in Flanders. Military operations had been terminated almost everywhere. The cantons of mountainous Switzerland and Scotland, where the debris of a few European families still persist today, were alone in being spared by the invaders. The Sultan came in person to take possession of his new empire.

When he reached the shore of the North Sea, in the vicinity of Blankenberghe, the conqueror, halting his escort, launched himself at a gallop to the edge of the beach. With his horse's hooves in the foam of the waves, he remained silent and motionless for a long time contemplating the waves, whose glaucous gleam he had never seen, and the cold, gray and misty sky from which the pale sunlight of septentrional regions descended.

Before the unknown of the desert horizon, it seemed to him that he had pushed his victorious march to the limits of the world;[50] the pride of satisfied domination swelled his heart. It was then that he dictated to the marabout Hassan-ben-Nafich the famous proclamation whose text has been preserved, and by which a cycle of history was closed;

"In the name of God the all-powerful and merciful!

"Praise be to him! Glory to his prophets! Glory and benediction to the believers who have vanquished beneath the sacred standard! Iron, fire and blood have erased putrefaction from the earth.

---

[50] Given that the story is essentially a parable, it might seem churlish to wonder whatever happened to the Americas, but still…

"God is above us; and he has guided me, Ibrahim, by his hand to the furthest confines of space, to exterminate the Infidels who scorn the holy word, and who abandon themselves to vain sciences extracted from books, to softness and idleness.

"In the name of the unique and venerable faith, I shall abolish the last vestiges of their corruption; I shall grind into the dust that paltry and enervated race, and I shall share out the rich kingdoms that they possessed between the strong and the brave; I shall reduce to oblivion the perverse knowledge in which they gloried; I shall destroy the monuments of their luxury; and I shall build in their stead thousands of eternal sanctuaries, from which prayers will rise up to the heavens.

"Go! And obey what I have said! Cultivate the soil that belongs to you henceforth. Resign yourselves to poverty or grief. Listen to the leaders who command you. Enjoy the pleasures of life and have no fear of death. Human destiny is not in human hands. And if it is written that you shall perish one day in battle, paradise is in the shadow of sabers!"

And now, alas, nothing remains standing of that which was built by the labor of centuries. The invaders have trodden underfoot the most admirable work of human wisdom. A gross morality, sanctioned by belief in God, has replaced the delicate scientific tolerance of yore; criminals are punished; indifferent to amelioration or general wellbeing, people occupy themselves with observing a pretended divine law, the rational foundations of which they neglect to analyze; they submit themselves to governmental authorities that they do not even debate; they only esteem the virtues of brutes—faith, patience, sobriety and courage—and only practice vulgar duties. Glad and proud of their strength, unconscious of their servitude, their ignorance and their poverty, unacquainted with the marvelous subtleties of the modern mind, which they disdain for lack of comprehension, they boast of having annihilated Europe; they have installed themselves there, organized themselves there and are multiplying there with the fecundity of inferior races. And even the most intelligent among them would be incapable of citing the minerals of which Sirius is composed...

The barbarians have reconquered the world. Civilization is dead.

Jean Jullien: *An Investigation of the World of the Future*
(1909)

I. The Prophet

A few years ago, the editor of the *Universal Informer* commissioned me to make an investigation of the United States. It was a matter of interviewing thinkers, scientists and scholars such as James Milner, Professor Fuss, the engineer John Eddy—all the geniuses in whose brains the destiny of the future world is unfolding. I have, in consequence, not done what my colleagues in reportage do, giving a glimpse into the present states of minds in the Great Republic, but have re-searched what it will be tomorrow and thereafter.

From that excursion into the other world I will report the materials necessary to establish an exact picture of its society, as it will function when we have disappeared. You will admit that, for a newspaper, that is definitely the last word in infor-mation.

My first impressions were rather discouraging. The med-dlesome formalism of an administration given free rein, the affectation of an unfortunately superficial correction, the rush of crowds after bluffers and a thousand other features of its mores suggested to me a civilization in decline, in which the brutal release of individualism, reinforced by imperialism, marked a return toward a certain savagery. I did not, however, attach any more importance to the eddies of that crowd throw-ing itself into life and fighting over it, in the midst of eternal conflicts of interest, than to the eddies of the sea breaking untiringly against the rocks. The masses live their own times; they do not prepare the future. Only minorities work for that, grouped around men of science or art, builders of hypotheses or utopians, whose dreams are the next realities.

In the Union more than anywhere else, it is necessary to recognize, the most vertiginous conceptions easily find ways to emerge from the domain of the abstract and speculative, while, in our old world, they incubate for centuries. There, a sense of practicality has taken possession of the most disinterested minds; people are not content to caress chimeras; they domesticate them and bring them down to earth.

How many futile words have been pronounced here and among our neighbors regarding the march of progress? How many projects, each more wonderful than the last, for the reform of society? How many popular orators promise happiness and how many poets sing about it, who see nothing more therein than words? How many prophets announce the new life, who obtain nothing from their apostolic mission but the disdainful shrug of our fellow citizens' shoulders? What hope is there, anyway, for a civilization like ours, where *inventor* is synonymous with *crackpot*?

It is not like that in the United States. Prophets are not armchair apostles; they act; they draw crowds, become forces—and the trade is, in fact, quite lucrative. Could I do better, in order to be informed as to the future, than to address myself to one of these seers?

I have little confidence, I must admit, in those variously inspired people who tell you things, with an imperturbable aplomb, that cannot be checked, and who have thrived on credulity for as long as humankind has existed. But I was told about a prophet, a man of science, and the man in question seemed to me to be so extraordinary that I did not hesitate to consult him.

He lived in the vicinity of Kansas City, and answered to the imposing name of Hierophas. I expected, as you might imagine, to find a thin old man with a long white beard living a solitary and ascetic existence of privation and mortification in his Thébaïd, in order that his mind might focus on the future

130

with all its acuity of perception. How surprised I was when I arrived at the door of the most sumptuous of cottages.

A tall ostentatiously-uniformed black man came to open the door by a crack and ask me whether I had an appointment. I replied that I had something better than that, and handed him the card that accredited me as a representative of the *Universal Informer*. The black man examined it attentively—he must not have known how to read—passed it to a groom, who disappeared, and opened the doors of the waiting room with an expansive gesture.

Scarcely had I had time to admire a few nice paintings and other art-works imported from Europe than an usher introduced me to the reception hall. Imagine a throne-room for a petty monarch, with the ambience and mysterious solemnity of a sanctuary. Hierophas took great care with his stage-setting. I expected to see him appear in antique garb, emerging from a trap-door, but he was a middle-aged gentleman of commanding bearing, who, in a grey jacket with a carnation in his buttonhole, simply came in through the door.

"Delighted, my dear sir," he said to me, like an old acquaintance. "I was expecting your visit."

Slightly surprised, I looked at him. Blue eyes softened a slightly ruddy face, at the base of which a carefully groomed blond beard fanned out; the lips were smiling with genuine affability. After all, there was nothing astonishing about a prophet anticipating my visit; and without asking anything more, I shook the hand that he offered me. He assured me that he was most honored to receive the representative of the *Universal Informer*, the only French newspaper that was worth the trouble of being consulted, and that he was entirely at my service.

I hesitated to reply. Should I address him as Master, Professor, Doctor, Reverend or simply Sir? Hierophas did not seem to be hostile to advertisement, and I concluded that he ought not to be insensitive to flattery, and gratified him with the Biblical title of Prophet. It seemed to me that he found it quite natural.

"Prophet," I said, "it would be childish to try to conceal the object of my visit from you. You have foreseen it, so you know as well as I do what I expect from you." He nodded his head in agreement. "I am, therefore, ready to consign to my notebook the oracles that condescend to escape from your august mouth."

He immediately burst out laughing, with frank amusement, put his hand on my arm in a familiar manner, and said: "My dear chap, don't be so pompous." He was definitely a straight-talking prophet. Instead of going up to his throne, he sat on the corner of the table at which I had installed myself in order to take notes, and said, cheerfully: "Write. I'll dictate."

He commenced thus:

"My visit to the prophet Hierophas was a bitter disappointment to me. I thought I would find myself in the presence of a pontiff and I found myself confronted by a charlatan, or at least a hoaxer."

I stopped writing and protested strongly.

"Don't deny it," he said, amiably. "I can read you like a book with large print. Yes, I live in a palace that astonishes you; I have a black porter in gaudy livery, who makes you smile, and this room looks like a stage set to you; yes, I dress ostentatiously and make sibylline pronouncements with a distant expression—because, if I behaved otherwise, no one would want to believe my predictions and I wouldn't have a single client. You see, my dear chap, the great inferiority of science is in forsaking stage-setting and presenting its truths naked."

I was no longer smiling, and I looked in amazement at the man who had evidently read my thoughts.

"For you," he continued, "who have sent to me by the *Universal Informer* and I divine to be sufficiently well versed in scientific matters, I don't have to surround myself with all that phantasmagoria. I received you immediately, because I had nothing to prepare, quite simply, because I have nothing to hide, and I introduce myself to you, not as the prophet

Hierophas but as who I am: William Smithson, mathematician."

I was still stunned by that unexpected declaration when a girl opened the door. "Papa," she said, "are you coming to lunch?"

"I'm coming," Mr. Smithson replied. He turned to me. "Will you stay for an informal lunch?"

I excused myself, invoking some pressing engagement.

"Don't disguise your refusal with a polite pretext," he replied, smiling. "Accept, or I'll think that I've annoyed you be telling you the truth. Then again, we haven't had time to chat. I want to explain my method in detail, in order that the *Universal Informer* can defend it before the world, as I shall defend to scientific sincerity of my predictions before you."

Conquered by the strange perspicacity and the captivating frankness of my interlocutor, I allowed myself to be drawn into a conservatory, in the middle of which the lunch table had been set. The prophet introduced me to Mrs. Smithson, who was supervising three young children as they ate. She smiled at the compliment I addressed to her, invited me to sit down next to her, and immediately started a conversation about France, its mores, its art and its literature.

Mrs. Smithson was a tall woman, with a slim but full figure, as gracefully abrupt in her movements a thoroughbred mare. Brown-haired, with a rose-tinted pale complexion and bright lips, she had enigmatic eyes: very beautiful, clear and innocent eyes, but impenetrable, which were not the windows of the soul but mirrors reflecting a sun. Her sarcastic smile, characterized by an advancement of the lower jaw, revealed solid teeth that were a trifle long, but dazzling. She represented a certain type of American beauty She also had a fine mind, very cultivated, not lacking in irony or mischief.

She told me that French novels seemed to her to be detestable. Were their readers only interested in vile adultery? Was it usual, in France, for women to deceive their husbands? Did they always find someone with whom to deceive them? Shocking! In America, the respect due to women was differently conceived—but she let it be understood that perhaps French manners did not displease her overmuch.

While we were discussing that subject in the fashion of Marivaux, the children disappeared, taken away by a governess, and the prophet left us to give an audience. I remained alone with the charming woman, and the conversation immediately took a more gallant tone. She stared into my eyes with a challenging expression, leaned closer to my ear in order to say things that she thought daring, and then leaned back with the stifled giggles of a provocative flirt. The most naïve and the most foppish would not have scorned the opportunity, and although I am not one of those lady-killers who imagines that he can conquer a woman at first sight, I was obliged to recognize that the lovely Mrs. Smithson was making advances to me.

It would have been necessary to have neither eyes not ears to be insensible to the attractions of her vital beauty, to have neither warmth in the heart nor blood in the veins not to be seduced by the envelopment of that siren in the inept gaucherie of an honest woman. One idea, however, held me back. If I became smitten with his wife, Hierophas, who read me like a book, would certainly perceive it—and then what would happen?

The more I restricted myself to respectful banalities, the bolder she became, and the more she developed her supple and undulating grace, playing the tease. I thought, however, that Smithson, in his quality as a diviner, had doubtless foreseen the welcome his wife would give me, and knew in advance the little scene that was being played out a few yards away from him. What kind of man was he, then? What role was he making me play? I was only twenty years old, and such adventures cannot help being disturbing, when one is abroad—especially in America, where one can so easily encounter the barrel of a revolver.

I advanced, meanwhile, to the ultimate limits of admissible gallantry, but quickly understood that I could not remain there without seeming absolutely ridiculous. Too bad—I launched myself into a crazy declaration, which she received point-blank, her eyes half-closed, with an extreme joy. I was about to become more pressing when the prophet came back in.

Absorbed in the oracle he had just rendered, he appeared not to notice anything, and talked to us about the pleasure that he experienced when he was able to offer his clients fortunate predictions.

"You're a prophet of good omen," I said to him, smiling.

"A prophet, no, my dear sir," he replied, with slight impatience. "Once again, strictly speaking, I'm not. I don't claim, like many of my colleagues in whom the Magi of the Old Testament live again, to be inspired by God—nor by the Devil. I have nothing in common with astrologers, diviners, sorcerers, necromancers and other charlatans. I possess neither the unhealthy gift of foresight of the ancient pythonesses and convulsives, nor the second sight of somnambulists and hysterics. I practice prescience."

Now, I thought, *it's getting interesting*. And I had a strong desire to take out my notebook in order to take notes. A scruple restrained me. I looked at Mrs. Smithson. She was leaning backward on the cushions, eyes closed, lips smiling, as if still under the spell of the confessions she had heard. I was ashamed of doing my professional duty in front of her, and did not want her to be able to suppose, for an instant, that I attached more importance to her husband's words than hers. It was certainly very agreeable to see her thus, bit I could not entirely forget the objective of my visit; and although not very well of, I would have given a considerable sum for some household obligation to have summoned her into the next room and permit me to become the reporter glad to take notes about prescience. Unfortunately, it is only in the theater that characters exit when desired.

I could not, however, remain silent. By way of compromise, I declared that prescience seemed extremely interesting, but that it was impossible for me to deny the delightful attraction of the unexpected. Our lives would be rather dull if we knew the day before exactly what we would be doing the following day, and were unable to abandon ourselves insouciantly to the sweet joy of living.

"Ha ha!" said Smithson, smiling. "I see that you've been getting along well with Laura!"

"Why do say that?" I asked, a trifle anxious, while the lady's large eyes settled gently upon me.

"Because my wife doesn't believe in science, and remains attached to superstition."

"That is to say," she put in, "that I don't believe in your predictions."

"A French proverb declares that no one is a prophet in his own country—all the more reason why he should not be one in his own house," I hastened to remark.

"Note that I affirm nothing; affirmation is only for the ignorant; science always doubts. Although I talk about the future, I don't claim certainty; I merely calculate probabilities to the nearest ten thousandth—and human life is no more than probabilities!"

Apparently, I was not concealing the interest I was taking in her husband's declarations well enough. Mrs. Smithson got up abruptly. "So you think Monsieur will be amused by all your stories!"

"I don't doubt, my love, that your conversation would be infinitely more agreeable to him than mine—except that Monsieur has come here with certain preconceived ideas, of which I want to disabuse him completely. Let's go into my study."

"I hope that you won't steal Monsieur for too long, in order that we can resume the conversation that you interrupted untowardly?"

"Yes, yes—that's understood."

I followed Smithson into his study like a man who, sensing that he is a victim of circumstances, no longer seeks to resist them. It was a large, well-lit room, simply furnished with tables like those architects use, and tall stools. The entire back wall was taken up by a blackboard, on which was displayed a scaffolding of formulas and symbols alternating with cascades of numbers. There were statistical tables, innumerable filing cabinets, enormous ledgers and calculating instruments such as one sees in physics laboratories or observatories, and bundles of electrical wires were branching out in all directions. He was certainly a modern prophet.

"My method," he began, "is exceedingly simple. It closely resembles the one that meteorologists employ to anticipate the weather. Those scientists study the situation of the heavenly bodies, the state of the atmosphere, calculate the direction and speed of currents, the action of multiple influences, and finally refer them to statistical analysis."

"Which doesn't prevent them, as we say back home, from often sticking a finger in their eye."

"Once again, Monsieur, absolute certainty does not exist. For my research, I have completed the studies carried out on the physical word by analogous studies of the intellectual and moral worlds, that's all."

He took me to a window, showed me a building that resembled a factory, and told me that there, every day, five hundred employees recorded the ideas and facts that came to their attention, and classified them into categories and tables reproducing the approximate movement of universal life. Others drew up diagrams of currents of opinion and various influences, so accurately that when a case was submitted to him, Hierophas was able very rapidly to identify similar cases, and, given the present direction, calculate the probabilities. He added that an extensive training had rendered him very sensitive to the kind of radiation emanating from facts that is known as "ideas in the air," and that with his profound knowledge of men and things, he sometimes arrived instantaneously at the solution to a problem. But that was only a conjuring trick; his method was entirely founded on observation.

"Then you'll be able to tell me what the situation of humankind will be one or several centuries hence?"

"Indeed I can. But you don't expect me to reply to you immediately? Then you'd have the right to take me for a trickster! The question is one of the most colossal that can be

137

asked. To resolve it will require considerable research and innumerable calculations; I don't know how many years it would take me to make them, but the problem doesn't frighten me, and it's very possible that I'll study it."

Then he started talking to me gaily about the ridiculous questions he was asked every day. As he was telling me about the misadventures of a farmer's wife, who had wanted to know, at any cost, how many eggs her chickens would lay, an electric bell vibrated precipitately, several times over.

"That's my wife getting impatient," he said, "and thinking that our discussion in lasting too long; let's go find her."

Those words, bring me back to the reality of a situation that I had gradually forgotten, caused me to shiver. Now that I had learned what I wanted to know, however, I was determined not to take my flirtation with Madame any further. I would offer her my compliments—I could hardly do otherwise—and I would take my leave.

"There's one curious detail," said Smithson, linking arms with me in a familiar fashion in order to take me to the drawing room. "Just now, my wife declared that she didn't believe in my predictions. Well, she's not entirely wrong. Can you imagine that, with respect to all the people closest to me—my wife and children, for example—my vision, so clear with respect to others, become almost completely obscure. Sentiment disturbs it, as a magnet confuses a compass needle."

"The ancients were right, then, to put a blindfold over the eyes of love."

"Yes, it's always blind!"

The tone in which he had produced the last phrase might equally well have indicated an intimate dolor, pity for his wife, a threat to me, or perhaps all three. With that devil of a man, who saw through all games, how could one tell which one he was playing?

In the drawing room, sparkling with light, I could see nothing but Mrs. Smithson. She was in evening dress, her shoulders bare, her perfectly contoured neck emerging from a bodice of flowery satin, molded over rounded forms. Again I met her large, bottomless eyes, her ironic smile and her dark hair, artistically decorated with orchids.

Smithson rapidly made himself scarce, in order to receive the daily reports of his secretaries.

Alone again with that half-naked woman, on whose forehead our artists would have put a crescent, so symbolic was she of nervous pride—not the banal Diana but a Diana of the north with snow white flesh—I forgot my resolutions and did not defend myself against rapture. A flood of enthusiastic acclamations rose to my lips, and as, fortunately, English is as familiar to me as my mother tongue, I multiplied the susurration of admiring words, mingled with exclamations of languid finality that enveloped her like a caress: perfectly lovely! She received my compliments with the satisfaction of a sovereign who knows what is due to her, but who was nevertheless slightly surprised by the exaltation of my emotion.

Then, she turned her head, and said, with a delicate flick of her fan: "Oh, you Frenchmen!"

Her smile was more sarcastic, her eyes went in search of some unfathomable ceiling, and I could not make out whether the reminder of my nationality signified that she was tormented by my words or my gallantry.

Smithson came back, very correct in a florid smoking-jacket. My decision was made; I thanked him for his cordial reception, and the kindness with which he had informed me; I bowed to Madame and made as if to leave.

"Oh, no, no!" cried the gentleman prophet. "You're our guest, you're staying with us! We rarely have the opportunity to welcome a Frenchman here, and you wouldn't want to deprive us of that great pleasure. I have, in any case, more information to give you about prescience, and my wife won't be displeased to find out a little more about French mores."

Mrs. Smithson nodded, and, very embarrassed, I replied that I would like nothing better, but that it would be very difficult for me.

"Come on, my dear chap—no one, so far as I know, is expecting you? It's getting pitch dark, we live some way from the town, and I was so convinced that you'd stay with us that I permitted myself to send your carriage away."

I remarked politely that it was not very honest, in order to justify his predictions, to make it impossible for people to carry out their plans, but that, having said that, I greatly appreciated the honor that Hierophas was doing me in receiving me beneath his roof. He had to know that, deep down, I was not excessively annoyed. I was seduced by the prospect of resuming the flirtation, of seeing that honest wife ignite, like a grey ember stirred by a gust of wind, in the breath of passion, and of finally deciphering the enigma of her eyes.

Supper, in the midst of flowers, was very cheerful. Smithson, as a philosopher who knew the vanity of life and was not harassed by the pursuit of a ideal, seemed to be joyfully practicing the principle of *carpe diem*. His wife laughed at my merest remarks, and I must say that I deployed a firework-display of pleasantries by which I was dazzled myself. That prolixity, which greatly amused my hosts, came, I now understand, from the need I felt to daze myself and no longer to analyze my impressions.

I slightly cloud passed over when I was served, under the label of Champagne, an alcoholic tisane from California, which I declared inferior to our national product. Mrs. Smithson saved the situation by saying, with a slightly malicious intent, while her nose was in her glass: "Wasn't it one of your poets who said: 'what does the bottle matter, so long as one gets drunk?'"[51]

"I congratulate you, Madame, on knowing our national literature so well, but intoxication that is not poured out by beauty is, for me, merely a brutal delirium, and that beauty is the guarantee of the sublimity of my joy, for a golden ewer with rare sculptures can only contain a nectar worthy of the gods!"

---

[51] Alfred de Musset, in "La Coupe et les lèvres." The line became a favorite cynical euphemism.

I proclaimed that with such conviction that Madame's drink went down the wrong way and her husband the prophet was gripped by an outburst of laughter that was prolonged like a hurrah in a crowd.

After supper, Laura sat down at the piano, excusing herself for only being familiar with the German repertoire. While her fingers flew nimbly over the keyboard and melancholy ballads succeeded the broadly overlapping chords of passionate sonatas, Hierophas and I, seated on the same sofa, silently blew away the smoke of our cigars. He was doubtless absorbed in his calculations, while I was pursuing my flirtation. Each note seemed to vibrate for me alone. I felt that she was smitten, as I was smitten, and that her heart was coming to me on the wings of the music, just as the blue spirals of smoke were bearing mine toward her.

"My dear friend," said Smithson, suddenly, "I've been thinking about the question you asked me a little while ago."

"What question?"

"About the future of humankind."

"Oh, yes…yes."

"Tomorrow morning, perhaps I'll be able to give you a more categorical reply, but at first glance, this is what I observe: the gods having rendered the earth inhabitable, humans have gradually recreated it. The forces of nature have been tamed by mind, if not entirely, at least in part, and…are you listening to me?"

It was not only the piano but her voice, a warm mezzosoprano that filled the room with tremulous and tender notes.

"Yes, yes!" I hastened to reply to Smithson, who continued.

"Follow my reasoning carefully. After the great physical discoveries will come the great metaphysical discoveries, which, even more than the former, will transform the world. We shall thus advance to the limits of the unknowable, and…are you with me?"

She had made a selection of the most fiery declarations of love, and I experienced I don't know what mad desire to respond to that voice, which was proclaiming in vain the ardor of its flame. Without being aware of it, I repeated with her the words: "Yes, I'm yours."

"I think," said Smithson, laughing, "that you're a little distracted."

"The music is so penetrating," I stammered, understanding my gaffe.

"I'll wager that you're in love?"

"Me!" I felt a shiver run down my spine. Repaying the audacity, I added, laughing: "I won't take the bet, because you only bet on sure things, since nothing can be hidden from you."

"I congratulate you on being in love—it's the noblest passion of all; I hope you'll be happy."

It was on the tip of my tongue to ask him whether I would be—he ought to know! To address that question to a husband, however, seemed to be to be in doubtful taste, and I relied with a vague exclamation.

"Is one ever sure of being happy?"

"Yes, sometimes," Smithson replied—and he dispatched his smoke slowly toward the ceiling, smiling at agreeable memories.

That prophet, that prescient, was the blindest and least jealous of husbands! He was truly soaring above contingencies. He read the future and did not see the present: his wife's flirtatiousness and our exchanged glances. He did not understand my disturbance at all. I felt sorry for him.

When she had finished, as I congratulated the cantatrice, I told her that her song had given birth to an emotion within me to which her husband could testify. Laura denied being a great artiste and claimed that in order to have been moved I must have been very obliging. I was about to say something stupid when some neighbors arrived to talk to Smithson about local business. As such questions were no more interesting to Laura than to me, we took refuge in a corner of the drawing room and resumed our intimate conversation.

She explained that, living in an environment where everything was foreseen, the unknown, that universal alarm, had a charm for her that she could not resist. For her, I was the unknown; an invincible force had driven her toward me, and my gallantry had done the rest. Incidentally, she told me that William and she had separate apartments, and that the room set aside for me was only separated from hers by a glazed corridor.

I limited myself to repeating that she was the most beautiful, most adorable and most marvelously amiable of all the women I had encountered thus far. I would have liked to silence the immense love that, on seeing her, had struck me like a thunderbolt, but I could not do it. By retaining me in hr proximity, she had prolonged my happiness but aggravated my torment, and I would only leave the house in permanent despair. Perhaps I put a little more emphasis into it than sincerity, but she didn't appear to perceive it.

The prophet bid his neighbors farewell.

Laura stood up, passed close to me, and leaned over to whisper in my ear: "One o'clock in the morning." Then she slowly drew away, to say goodbye to the people who were leaving.

I remained nailed to my chair by shock. Laura had given me a rendezvous, and a nocturnal rendezvous, which could only take place in her bedroom! My first reflection was to think that these American prudes so strict in their "respectability," so prompt to be shocked when one mentioned Parisian women, could certainly give them pointers! I could not imagine, in fact, that one of our honest bourgeois wives would fall into the arms of anyone like that, after a few minutes of conversation. The sphinx had feet of clay! Which didn't prevent me from glorying in my conquest—one doesn't meet the wife of a prophet every day—and reveling in the thought of the promised felicities.

Having exchanged good nights with my hosts, accompanied by warm handshakes, I found myself alone in a very elegant apartment, naturally provided with all desirable comforts. Then I reviewed the multiple incidents of the day; they appeared infinitely less odd to me.

I was now certain that I had stupidly allowed myself to be caught by a flirt, an expert and exceedingly cunning woman who was drawing me into a wicked escapade. Her gracious welcome, her smiles, her glances, her beauty—everything seemed suspect to me. That insistence on my staying, the skill in engineering private conversations, that outrageously low-cut dress and those lascivious songs—was all of that not a task of seduction planned in advance? Besides which, could there be anything unexpected in that house?

An atrocious idea crossed my mind: perhaps she was following a plan concocted by her husband. Yes, yes, the fellow's joviality rang false and his cordiality was only feigned. True, I had not familiar with prophets, but it seemed to me that such a man would not put himself out for a mere reporter, explain his working methods to him, introduce him to his wife, allow her to flirt with him—for he could not have failed to notice it—and then entertain him under his roof. What did it signify that he had sent away my carriage, and made me drink, in spite of myself, strange alcohol decorated with the name of Champagne? And the care he took to tell me that he could not foresee anything that concerned his wife—was that not to give me to understand that I could pay court to her without fear?

I threw myself down on a chaise-longue, certainly not to sleep but to collect myself and concentrate my ideas.

There was no need to seek any further; I had fallen into a trap. What were their objectives? What did they expect of me? Did they want to make me sing? They couldn't suppose that I'd roll over for money. Did Smithson want to take revenge on his wife? He couldn't have expected my arrival.

Aided by the darkness and the silence, the most extravagant thoughts crossed my mind. Sinister anecdotes crowded my memory. Who could tell, with these eccentrics, what one might expect? I could already see myself riddled with bullets or lacerated by stab-wounds.

I thought about running away. Through the house? That was unthinkable; I might get lost in the maze of corridors and stairways, and bump into the porter, who would mistake me for a thief and shot me dead. Jump out of the window? I looked out; it opened into an interior courtyard.

The best thing to do was to stay in my room, lock the door and wait for morning. In order to put this very reasonable plan into execution, I went to lock the door. There was no key!

Firmly decided not to go to sleep, and to remain ready for anything, I paced back and forth, wondering whether it might not be prudent to barricade the door with furniture. No, in spite of appearances, I might be mistaken, and then, how ridiculous it would have been to erect such defenses.

My watch showed a quarter to one. Already! Laura would be expecting me in a quarter of an hour. Would she be the only one expecting me? Whether she was sincere or setting a trap for me, she would be expecting me, I was sure of it. At that moment I imagined her there, all ready, at the other end of the corridor, her beautiful body draped in a light and transparent fabric, lifting up her loose tresses with a gracious gesture and darting a last glance at her mirror. Then I saw her curl up, tremulously, in a profound armchair and smile within it, that dazzling smile which transfigured her beauty. Her feverish eyes, fixed on the face of a grandfather clock, following the progress of the hands... By the undulation of lace I sensed her breathing becoming gradually weaker. I saw her beautiful arms, so pure in their lines, coming apart like wings, and extend toward the unknown—toward me—while her lips came together to blow me a kiss.

Shall I lose that delightful Laura forever because of a stupid and unjustifiable pusillanimity? Shall I exasperate myself and curse myself in a vain attempt? I've certainly seen what I've seen, heard what she said to me; thunderbolts are undeniable: she loves me! She loves me and I'd be stupid not to respond to her love, to let her go because a hallucinatory wakefulness has given birth within me to chimerical dreads. No, a thousand times no! Shall I tell her tomorrow that I was

145

afraid? A truly fine defeat for a gallant man! All the more reason to do it if there's a risk to be run. That woman, sincere or false, has trusted me, and I can't appear to her to be a coward or an imbecile.

The hands of my watch were approaching one o'clock. What if I were going to my death, though? Damn it! The husband was one of those idiots that can be fooled with impunity. Was it not the height of cynicism to take the wife of one's host? Get away! Is there a morality for love?

The d'Artagnanesque side of my character got the upper hand, forcefully, and I opened my bedroom door.

Moonlight coming through the windows that lit the corridor described large black arabesques on the floor. I slid along the wall, muffling the sound of my footsteps as much as possible, pricking up my ears at the slightest suspect rustle. I reached the blissful door.

It is no exaggeration to say that at that moment, my heart was beating as if to burst. I scratched softly; no sound replied to me; no light filtered through the cracks.

Softly, I called: "Laura, my darling?"

Nothing.

I presumed that Laura, by virtue of some residue of respectability, preferred silence, darkness and mystery. Boldly, I pushed the door. It opened. Hesitantly, I advanced into the darkness, dreading at every step that I might bump into a item of furniture.

"Laura?" I repeated, tenderly. "Laura, my darling?"

Emotion must have paralyzed her throat, for, after a few seconds, I perceived the hoarse sound of her respiration. Cautiously, I approached the bed. I reached out a hand; I felt a dangling arm: her arm, rather strong, with pure firm lines. I seized it, and covered it with kisses.

Abruptly, it tore away from my caresses. The bed shuddered, as if she had leapt out of it. Electric lamps lit up and I saw, standing by the bed, in his sculptural nudity, the black man who had opened the door to me!

Alarmed, he had flicked the switches, and grabbed a revolver. I stopped him with a placatory gesture; he recognized me.

How could I explain my presence? I could not confide to him that I was going his mistress's room and that, having mistaken the door, I wished he would tell me where I was. I gave the excuse that I was looking for a bathroom, to which he gave me directions tremulously, and I found myself back in the corridor.

What should I do? Knock on another door? It seemed to me, now, that it was a nearby door that she had indicated to me. No, though. What if, this time, I were to go into the prophet's room? I retraced my steps. And, although it was exceedingly cruel to tell myself that Laura might perhaps be there, impatient to see me, I went back into my room, furious with myself, ashamed of the ridicule that would shower upon me if rumor of the adventure got around.

In the morning, I had resolved to cut things short, to leave without even seeing my hosts, and send them a letter explaining the plausible reasons that had motivated my precipitate departure. I forgot that in that house, one could not do anything that was not anticipated.

Scarcely was I in the hallway than I saw Smithson and his wife advancing toward me, with their hands outstretched, thanking me effusively.

"For what?"

Finally, the prophet spoke. "Yesterday, when I received your card, I was with Laura. 'A Frenchman!" she said. 'Will you introduce me to him?'

"'Do you intend to deceive me with him?' I asked.

"'Why not?' she replied.

"Confronted with that threat, I declared to her that, in spite of everything she could do, I was certain that she would not deceive me. She replied that she did not believe in my prophecies, and that, if she wanted to, she would deceive me. My prediction, and I thank you for it, has thus been realized this time, since Laura did not leave my side last night."

"And I have won my bet too," continued Madame, "since, if I had indicated the door to my room last night, instead of that of my servant, you would at the present moment, William, be well and truly deceived; while my servant would have been spared a shock."

I must have had an expression so pitiful, and a manner so disconcerted, that the adorable Laura thought it necessary to offer me excuses.

"Alas, Monsieur, I am indeed not the Messalina you thought you had encountered; I'm merely an honest mother, who permitted herself to play a joke on your complacency—a cruel one, I admit—and who sincerely begs your pardon. I would have been horribly vexed if I hadn't succeeded in seducing you and I would rather you were dead than had failed to come to knock on the black man's door. Be assured that I shall conserve a precious memory of all the gallant things you said. I hope that, for your part, you will also recall our flirtation with pleasure."

And Laura held out her pretty hands, which I kissed respectfully.

"I don't want to be in your debt," Hierophas said to me, "And I don't want you to harbor any resentment with regard to an adventure from which none of use emerges entirely honorably. This is my response to your question about the progress of humankind. Humankind is in decline in Europe, Asia and Africa; it is making progress in America."

"Which means?"

"That humankind will become American, or disappear!"

II. The Reverend

Setting the ridiculousness of the adventure aside, I had every reason to congratulate myself, since the prophet had indicated to me mathematically the direction in which humankind was progressing. It remained to discover how it would progress on the new path. It seemed to me that a visit to the

New Life Club would fill me in on this point; a friend in Cincinnati offered to introduce me and serve as my guide.

At first sight, the club in question resembles all the rest—and God knows how many of them there are in the territory of the Union—in making the same bluff: pretention to colossal proportions, insolent and garish luxury. It goes without saying that a multitude of black men and innumerable servo-motors permit every member to satisfy his most capricious whims rapidly and effortlessly, each to his own: work, play, read, chat, argue, eat, drink, sleep, dance, play sport, watch various spectacles or flirt, if the inclination moves him. My introducer gave me a thousand details about the organization and told me that the club had been founded according to the principles of Reverend Lowster of Cincinnati.

Although I had never heard mention of the Reverend, I did not want to appear to be ignoring his work, and declared that, without permitting myself to criticize such respectable principles, his "new life" seemed to me to be strangely similar to the old.

"How alike you all are!" my Yankee replied, with the loquacity of a do-gooder. "You stand in ecstasy before a working machine, the flood of light that springs forth, the cylinder that records speech, the invisible wave that carries it, the automobile that devours distance, the airplane that takes flight—all of those that are children's toys. Science amuses you, and for you, moral discoveries pass unperceived. Know, then, once and for all that science has given all it could; it has gone from the heaviest substance to the imponderable, and we say to it: 'Stop! Your role is over!' To tame the force—blind, like all forces—that we call nature, there is no longer any but one force in the world: that is moral force.

"That's why we reckon that Reverend Lowster had one of those inspirations of genius that are very rarely encountered in history, when he demanded of all the members of the circle to make an undertaking to leave nothing to chance."

"You'll excuse me," I replied, "but I don't really see how that can greatly modify the behavior of your compatriots, who are not given to treating things lightly, being practical men who calculate and carefully weigh the pros and cons before launching themselves into any project."

"Yes, it doesn't seem like much, and yet it's a considerable matter for the future of our race," said the enthusiastic disciple of Reverend Lowster, with the discreet smile of a polite gentleman who dares not mock overtly.

We were going through a reading room; he fell silent, and I took advantage of it to admire a collection of Bibles, ranging from the most ancient parchments to very recent editions. There were handwritten pages there, and other printed with an amazing perfection and beauty, marvels of miniaturization, design and engraving and masterpieces of binding, such as I had never seen anywhere else. One might have thought that those simple books revealed in themselves as much enthusiasm and mystic grandeur as our Gothic cathedrals. I was slightly surprised to see the respectful indifference of the readers in their regard. They probably all knew the Bible by heart, for none of them was reading it. On the other hand, they were competing for the magazines, newspapers and illustrated periodicals of the entire world, including those sheets of very special artistry that are produced in Paris for export.

We passed into a walkway ornamented with frightful antique moldings and mediocre but vast paintings; my guide stopped and turned his long jaundiced and almost hairless face toward me.

"Yes! You think that the promise we make, which you will take if you want to be admitted, is a derisory formality? I beg you—as a Frenchman, who, in consequence, doesn't reason very often—to think about what a life might become in which all the actions...all of them, you understand...are only accomplished with attention, reflection and judgment."

"It must be extremely tiresome!" I exclaimed. "The live we lead isn't exactly full of fun; if it were to augment our annoyances, our cares, our preoccupations and our alarms, then it truly isn't worth the trouble of changing. The sole charm of life, my dear colleague, it to let oneself live!"

"Not at all! The worst danger we face is that of thus abandoning ourselves to the suggestions of instinct and the illusions of sentiment!"

"I believe I perceive," I replied, "that your club is a puritan society of temperance and continence, doubtless vegetarian, anti-alcohol, anti-tobacco, anti-everything you like: a union of neo-quakers forming one of the thousand varieties of the salvationist species."

My man shrugged his shoulders and accelerated his pace. He opened a door in order to usher me into an empty, sonorous and chilly conference hall, in which the voice of an orator could not resound very often.

He pointed at the speaker's podium and said: "It's there that Reverend Lowster developed his idea for the first time, defined the action of our moral force and revealed the goal that we ought to pursue—a goal far more elevated than you suppose."

"I'd be very grateful to you if, even though you think me unworthy, you'd care to acquaint me with it?"

My loquacious journalist did not need to be asked twice, and, taking Lowster's place, he said:

"These are the Reverend's own words: 'God has said: multiply and increase. Now, what do we see today? We are multiplying, but we are decreasing. Why? Because, although we apply all our efforts to make our businesses prosper, we leave to nature—which is to say, to chance—the care of making our species prosper and our race increase. Blind nature goes straight ahead and sows life without worrying about the terrain on which it falls, without worrying about the consequences; whether the seed produces the blind or the lame, cretins or cripples, is irrelevant; all that matters is that it grows. Now, is it at hazard that the laborer throws seed into a field? No. If Scripture remade the base and vile calculation of interest, it would not say that our descendants ought to be the produce of a hazard too often regretted, but the beautiful harvest of a planned insemination, made in favorable conditions. Thus, to follow the path of God and work as honest Yankees for the future of our race: Leave nothing to chance!'"

This little sermon, pronounced in a pastoral tone, instead of enlightenment, served only to sow confusion in my mind, but, as I had noticed a number of old ladies in the reading room, I thought I understood."

"I get it," I said. "Your club is a model matrimonial agency."

"Not at all! Listen to me closely: we want to found a race of elite men and women, capable of playing the formidable role that the future reserves for them; for that, we have such a mixture of bloodlines among the inhabitants of the Union that it's indispensable to maintain a pure Yankee race."

"I must say right away...I confess to your humbly that I would never have been able to suppose that the Reverend Lowther, in order to ameliorate the American race, would use a method more specifically reserved for the equine race."

My amiable guide seemed indignant at my assumption. His jaundiced face blushed a prudish orange. He made one of those American grimaces that is to ours what a leaden cloud is to a light mist. Then his pursed lips let fall these scornful words: "Reverend Lowster does not understand selection in the same way as Parisian *devils*!"

"How the devil does he understand it, then? If he proscribes the game of love as a game of chance, and banishes all calculation, I don't really see what's left."

"Moral force!"

I stared at my interlocutor. "My dear chap," I said, "I know that you like to mystify those of our colleagues who come from the far side of the water to see what is happening here. In France, a number of investigations of the United States have appeared in which it is obvious that my compatriots have been played for fools by yours. I reply to you that mine will not be one of those, and that you will not claim the head of the correspondent of the *Universal Informer* with impunity."

Having said that, in a slightly dry tone, I followed him into the lunch room.

There, I was not a little astonished to see young and elegant unmarried women, some with flame-colored hair and languid eyes, others brunettes with white complexions and fiery gazes—who, according to all the evidence, were pursuing violent flirtations with furiously enterprising gentlemen.

"Well, my dear friend," I said, jogging the elbow of the Reverend Lowster's disciple, "here are some individuals who see to me to have left their moral force in the cloakroom."

"Don't you believe it. They're all good Yankees, for the most part special people. Some of them are worth I don't know how many millions of dollars! None of them will allow themselves to be surprised by chance; they're all too well aware of what they owe to the Republic, and are awaiting favorable conditions to endow it with elite citizens."

My curiosity was boundless; I wanted to know what those conditions were, hoping one day to impart precious knowledge to my fatherland, which might perhaps permit it to regenerate itself too. But Reverend Lowster had gone into such minute detail and the conditions required, as listed by his disciple, were so numerous and so contradictory, that it seemed to me to be impossible, at first glance, that the two subjects indispensable to the…regeneration could ever encounter one another simultaneously in favorable conditions.

We then found ourselves perched side by side on those high bar-stools without which one cannot drink a good cocktail. And it was not by chance, as you can imagine, that we started drinking. My transatlantic colleague had observed my fit of bad temper, and, perhaps fearing that I might see through the whole bluff of morally regenerative heroism, that I might perceive the all-too-human realities behind that décor of evangelical respectability, wanted to get back into my good graces. Perhaps he had judged it prudent thus to facilitate the acceptance of explanations that really were a little difficult to swallow.

I had listened to him without saying a word, and when he had finished, I paused for a while with my nose in my glass, wondering whether I ought to get indignant or laugh.

This Reverend was a brave and worthy pastor, whose sincerity, so far as I was concerned, as not subject to a shadow of a doubt, but who, in wanting to reconcile divine precepts and worldly restrictions, had not seen any further than his apostolic and regenerative zeal. Obviously, he was not the first who had sought to tame nature by means of will-power; the others, it is true, had not preached a crusade against chance or founded a club—but they weren't Americans! More modern than all those saintly individuals, Lowster had not entered into an overt conflict with nature; he merely aspired to domesticate it. Like the engineers who had taken possession of the lightning in order to serve as the motor of industrial progress, he had taken possession of that other lightning which is love, in order to make it serve for the amelioration of his race. The project was grandiose; the execution seemed to me to leave much to be desired.

"That's made you think," my companion went on, thinking that he had triumphed over my skepticism.

"Yes," I replied. "Everything you've told me is very wisely thought out—but don't you fear that Reverend Lowster of Cincinnati, in obedience to God's second principle, has misunderstood the first, and that, in trying to ensure the physical and intellectual development of the race, he might injure its multiplication?"

"Multiplication is the affair of the masses, of the poor, the wretched, manual workers—proletarians, in a word—who, as the name indicates, whatever we say and whatever we do, will always pullulate. We reserve ourselves, for giving birth only to a few geniuses—leaders of men."

"I don't doubt that in future, posterity will be very grateful to you for the efforts you're making to elevate it to presently-inaccessible heights of human thought; unfortunately, the results seem to me to be rather problematic."

"Why is that?"

154

"Because you're demanding from your initiates a sacrifice beyond their moral force."

"One can always be master of one's sentiments."

"That's possible; but Scripture itself recognizes that certain temperaments are subject to an insatiable avidity, and..."

"For those, 'there are accommodations with heaven,'" said my Yankee, softly, in excellent French.[52]

"Of course!" I cried. "Now I understand how the New Life Club works!"

"Would you like me to put you up for membership?"

"No, there's no need," I said, shaking his hand. "Only, when you've created the geniuses, be good enough to send me a telegram."

III. The Professor

Finding myself at an American exhibition, hazard linked me in conversation with a young Yankee, very blond, very tall, very muscular and exceedingly clean-shaven, who passed indifferently and stiffly, looking straight ahead, through the midst of the most authentic marvels. When I expressed my astonishment at the scant interest he seemed to be taking in the enormous exhibition he said:

"All that you see here: these incomparable works of art, these titanic achievements, these stupefying inventions, this colossal effort of human genus; is nothing—nothing!—compared to the discovery of Professor Fuss. Remember the name of that great genius, which, in a few years time, will equal those of Galileo and Newton, if it does not surpass them."

---

[52] This euphemistic phrase had become very widely used by the end of the 19th century, and its origin had probably been forgotten as an irrelevance. The earliest printed version I can identify is in Frank Puaux's *Histoire de la Reformation Française* (1868).

155

"Tell me quickly," I demanded, "of what the discovery of this illustrious scientist consists."

"A man of science first and foremost, Professor Fuss is a patient observer and a meticulous experimenter. He does not want to reveal anything of his endeavors before having checked and rechecked the results of his research and acquired absolute certainty."

"Can't you at least indicate the direction his research is oriented?"

"That's impossible. I promised to maintain secrecy. Go see him; he's a very affable man, and perhaps for you—who are French, and hence skeptical—he'll make an exception to the reserve he maintains with his compatriots, whom he knows to be too prompt to enthusiasm and too prone to put a discovery into action before it is complete."

"Where does this extraordinary men live? I'll go as soon as possible."

"He's quite simply the Professor of Experimental Physiology at the Free University of Denver, Colorado. Mention my name when you introduce yourself and you'll be well-received, I can assure you."

The young Yankee scribbled a few words on a card, which he handed to me, and for which I thanked him with the sincere effusion of a reporter notified of an unknown prodigy, an impending sensational event or a strange, mysterious and formidable person to interview.

Two days later, I took the train to Denver, and, scarcely having disembarked, took a taxi to the Free University, which occupied a series of veritable palaces in the middle of an immense park. Fortunately, Professor Fuss was in his. I sent him my card, along with the one the young Yankee had given me. A few minutes later, a gentleman whom one would not readily have taken for a flunkey took me to a kind of bar. In the middle, standing on crooked legs, was a small man, certainly of mixed race, with a large forehead and energetic features, whose singularly keen eyes and disquieting rictus rendered him strange. In a flannel shirt with the sleeves rolled up and his braces showing, he seemed to be awaiting a sparring-partner for a boxing bout. That was Professor Fuss.

Aha!" he said to me. "You're a Frenchman, and a journalist. I'm doubly pleased to meet you. It's lunch time; if you'd like to come with me, it's no trouble. Choose what you please; the victuals you see here are at your disposal."

My Yankee had not deceived me; the professor had an ironic affability. Once having greeted me, however, without paying any more attention to me, he attacked a ham, detaching a large slice therefrom, which he set about consuming, while muttering bitterly.

"Oh, France...I know it. I've been there, to France. What a sad country! The French really are the worst people. An exhausted race, finished. There are no longer any people or ideas there—nothing!"

I tried to protest and cite the names of our most eminent and respected masters.

"Get away! Scientific smugglers all! Because they dress themselves up with titles and are heaped with honors, they think they're something! No, they're donkeys, pack-donkeys—and what's worse, impotent. And as, in spite of their stupid pride, they sense their inferiority, they force themselves by any means to prevent the hatching of genius. Any slightly elevated concept surpasses them, any boldness confuses them. Not only don't they dare to confront the questions that emerge from the banal cycle of our familiar knowledge, but they deny others the right to search the unknown, to go any further in the science of life. And they laugh—yes, Monsieur, they laugh and shrug their shoulders—when a man like me comes to talk to them about research as simple, as logical and as far-reaching as that to which I devote myself. How stupid!"

His words were pierced by an evident rancor. I inferred that the illustrious professor most have been turned away, more or less politely, by our official scientists. I came to their defense hotly, affirming that there must have been a misunderstanding, and that, on the contrary, our great masters were often very quick to appropriate a foreigner's ideas, and that, in any case, their well-known courtesy was not in accordance with what he was saying about them. I made an effort to get back to the point, and asked him, if it was not too great an indiscretion on my part, to indicate to me, as a layman, if not the actual nature of his research, at least the objective toward which it was directed.

"I'm work," he replied, "for the improvement of the human race."

"An admirable problem," I exclaimed, "but how arduous! For centuries now, elite thinkers have been striving to find a solution for it, and we haven't glimpsed one yet."

"Because they're going about it the wrong way," the professor replied, curtly.

"Really?" I said, giving my voice the flattering, respectful and pressing inflexion of an interlocutor burning to know more.

The little man poured the contents of various bottles into a tall glass, added ice cubes and stirred it slowly. A sarcastic smile cleared the grimace from his face.

"Well," he said, "you Frenchmen, since your Revolution, imagine you can arrive at that improvement by means of words and phrases. Wrong, Monsieur—a grave error. If the prejudice inherent in your race weren't blinding you, you'd recognize, as I do, that in your country, in spite of the efforts of legislators, the moral level is unchanging, intellectualism is stagnating and inferiority remains. The German have tried scientific culture, and the English physical culture, without achieving better results. The history of all times and all nations proves to us that we rotate invincibly in the same circle, fall back into the same errors and the same faults as our predecessors; and everything leads us to believe that our heirs will do the same. In any case, that observation can only astonish a superficial observer; for anyone who knows, can see and can reason, it's obvious that it can't be otherwise."

Emphasizing every word, Professor Fuss repeated: "It can't be otherwise," and set about absorbing the iced mixture in small sips.

"Dare I demand, Master, why that is?"

"It's simply because our brain isn't capable of anything more. It's so crammed and stuffed with knowledge of all sorts that it's no longer possible to get the slightest new idea into it. Cranial capacity has its limits; they're bursting!"

"But you, Professor, are living proof to the contrary?"

"The man of genius is an exception. It has been said, quite justly, that he's a monster. His case is a subject of teratology; I'm not talking about that. I'm concerned with normal brains. Well, in France, for example, you talk a great deal of implanting general ideas in the minds of your compatriots: of universal good will, humanity, justice, solidarity and I don't know what else. It's absurd! It's tantamount to wanting the contents to be greater than the container. These conceptions are treated as utopian, and that's perfectly reasonable. Before demanding a machine to produce more, it's imperative to increase its power. Before trying to inculcate more elevated notions into individuals, it's necessary to enlarge their skulls."

With these concluding words, Professor Fuss stood up. Terrified by the operation of enlargement to which the little man wanted to subject our poor normal heads, I wondered anxiously whether he might have lost his own. I looked at him attentively. Nothing in his tortured expression—that of a scientist—his strict attitude, his cold and correct elocution indicated derangement. I risked a question.

"Undoubtedly it would be desirable to augment cranial capacity, but I can't quite see what orthopedic apparatus one could employ to obtain such a result?"

This time the Professor deigned to smile broadly.

"What do you expect to find? It's not a question of apparatus, nor of operations, and you have nothing, my dear Monsieur, to fear from me. I only act on skulls that are not yet formed. For the others, alas, I can do nothing, and you'll have to resign yourself until death to the small mind that you have."

"I'm in despair, my dear Doctor," I said, smiling in my turn, "but only up to a point. I know now that your discovery doesn't affect me directly, that you're improving future beings; my curiosity is all the more excited, and the interest provoked by your research is so powerful that you can't refuse to satisfy it. Explain to me, I beg you—in a few words—the principles of your procedure."

"It's just that my procedure, as you call it," said the professor, visibly embarrassed and desirous of cutting the conversation short, "is still in an embryonic state. Then again, in order to go into more detail, I'd have to give you a veritable lecture, using technical terms with which, for the most part, you're probably not familiar."

"Master, I confess my ignorance frankly—but let me say that high science is astonishing in its clarity, and I have no doubt that a scientist like you can make himself understood to an ignoramus like me."

"All right—so much the worse for you; you asked for it. Let's go into my study."

Professor Fuss's study occupied a large, brightly-lit room. Everything there was methodically arranged. Even on the work-desks, there were no scattered papers, manuscripts in confusion, or piles of books. Low bookshelves within arm's reach and display-cases garnished with skulls and molds of the brain. On the walls, a series of frescoes, not too bad, whose subjects were borrowed from natural history. Comfortable seats almost everywhere, matching the form of the body, permitting the sitter to adopt the negligent poses that American affect.

The professor indicated one of those seats to me, and I sprawled in it. He offered me a cigar, and I lit it. Then he went to perch on a high stool facing me, and tucked his knees under his chin.

"You can easily conclude from what I've already said," he began, "that to improve the human race, one cannot think of utilizing humans as we know them. We must therefore modify them, and by that means create individuals of a superior order—supermen, as that lunatic Nietzsche said, who got the problem backwards. Now, we know that selection, education and different cultures only produce insignificant modifications. A pear-tree, no matter how you treat it, won't produce melons. What can be done, then? The answer comes quite naturally to mind: since one can't modify humans after birth, let's modify them before. We shall thus prepare in the egg the giant race that will succeed in emerging from the narrow circle in which we have been turning, like lamentable squirrels, for forty centuries: a race whose vast minds will be capable of embracing the knowledge of space, time, the universe, nature, matter, mind, life, death and destiny—things that are presently dead letters so far as we're concerned."

"They'll know everything, then?" I said, enthusiastically, sitting up in my chair.

"I can't guarantee that; I can only affirm that they'll know infinitely more than we do."

"Illustrious Professor," I said, "if you have the possibility of realizing such a prodigy, publish it quickly, everywhere in the entire world! Everyone will be proud to cooperate in what may be called a veritable renaissance. For my part, I declare myself entirely disposed to assist you, according to my means, in the fabrication of supermen. Tell me how."

From the height of his perch, Professor Fuss looked at me with owlish eyes, and his rictus was aggravated by a mocking laugh.

"Oh, you Frenchman!" he said, as if he were saying, 'you imbecile!' "You're as frivolous and grotesque in your skepticism as in your over-enthusiasms. Do you think it's sufficient to take such and such a measure to procreate beings of a superior order at will? That would, of course be easy, and my merit, would be slender, given that, since the world has existed, all modes of procreation are known and practiced daily... No, Monsieur, no, the matter isn't as simple as it appears to you. It requires long preparation, and entire exceedingly delicate operating manual, and can only be applied to rare subjects."

The words "operating manual" calmed my excitement down completely. I slumped back in my chair, determined this time not to interrupt again, to let the professor continue the revelation of his stupefying discovery to the end.

"Have you heard mention," he asked me, abruptly, "of *marine genesis?*"

I made a vague gesture, a sort of flutter, which testified to the perfect bewilderment into which that question put me.

"That doesn't surprise me," the terrible little man continued. "It was one of your compatriots who invented the theory,[53] and Frenchmen, while they mock our efforts, are generally ignorant of those made in their own land. Well, look at this succession of pictures." He pointed at a fresco, which, like a *danse macabre*, ran in a frieze around the room. "First, you see the envelope of our planet as it cools down. Here, it's sufficient cool to allow life to become manifest. Here is the simple cell that gives rise to more complicated ones. The first algae arrive; our great ancestors the mollusks, reptiles, fish, saurians, and finally mammals. The chain continues, as you can see, all the way to humans, passing from the rudimentary state to an increasing degree of perfection. Perhaps you will think the transition from fish to mammal unjustified, but your compatriot has sagaciously observed that the transition is accomplished every day before our eyes when tadpoles are transformed into toads or frogs. That's what is known as marine genesis."

"For my part, Master, I declare that I don't see anything inconvenient about our being descended from fish. That detail might even explain the tendency that certain individuals have to swim under water, and legitimate such ichthyological terms as serve to designate individuals of either sex whose morality drifts downstream.[54] I don't quite see, however, what rele-

---

[53] Benoît de Maillet.

[54] The term "shark" springs to mind, but Jullien is presumably referring to the fact that *maquereau* [mackerel] is also used in French to refer to a pimp or brothel-keeper. It is also signifi-

vance these considerations have to the improvement of our species."

"Don't makes jokes, and wait—we'll go into my laboratory. All right?"

The laboratory, into which I went after the Master, was installed in an immense gallery, almost entirely glazed. A dozen laboratory assistants were at work there, some doing histological research, others chemical analyses, others on anatomical preparations, etc. He went along the whole length of the room, darting glances to the right and the left at the work of his assistants, giving instructions as he passed by, and led me to a kind of shelf-unit on which bottles were aligned.

"You see these crystal jars," he said. "They contain a collection of fetuses going from conception to parturition. If you care to take the trouble to examine them, what will you observe? You'll observe that the human ovum, fertilized by an infinitesimal worm, successively takes the form of a mollusk, a fish, a tadpole and a quadrumane, etc. Do you grasp the correlation? In nine months, the human seed passes through all the transformations to which the species has been subject in a long sequence of centuries."

"It's a reduction of evolution," I said. "Transformism in two hundred and eighty-some days."

"Very good," said Professor Fuss, sketching a bow in my direction, glad to see that, in spite of the narrowness of my skull, I had understood his demonstration. "Now, follow my reasoning carefully."

"I'll follow it step by step."

"In order to arrive at the human condition, therefore, the cell is extraordinarily modified and, so to speak, improved. Who can affirm that it has arrived at the end of it evolution and that we are the definitive form? To formulate that proposition is to display illogicality. What will the superior phases be that we will reach in several thousand centuries? No one can

---

cant that what might be called a "come hither look" in English is described in French as "making carp's eyes" at someone.

flatter himself that he knows. Perhaps we'll acquire organs of which I have no knowledge, corresponding to needs of which we have no suspicion. In any case, it's probable that today's 'unknowable' will no longer be a mystery to us then. Suppose—which is perfectly permissible—that the difference between humans a hundred thousand years hence and those of today will be similar to that observed between a present human being and the cellule. Now imagine, if you can, what that prodigious being might be!"

And Professor Fuss folded his arms, while directing the fire of his pupils at me.

"I can't," I replied, lowering my head. "My brain refuses."

"Certainly," he said. "I don't flatter myself that I can make humankind overstep a separation of so many centuries, but I think I can advance the desperately slow work of nature considerably."

"Aha!" I exclaimed. "You're finally getting there!"

"The method is quite simple, as you shall see."

"Except," I added politely, "that it was necessary to think of it—Columbus' egg again!"

"I'll keep to reasoning that a child could understand. If, in two hundred and eighty-some days, as you out it, a fetus goes through all the cycles of the transformation of the species, in twice two hundred and eighty-some days—about five hundred and seventy—it will go through twice as many. Which is equivalent to saying that it will surpass them by as much. Thus, by prolonging fetal life, we ought logically to obtain products that will be what we would normally become in fifty, or a hundred thousand centuries. Do you understand?"

"I was momentarily confused by the eminent professor's arithmetic. He savored my bewilderment, twisting his nutcracker chin, and his triumphant rictus seemed to be saying; "Well, my little Frenchman, you weren't expecting that, were you? You thought I was bluffing, and you made jokes, facetious reporter! Now you're stuck, my lad, and you can only bow down before my science."

"Most illustrious Master," I said, determined not to spare the epithets any longer, "I can't translate into congruous terms the profound admiration by which I'm penetrated for your conceptions of genius; unfortunately, between your sublime theory and the practice, doesn't there exist a certain abyss, which one might think unbridgeable?"

"I shall bridge it!" declared Professor Fuss, with impressive assurance.

"Permit me one reflection, however; it seems to me to be difficult to force a tenant to remain in his lodgings once the term of his lease has expired, when he has handed in his notice and wants wholeheartedly to move house."

"Wrong, Monsieur—a grave error. I already have a quantity of observations proving the contrary. And if I could take you to visit my clinic, I would introduce you to patients whose parturition has been delayed by ten, twenty, thirty, fifty and sixty-six days—but I fear the emotion that might be caused to my patients by the sight of a stranger, and I've made it a rule only to let my assistants go into my clinic." The professor drew me back toward his study. "Besides," he added, you know more about it than I've told anyone else. And I repeat to you that I don't want to publish my discovery before having carried out more experiments and obtained results as numerous as they are incontestable."

"And do you already have conclusive evidence?"

"Yes, most certainly. Prolonged fetuses have already given me individuals that are utterly remarkable. For now, it's necessary to await the products of greater prolongations. The difficulty, you see, isn't the prolongation, it's rendering the gestation forceful, active and creative; I'm almost there."

"I don't doubt, Master, that you'll get there soon. And in a short time, your name, as your friend told me, will surpass in glory those of Galileo and Newton."

"I believe so," said the professor, sincerely. "For after all, Galileo was only an observer, Newton a calculator, while I'm a creator! They only brought human beings a few parcels of truth; I'm giving them the possibility of knowing everything. They left them human; I'm making them gods!"

With these words, pronounced quite naturally and without emphasis, Professor Fuss gave me to understand that the conversation had gone on long enough, and guided me toward the exit door.

I thanked him for the benevolent welcome he had given me and the signal favor with which he had gratified me, in condescending to explain his discovery in outline, and apologized for having taken up his precious time.

"It wasn't a waste of time for me," the little man replied. "You're going to write an article about my discovery. You'll treat it lightly, I'm sure—otherwise you wouldn't be French. But the scientists of your country, who will be able to read between the lines, will learn who the man is that they turned away, and I'll be avenged for their impertinence. Above all, tell your compatriots that Professor Fuss is not a madman!"

"I promise you that, illustrious Master! Will you now permit me to communicate a doubt that has just occurred to me, regarding the excellence of your method?"

"Go on."

"Don't you fear that, by prolonging the gestation to two years, the time necessary for the fetus of an elephant to reach term, that you might reproduce that proboscidean pachyderm? Perhaps we're the intermediary between the cellule and the elephant?"

Professor Fuss gave me a terrible sideways glance, said, in a dry tone: "Goodbye!" and closed the door in my face.

At the time, I was resentful of the young Yankee for having made me go all the way to Denver Colorado in order to talk to that maniac. Since then, I've decided that the adventure ought to take its place in my enquiry. What if there's some truth in what Professor Fuss told me?

IV. The Pedagogue

Duly well-informed about new methods of manufacture, I set out to document the fashion in which future American generations would be educated. I visited a number of coeducational or specialized schools, more or less devoted to sports, in the East and West of the United States, in which various notions were force-fed to boys and girls until I was exhausted, without succeeding in discovering any pedagogical system that was truly new.

I don't know why, one day, as I was perusing the eighteenth page of a petty daily newspaper, I was struck by the phrase "intensive culture." I read the article, thinking that it was a matter of some horticulturalist or market gardener practicing what we in France call "forced culture"—which is to say, forcing a plant to produce more abundantly in less time. After a few lines, I perceived that it was a matter of young human plants. Right away, I had found my story, and the first train took me to Boston, whose suburbs were host to the unique establishment.

It was rather difficult for me to discover the address, and I thought I observed that the exceedingly universitarian city was manifesting a certain aversion to the communication of that kind of information. After long detours, I finally arrived at a massive and ponderous Gothic edifice, which wanted to be imposing but was merely overwhelming. I went in, asked to talk to the director, and, at the sight of my card, was shown into a rather nice waiting-room.

A few moments later, the door opened and I saw coming toward me, tall and sculptural, head held high and chest pushed out, an elegant young woman whose mahogany-colored hair had golden gleams, like a diadem: *incessu patuit dea*.[55] After an "Oho!" of surprise, I silently voiced, on seeing her at closer range, the "Aha!" of a satisfied amateur. Take my

---

[55] A quotation from Virgil's *Aeneid*: its literal meaning is "the [true] goddess revealed by her gait."

word for it, she could have rivaled the most highly-rated professional beauty in the Union. I bowed to her, as I would have done to an empress, and presented her, as a supplication, with a request for an interview with the director of the establishment.

"That's me," she replied, in French.

If my surprise on hearing her express herself in my language was considerable, it was no less so on learning that this superb individual—bearing as much resemblance to our schoolmistresses, qualified governesses and other educatresses as an archduchess to a kitchen-maid—was directing the intensive culture of American youth.

"I like the French a great deal," she continued, with a smile full of benevolence. "All in all, they're the most interesting products of the decomposition of the Old World. A former student of Radcliffe, I was an assiduous follower of the lecture courses given every year at Harvard by your compatriots, and I owe them many joyful moments."

On thinking about the men, as eminent as they were grave, who had lectured at Harvard in the name of France, I understood that Madame the directress's gaiety must have been of a very special kind, but, as she seemed satisfied with it, I raised no objection.

"Yes, they have served me as living examples in order to help my students grasp the pretentious and grotesque drone to which knowledge has been reduced in your country."

"Precisely!" I exclaimed, catching the ball in mid-air. "Recognizing our inferiority, I have come to you to ask you, if it's not indiscreet, what your methods of education are."

"There's no indiscretion; my method is an extremely simple one, within the range of all; it's sufficient to want to apply it. Sit down."

I obeyed this injunction passively while she briskly went this way and that, giving orders, and the returned to stand in front of me, tapping her feet like a spirited thoroughbred.

"First of all," she said, "a few preliminary questions. You're astonished to see me, Hira Green, a woman, at the head of this college?"

"I admit it."

"You're not a feminist?"

I protested my preference for the equality of the sexes; she turned her back on me scornfully.

"No, Monsieur," she declared, forcefully, "the sexes aren't equal; you're repeating a stupidity, and only backward people can sustain such a idea."

"Oh!"

"Consider, in fact, the progress of society. Once, women were enslaved, and still are in backward countries; they were obliged to obey their husbands. Progressively, they have risen, and have become the equals of men—but the ascensional movement did not stop there; women have overtaken men, and their great superiority is now incontestable. To take account of that, one only has to consider the order of events; men have made strength render all that it could, and it's now the turn of the mind; now, no one has a finer, livelier, subtler and more perspicacious mind than a woman; it is up to women to guide humankind.

Hira Green pronounced these words with such authority that I could find no response. She was truly dominating me and I felt that before her I was nothing but a schoolboy, a little scamp. I nodded my head.

"For that reason, I have reestablished the division of the sexes; those who ought to obey will no longer mingle with those who ought to command; familiarity engenders disrespect and authority becomes more powerful the less one sees of it— as is the case with God."

I nodded again, without formulating the slightest reservation.'

"Your objection has its merit," she continued, parading her irony superbly before me. "Women have smaller brains than men, that's notorious, so how can they develop a greater intelligence? You're unaware of the physical, not to say physiological, means that we possess."

"Ah yes: gymnastics and sports."

The directress looked at my pityingly and scornfully—but it was a beautiful expression, all the same—and then she continued.

"It has been a long time since we abandoned sports, which develop the muscles at the expense of the brain and were the cause of countless maladies of the heart. The physical agents that we employ are surgical in nature; trepanning and craniotomy permit us, by undoing the sutures of the cranium, to give the skull the capacity we desire. Think about the enormous quantity of knowledge that has to be stored today—knowledge whose abundance is increasing further every day; the old brain is no longer sufficient, we need a larger one. So that minor operation, very simple and free of danger, is obligatory, like a vaccine, for all the girls who come here, voluntary for the boys.

That was Professor Fuss sunk!

I made no reply, but my silence doubtless had an eloquence that I did not suspect, for my Amazon, as if stung to the quick, exclaimed: "Oh yes, you're telling yourself that by thus deforming the head, we're destroying the appropriate proportions of the body, the harmony of the face, and thus rendering ugly those who ought to tend to perfection in their entire being. Well, look at me!"

She took a few steps, with her head held high and her back arched, with undulating movements of the rump and tensions of the hock that reminded me of a large chestnut filly, superb in appearance and perfect in form, that I had once known very well. I declared the ensemble irreproachable.

"Now feel my skull," she said, lowering her had toward me. "I was one of the first to have the operation."

Not without a certain tremulousness, I plunged my fingers into the gold of the mahogany tresses and felt a skull that was evidently a little larger than average, but which did not present, I can attest, any bumps or depressions, and was of a

170

rather fortunate brachycephaly. But what gave me pause was the nape of the neck. Oh, those American napes! Very pale and exquisitely shaped, they lurk beneath the brown fleece, appealing for a kiss, which I certainly would not have hesitated to deposit, if it had not been a matter of a dominatrix who might have taken that humble tribute for the bloodiest of insults.

Hira Green stood up disdainfully, continuing to reply to remarks that I had not made.

"You're right; capacity isn't everything: what a beautiful head, but brain, none! What is, in sum, the cerebral matter? A triglycerylglycophosphate of trimethylethylammonium, of which it's sufficient to make the human organism produce a greater quantity."

"Yes," I hazarded. "It's been claimed for a long time that the human body is a laboratory."

"It's a nonsensical claim. The human body is a continuous reaction, and we have to combine the nutritive elements in view of that reaction. That's why the alimentation of our pupils is regulated in such a manner that the elements they absorb, in reacting with one another, produce cerebral matter in abundance."

A distant memory came to mind; how pitiful, I thought, in comparison to these chemical products, must be the effect of the modest haricot beans responsible in our boys' and girls' schools for furnishing the cerebral matter of the pupils.

"Once we've prepared our students in that manner, instruction may begin; the terrain is appropriate to intensive culture. You are of the opinion, are you not, that the brain must primarily play the role of an accumulator?"

I protested that such had always be the idea at the back of my mind.

"To inform is to charge that accumulator. This is how we proceed in that task. We begin from the observation that all infants like things that stir and move, going from one point to another: dancing puppets, animals, boats, railway trains, etc.—that, in sum, they are passionate about motion."

171

"Many so-called reasonable people have that same passion nowadays," I put in.

"They're big kids, that's all. Add that an infant registers much more by means of the eyes than by means of the ears. We therefore make as much use of the cinematograph as possible, which has the advantage of going quickly, for instruction in history, geography, natural history, etc. The phonograph can be combined with it; it renders greater services in the study of languages. For reading, writing, drawing, calculation and all the exact sciences we use machines successfully. They have the great advantage over teachers of amusing children instead of boring them and demanding less mental tension by materializing, so to speak, the most abstract notions. Machines are more precise, constant in their regularity; they can repeat the same thing a hundred or a thousand times without becoming impatient—and I can't imagine how mathematics can be taught in any other way."

I took advantage of a pause to remark that this intensive culture only applied to what might be called the passive component of education; that the storage of ideas wasn't everything; that it was also necessary for the mind assimilating them to produce new ones.

"Patience, Monsieur; I'm getting to that," was the reply I received, in a rather dry tone. "Until today, assimilation, as you call it, had been horribly difficult; pupils forgot as quickly as they learned; only memory labored and knowledge evaporated, so to speak, without having penetrated the brain, without even having impregnated it. that's because achieving assimilation requires a effort of intelligence and will, an effort often repeated because of fatigue, anemia and decline, the atrocious overwork that causes the finest faculties to deteriorate. We have avoided those dangers, and, while pupils learn more, they suffer less fatigue. For that, we simply employ hypnotic suggestion; you see how facile it is. No more recalcitrant intelligence, no more ill will, nor idleness; our students assimilate without effort—unconsciously, as it were—the most arduous knowledge. The method has the enormous advantage of only enabling the assimilation of useful knowledge and suppressing a host of accessory nonsense that only serves to envelop an idea as the sugar-coating envelops an almond in a box of candy. We get straight to the facts and only inspire thoughts that are elevated and practical—American, in a word."

"And good too," I added.

"Of course. But there we touch on the part of education that consists of making the brains of our pupils productive: the goal of intensive culture. That's utterly straightforward. When the brain is left to itself, the secretion of thought requires a considerable effort, with an elevation of temperature and disturbances in circulation—congestions that often cause very serious disorders. We therefore have recourse to the indicators that act upon the senses, such as paintings, music, perfumes, etc., the stimuli that act on the nervous system: differences in temperature, pressure, light, electric effluvia, X-, Y-, Z-, A-, B- and C-rays etc., and also to certain physical exercises—marching for example—and certain aliments, certain beverages like coffee and the products of fermentation, even on occasion to hashish and opium. We thus produce a kind of erethism of the imagination; and when the imagination is ready, the sentiments are set in motion and the reflex of consciousness regularized."

"The reflex?" I queried, think that I had misheard.

"Yes, consciousness is only a reflex—everybody knows that. Our subject thus advances in the given direction with her own means, according to the assimilation and consciousness she has stored. We have obtained amazing results in his way and produced absolutely remarkable women: inventors, mathematicians, financiers, economists, merchants, agriculturalists—even actresses."

"And directresses," I added, with a gallant smile, which was greeted rather coolly.

"You know as well as I do, now, the basics of intensive culture in practice; the only delicate matter consists of bringing the various instruments into accord with the character of

173

the individual—for we have a horror of uniform education, which cannot take account of the qualities and faults inherent in every individual. And we would be very discontented if, in making an abstraction of natural gifts, all our pupils were educated according to the same model."

"I suppose, in fact," I said, "that you must include in the number good housekeepers, who know how to cook, do laundry, set a table, care for children..."

Hira Green looked me up and down with a scornful smile. "All that is men's work!"

Then, turning her back on me, she went out, telling me to wait a minute. She reappeared a few moments later, this time followed by a dozen young girls, to whom the amiable directress introduced me thus:

"This is an individual of the French race—which is to say, a rare specimen of the decrepitude of our species. Interrogate him; make notes. I leave him to you."

The pupils had surrounded me, opening their eyes wide, rather as if they found themselves in the presence of an anthropomorph. The situation would have been amusing if it had not seemed too grotesque. I was, moreover, less than reassured in being a prisoner of these Amazons, all modeled on their directress, and who did not seem to want to comprehend the joke.

Fortunately, as soon as Hira Green had turned her back, their physiognomies changed as if by enchantment; the faces became smiling and impudent, and the compassed reserve was succeeded by an amiable impishness. The jostled one another politely, like young hinds in a narrow passage, each wanting to be the first to question me. They rivaled one another in suppliant grace; their voices were as soft and lively as birdsong; and their wide eyes obstinately sought mine, in order to ask me to reply to the questions that they were all asking me at the same time.

I, who had interviewed so many people in the United States, was interrogated in my turn by a dozen Yankee girls at the same time. And what was terrible in my situation was that those women of the future were all absolutely charming, and I did not know to which to address myself by preference.

The injunctions became pressing, however. They took on a slightly more imperious tone, and I sensed all of the distance that would soon separate American women from the men. To tell the truth, their hauteur and scorn did not surpass in its impertinence that of our coquettes; the latter subjugate us by the charms of their sex; the former were dominating me by the vivacity of their intelligence, but were no more disagreeable for that—quite the contrary.

I asked them humbly to be so kind as to interrogate me one after another, promising to do my best to answer. The questions they asked me were in the vein of the following. Was it true that in France it was still young men who chose their wives? Was it true that women there had to obey their husbands? That a husband had the right to kill his wife? What was meant by French gallantry? What did it mean to amuse oneself? Was love really the only preoccupation of the French? How did they understand it? Etc., etc.

It was really not worth the trouble of enlarging their craniums, of stuffing them full of any kind of phosphates, of inculcating them with the exact sciences by means of machines, cinemas and phonographs, of suggesting new ideas to them and employing indicators and stimuli, in order that they too should arrive at questioning me about love!

That sentiment, which seemed to them to be an obsolete archaism, about all of whose effects and ill-effects they knew historically and scientifically, and which was for them the amiable accomplice of maternity, resumed all the allure of forbidden fruit. Those great-granddaughters of Eve had the curiosities and ingenuous anxieties of the good old days.

As every theoretical instruction is completed by practical exercises, they drew nearer to me in a feline manner, their gazes suppliant, offering me their cheeks. There was no scope for hesitation; I kissed them all and ran away, as if I had thirty-six thousand devils on my heels.

At the extremity of a corridor Hira Green appeared before me, blocking the way.

"What about me?" she cried.

"You?" I replied. "I have a very bad character, and never do anything when I'm ordered to."

"In that case," she said, softening, "I beg you."

I could only oblige, and I believe that my kisses commenced on the cheek were prolonged as far as the nape of the neck—but this time, I got away, while the directress of the establishment of intensive culture shouted after me: "*Au revoir!*"

V. The Engineer

I had learned in Denver that John Eddy had installed himself some time before in a territory that was very sparsely populated. Once in the Far West, I immediately set out I search of the celebrated engineer, very hopeful of obtaining from my visit a few useful notes about the organization of the world of the future. In that region, barely furrowed by few poor trails that marked out occasional embryonic villages, it is difficult for a traveler to obtain information. Moreover, John Eddy, having retreated so far in order to avoid the curiosity of his compatriots, carefully concealed his address. So it was by chance that I picked up his trail. I immediately hired a guide, who, for an immoderate price, consented to take me through the mountain country the bordered the prairies, and we left.

After a long day of exceedingly difficult travel, we arrived at a farmhouse, similar to three or four that we had previously encountered, but better constructed. According to the directions, it had to be John Eddy's. We introduced ourselves as travelers asking for shelter for the night.

I was allowed into a hallway where I saw the conditions of hospitality pinned up in three languages: English, German and Italian. It was afforded according to a fixed but high tariff. I obtained tickets for our rooms and supper, and for fodder and stabling for our horses, from automatic distributors. After briefly freshening up, we sat down at table.

No one asked who we were or what we wanted. Serving-women busied themselves with their occupations without paying any more attention to us than they would if they had known us for a long time. We had encountered those alert and vigorous female servants everywhere, in the hallway as well as the dining-room and the stables. It is necessary to say that a nearby waterfall had singularly simplified the service, for electricity was distributed in abundance and in all its forms: light, motive force, heat, ventilation, telephones, etc.

When we were sufficiently restored, my guide felt the need to go to bed, and I allowed him to retire alone, counting on taking advantage of being alone with the serving-woman in order to question her and find out from her how to get to see her master. At hazard, I had filled my pockets with the catalogues of illustrious French manufacturers, and although it was improbable that a French company had ever had the audacity to send a commercial traveler to the Far West, I introduced myself as such to the serving-woman.

Without pausing in clearing the table, she was letting me speak with the indifference of a deaf-mute, when a tall fellow came in, in short sleeves, who looked like some kind of civil servant. I called to him and asked him whether the boss—whose name I was careful not to pronounce—might like to see some quite extraordinary models of dynamos.

"No," he replied, in a tone so lacking in courtesy that I countered, rudely:

"How do you know? Are you going to ask him?"

"No," he said, a second time, with equal affability, and turned his back on me.

"Oh!" I exclaimed, getting to my feet. "Why don't you want to go?"

"Because I'm the boss."

"What?" I stammered. "You're John Eddy, the engineer?"

"I'm Mr. Eddy, the famer."

"Presently, perhaps—but you're the author of works on radiant matter of which I've heard mention even in France."

"You're French!" he said, with a smile, demonstrating that he was flattered, all the same, to know that he was appreciated by a modest commercial representative from the Old World. But it was only a flash; his face immediately darkened again. "Don't talk to me about my works. Since Joe's death, I don't want to her any more mention of them. As for your dynamos, you can send them for scrap—the French manufacturers are fifty years behind ours."

I made the remark that there had been very few dynamos fifty years ago; he replied that it was America that was fifty years in advance, and turned his back on me a second time. Then, abandoning French industry completely, I deplored the death of Joe, which would deprive humankind of unsuspected discoveries. I expressed astonishment that the death of a friend or relative, even a son—the foreseen and inevitable fate of everyone alive—could suppress a scientific mind as distinguished as that of John Eddy.

"Joe was more than my son; he was the child of my mind, the finest of my works."

"There are no exceptional beings; you'll find someone else."

"It's possible. But Joe's death was more to me than the disappearance of an individual; it was the death of my ideas, the negation of my theories, the contradiction of my experiments; it was error! Error—do you understand all the horror there is that word for someone who believed himself master of the truth? Joe's death, for me, was the death of truth."

"A disaster?"

"A very great disaster!"

"Disasters aren't always irreparable. Look at San Francisco, more flourishing now than ever. It will be the same for your discovery, I'm convinced, on seeing the man that you are."

I had, in fact, been admiring for some time his fine build—than of a blond athlete in the prime of life—and his bony face, with a determined chin and dark blue yes, as profound as a night sky in which a first magnitude star is shining.

"I'm beginning to hope," he said to me, confidentially. "I think I'm on the right track, and I thank you for giving me confidence in that idea."

He shook my hand.

The ice was broken. Passing from anxious reserve to confidence, the eminent engineer became charmingly loquacious. Deep down, like every researcher, he seemed delighted to meet a stranger to whom he could confide his hopes without having to fear indiscretions.

"Perhaps you can understand me, given that you appear to have a few vague scientific notions and you belong to a country where an endeavor isn't always judged on the immediate benefits it brings. Would you like to smoke a good cigar with me?"

I accepted, as you can imagine, and he led me through a long glazed corridor into a sitting-room adjacent to his laboratory. I installed myself in a rocking-chair, while he chose from among his Havanas.

"Bluffers will tell you that, after long study sand patient research, they succeeded in establishing their thesis. Personally, I confess that the idea came to me quite suddenly."

"A stroke of genius."

"Exactly." He offered me a cigar. "Here—I can recommend this one."

Then he went to a table on which there was a collection of the glass receptacles that chemists call evaporating dishes. He examined them closely while talking.

"I said to myself one day that, human effort being due to mental effort, just as the effort of our machines is due to electrical energy, that it might be possible to accumulate one as we accumulate the other. You can see the application right away: it's sufficient for me to put a subject in contact with one of my accumulators to make him, immediately, a man of indomitable energy, a hero—just as it's sufficient for me to establish a contact that makes this extinct lamp into a dazzling beacon."

179

As he spoke, John Eddy caused a flood of light to spring forth, which doubtless permitted him to discover a slightly ironic smile on my lips, for he continued: "Don't laugh. Believe me, the similarity of the two energies is real. One can collect them, the one just like the other, and store them—that wasn't my error."

"But for a long time," I said, "in the Old World as in the New, we've possessed accumulated energy. Our Cognac and fortified wines, your gin and your whisky are nothing other than bottled energy; don't physicians employ subcutaneous injection of energy-giving liquids with invalids?"

"My dear sir, you're talking about artificial energy, temporary overexcitation, not a continuous current. The source of mental energy is within us; it's within us or other animals that it's necessary to look for it."

John Eddy began pacing up and down from one side of the room to the other, interrupted by abrupt halts and sudden resumptions, launching utterances as they came to him, between puffs of smoke.

"Some people develop a considerable sum of energy; on the other hand, others are almost completely deprived of it. What happens? The energetic people influence others and cause them to act. That influence can even be manifest without the energetic persons being invested with any authority whatsoever, and sometimes without their being aware of it. It emanates from them, and is, so to speak, a radiation. A few make use of these effluvia to make weak or sleeping subjects act according to their will. Others claim to collect its image on the sensitive plate of a photographic apparatus. I tell you that I have succeeded in storing that force, more fluid than electricity, the most subtle radiant matter that there is."

He stopped to measure the effect he had produced; I didn't bat an eyelid. I was in luck, for he was about to enter into a minute description of his apparatus when he changed his mind.

"No, in spite of your technical knowledge, you couldn't follow me in such an arduous explanation, bristling with numbers. Simply know that with the aid of instruments of a extreme sensitivity, which I had constructed, I searched for the most abundant sources of vital energy in order to charge my apparatus.

"I was able, thanks to my indicators, to realize that mental energy isn't always in proportion to physical strength. I established that a small continuous effort expends much more energy than a considerable transient effort. Finally, I recognized that some subjects, in certain circumstances, lost all their energy, while others, who lacked it, suddenly developed it in prodigious quantities in the same circumstances. The greatest producers of vital energy are the instincts of self-preservation and reproduction, necessity, misery, self-interest, ambition, jealousy, pride, etc. etc. Either by utilizing those intermittent sources or making appeal to powerfully energetic people, I was able to charge the gelatine layers of my accumulators and conserve it without too much leakage. I had attained the objective that I had set myself.

"I then established my theory, thus arriving at a rational and scientific explanation of all the phenomena of physiopsychology: suggestion, telepathy, thought-transmission, second sight, spiritualism, magic, etc.—all the facts for which ignorance and superstition attempted to find a divine or satanic explanation. I explained genius—which, I can assure you, I have created! I had found the link between matter and mind, the source of life!

"These results, which became public without my knowing it, made a certain noise in the world—as they must have done since you heard mention of them in France, the country where people know less about what is happening elsewhere. Also, if you'll excuse me for saying so, the French imagine that they've discovered everything!"

Slightly stung by this brutally-unleashed dart, I replied that we had, in fact, not discovered America, but that we knew about it, while his compatriots, especially those who had discovered bluffing, would never understand good old France.

These words generated a certain chill, and I feared momentarily that I had gone too far. John Eddy searched for a reply that he obviously did not find. In the end, he threw himself down in a rocking-chair.

"You're great jokers," he said, "and you've played the game well, since Joe is dead! But wait—I'll have my revenge."

After having comforted himself thus, he continued his confidences—and I sensed that nothing could have prevented that solitary man from talking, having doubtless not had an opportunity for a long time to exchange so many words.

"My first attempts at application, using black men, weren't very encouraging. I decided to study the action of my accumulated energy on white men. I rendered the will of subjects absolutely passive, I gave strength to the weak, one person in despair recovered a zest for life and resumed the struggle—but the most conclusive results I obtained with Joe. You haven't heard mention of Joe, our great cycling champion?"

"What—that's the Joe you mean? Not only have I heard mention of him, but I've seen him executing vertiginous circuits of the track after a six-day race. He was truly prodigious."

"Exactly. And when you know what that boy was before he met me, you'll understand that the word is no exaggeration. Joe started out as a simple shoe-shiner; then he became a messenger-boy, and made use of a bicycle to carry out the commissions he was given. He was a weak and uneducated young fellow, with no drive, destined to live his entire life in the New York mud. One day, he came to my house to deliver some message or other, and I recognized him as a complete degenerate, and told myself that I'd never find a better experimental subject. If he was a good receiver of energy and I succeeded in transmitting enough into him to make a man of him, the proof would be convincing—and I could then launch myself with impunity into more grandiose applications, you understand.

"The effect was, so to speak, a bolt from the blue. You need to know, now, that the energy received from my accumulators supplements the effort that the subject is making at that moment. Because Joe's efforts consisted of transporting himself as rapidly as possible from one point to another, the mental energy he received increased the rapidity of his journeys a hundredfold. In a few days, he became the fastest and most indefatigable cyclist in the Union.. From then on, he devoted himself uniquely to that sport.

"In three months, he had beaten all his rivals, enriched his managers and accomplished implausible journeys without his extraordinary resistance ever being found wanting. I say extraordinary, for the effort produced far surpassed human strength, and is exploits were veritably superhuman."

"What could such a man not have accomplished," I exclaimed, "if, instead of applying himself to make wheels turn, he had employed his…I beg your pardon, *your* energy…to some great endeavor?"

"I've already had the honor of telling you that this was a first experiment, before permitting myself to undertake anything important."

"But since you've achieved that result, why are you waiting before endowing humankind with one of those geniuses who would be able to complete the conquest of the unknown?"

"Because, once again, Joe is dead."

"Even if he is dead, the result was nevertheless attained; your theory remains intact; I can't see the error."

"Wait—I'm getting there. Joe knew all triumphs and earned colossal sums. Acclaimed everywhere, and fêted, men fought for the honor of shaking his hand and ladies turned the most troubling gazes toward him. Joe seemed not to hear or see anything. One evening, however, one young woman more enthusiastic than the rest flung her arms around his neck. He couldn't tear his gaze away from the two dark eyes staring into his. He shivered all over when he felt the young woman's lips on his cheek, and held her, in bewilderment, pressed against his bosom, stammering words of love."

"The thunderbolt!"

"You couldn't put it better. It was, indeed, a thunderbolt, which shattered his energy. From that precise moment on, I felt him grow weak, and he, the unbeatable champion, knew defeat!"

"Did he at least know the sweetness of shared love?"

"Certainly."

"That explains everything, then!"

"Not at all; his condition remained the same before and after his marriage. I doubled and tripled the charges in my accumulators without obtaining the slightest modification."

"Listen, then—I can understand well enough that, sated with what we call glory, he was content to spend happy days with a beloved wife."

"If he spent happy days, they were of short duration. The lady disappeared one morning with a boxer, the victor in a sensational match."

"She loved sports too much."

"Joe was plunged into despair."

"That, if ever, was the moment to give him a strong dose of energy."

"I didn't fail to do so, but my accumulators emptied and the mental weakness was still getting worse. Soon, the distress was supreme, and the man, undoubtedly the most energetic that had ever existed, was so stupid and cowardly as to put a bullet in his brain."

"Damn! The failure of energy…of your energy."

"Right!"

John Eddy resumed pacing back and forth, his hands behind his back and his head bowed.

"What haven't you experimented on another subject?" I asked.

"So that a passing woman can destroy my work with a smile? No, there was something better to do, and I've done it. My error came from assuming that feminine energy is identical to masculine energy—and it's not. The error was unforgivable; after all, the debilitating effect of womanhood isn't a recent observation. Don't we all know that Delilah abolished

184

Samson's energy, and that antiquity symbolized the phenomenon by making Hercules fall at the feet of Omphale? Firstly, therefore, it was necessary to study feminine radiation, and then to seek to combat its detestable influence."

"Don't regret your error too much, illustrious master; it won't be a trivial discovery if you succeeded in neutralizing the influence of women, rendering us insensitive to the temptations and seductions of beauty, youth and grace, to coquetry, smiles, murderous winks, intoxicating words—in a word, to love! You'll certainly be able to boast of having delivered humankind from the most terrible of its afflictions, and I don't doubt that you'll obtain a resounding success, on this side of the Atlantic as on the other."

John Eddy shrugged his shoulders and continued.

"On this farm, as you've perhaps noticed, I only employ women. By physical effort, or efforts of intelligence and will, I oblige them to develop their energy, which I collect in certain accumulators. Now, listen to me: whereas negative electricity combines with positive electricity, male radiant matter, according to my numerous observations, brought into contact with female radiant matter, is immediately absorbed by the latter. That explains the death of my poor Joe."

"But don't you fear," I said, "surrounded as you are by young and vigorous women, seeing your own energy absorbed and ending up as miserably as your subject?"

"No," he said, smiling, "and this is why. The Mormons here and the pashas in the Orient, although living in the midst of numerous wives, nevertheless retain complete mastery of themselves. Do you know why? It's because—nothing is easier to demonstrate with the aid of my apparatus—the absorbent feminine radiations neutralize one another! So, I can continue my work among these women with impunity."

"Just now, you explained scientifically the antinomy that exists between men and women, now you're providing a scientific reason for jealousy between women, their systematic and reciprocal denigrations. You're demonstrating experimentally the philosophical aphorism: woman's worst enemy is woman. You're a profound psychologist."

"No, my dear sir, I'm an engineer. Draw speculative conclusions if you wish; personally, I never emerge from my laboratory. All that I can tell you with certainty, at the present stage of my research, is that all that is needed to prevent the absorption of feminine radiation is that same radiation."

"But that's a rehabilitation of polygamy! And husbands who deceive their wives simply become individuals who don't want to allow themselves to be absorbed."

"I'm not concerned with sociology. In possession of these facts, I undertook a new series of experiments, in order to discover whether any kind of animal energy could resist the absorption. First, I employed that of the horse—several horses; hundreds of horses—without achieving any result. After that, I tried various carnivores—ferocious beasts, big cats—but they gave me nothing more. Are you following me? This couldn't be more serious?

"Finally, I had the idea of collecting the energy of reptiles; this time I'm undoubtedly on the right track. I am, moreover, in accord with the Bible. When it informs us that, of all the animals in Paradise, only the serpent succeeded in tempting Eve, the first woman, it is indicating to us quite clearly that only the energy of the serpent can neutralize that of a woman."

Having said that, the scientist took me to the table on which I had seen, as I came in, evaporating dishes lined up, half-full of variously colored gelatinous substances. They were his accumulators. With the aid of violin strings, he put a male accumulator in communication with a female accumulator; then, when the energy of the former had absorbed that of the latter, he introduced a reptile current—and the absorption ceased!

"You see; it's convincing—and now I can try it on living subjects."

John Eddy took me by the am then, amicably, and led me to the box of Havanas. Then he offered me various drinks, congratulated me on having come to the Far West, blessed the hazard that had cause me to stop under his roof, and thanked me effusively for the encouragement I had given him. Then he asked me, point blank, whether I wouldn't be proud to be the first person immunized by the reptilian current against feminine radiation? The experiment would be all the more conclusive since I belonged to a vice-ridden, degenerate and, so to speak, finished race.

After assuring myself that the celebrated engineer was not a deadpan humorist who, as we say in familiar terms, wanted to get a rise out of me, I begged him to excuse me if I refused. We were so low on the scale of beings that it was scarcely worth the trouble of attempting a regeneration, and also so backward that we would much prefer to die of love, like Joe, than be deprived of it. In addition, exhausted by fatigue and only possessing a relative energy, I asked his permission to retire to my bedroom.

"All right," he replied, dryly.

Before going out, I heard him murmur between his teeth: "How stupid these Frenchmen are!"

VI. The Humanitarian

The *Universal Informer* published the following article under my signature.

The questions of mutual aid and solidarity are much discussed at present. The reconstruction of the Parisian hospitals has just been decided, and the creation of new asylums; it is therefore not impolitic to cast a glance on the innovations introduced abroad in the matter of social assistance. Among the innumerable supportive institutions of more or less original design, I shall permit myself to draw the attention of interested parties to Psuquet House in Denver, Colorado, on the functioning of which the specialist journals of the United States have not spared their eulogies.

It is to the initiative of one of our compatriots, Victor Psuquet, that we owe the foundation of that asylum, which is truly unique in the world. Born in a small shoemaker's shop in the Rue de Verrerie, Victor did not seem to be destined for a life of adventure, but, having launched himself body and soul into the great conflict of '71, without being excessively troubled, he nevertheless left the country.[56] He thought that on the other side of the Atlantic he might be able to realize his dream and live freely in the midst of a free people. I will not astonish anyone by declaring that his disappointment was as complete as possible. The only liberty he encountered in America was that of dying there of starvation. He found it large and empty, devoid of a friendly hand reaching out to help him, disinterested advice to comfort him or a compassionate gaze turned toward him.

That isolation, combined with bad luck, aggravated by domestic troubles, led to Psuquet to a profound discouragement. He wandered from town to town, trying to get to the new lands of the West, where he hoped that fate might be kinder to him. On the contrary, the further he went, the harsher the struggle for disappointing existence became. Neither fatigue nor physical suffering defeated him; his health was robust and he had good arms, moved by solid muscles; but his moral strength weakened from day to day, and ended up abandoning him completely.

Once he was fully convinced of the futility of his efforts and the persistence of his bad luck, he resolved to put an abrupt end to his miserable existence.

By what road should he return to oblivion? Victor Psuquet did not hesitate for long. One morning he unbuckled his belt and hanged himself high and short from the principal branch of a tree by the roadside.

Either by virtue of haste, or lack of practice, the belt did not run smoothly through the knot, and our man remained

---

[56] Most of the leading participants in the Paris Commune had no choice about leaving the country, being transported to New Caledonia.

suspended by the chin, striving in vain to tighten the noose with his hands.

An obliging passer-by came to his aid, but had no better success in hanging him. "This is ridiculous," the latter declared, opening the buckle that retained Victor Psuquet between heaven and earth with a thrust of his knife. "One doesn't hang oneself with a belt! How the devil can you expect that to slide?"

The failed hanged man fell at the foot of the tree, only slightly suffocated.

"Wait for me there," said the other. "I'll go fetch a stronger rope, which we'll soap, and you'll see how smoothly it will run!"

He did, indeed, come back, carrying a very long rope, and set about knotting it conscientiously, while the despairing Victor apologized for the trouble to which he was putting the excellent Yankee.

"Why, only too happy to render you this small service, my dear Monsieur," the man replied. "You have, I suppose, a conscience burdened with a few vile misdeeds and want to acquit yourself with regard to society. I approve—it's always necessary to pay one's debts."

"No!" exclaimed Psuquet, sharply. "I haven't committed any crime; I've never wronged anyone. I'm an honest man!"

"You've doubtless contracted an incurable and exceedingly painful disease?"

"Not at all!"

"You're convinced at least, that you're going to a better world?"

"I don't believe in God or the Devil, and I've always considered the afterlife as a sinister joke."

"Then you're an imbecile, my friend," the hangman went on, while fitting the rope to the branch, "and in that case, you're absolutely right to leave us; your disappearance won't be any loss to anyone."

Victor protested, spoke about his misfortunes and bad luck, and described his misery, his destitution, his confusion and his distress.

"And you're despairing over so little?" said the unknown. "I've gone through worse myself! You see, comrade, as long as one is healthy, nothing is lost. Those who get discouraged are mystics or imbeciles. Only ask of life that which it can give us, and struggle until the end; something trivial can sometimes turn a life upside down! Would you be so kind as to put your head into this noose—I'm in a hurry!"

Psuquet, however, no longer was. Life suddenly appeared to him in a new light. He was in much less haste to quit it, and confessed that to his interlocutor, who went red with annoyance and cried indignantly:

"What! I've gone to all the trouble of hanging you, going in search of a rope, soaping it, knotting it, attaching it, and you don't want to hang anymore? No, you wouldn't do that. You assured me that you were honest; you wouldn't do me such a grave injury. Just think—after the operation, my rope, cut into little pieces for the Italians who pass by here in considerable numbers, would have brought me at least twenty-five thousand dollars!"

"I admit, honestly," Psuquet said, "that I owe you some compensation. Employ me as you will, until my debt is completely paid off."

The American protested forcefully, but Victor would not change his mind.

That is how he entered employment as a laborer in a mill, of which he eventually became the owner. Later, he bought neighboring mills, rival mills, distant mills, and finally founded the Psuquet Company, whose innumerable mills turn over the entire extent of the Union, and bring him millions.

As one can imagine, Victor Psuquet did not forget the incident of the hanging. He told the story gladly, and cited it as an example to those gripped by discouragement. In order to increase the good effects of his advice, he wondered whether it might not be a good idea to create veritable hospitals, with consultations and treatments for moral suffering, as there were for physical suffering. A puritan to whom he communicated that idea suggested to him that hospitals for sick souls had been functioning for a long time, churches and temples being nothing else, and that their ministers could be considered as spiritual physicians *par excellence*.

"No, no," Psuquet replied, "they're nothing but charlatans. Their remedies are sovereign for another world, to which none of us plausibly go, but for the one in which we live, they're absolutely worthless. I'd like bewildered unfortunates suffering from pain, grief, ennui and misery to be able to find something other than banal consolations, an appeal to stupid resignation or the fallacious illusion of chimerical hopes. I'd like a meeting of businessmen and thinkers, scientists and lawyers, manufacturers, tradesmen and philosophers to be able, every day, to give them the practical and disinterested advice that their condition demands, and, if necessary, to undertake complete moral cures.

On his death, which occurred inopportunely in 1901, a voluminous file was found among his papers bearing the title, in capital letters: *Psuquet House*. It was the plan of an asylum for the desperate, worked out in great detail; not only had he determined the construction of the buildings and their interior dispositions but, in a long memoir, had scrupulously described its organization and functioning. As he bequeathed a considerable sum to permit the execution of the project and provide for its maintenance, the architects and entrepreneurs set to work immediately, and notable individuals identified by him are preparing to exercise their new functions.

Today, Psuquet House in Denver is a model establishment of assistance. Anyone can knock at the door, provided that he say that he is unfortunate. Whatever his nationality or religion, whatever his past, the newcomer is sure to find practical advice to get him out of difficulty or soothe his distress, and, if his case is serious, hospitalization for one or several days.

Is there any need to add that the success and fashionability of Psuquet House is increasing by the day, and that similar foundations are being created in the principal cities of the Union. It should be noted that, since it opened, crime has been reduced by sixty-five per cent in Colorado, and that suicide has completely disappeared there.

VII. The Doctor

A newspaper recently announced the creation of a Milner Institute in the vicinity of Paris—at Villemorin (Seine-et-Oise), to be precise, where a rich landowner has put his château and its grounds at the disposal of the organizers. I ought to say that this announcement passed virtually unnoticed; the immense majority of French readers have no idea of what Dr. James Milner's treatment consists. As I was able, in the course of my investigation of the United States, to visit the prototype establishment, in all its details, I have made it my duty to inform my compatriots as to the functioning of a Milner Institute—or a Love Institute, as they say over there.

Let me permit myself, before introducing the man and his work to you, to enter into a few general considerations necessary to the full understanding of the great and noble ideas that presided over the elaboration and scientific organization of the new institution. Without these explanations, Dr. James Milner's foundation might pass, in the eyes of Europeans, for one of those eccentricities to which certain Yankee lunatics devote themselves—and nothing could be further from the truth.

You are aware that, for a long time, the Americans have advantageously put into practice the great discoveries of the schools of Nancy and the Salpêtrière with regard to suggestion and hypnotism. A new path has thus been opened up to their "devouring activity," and psychic industry—if I might label it thus—has been born. Starting from the principle, albeit eminently contestable, that the majority of miraculous cures are phenomena of hypnotism, and that the faith that saves is merely autosuggestion, they have sought to reproduce the same phenomena by creating religious exaltation scientifically.

The Christian Science movement, which has made such rapid and prodigious progress in the Union, has no other cause; and it is entirely natural that public favor should rally to that movement, which, by suppressing physicians and pharmacists, fully realizes the precepts of the Salerno School: *cito, tuto et jucunde.*[57]

As always, the ameliorations observed in some invalids, particularly predisposed by their nervous condition, have been celebrated with the help of loud advertisement—and you know how good Americans are at that—while numerous failures have been passed over in silence. In the same way, the names of a few believers escaped from tempest can be read on the walls of votive chapels, and one does not remember the multitudes of suppliants that were swallowed up. The infatuation with the new method was all the greater because people sensed the intervention of an occult power therein, and, while being quite natural, it seemed not to be. The marvelous has always seduced the crowd.

It is easily explicable, in fact, that very powerful wills impress weak or sensitive characters, and exercise such a powerful empire over them that they can cause them to act, even against certain instinctive tendencies. Such is the debilitated or depressed person who immediately reacts and makes an effort; or the person in despair who regains courage; the mental having as always, a considerable influence on the physical, health improves. In the presence of these excellent results, a commerce in will-power, so to speak, has been established between those who do not have enough and those who have it to spare. Then, these powerful wills no longer even needed to be exercised directly in order to achieve good results; absolute confidence in the practices they indicate suf-

---

[57] "Quickly, safely and pleasantly" (with respect to medical cures).

ficed. The new faith set out to save like the old; the psychic industry was created.

Until recently, all the efforts attempted on this path have converged on one single goal: to soothe, or to heal. In a word, it is the practice of psychotherapy. It is Dr. James Milner who has the honor of being the first to direct his efforts in a directly opposite direction. Instead of combating maladies, he provokes them. One can see immediately what an immense field, fertile in unsuspected discoveries, the scientist will open to science by means of this notion of veritable genius.

Good American as he is, though, the Doctor does not consider that an idea exists, however admirable it might be, so long as it remains in the realm of theoretical speculation and has not received the consecration of practicality.

A primary question arose: what malady was it preferable, from the humanitarian point of view—the doctor is a philanthropist—to suggest to his clients? After long calculations, which you will excuse me for not going into, and mature reflections, which I cannot summarize in such a brief article, James Milner succeeded in determining scientifically that the malady in question was love.

The scientist, in fact, considered love as form of mental alienation. "Observe," he wrote in his introduction, "a subject afflicted with the malady in question; you will notice that all his psychic forces are applied to a single object, which takes on immeasurable proportions and ideal forms in his eyes. According to him, that object is of implausible perfection, sublimely beautiful, encapsulating the past, present and future, greater than the world, than life or death! It is all of happiness. Are those not the words of a lunatic? If that dementia sometimes leads to the most atrocious forfeits, it also produces superhuman feats, engenders immortal works of art, and, all things considered, the harm it can do is trivial by comparison with the enormous benefits that humankind may reap therefrom."

After that exceedingly neat description, the doctor observes that in our epoch, especially in America, love is increasingly in decline. The relentless conflict of interests, the material cares of existence, egotism, flirtation, the thirst for brutal enjoyments and the vulgarization of rational and scientific ideas, have distanced individuals therefrom. People no longer have time for love; they no longer want to love; they are afraid of love. More often than not, people marry without love, and if, by chance they are afflicted by the malady, they seek to be cured of it more rapidly by means of separations, voyages and even deliverance by single or double suicide. James Milner therefore thought, with good reason, of taking his place among the benefactors of humanity by founding an institute designed to propagate among his contemporaries true, intense and durable love.

He is not one of those who imagine that, in order to attain that end, it is sufficient to write the word love in a code of behavior—as if one could love in the name of the law! Nor is he one of those bedroom moralists who lament the lack of sentimentality in our time, or one of those sociologists who make speeches about neo-Malthusianism or repopulation. James Milner is a man of action, who, having had an idea, makes haste to realize it. Today, the Institute exists, and is functioning; and it has already produced such fine results that institutes are under construction in various countries, and it is proposed to establish one near Paris. Will the obsolete and routine mores of the Old World permit this innovation to prosper here? I don't know; all that I can affirm is that, thanks to the Love Institute, a complete transformation is now in progress in the American family.

Dr. Milner's Institute is located a few miles outside Denver, Colorado, in the middle of a park in which vast lawns surrounding clusters of exceedingly old trees create cheerful views. The assembly of buildings, according to plan, affects the form of a heraldic fleur-de-lys. The administration and general services, a large hall with an elongated oval shape and a chapel design the median section, to which are attached, to the right and left, at the lower part of the convexity, two wings curved like palm-leaves.

195

At first glance, the sight is neither cheerful not severe, but surprising. On a stone foundation forming a terrace all the way around, various constructions are erected, made entirely of iron and glass. The effect of those vast windowless—or, if you prefer, entirely windowed—edifices is strange, for the walls are comprised of two mirrors between which warm air circulates in winter and air cooled by refrigerators in summer. Except that the architects have succeeded in relieving the iron of its rigidity and the glass of its flatness, and, in spite of the geometry, have made both so flexible that they come together in perfectly harmonious lines. One might think that Dr. Milner, by means of that mode of construction, wanted to symbolize love, which unites with so much grace the brutality of man and the fragility of woman.

As soon as I had climbed the steps of the perron and gone into the entrance hall, I experienced a singular impression; it seemed to me that I too was made of crystal and that all my thoughts, even my secret ones, were legible through my face. The iron and glass outside were complemented by oak and polished brass within, which gave the whole a complete beauty made of light, simplicity and…I might almost say honesty; which did not exclude either charm or comfort. The anticipations I had formed regarding the work of James Milner—and I must confess that I had imagined that the institute was not at all serious, and that it would be more reminiscent of a tea-shop—disappeared. My skepticism was vanquished; I was conquered, or perhaps hypnotized.

On the presentation of the letter granting an audience to the representative of the *Universal Informer*, an usher took me to the director's office. At the precise minute that he had fixed, Dr. James Milner had me shown in.

Before I had time to greet him, he said volubly: "You're at home here, Monsieur. You can go anywhere; we have nothing to hide. One of my secretaries will accompany you in the different services, and will give you all the explanations you desire. Goodbye."

196

With those words, the tall clean-shaven old man, with a Benedictine face, rotated his armchair through ninety degrees and resumed work. Giving up on posing the questions that I had prepared in view of a sensational interview, I bowed, and was beginning to formulate vague thanks when a tall young man, very bond, very polite and also very clean-shaven, whom I had not heard approaching, said: "At your service!" And he added, as if handing me a card: "Mr. Steeg."

Mr. Steeg might more accurately have said "at my service." In fact, he went out first and I followed him. We went back across the hall, and back down the front steps; he stopped in the grounds and showed me the ensemble of the buildings.

"The right wing, which you see here," he told me, "is reserved for gentlemen, the left wing for ladies, and the central section, which contains the general services, is communal to both sexes. All the operations carried out in one wing are carried out in *exactly* the same fashion in the opposite wing; the locations are identical, the feminine personnel of one corresponding to the masculine personnel of the other, and the formalities are the same. Knowing one, you know the other. We shall, therefore, go into the building on the right, and you shall see, in order, the trials to which our clients must submit."

It was necessary for me to speak English as well as I do to follow Mr. Steeg's explanations. I thought, however, that I had not understood him very clearly when he spoke about the distinct affectations of the two wings. For the second time, in the United States, I saw an inviolable line of demarcation drawn between the two sexes. And while steering me toward the building reserved for male clients, I wondered whether love was not born of that separation, and whether we were still in the old story of the forbidden fruit.

In the vestibule, my guide took me to an enormous register in which the clients had to write this short sentence: *I sincerely desire to get married*, followed by the date and a signature.

"Dr. Milner," Mr. Steeg explained to me, "deems that one cannot make people happy against their will, and the first condition he demands of his clients is to want to be happy, sincerely and reliably. He thus renders a signal service to young men and young women who either do not have the time to search, or to exhaust themselves in vain research; instead of wasting their time or languishing, they have only to write their names here."

"Well," I said, laughing, "I'm strongly tempted to write my own name. I've had every intention of marrying for a long time, but have never encountered the opportunity."

"At your service—the register is open to anyone, without distinction. Inscription only costs five dollars, which is non-refundable."

I thought that obtaining for twenty-five francs the guarantee of a legitimate wife, who loves you and whom you love, wasn't too expensive. I wrote my name and put the five dollars into the hands of a cashier, in return for which he gave me a red file bearing the number 128,637. That was the registration number that would replace my name in all the subsequent operations.

"Let's go on to registration," said my guide. "Here the candidate is required to furnish certain documents: firstly, a certificate of bachelorhood, widowhood or divorce, as the case may be; secondly, a certificate of morality; thirdly, a certificate of means of existence, profession and assets; fourthly, a birth certificate, etc."

"Damn it!" I exclaimed. "I'm thwarted at the first step. I never thought that Americans were so bureaucratic. Your Dr. Milner must surely have French blood in his veins. One doesn't usually have to jump through so many hoops when one gets married—one finds a clergyman and that's that."

"We don't forge unions like that, Monsieur," replied the master's secretary, dryly. "You have only to take a walk in the park and you'll meet women who, in order to marry you, would even by-pass the clergyman. For us, love is required."

"Is love the result of formalities and stupidities, then?" I said, rather vexed.

"No, Monsieur, these formalities are necessary for us to obtain the guarantees that we need."

Not wanting to have wasted my twenty-five francs, I emptied the compartments of my wallet on to the clerk's desk, including my passport, my press card, several other cards attesting that I was a member of literary societies or professional associations, an old stage-pass, letters from officials accrediting me with respect to famous individuals I was to interview, a rent-book, a polling card, various papers demanded by our postal administration, customs or pawn-shops, an insurance policy against accidents, and letters and a card from our consul in Denver, Monsieur Philémon. Phlegmatically, the clerk placed them all in a folder bearing the number 128,637 and gave me a receipt, on payment of a further five dollars.

Mr. Steeg was then kind enough to explain that all the documents would be placed in the hands of the agents responsible for checking their authenticity. After a lapse of time, which was unlikely to be less than twenty-four hours, my registration number would be attached to one of the notice-boards labeled Admitted or Refused. The most minimal deception would lead to refusal.

"Damn! In forty-eight hours I have to be more than a thousand miles away. Isn't there any way of speeding up the checks?"

"I'll ask," said the obliging Mr. Steeg.

After a long negotiation, the chief checker agreed, in view of the fact that I was a foreigner, to simplify the operations. By way of compensation he required me to make a certain number of sworn statements, and I soon saw my number on the board of admissibles. I hurried to the clerk, who, with the same phlegm, returned them to me and handed me a red card—those given to ladies are blue. The card, bearing the number 128,637 at the top, was divided into two columns, one entitled Description, the other Request. In each column the same 175-item questionnaire was printed. That's what I said: a hundred and seventy-five. The checking clerks had already filled in the blanks with respect to my age, date of birth, nationality, resources, and so on. The remainder would be filled in by the members of the medical committee, at a cost of ten dollars.

My guide had warned me that the medical examination was very meticulous, the slightest error leading to the payment of damages and compensation, but I had not imagined its extent.

After having passed through a very comfortable cloak-room I presented myself, as naked as a worm, before the medical board. They sounded my chest, palpated me and interrogated me with an indiscretion that, in any other circumstances, would have seemed to me to be revolting. When the gentlemen had established well and truly that I was not carrying any disease, that I did not manifest any physical, intellectual or moral infirmity, or any hereditary or acquired defect, they passed me on to the description service, properly speaking. That was more complete, since it was concerned with character, ideas and moral qualities, than Dr. Bertillon's anthropometric method. My face was photographed head on, in profile, at an angle and from the back; imprints were taken of my hand and one of my kisses; I was made to write a few affectionate words addressed to an unknown woman, in order to give an idea of my character and my style. I had to speak into the recording cylinders of a phonograph. Finally, my card was handed back to me, bearing responses to the 175 questions relating to me. That cost me another ten dollars.

I found Mr. Steeg in the gentlemen's hall.

"Well," I said to him, "to what further persecution are you going to subject me? I have to tell you that I'm beginning to find the joke a little long-winded."

"My dear sir, you now have forty-eight hours to inscribe in the second column of your card, headed Request, the description of the woman you desire to take as your wife, as well as your plans for the future. The forty-eight hours is obligatory."

"But in forty-eight hours I'll be the two thousand miles away! Come on, Mr. Steeg, since I'm a foreigner, can't the delay be reduced to five minutes? A long time ago I've had a perfectly exact idea of what I'd like in a woman, and if you'll permit, I can fill in the 175 blanks of the request immediately."

"Monsieur, these delays have been calculated and fixed by Dr. James Milner himself. We have often been asked for prolongations, but never for abbreviations. The lapse of time is necessary for the candidates to be clear as to what they ought to request. We have, moreover, amphitheaters for their information, in which daily lectures are given on psychology and physiology, designed to show them the reasons and causes of affinities and repulsions, to teach them how to form and continue happy unions, of what perfect accord consists, and, in brief, to communicate to them a host of other eminently practical notions regarding the social and intimate relations between the sexes, of which your European newlyweds have no notion."

I replied that, like the young people of Europe, I had instructed myself by practice—which as, I agreed, detestable and dangerous, but which was nevertheless capable of advantageously replacing lectures.

Only the intervention of the supervisor in charge of the men's quarter was able to spare me the forty-eight-hour delay. I immediately began writing the 175 responses to the questionnaire relating to the person I desire to take as a wife. Mr. Steeg advised me not to be too demanding, not to expect perfection, for I would then risk remaining unclaimed. It was necessary to know how to be content with certain qualities and to overlook a few petty faults, thus arriving at a very satisfactory compromise. I followed his advice and handed a completed card to the supervisor himself, who was kind enough to write "urgent" on it.

"Now," my guide continued, "Your card will be handed on to the correspondence service. All the cards are centralized there, the red on one side, the blue on the other. They're classified in pigeon-holes by age, and within each age-group by height, muscular strength, weight, hair- and eye-color, the size of the ears, the shape of the nose, dentition and all other intellectual, moral and social characteristics. Between the male and female racks of pigeon-holes are long tables at which the clerks work. This is what their work comprises:

"You card, for example, is given to a clerk on the red side. He immediately searches, according to your description, for the place you ought to occupy in the pigeon-holes. One of two circumstances might then arise; either the pigeon-hole already contains one or more requests corresponding to your description, or none, If it contains one, the clerk will seek information from one of his colleagues on the blue side as to whether the person who has made the request corresponds to your request. If there is no request in your pigeon-hole, or if the description differs from the one you have stipulated, the clerk simply transmits your request to the blue side. There, a search is made for the descriptions that most close match our desiderata—for it's materially impossible to fulfill the 175 conditions you stipulate exactly. The chief of the service examines the descriptions himself, compares them with yours and chooses, as a last resort, the one that ought to be introduced. If he judges that the physical, intellectual or moral divergences are too great, the cards are replaced in their respective pigeon-holes and the client is asked to wait."

"Wait? You're joking! I won't be here! I'm expected in San Francisco; I have to go, and I think it's in rather bad taste to have made me hand over seventy dollars"—I have forgotten to mention that my card, in order to be passed on to the correspondence service, had required a forty dollar fee—"under the pretext of furnishing me with a legitimate wife, and not even showing me one!"

"Don't get annoyed, 128,637—thanks to the supervisor's note, they'll hasten the correspondence, although the work generally takes at least twenty-four hours. You might be lucky enough to find a request in your pigeon-hole, with a description corresponding to the one you desire. Just be patient."

"Be patient! With you it's always necessary to be patient!"

"Knowing how to be patient, my dear sir, is the secret of happiness."

I was beginning to reflect bitterly on the naivety with which I had allowed 350 francs to be extorted from me when an electric bell rang in the waiting-room and I saw my registration number light up on the blackboard!"

"What does that mean?" I asked Mr. Steeg.

"Hurrah!" he exclaimed. "It means that the correspondence service is in possession of a card satisfying your request."

"Really?" I said, nonplussed. "What now?"

"Now, we go as quickly as possible to the communication hall, where you'll be given the card in question, while yours is handed to the designated lady in the other communication hall—if, that is, you're fortunate enough that the person is in the institute a present."

We went into a hall adjacent to the central building and, for twenty dollars, I was handed a blue card bearing the number 203,005. I would be lying if I said that, at that moment, I did not feel a small shock in the heart, followed by a slight tremor. I studied that card with an insurmountable emotion, all the more so because, on the other side of the central building, in a similar room to the one in which I was standing, I knew that a young woman was holding in her hands, perhaps with a similar tremor, my own red card.

I read the description. The requisite social conditions were almost fulfilled. The physical part responded quite well to what I had requested, but from the viewpoint of character, there was some divergence. The qualities seemed less accentuated and the ideas less absolute. I noticed, too, that Mademoiselle 203,005, in the almost exact portrait she had drawn of me without knowing me, had noted preponderant virtues that only existed in me in an embryonic state. Mr. Steeg assured me that it was always thus, one had to think oneself lucky to obtain an almost exact match. Love would do the rest!

I reflected that, in sum, the honorability and morality of the young woman were guaranteed, that there was no deceptions in the social and pecuniary situation, that a committee of female physicians had certified that she had no infirmity or defect, hereditary or acquired, that the anthropometric service had indicated her physical and moral state to me exactly and impartially, and I could see, moreover, that her description was very close to the ideal woman of whom I had dreamed. Who, in the ancient world, could flatter themselves that they were going into a marriage with such assurances? And when I thought that the young woman, for her part, was probably of the same mental disposition with regard to me, a mad desire overtook me to make her acquaintance.

"Ask to see the photograph and documents first," Mr. Steeg advised me. "They're usually handed over twenty-four hours after the card, but for you..."

On seeing the photograph, I started. I recognized her! I definitely recognized her; I recognized that Mademoiselle 203,005, whom I had never seen! I understood that I was rediscovering in that unknown woman the original beauty that my dream caressed. I looked at the full face, the angled shot, the profile and the rear view; they were exactly what I had requested, if I were not the victim of a suggestion that made me see my own dream where there was thing—but no, the photograph was quite real.

The hand had left a firm and frank imprint on the paper; the imprint of the kiss was soft; the writing was unpretentious, the style simple and quite natural. The voice on the phonograph seemed to be a trifle nasal, but the clerk assured me that it was due to the instrument, and I was not dismayed hear her say, with the tender and strong inflections that give such a powerful relief to the English language, the sentence: "Sir, I've never seen you, but since you respond to my ideal, I've known you for a long time. I hope that you can say as much about me."

"Yes, yes!" I exclaimed. "That's absolutely what I think about you."

Meanwhile, the phonograph continued: "If so, it will be very pleasant to meet you, and to unite my destiny with yours."

"Where is she?" I said, hurling myself toward Mr. Steeg. "Where is she? I want to see her, immediately—immediately, do you hear?" My voice became threatening. "I want to; I demand it! And don't tell me that I have to wait twenty-four or forty-eight hours, according to Dr, Milner's calculations—I couldn't care less."

"Calm down, 128,637, calm down! First, we'll see whether 203,005 consents to the introduction." And he went to telephone the introduction service.

In truth, I no longer recognized myself—me, normally so patient, who had come to the Institute as a skeptic and had written my name down as a joke—now that I was taking things terribly seriously. I became irritated, carried away; a strange fever gripped me while I waited for 203,005's response. Finally, an electric bell sounded; the demoiselle agreed to the introduction.

"All you need now is Professor Milner's authorization," added the terrible Mr. Steeg. "We'll send him the two cards; he'll study them and make the final decision."

"To the Devil with your Dr. Milner. So much fuss to get married! It's worse than the idiotic formalities of the Old World."

"I will simply point out to you, Monsieur," said my guide, with a pinched expression, "that it's scarcely four hours since you came into the Institute, and that in an entire lifetime, a man of the Old World does get to know his wife as well as you already know yours."

"Without having seen her!"

"You're going to see her; I can hear the doctor's bell authorizing the introduction. Come this way."

Stupidly, I imagined that my companion was going to introduce me into the grand hall, where I would hear loud music, and that, at concert, a performance or a ball, I would be introduced to the demoiselle as it is done among us. What an error!

The garden that was underneath the hall, with its sports pitches and its multiple amusements, was reserved for fiancés and their families; they stayed there until they were married. All around there were conversation or reading rooms, meeting rooms, restaurants and bars.

Mr. Steeg invited me to have a cold drink, which I did not refuse, as I was beginning to be inconvenienced by the surges of heat that were rising to my face.

"Come on," he said to me, smiling, "be brave. You've now arrived at the final test, with a rapidity that constitutes a veritable record; it usually takes at least a week. Ten dollars to the service electrician, and you can go into the introduction room. Moreover, they're the last ten dollars you'll have to spend; they complete the hundred dollars we demand of you, and from now on, all remuneration is at your discretion."

"Who cares!" I exclaimed. "If it costs me another hundred dollars, I want to see her."

"Go in!"

Picture a large rectangular room, separated into two by a metal sheet, hidden on both sides by blinds. Each of the two subjects is introduced to one side. There is complete darkness; the blinds are raised, and then, thanks to cleverly contrived lighting, one or other appears, in turn, brightly lit, while the other, remaining in darkness, can study them without the agreeable or disagreeable impression they feel being perceptible. If both are satisfied with that first glimpse—that's the right word—they're authorized to speak, but in darkness, aloud, and through the metal sheet. The operator reminds them that they must not reveal either their name or their address, nor say anything whatsoever contrary to morality or good manners. He starts the conversation, which can last as long as the clients wish.

How can I translate the excitement and delight I experienced when I saw, in the darkness that enveloped me, the radiant and quasi-unreal apparition of 203,005? She was exactly as I had imagined. Elegant, without sacrificing anything to American bad taste, sitting in a rocking-chair, she was swaying, smiling in the light that inundated her. Her slender and supple grace, her vivid dark-eyed blonde beauty, realized so completely the conception I had of the desirable spouse that I seriously believed that I was the victim of a hallucination.

I rubbed my eyes; the apparition vanished—and I was inundated with light in my turn. Surprise and joy must have given my wonderstruck person a slightly bewildered expression. When I was allowed to see the woman to whom my arms were reaching out reappear, she was standing much closer to the metal sheet and seemed anxious, troubled and emotional. Yes, she was emotional—but certainly not as much as me. What would I not have given to be outside that cage, far from the Institute, and to be able to say to her at close range the thousands of affectionate things kept in reserve for such a long time in the depths of my heart, while thinking of the moment when my dream would be realized. But was it not a dream?— that precipitate succession of scarcely events, providentially bringing together two beings born for one another.

"Come on, sir," said the operator, when darkness had enveloped us again. "Tell Mademoiselle how glad you would be to have her for a fiancée—and you, Miss, tell the gentleman how delighted you would be to be his fiancée."

No, nothing, nothing, can give an idea if the delicious charm, the supernatural charm that that first conversation in darkness, through a metal screen, had for us. It was the sincere, tender and mysterious outpouring of two hearts drawn to one another; it was love in its purest and most sublime manifestation. We had nothing to ask one another; we were each familiar with our different ways of seeing and we knew the smallest details of our projects; the conversation continued without pause nevertheless, without embarrassment, as if between two comrades of twenty years who had met up and had nothing to hide from one another.

I was no longer thinking either about the mission that my editor had entrusted to me, or about my interviews, or America, or the Milner Institute, or anything else whatsoever. My only thought was for the adorable being who was close at hand. There was no mistake; it really was love in its full force, indisputable love—and the most marvelous thing of all was that there was no doubting that the sentiment was shared by the person who was its object!

Our two hearts communicated in the same love, and our souls were fused by the mystic betrothal. A divine moment, that I, so pressed for time a little while before, would have liked to prolong indefinitely, and which the operator brought to an untoward end by announcing to us that the session was concluded.

I emerged from the introduction room like a madman, hurled myself toward Mr. Steeg and grabbed his arm forcefully. "Swear to me," I said, "that in all of this, there's no magic or trickery, that the cold drink you had me drink hasn't produced these intoxicating hallucinations, that I'm not dreaming, that everything I've seen is real, and that I can see her again."

He contented himself with shrugging his shoulders and smiling. "You can see her again when you wish, but not for forty-eight hours."

"I'll wait!"

"You understand that the doctor absolutely demands that delay, to avoid any surprise and any over-enthusiasm that might subsequently cause regrets. During those forty-eight hours, you'll resume your normal existence, you in Denver, your fiancée in the city where she lives. If, after that brief lapse of time, you're both in the same mental disposition, you'll meet up again in the festival hall."

"I'll be able to take her by the hand? Hold her in my arms? Whisper in her ear and tell her anything I wish?"

"Of course. Come on, calm down, reflect deeply, and if you return in two days, bring relatives or friends who can serve as witnesses. Good night, sir."

I was in the grounds. I walked straight ahead without knowing where I was. It was absolutely impossible for me to fix my attention on any idea that did not bring me back to her. Incessantly, I saw her again, close by; we were still talking. I repeated to her that I loved her, and as it was impossible for me to call her by her name—which was a cruel torture for me—I lavished the sweetest names upon her, and pronounced the number 203,005 ecstatically, so forcefully that the people who encountered me must have taken me for a madman obsessively repeating an imaginary telephone number.

I forgot meal times and bedtimes; I forgot my correspondence and the train I was supposed to catch. My professional duties seemed to be negligible. What did it matter if I were sacked by my boss, that my future was shattered? I loved her.

I still ask myself how I lived through those two days. All that I know is that at the appointed hour, I presented myself at the Love Institute, accompanied by our amiable consul, Monsieur Philémon, and his secretary.

Mr. Steeg took me to the festival hall, where a number of people were already assembled.

"Look for your fiancée," he said, smiling, "and above all, don't make a mistake, for you'd be liable to pay damages and compensation."

"Have no fear!"

Monsieur Philémon and his secretary stayed with Mr. Steeg, and I made a tour of the garden with the multiple attractions that occupied the central part of the hall. I slipped through the groups of spectators, inspected the people seated in the pathways, followed the progress of games of tennis and golf and searched the booths, telling myself that she was undoubtedly devoting herself to the same investigations with a similar impatience.

After several circuits, I told myself that perhaps we were both moving in the same direction, and might continue thus without ever meeting. I turned round, and it was a good decision; after a few minutes we found ourselves face to face.

"203,005!" I cried.

"Call me Mary," she said, daintily.

"Mary, oh my dear Mary," I murmured, covering the hand she held out to me with kisses.

"And what should I call you, Monsieur 128,637?"

"Jean!"

"Oh! Jean—that's very pretty, Jean; I like it a lot." And she squeezed my hand between hers, forcefully.

My adorable fiancée seemed even more beautiful, but a trifle pale, and I became anxious about her health.

"Oh, those two days!" she said, uttering a profound sigh. "What torture!"

"Yes, but it's over now; we won't be apart again."

"Oh, no, never again!"

We went into a conversation room in order to communicate to one another all the affectionate things that we had planned to say, and our hearts overflowed. Mary confided to me that it had always been her dream to marry a Frenchman. I confessed to her that, finding out Parisian dolls and the emancipated dimwits of our bourgeoisie unbearable, I had always had a weakness for American women. It was decided that we would hasten the conclusion of our marriage as rapidly as possible.

Immediately notified, Mr. Steeg took us into a room where my fiancée's friends and relatives were already assembled, along with Monsieur Philémon and his secretary, my witnesses.

The introductions were rapidly made, and my amiable guide said to me, with a smile: "Well, now you'll be married."

"Immediately?"

"Immediately."

"And there aren't any dollars to hand over?"

"Not one."

"That's admirable."

"Except that, before going into the marriage office, where almost all the formalities demanded by different nations can be completed, would you, Monsieur, and you, Miss, write rapidly in this register the following declaration: 'I, the undersigned, freely declare that today, I take for my wife, or husband, Miss, or Monsieur…then the name…whom I love and desire to love for as long as possible,' Sign and date. Come on, hurry up!"

I could not help remarking to the honorable Mr. Steeg that he was now the one hurrying me and reminding me a little too much that time is money.

"No," he replied, "time is love!"

I confess that that reply, made by a pure-blooded American, left me nonplussed. You can clearly see that, as I said at the beginning, something has changed in the mores of the Union.

My guide had told me that pastors of all religions were attached to the establishment, and that we had only to choose. The various ceremonies were very rapidly expedited, and my wife and I soon found ourselves in a lunch-room, surrounded by relatives and friends addressing their sincere congratulations to us.

At that moment, I thought about Dr. Milner. I recalled the mocking skepticism with which I had come into that house, and the malevolent and odious assumptions I had made. I was profoundly sorry for that, and asked Mr. Steeg's permission to go and offer my apologies. Perhaps, too, I had a hidden agenda, wondering whether everything that was happening around me might be a dream, and that the doctor, on seeing me again, might liberate me from the suggestion that he had imposed upon me.

I found the tall old man sitting in the same place in his study. He rotated his armchair through ninety degrees, and before I had opened my mouth, said: "Well, Monsieur Journalist, are you convinced?"

"Oh, Doctor," I stammered, "How can I thank..."

"No," he said, "it's me who should thank you, for you've provided a striking confirmation of the excellence of my method. Goodbye."

And he reversed the quarter-rotation in order to go back to work.

Before we separated in the entrance hall, Mr. Steeg took us to the various insurance offices. Insurance on life and love, insurance against accidents, maladies and divorce, maternity insurance with a progressive endowment at the birth of each child; we took out everything. He took us through the consultation rooms, where experienced men and women were giving useful advice on conjugal happiness to those who came to ask; then we deposited our cards in the archives, after having taken copies.

Not knowing how to thank the excellent man who had served as my guide, I embraced him with hasty affection, affirming that I would never forget what he had done for me. He assured me that the commission he would receive on all the operations I had accomplished at the Institute would be ample compensation and, wishing us *bon voyage*, he allowed us to go down the front steps arm in arm.

"Have a pleasant journey!"

Curiously enough, we experienced a great pleasure in linking arms like that, but were not at all tormented by the frenzy to be "alone at last" that tortures newlyweds in our country. It did not displease us at all to mingle with the general agitation. On the contrary, leaning on one another, we advanced proudly into life, sure of our love and convinced that it had the strength to vanquish all adversities.

Since that day, it has not failed for a minute, and we have already received two birth endowments.

After that, how could I not desire for my country the prompt organization of the projected Milner Institute in the vicinity of Paris? Is it not the indispensable preparation for that law of love so often talked about but impossible to apply? I have not hesitation in repeating that the man who has penetrated the arcane of the human heart with so much perspicacity, the man who has calculated so accurately the slightest stirrings of the soul and the effects of automatic suggestion, is a great businessman and, above all, a man of genius, and that future humankind will be grateful to him for what he had done for it.

VIII. The Merchant

From New York I sent the *Universal Informer* the following dialogue, supposedly overheard on a Parisian boulevard:

"You believe in it, then—in suggestion?"

"Yes, I believe in it—which is to say that I believe in nothing else."

"You really think that an invisible force can be imposed upon us and make do things that we don't want to, and perhaps even couldn't do before? You're a sucker!"

"I think that a powerful will, supported by a real or feigned authority and seconded by a firm aplomb, and obtain a considerable empire over a weak will. I think that miracles are almost all effects of suggestion, and that the marvelous cures still obtained today by entrepreneurs of pilgrimages in their baths of stagnant water are phenomena of the same order."

"You're talking about visionaries, mystics, simple minds and wise heads that cut into the supernatural and who always have been able to do it—but what about the others?"

"Witchcraft has no other causes."

"That's ancient history!"

"Look at what is happening today for physicians. Do you imagine, by change, that it's their drugs that are effective? Nine times out of ten, the mere presence of the doctor soothes the patient by suggestion, and that's so true that some sufferers, on going into the dentist's, no longer feel toothache."

"You're referring to a very special category of individuals—the sick. When one's suffering one's ready to accept the most abominable healers' tricks and allows oneself to be influenced by anyone. For people healthy in mind and body, though, your suggestion is nothing but a vile bluff, a charlatan's trick. It'll never find any application in normal life."

"I am, my dear chap, absolutely convinced of the contrary, and that, in a future perhaps not very distant, mental energy will be distributed to homes like electrical energy. And there'll be mental bistros on street-corners where you'll be served small glasses of will-power, as you're served brutishness, folly and plum brandy today."

"Permit me, my dear friend, while awaiting more ample information, to file your certainty along with the fantastic conceptions of our fashionable humorists. When we see merchants of will-power on the boulevard, it'll be hotter than a brick-maker's kiln!"

"In that case, the temperature might well be going up faster than you suppose."

"Why's that?"

"Because there are already people in the world trading in will-power."

"Where? I'll run and get some."

"Oh, it isn't here, of course, in a backward nation on its last legs, a nation stuck in its old routines by its old fogies. You have to cross the Atlantic, to go among the people of the future, in the United States."

"Always those damned Yankees."

"Always them. In fact, it's in...I can't tell you the name of the city in the Union that gave birth to the new kind of trade; newshound as you are, you'd soon have ferreted out the businessman in question and I'd be guilty of having given him free advertising—which is unpardonable for reporters like us. All that I can certify for you is that my information is scrupulously exact and that fact I'm giving you are guaranteed authentic."

"Go on, I'm listening."

"So, in an American city, no less—since it has its half-million inhabitants—there is a very well-patronized merchant of will-power for ladies..."

"Why for ladies? Are they the only ones who need it?"

"No, alas—but we're at the beginning of an industry. At present, it's quite possible that certain gentlemen have recourse to the aforementioned merchant of feminine will-power—I wouldn't know. Let's get back to the ladies. These ladies, like all those in a big city's high society, are literally monopolized by social obligations: morning sports, a succession of couturiers and suppliers, receptions, visits, exhibitions, fêtes, lunches, dinners, soirées, performances, balls and the rest. It gets to the point where they can't find time during the day to isolate themselves in a discreet location and obtain some relief."

"That's of no great importance. Seven out of eight society women can easily dispense with reflection."

"You're not following me. It's not, strictly speaking, a matter of reflection; take 'relief' in a less elevated sense, as down-to-earth as you can. It's rather delicate to explain— please try to understand without me spelling it out. When a machine works for a long time without stopping, it gets overheated, and ends up breaking down. Well, that's exactly what happens to these ladies."

"Ah! Yes, yes, I've got it. They're in the condition of the legendary Curé Comparet,[58] who had a stubborn constipation for twenty years. It's not a hanging matter, and it's not rare. Fortunately, we have sovereign medications to vanquish that resistance today—exquisite waters and delicious candy, not to mention melon."

"Oh, my dear chap, how far behind the times you are, how unready for the world of the future! Taking medicine when one already has a stomach ravaged by overly succulent fare and overly alcoholic beverages—you can't think of that."

---

[58] The clergyman in question, allegedly the parish priest of St.-Romaine-des-Îles, figured in a massive advertising campaign, offering a testimonial to the effect that Du Barry's Food (a quack medicine) had saved him from twenty years of dyspepsia and various other ailments. At the turn of the century there were very few effective medicines, and only two groups stand out as having any real virtue beyond the placebo effect: opiates and laxatives. The coincidence was to some degree fortunate, as taking opiates on a regular basis tends to cause dire constipation.

"I've heard it said that massage is quite effective."

"Massage? Shocking!"

"We also know, by virtue of what happened to Panurge when the cannon was fired, that 'the retentive virtue is dissolved' by fear, and that certain reading materials, even the sight of certain people, produces the same effect."

"No, my dear chap, no—you haven't got it; in this, as in everything, 'to will is to fulfill.' Everything depends on an effort of will. If these ladies, although wanting to, can't, it's because their will is insufficiently forceful. They need to find a surplus somewhere, and then they go to the will-power merchant. That honorable dealer, who is neither a physician, nor a pharmacist, nor a masseuse, nor a somnambulist, nor a witch, not anything similar or approximating thereto, is a woman of the world, and had no other means of action but will-power. She simply suggests to her clients a force of will sufficient to vanquish the resistance and arrive at the result their own will was unable to obtain. It only costs five dollars."

"Twenty-five francs for a result that generally costs fifteen centimes is expensive!"

"Which doesn't prevent the will-power merchant's *cabinet*—and you'll admit than the word '*cabinet*' was never more appropriate[59]—always being full. The city's aristocracy meets up in her salon—for people come back, the dose of will only operating once—and over there 'one doesn't find that so ridiculous.'[60] It requires backward people like us to laugh at it."

"I'm not laughing at it—but I'd be curious, all the same to know how the honorable lady discovered this new profession. Was it revelation, inspiration, science, calculation or pure chance?"

---

[59] The pun does not translate: in French, *cabinet* can mean both a consulting-room and a toilet.

[60] Another phrase in common ironic usage, probably originating from an earnest but facile comment in Baron Reiffenberg's *Archives philosophiques* (1826).

"I can't enlighten you on that point; what I can certify is that, at present, she's enjoying great success, and that, as we speak, numerous rival boutiques are probably being set up. Don't you realize now that what is so successful in this particular case might be equally successful in a thousand other cases in which will-power is lacking? Can you see now that commerce in will-power isn't a chimera—that it is, on the contrary, bound to have a considerable extension some day? And do you understand, finally, that suggestion isn't a hoax?"

"Say no more, my dear chap. It seems to me that I can already see shops opening up on all sides with attractive advertisements: *Unbreakable wills guaranteed. Wills of iron. Extra-Strong Wills. First-rate Wills. Big Sale of Good Wills!* And in the age of apathy and cowardice we're going through, I can see overflowing shops making scandalous fortunes in a matter of days."

IX. The Monopolist

My investigation for the *Universal Informer* would have been incomplete if I had not managed to discover the state of mind of one of those enormous monopolists who have organized trusts. Having formed my resolution, I no longer hesitated, and departed for Chicago with the intention of interviewing Burcket—the great Burcket, nicknamed "the hog king."

I was initially surprised by the warm welcome accorded to me by that excellent man, in his veritable palace on Four-Hundred-and-Thirtieth Avenue. No expansive southerner has ever greeted one of his old comrades with more enthusiasm and joy than Burcket lavished on me. My amazement peaked, however, when the billionaire, full of cordiality and French good humor, told me that he was my compatriot!

As supportive proof, he gave me the following manuscript, to which he had consigned his surprising story:

I'm sure that by making a slight effort of memory, you'll recall the name of Pierre Labrique, which is mine. Twice it had the honor of widespread publicity. The first time was…I can't remember the exact date, but it was at least twenty years ago. At that time, pale young adolescents, faces thinned by long hair drooping like weeping willows, gazing into the distance, with a phantasmal gait, were intoning rhymes in the smoky basements of the Latin Quarter. We were translating, in impenetrable stanzas, the emotions of our Self, wandering in the obscure park of the Ideal amid lilies and swans while the water of fountains pearled over the crystal of lakes!

Without flattering myself, I can avow that I had become jolly good at giving the most banal thoughts an unfathomable profundity. My lyricism plunged the youth of my generation into an admiration that increased as it became less intelligible, and Verlaine said, without laughing, to anyone who cared to listen, that I was "the genius of the abstruse."

My mistake was to believe that that was "arriving"—or, rather, that I had arrived at the first flap of the wing at the summit of Parnassus. A little book of verses, *Waves and Frissons*, printed in an edition of fifty copies, completed my intoxication. Petty literary magazines sang my praises. I was mentioned in the large dailies. And I still possess the handwritten letters of true masters—Academicians—who consecrated me as a poet.

Ah yes, a poet! I was one to the marrow of my bones, and the scorn that down-to-earth humankind and its prosaic needs inspired in me soon caused a breach with my family. My father, a small businessman, had always counted on me, his only son, being his associate and successor. One morning, I told him that a poet of my ability couldn't accept the existence that he had intended for me, and after a painful scene, I left the paternal ground floor to install myself in a sixth-floor room close to the stars.

That rupture, I believe, dealt my father a blow from which he never recovered. The worthy man had done everything possible to give me a complete education. All his hopes were invested in me. When I was no longer there, he became discouraged, neglected his business, which went into a decline, and eventually died facing certain bankruptcy. My mother followed him a few months later.

I had wanted to be free, and I was, more than I would have wished, left alone—absolutely alone—in Paris. To tell the truth, like everyone else, I still had a few relatives in a distant province, but I didn't know them. As for friends and neighbors, my father's suppliers or clients, I preferred not to know them.

A few scraps of inheritance wretched—not without difficulty—from the voracity of the men of law gave me a little time to sort myself out; which is to say that, when the time came to settle my bills, I didn't have to pretend to be digging deep into my pockets. The bad times came all too soon! In truth, although my verses were highly praised, no one bought them. The periodicals that enthusiastically opened their columns to me kept their cash-boxes firmly shut. The publication of my second collection, *Lights in the Darkness*, was a disaster, and obligatory borrowings considerably diminished the number of my admirers.

I knew well enough that a good poet has to be a vagabond, only rich in his dream, and that he must scorn monetary contingencies. Perhaps that was possible in the epoch when feudal lords entertained troubadours. Today, the parasitic poet has had his day, and the starveling poet too. The Bohemian life, although so recent, seems a prehistoric concept. Thanks to the repeated cramps of my empty stomach, I understood that our democratic and bureaucratic society was hermetically sealed to those who seek to give a little of themselves to the ideal.

In my distress, I went to ask for help and advice from one of our poets whom I considered to be the most uncontested of our masters. In the matter of aid he could do nothing, his staff of secretaries being complete for the moment; as for advice, he gave it to me generously. According to him, it was necessary to have an annual income of at least twenty-five thousand francs to permit one to write verses. Poetry did not sell. Only Victor Hugo had sold, and only because he had written novels too. "Life is prosaic; to live, one must write prose."

Write prose! A girl to whom I had promised the dignity of being my Muse had already told me that I ought to give up verse! Write prose! And realism too—why not? Write prose, when lyrical inspiration had never been as imperious and proud!

Well, since the necessities of existence condemned me to it, and since it was a question of life or death, I set down my lyre on the glorious pedestal of my past and took up the acerbic pen-holder of the man of letters.

If only I had preferred death to prose! I set to work with furious determination; they wanted prose, they would have it! One person advised me to write short stories for periodicals, another to harness myself to a novel, a third to work for the theater, where crazy sums could be made. I resolved to buckle down to all those tasks, and the quantity of paper I blackened in a matter of weeks was incredible.

It was certainly not inferior to what I read in periodicals or saw in theaters, but I soon had to recognize that it is easier to produce masterpieces than to place them. I was sent packing more or less politely, especially when I had the misfortune to mention that I was a poet. To relieve themselves of my persistence, editors published a few short stories; as for novels, that was out of the question—I had no reputation! In vain I assured them that the publication of my work would give me one; no one would listen.

A feuilleton-dealer to whom I was introduced by a grocer to whom I owed a little money made me a firm offer for fifteen thousand lines. He resold them verbatim to a daily that paid him two francs an episode for them, but only gave me a derisory sum. Another illustrious man, an up-and-coming dramatist, bought a four-act comedy from me for five hundred francs, which consolidated his fame and was a rare commercial success

I ought to tell you that I had previously observed that, in order to be put on in any theater, it is not necessary to offer it a good manuscript, but simply a financial arrangement. Now, the state of my finances attesting to an intense crisis, I had no hope in that direction.

Everything that I had produced thus far could still pass, strictly speaking, for literature. Afterwards…great gods, when I think of it—what abomination! Obliged to "cook with tiny *canards*,"[61] if I might express myself thus, to report on society events, market prices and gossip, to interview personalities worthy of reportage in a fawning manner and plagiarize *Larousse* outrageously, like my great colleagues. Then, haunting the streets as poor wretches haunt the woods, I picked up shreds of rumor, which I hawked from editor to editor. Glad when a colleague in misery had not arrived ahead of me bearing the sensational news redrafted in publicans' slang.

Yes, I was reduced to those expedients and many others, going so far as to produced imbecilic monologues for dubious characters. You'll admit that, except for murder or theft, I couldn't have sunk any lower.

My comrades no longer knew me; my admirers had never known me! And yet I was still the author of *Waves and Frissons* and *Lights in the Darkness*. Tears came to my eyes when I thought about that.

The little Muse, unable to cope with the irregularity of meals, disappeared; and that departure turned my thoughts so dark that death—the death about which I had so often sung, beautiful death—became my only hope.

Although I gladly accepted the dispersal of my genius in oblivion, like a soap-bubble iridescent with the most delightful colors vanishing into the ether, I became nauseous at the idea of suicide. Suicide is a crime and all crime is ugly! I was also reluctant to be the artisan of my end. I did not want that at all; I even professed for myself a particular esteem. Besides, had I the right to extinguish the divine flame that burned within me?

---

[61] Again, the pun does not translate, *canard* [duck] being a slang term for (among other things) a disreputable newspaper.

221

Then again, was there anything more vulgar, more bizarre and more prosaic than suicide? That means of finishing with life, within the range of any idiot at all, which financiers employ to balance their accounts, could not be mine. No, I would not climb over the parapet of a bridge! No, I would not throw myself under the wheels of a locomotive! Merely thinking about the mocking articles that would announce the fat in the press, I was disgusted.

Others, if they wished, could soil their hands with my blood; I only demanded not to have "committed suicide."

The thing was not as easy as one is led to believe; it's a matter of luck. It's claimed that the streets of Paris are unsafe by night—what an error! On the darkest nights I roamed the most eccentric quarters without encountering an apache bent on planting his "spike" between my shoulders. The drivers of automobiles are also, whatever anyone says, extremely honest men. I walked up and down the Avenue de la Grande-Armée for an entire afternoon without one of them consenting to run me over. I could not, however, ask a policeman to put a revolver-bullet in my head.

Momentarily, I had the idea of having myself admitted to a hospital. Enjoying a robust constitution and not possessing, in spite of my thinness, any infirmity, it was a safe bet that the physicians would discover an incalculable number of diseases and enable me to pass from life to death *secundum artem*.[62] It would have been amusing to mock the pontiffs of science in that fashion, except it would be a slow death and I preferred to finish things at a stroke.

I dreamed about a gigantic pile-driver squashing me flat.

After mature reflection, the exceedingly simple idea occurred to me that it was unnecessary to search for an executioner, that in a society as well organized as ours, where it is forbidden to poets to live, facilities must to be provided for them to die. I searched hard, but our civilization, much inferior

---

[62] Literally "according to the art," but used to mean "in the customary manner."

to barbarity, only offered me two admissible and truly expeditious means: rifle fire and the guillotine.

Poets are not generally given to heroic gestures. My bellicose sentiments are non-existent, and I couldn't see myself going to the colonies to make war against inoffensive natives, given that we no longer make war in Europe. There remained the guillotine—but Monsieur Deibler doesn't cut off just anyone's head.[63] One can't go to hum as to a barber and ask for a "haircut and shave." It's necessary to be sent to him by eminent magistrates with the recommendation of the President of the Republic, and for that, it's necessary to have committed a notorious crime.

Was it really indispensable to have committed a crime? There are so many judicial errors! I could accuse myself of imaginary crimes, or declare myself guilty of crimes as yet unpunished. But that would mean lying, and lying is also ugly. Could I not, at least, be compromised by some dark affair? As, once one has a finger caught in the gears of justice, it does not make much for the entire body to be drawn through them, I had a good chance of not getting out of it. That was no longer a banal judicial error; the innocent went to the guillotine and took a kind of bitter pleasure in seeing the judges go astray. His end would be reached on the day when they pronounced an iniquitous sentence upon him. He wagered his head against the truth; the gamble was not lacking in poetry, nor in grandeur.

---

[63] The official executioner in Paris at the turn of the century was Anatole Deibler, who had taken over the position from his father. He was unemployed between 1906 and 1909 when exercise of the death penalty was suspended by the President of the Republic, but the latter was forced to recall him to duty by the public outcry following a particularly nasty murder committed by Albert Soleilland. The narrator is harking back to an earlier epoch, but the story's original readers would have been in the midst of the controversy.

Curiously enough, as soon as the idea of being guillotined had entered my head, not once had I thought about the dishonor that might by reflected on my family and myself. I delighted in savoring in advance the refined vengeance that I would be taking on the stupidity of my contemporaries. For me, the worst that might happen was that a pardon might throw me back on to the streets. But in that case, since documentation is now required, I would have first-hand experience of the justice system, and would be able to make a living.

Between unpunished crimes that had made some noise, I had an embarrassment of choice: murdered prostitutes; men cut into pieces. It was definitely only stupid villains who got caught, and they were in a tiny minority. I wanted a crime of a good sort, a crime hiding a dark family drama, a fine crime—which was not a crime of passion, for then I would surely be acquitted.

At the time when I was still ghost-writing, I had gone several times to the home of the well-known stockbroker Monsieur D*** in Montmorency, who dabbled in literature and passed for a protector of young women. There I had heard long discussions of different hypotheses relating to the Hurelle affair. Do you recall the famous Hurelle affair, also known by the sensational title of the *Mystery of the Plaine Saint-Denis*? The body of a famous banker, Monsieur Hurelle had been found with a single stab-wound, on an embankment of the Northern railway, at a place where the tracks crossed. Monsieur Hurelle was a country neighbor of Monsieur D***, and the murder had interested him greatly, so I had first-hand information about it.

The affair made an enormous noise. It was seen successively as a family drama, a case of mistaken identity, a political plot, the vengeance of a husband or a ruined speculator, etc. The imagination of the reporters could be given free rein, for no clue emerged to support one version or another. The finest sleuths were unable to turn up anything, and the police and the law floundered in competition with them.

Incontestably, it was a fine crime. But how, with respect to a matter forgotten for so long, to which I had absolutely no connection, could I attract the sword of justice to hang over my head?

Entirely at hazard, I re-raised the affair in a bar in the Rue Montmartre, near the Croissant, where we sharp-shooters of reportage met in order to extract information from one another. For no particular reason, I exclaimed: "It's just like the Hurelle affair; they're searching though a heap of explanations, each more complicated than the rest, when he was simply a mug ready to be knocked over, and the compromising documents he had in his wallets were his banknotes! I'll say no more—make of it what you will."

I was secretly convinced that, falling upon avid ears at a time when there was a shortage of news, that indication would run its course, and it did.

I had often suspected some of my colleagues of having acquaintances in the Sûreté—one always thinks that about silent comrades—and I had palpable proof of it. At the same time as an item appeared in various newspapers announcing that the Hurelle affair, so often resumed, had taken a new direction and that the magistrate finally believed that he was on the track of the real guilty party, I received a note from Monsieur Meynadier, the famous examining magistrate, inviting me visit his office the following day at two o'clock.

Things were working out even better than I could have hoped. But what was I going to say to the judge? I had not expected the summons so soon, and had nothing prepared.

At two o'clock I arrived at the meeting. Monsieur Meynadier, who was very busy, made me wait in the corridor until half past two. Finally, I went in. The judge enveloped me with an investigative gaze, then, shrugging his shoulders, like a man carrying out a task whose utter futility he has foreseen, after a summary confirmation of my identity, he said to me in a hasty and indifferent tone:

"In a bar in the Rue Montmartre you said something that encouraged the belief that you know something about a murder committed on 31 July 1900 on the train that that left Enghien-les-Bains at thirty-two minutes past midnight for the Gare du Nord, the victim of which was Ferdinand Victor Hurelle, banker, of the Boulevard Haussmann, Paris. Tell me quickly what you know, for I'm very busy at the moment."

The scornful welcome annoyed me and I replied, very grumpily, that I knew nothing, absolutely nothing, about the crime he had mentioned. I had chatted about the Hurelle affair with my comrades, as I would have chatted about any other famous affair. I did not understand why, on the denunciation of an over-zealous informer, I had been summoned to give an explanation of what I had said. One would never finish if one had to account to the law for everything that one said. Besides which, I had better things to do than spend entire in the corridors of the Palais. I had a living to earn.

"Come now—don't get upset," said Monsieur Meynadier, stirred by the violence of my protest. "I agree that what's happened to you is very irritating, but my duty is to seek enlightenment by all means possible, just as yours is to help me in my investigation. You've said that the police were on the wrong track, that theft was the motive for the crime; what is your basis for making such an affirmation?"

"It was merely an idea! I have no other information—none. I said that as I might have written a short story or novel—it's my profession."

"I understand that," said Monsieur Meynadier, who was beginning to take an interest in my deposition. "But why," he added, subtly, "in citing a crime still unpunished, did you chose the murder of the banker Hurelle—which goes back several years and has slipped out of memory—when you had so many recent examples available?"

"Because, Monsieur, I heard a great deal of talk about the crime in a house when, at the time, I went to Montmorency."

"Ah! You went to Montmorency in the month of July 1900?"

"July, August…you understand, Monsieur, that after so many years, it's difficult for me to be precise about the date."

"Undoubtedly…but tell me, what did you go to Montmorency to do?"

"My God, Monsieur, I can tell you that—there's no dishonor in it. I went to see Monsieur D***, the stockbroker, of whom you must have heard, in order to recite verses and to tout for some work. At that time, just like today, I was very short of money."

"We're saying, then," the judge summarized, "that in the month of July 1900, when you went to Montmorency to see Monsieur D***, you were without resources?"

"I beg your pardon! I had novels, comedies, dramas, and three volumes' worth of verse"—Monsieur Meynadier sketched a indulgent smile—"and only needed to place them."

"Yes, except that you hadn't succeeded. You were, therefore, as I said, quite without the means of existence." After a pause, he added: "Since then, what have you lived on?"

I started, exclaiming indignantly: "Are you subjecting me to an interrogation?"

"I'm exercising the authority that the law confers on me to discover the truth," the judge replied, dryly.

"It's quite unnecessary, for that, for me to tell you everything I've done."

"I deem, on the contrary, that such an account is absolutely indispensable to the continuation my enquiries, because it seems to me very surprising that you, Pierre Labrique, should be so well-informed about the motive for the murder in question, when the police know so little."

"Then…you think, Monsieur le Juge…?" I said, genuinely amazed .

"I don't think anything. Long practice in examination has taught me that you must obtain information about people who know a great deal about what has happened, and I want to know what your relationship to the affair is."

"I repeat to you, Monsieur, that it's purely a matter of hypothesis, and that no one has ever spoken to me about the affair."

"You're contradicting yourself—just now you affirmed that someone had talked to you about it in the home of Monsieur D***."

"As one speaks in a drawing room about the day's events."

"It really was the thirty-first of July, then?"

I had noticed that the simpler and more accurate my denials were, the more deeply the conviction of my guilt became anchored in the judge's mind. Let anyone tell me know about the omnipotent force of the truth! The energy that I put into defending myself against that unjustifiable accusation was replete with compromising irascibility, and my exasperation against Monsieur Meynadier's revoltingly cynical methods. It's true that indifference or despondency might equally well have been turned to my disadvantage. The quite natural refusal to name the people to whom I attributed the version of the crime—since they did not exist—completed my ruination.

"You persist, Labrique, in not wanting to reply?" the magistrate concluded, his lips pinched and his gaze menacing, with a categorical hand-gesture.

"I persist, having no reply to make, any more at present than I had just now."

"Well, my friend"—at this sympathetic word I sensed that my goose was cooked—"I shall find a means of making you talk. Firstly, I shall change your summons as a witness into an order for your detention."

And he began to fill in the blanks on an official form.

"This is odious!" I cried. "Abominable! We're back in the Middle Ages, the Inquisition! If you pursue the imagination, you'll have to arrest all the novelists, playwrights and poets!"

Monsieur Meynadier's affirmative smile suggested that one could do worse.

"And individual liberty?" I continued. "What becomes of that? It's not permissible for a magistrate to incarcerate a citizen for his own amusement; the Garde des Sceaux has issued a circular on precisely that point; it's an abuse of power, a denial of justice."

"Shut up, Labrique," growled the judge, rapping on his desk. "Don't make things worse for yourself!"

"I'll shut up, not because you have the right, but because you have the strength, and it's necessary to yield to strength; but I admire the revolting arbitrariness with which you attack a poor penniless devil of a writer."

"It's certain that if you were Monsieur Rothschild, you probably wouldn't be being charged with having killed Monsieur Hurelle in order to steal the cash from his wallet."

"What, me? I'm being charged?"

"Guards! Take the accused away."

For Monsieur Meynadier the matter could not be clearer. My brilliant poetic imagination, led astray by poverty, had conceived the crime. Informed by his neighbor, Monsieur D***, of Monsieur Hurelle's habits, I had taken the last train with him, leaving Enghien at 12.32 a.m.—a train that, on 31 July, would doubtless not have many passengers. Once my victim was drowsy, I had stuck him, stolen his wallet and, before reaching Paris, had thrown him on to the embankment on the Plaine Saint-Denis. That same evening I had returned to Montmorency, as much to create an alibi as to hear what was being said about the crime—which was very audacious, but accorded well with what was known of the psychology of murderers.

That having been posited, it only remained to find evidence. That was the A-B-C of the profession. The examination of my affair was, however, very laborious. I must also say that I became irritated by the game and that, in spite of my keen desire to be guillotined, I did my best to make my innocence obvious.

Everything was against me. In spite of everyone's good will I had not been able to establish my whereabouts in the day of 31 July 1900, while the judge, aided by police notes and the testimony of witnesses, established them hour by hour in an irreproachable fashion. A search of my room produced astonishing results.

First, all my rough drafts and manuscripts were put under seal in order to be searched minutely at a later date. Then all my letters and the like, which I had had the misfortune to throw pell-mell into a drawer, were seized. A few of them immediately caught Monsieur Meynadier's attention. Written on school notepaper, they bore no date or signature, but one could read sentences such as: *I'll meet you at the brasserie this evening to talk about it; Make sure that no one finds out about it; No, no, no sentimentalism; get straight to it;* and *No more hesitation; it's absolutely necessary to kill the fellow.*

It did no good to tell the judge that these notes had been sent to me by the novelists for whom I worked; he didn't want to believe it. He kept repeating to me incessantly: "Tell me who they are, then!" as if, even admitting that I had been able to tell him their names, the dear masters wouldn't have been the first to deny all knowledge of me!

A more serious discovery was that of a timetable for the northern railway bearing the date 1 July 1900. I remembered, in fact, that I had bought it at the time when I was going to see Monsieur D***. Finally, a crushing blow, there was a rusty knife with a slender blade and a safety-guard, which I used for scraping mud off my shoes. Engraved on the knife's safety-guard were the words: *Souvenir of the 1900 Exposition.* It had been given to me for a sou—for not severing the relationship—by the little Muse, one day when she had won it throwing rings at a stall in the Avenue de Suffren.

With regard to the possession of these objects and many others, I was obliged to furnish numerous explanations, of which the judge did not believe a word. When one attempts to dissuade a man haunted by a preconceived opinion, it's curious to see how everything that one might say only serves to confirm that opinion. In my case, the investigation of my past provided further corroboration.

The judge thus learned that a short time after the crime I had paid a few debts and had indulged in some expenditure that he qualified as foolish with a registered prostitute. The prostitute in question was none other than the little Muse, who had become very fashionable after leaving me. I succeeded in remembering that at that time I had sold the celebrated playwright the comedy that had made his name. I told Monsieur Meynadier that—who, on that occasion, could not help laughing, and replied, paternally: "Come on, Labrique, find something more plausible to tell me; you're doing no credit to your imagination, I assure you."

The task of defending me had been given to Maître Dupillet, a young advocate full of talent, but with an exaggerated politeness with regard to highly-placed people. Without believing in it overmuch, he protested my innocence fervently, and then always conceded the judge's arguments out of deference. He made, however, one reply that went straight to my heart. When my tormentor mocked my verses, he affirmed that our best poets could have signed certain passages of *Lights in the Darkness*—a eulogy that was, however, immediately turned against me.

"Do you recall, Maître," countered Monsieur Meynadier, "that great criminals have often been true poets. The most banal crime—Monsieur Labrique's, for example—does not exclude a certain poetry. I will even say that it is sometimes the result of it!"

Maître Dupillet conceded the point.

One day, when we were alone in my cell, he said: "Come on, Labrique, you're not unaware of how devoted to you I am, how passionate in the defense of your case, but permit me to tell you that your strategy of defense is detestable. You deny everything systematically; that's very bad. It's necessary to hold fire, throw off some ballast, confess a few peccadilloes. Monsieur Meynadier will be grateful to you, and we'll be

231

more easily able to throw him off the scent with respect to the major charge."

"What the devil do you want me to confess, since I'm innocent?"

"It's all right," he said, tautly. "I'll plead irresponsibility."

"Oh no, no!" I cried, swiftly, seeing myself locked up in a lunatic asylum until the end of my days. "I claim full responsibility for my actions!"

"Do you know that premeditated murder, without extenuating circumstances, means the guillotine?"

"I'm well aware of that, since..."

I stopped dead. The idea had occurred to me of revealing my suicide plan, and I perceived almost immediately that my advocate the truth would appear to be a wretched and ridiculous invented defense. He would have demanded a mental examination there and then!

"All right," he said, misinterpreting the reason for my reticence. "I can see that I don't have your confidence. Do as you wish; I shall act according to my conscience."

When an advocate at the Assizes talks to you about his conscience, no matter how prepared one may be, one experiences a slight chill at the back of the neck. The last word pronounced by Maître Dupillet was all the more striking because I was subject to a singular phenomenon. Until then, having the certainty of being able to reveal, sooner or later, how I had given birth to the suspicions, I had not paid much attention to the outcome. Now that I recognized the absolute impossibility of having the plausibility of my plan admitted, that outcome annoyed me. I would enter the annals of judiciary error, an everyday gaffe, a subject of scorn and ridicule.

I became less sarcastic, less mocking, more self-enclosed. Monsieur Meynadier observed that with satisfaction, and declared that after a few more days "*cuisinage*"—I don't know whether the word is French, but the thing is very judiciary—I'd be done to a turn.[64]

I won't mention either the young vagabonds or the old malefactors that were locked in my cell in order to discover my secrets. I shall also pass over in silence my successive confrontations with all the prisons of the Seine, containing bandits, cut-throats and pimps. I shall pass on to the witnesses.

After the procession of employees of the Hurelle bank, three-quarters of whom thought they recognized me as an individual who had come to solicit help from their employer, that of the employees of the northern railway began. Here I must remark on the extent to which punching tickets or closing carriage doors improves one's memory for faces. A good half dozen remembered having seen me on the train going to or coming from Montmorency—in which there was nothing extraordinary—and a controller affirmed that he had caught me one day in a first-class compartment with a second-class ticket (which was untrue) but that he could not say whether it was on the thirty-first of July 1900. The special commissioner at the Gare du Nord declared that my signature corresponded exactly with that of the supposed murderer furnished by the guard on the 12.32 train, who had since died.

Another dead man gave a crushing deposition against me—I mean the examining magistrate who had opened the first investigation after the crime. Among the pieces of evidence collected by him, a piece of paper was found to which he had not paid any attention and on that paper some lines of verse had been written, in my handwriting!!! There was no doubt about it; I remembered them perfectly, and it really was my handwriting.

---

[64] *Cuisinage* is not, in fact, good French, and although the examining magistrate is presumably deriving it from *cuisine*, much as an English policeman might refer to letting a suspect "stew," the narrator is obviously aware of its similarity to the English cozenage (i.e,. fraud)—hence the insult in the remark about the thing being typical of the justice system.

At the sight of that piece of paper, a terrifying hallucination took possession of my mind. I wonder whether I really had killed the banker Hurelle, in a crisis of somnambulism. It had been repeated to me so often and so firmly from all sides that I almost ended up believing it. On reflection, I realized that an over-zealous police officer had removed the piece of paper while searching my residence, and had slipped it into the file to add a little spice to it.

When I gave that explanation to Monsieur Meynadier, he had a blue fit. "It is not permissible to doubt the honesty of the modest and devoted auxiliaries of Justice!" I really was the most cynical and shameless of wretches.

The deposition of Monsieur D***, the stockbroker, was an agreeable diversion. Very simple and very correct, it declared that not only did he hold my poetry but also my character in high esteem. (I would never have thought that Monsieur D*** had so high an opinion of me.) To be sure, I had bold and subversive ideas that were not always to his liking, but he believed me to be absolutely incapable of committing the crime of which I was accused.

The judge paid no attention to this declaration, nor to those of my employers, comrades or eulogists, which were, for the most part, sympathetic. I say "for the most part" because a few did not miss the opportunity to play to the gallery, claiming that they had divined the soul of a villain in me a long time ago, citing in support insignificant facts that took on frightful proportions in their mouths.

The masters whose letters I possessed or in whose homes I had presented myself as a beggar, summoned to appear, did not take the trouble; either they had nothing to say or did not know me. And the little Muse, who had entered, as I have said, into the demi-monde, presented a certificate issued by a medical committee in order to excuse her from appearing. Talk about little Muses who would cut off your head serenely! Poor girl, I had showed her all the beauty of my dreams, and she was nothing but a wretched creature devoid of intelligence and heart!

I was also subjected to the physicians. They're more terrible than the magistrates. Judges always seem to be discussing hypotheses; doctors pronounce irrevocably. The first, an expert, affirmed that, according to the official autopsy of the late Hurelle and experiments that he had carried out on cadavers, the knife with the safety-guard found in my home could easily, by means of an abrupt half-turn, have caused the wound that had been attributed to a dagger.

The second was commissioned to examine my mental state. He carried out that task, the animal, in such a way as to render me absolutely insane, if I had had the slightest disposition. For him, I was a "lyric degenerate," probably the child of an alcoholic and a hysteric (my father never drank anything but water and my mother was exemplary in her gentleness and virtue throughout her life). He accorded me nevertheless the consciousness of my acts, but concluded that my responsibility was slightly attenuated.

The *cuisinage* finished by becoming exasperating. Replying fifty thousand times to the same questions in the same way, hearing discussions of verbal divergences rather than factual contradictions—which is those gentlemen's forte—and sensing that the truth I possessed would never succeed in piercing the mesh of error that was increasingly tightening around me, was a mental torture of which no one who has not been arbitrarily detained can have any idea.

The moderns have invented a torture more cruel than those of the boot, the rack, the water and red-hot irons: the slowness of the procedure. In the past, at least it was over in a single session, while I got to the point twenty times over of saying to Monsieur Meynadier: "Well yes, it was me—there! Let's not talk about it anymore and get it over with!"

Finally, the authorities decided that I would go to the assizes at the next session.

There is no need to describe that memorable sitting in detail. There is much exaggeration with regard to trials; personally, I was profoundly disappointed. Instead of being imposing, the apparatus of justice seemed to me to be grotesque, and the gravity with which the men clad in red or black approved the implausible fable imagined by Monsieur Meynadier appeared to me to be enormously comical.

Poor humanity, I thought. *How many errors as gross as the one of which I am the victim have scholars, pontiffs and the great not approved with regard to you? Who would dare to affirm, after the heavy scorn of these high competences, that the laws and principles that rule our society are not a tissue of lies?*

For I had no doubt that, from the president to the guard seated beside me, there was not one person who had not made up his mind about my culpability before the arguments began.

I was obliged once again to hear in detail the story of the Mystery of the Plaine Saint-Denis, heightened by dramatic phrases intended to impress the jury. Then came the multiple reports presented during the initial examination, and then the formal accusation. Finally, the president proceeded to my interrogation.

As there was a very good crowd, including quite a few ladies dressed up to the nines, the president—who, in order to seek the genesis of the crime, went back to the era before I was weaned—thought it as well to show off, by means of a few ironic pleasantries, the sparkling facets of his intelligence. Naturally, I served as the butt of his gibes, and bore all the expenses of that amiable diversion. The method seemed to me a trifle sharp, and I told him roundly that he had "the right to cut off my head, but not to poke fun at it."

That interjection had an effect on the audience akin to that of a cold shower. My advocate raised his despairing arms to the heavens, and the president conducted my interrogation rudely. He presented me as a third-rate actor of crime, avid for fame. I could not bear the idea, he said, that the author of a murder so cleverly conceived and so skillfully executed should remain unknown, and that, stuffed with vanity as others ere were remorse, it had been inevitable that, sooner or later, I would boast publicly of having committed it. The proof of that was that I had hoped, by having called as witnesses the greatest names in literature and the theater, to transform this vulgar murder, whose motive was theft, into a *cause célèbre*, or at least a "very Parisian affair."

I would have liked to argue against the formal accusation point by point, to demonstrate how absurd the charges laid against me were. As soon as I opened my mouth, my advocate precipitated himself toward me and begged me to be silent, while he president, revolted by my cynicism, threatened to continue the arguments without me.

The witnesses repeated under oath what they had said during the examination, but with less assurance. Monsieur D***, the stockbroker, seemed very annoyed to find himself mixed up in the nasty business. As for the experts, they were as categorical as possible. One juror, a builder, demanded a second opinion on the piece of paper found in the railway carriage. "One doesn't condemn a man," he said, "one the strength of a scrap of paper." The foreman of the jury, a man of letters, who could not forgive a colleague for dishonoring the profession, made the remark that I had confessed to once having written the lines, and that the piece of paper was a metaphorical sledgehammer as striking as it was just—and that in the end, as well as the paper, there was the knife! They passed on.

The prosecutor's speech was a pure masterpiece of logic, common sense and literature. After having addressed his congratulations to Meynadier for the sureness with which he had conducted the examination, and the president for his impartiality in the direction of the arguments, he appropriated both their theses and then raised, not without eloquence, the most transcendent sociological considerations.

My crime was a literary crime, if he might be permitted to express himself thus: the act of an intellectual whose mind had been led astray by the mirage of words and whose imagination had been perverted by poetic exaltation. A few truncated quotations from my works, and a choice of aphorisms and lines of verse perfidiously selected from my manuscripts, did not, according to the honorable magistrate, leave any doubt on this point. More fortunate that many other authors, I had had at least one passionate reader: the public prosecutor.

"Thus," he continued, "one is eventually convinced that one is living on a higher level than one's fellows and the law, for an ideal of beauty; one believes that one is in touch with the inaccessible horizon of utopia; and when one finds oneself at grips with the miseries of existence one resorts to crime as deliberately as an apache!"

Except that, while one had to reserve all one's commiseration for the apache, born in the utmost depths of society and grown up amid vice, it was necessary to strike, and strike pitilessly, the man who, possessing a certain culture, authorized himself by virtue of that superiority to avenge his disappointments and failure on the best and most honest father of a family. The just punishment, which he demanded that the jury pronounce upon me, would be a salutary example for the deviants, the fallen in revolt against society, who went to ignominy as one marches to glory!

The materiality of the facts was more than proven, thanks to the vengeful piece of paper that the murderer had left at the scene of the crime, like a visiting card, and the knife, by which, out of a refinement of pride, he had not wanted to be separated. Around these proofs, all the others were grouped, like the fasces surrounding the ax carried by a party of lictors.

The speech made a profound impression on the audience. Our most eloquent masters of the bar—which did not include my defender—could not have vanquished it. Maître Dupillet raised a smile when he praised my abilities as a poet; his insistence on talking about my disillusionment, my poverty— more horrible for me than anyone else, since I had fallen into the gutter from the heights of Olympus—provoked protests. Then he broadened his fire, declared that the excesses of my imagination revealed a congenital defect, an undeniable derangement, observed by the most celebrated specialists—and he sat down, exhausted, after having begged for the indulgence and pity of the jury.

When the president asked me if I had anything to add, I replied: "I am as much a stranger to the murder of the baker Hurelle as you are, Monsieur le Président. A frightful fatality is weighing upon me, but I am innocent; I swear that I am innocent."

That declaration merely aroused the indignation of the public. I distinctly heard cried of: "To death! To death!" and the president threatened to clear the room.

A few minutes later, found guilty of premeditated murder without extenuating circumstances, I was unanimously condemned to death.

I confess without boasting that the pronouncement of the judgment caused me scant emotion. I had expected it for a long time, and that was what I was there for. Incontestably, I had triumphed; I had attained the goal that I had adopted for myself; I had every reason to be satisfied. Well, I wasn't—not at all. It is true that all our hopes are bound to end in disappointment.

Condemned to death, huddled in a corner of my cell, I reflected strangely. Life no longer appeared to me from the same angle, and the prospect of having my head cut off by mistake no longer presented itself to me in its grandiose aspect of tragic beauty. I wanted to write my story, but what good would it do? Everyone would believe that the true story that I am telling today was only a fable designed to delay the execution of the judgment. I would die carrying my secret with me, and would be the real butt of the joke that I had wanted to play on society, since it would be forever unaware of it.

Then again, now that I was on the point of losing it, life—even the miserable life that I had led before my incarceration—seemed sweet. I told myself, having become fearfully positive, that it was necessary not to seek midday at two o'clock in the afternoon, that life was made to be lived, not to be dreamed. I surprised myself by making plans for the future, as if my days were not numbered, and I saw myself certain of winning fame and fortune. All those who have the intention of committing suicide ought to be locked in the condemned cell like that; I'll wager that after a few days of that regime, they would be completely cured.

It is easily comprehensible that in the isolation in which I was languishing, the slightest incident took on considerable proportions. On returning after the verdict I had found a little two-sou bouquet on my shelf. Those flowers troubled me, deep down, more than my condemnation. Where did they come from? Who had put them there? Was it a protest or a mark of pity? Someone, therefore, was thinking of my with sympathy, and that someone as undoubtedly a woman.

I must render her this justice, that not for an instant did I think that the little Muse could have chosen that gracious fashion of asking forgiveness for her weakness.

The next day, I found another bouquet on my shelf, but, oh! much finer than the first! I have never seen roses more resplendent, smelled carnations more deliciously perfumed—and there were lilies; yes, lilies!

I was moved to the point of tears. I put the immaculate petals devotedly to my lips and emotional stanzas rose up from my heart, as vibrant as a prayer of thanks addressed to my unknown friend.

It was the same in the days that followed. To all my questions, the warders remained mute. They knew, however, that the flowers had not fallen from the sky; their vigilance could not be deceived every time; they must therefore be in connivance with the person who brought them—unless it was a custom of which I was unaware, and which I did not find displeasing. I believe, in fact, that such a distribution of flowers in prisons would improve the most savage heart.

The terrible moment approached. My advocate did not hide from me that my petition for mercy had no chance of success. He addressed the vague encouragements to me with which one comforts sick people who are felt to be doomed. For myself, I tried to be reasonable, and said to myself that, after all, it was perhaps better to die than to seek to penetrate the mysteries that surrounded me on every side.

One day—and I mean one day, not one morning at dawn—I saw the governor come into my cell, accompanied by two other grave individuals (everyone is grave in that administration). I had a presentiment that my sentence had just been commuted to hard labor for life.

Terrified, before the governor could open his mouth. I said: "No, no, I don't want a commutation; I've been legally condemned and I demand to be executed."

"I haven't come to notify you of a commutation, Labrique," the governor said, eventually, "but to set you at liberty immediately."

He told me that the banker Hurelle's murderer, not wanting to allow an innocent man to be guillotined, had secured justice, after making a sworn written confession. That murderer was none other than Monsieur D***, the stockbroker! The wretch had thought he could avenge himself thus for an outrage committed by Hurelle upon a person who was dear to him. He had taken care to explain that the piece of paper found in the railway carriage was a copy of a ballad for which he had asked me—a copy that must have fallen from his jacket pocket during his struggle with the victim.

I was nailed to my stool, wondering if I were not the victim of a hallucination.

"Don't worry, Labrique," the governor went on. "Your trial will be rapidly revised; the law will compensate you for the wrongs it has done you; in the meantime, accept this."

He put a blue ticket in my hand.

I thanked him, without really knowing what I was saying, and allowed myself to be led unsteadily to the door. Blinded by the bright sunlight, I was hesitating over which direction to take when a footman approached me, asked whether I was Pierre Labrique, and invited me to climb into a coupé stationed not far away. A few minutes later, the mystery of the flowers was revealed to me.

Mrs. Burcket, the widow of the richest livestock-breeder in Illinois, had followed my trial with the passionate interest that American women put into delving into things that surprise them. Convinced of my innocence and revolted by the verdict, she had bribed the warders in order to get the flowers to me, had moved heaven and earth to contrive the revision of my trial, and was no stranger to the liberating resolution taken by Monsieur D   .

Today, the happy spouse of Mrs. Burcket, having become a Burcket myself for commercial reasons, I breed pigs in Illinois. I buy them, I sell them, I resell them, I export them, and the business is prospering; I'm the Hog King!

Poets will say that I've committed suicide. Obviously, it's true—but incontestably in the most agreeable fashion. The future belongs to monopolists!

Oh, poetry of the future world!

X. The Politician

I was sent to Pittsburgh by the *Universal Informer*.

Thanks to the generosity of the billionaire Carnegie (trusts, mining, currency dealing) who, having accumulated furiously, now feels the need to squander magnificently, the Old World—what am I saying? the entire world—will be endowed with an ultra-modern temple consecrated to peace. Completing the generous initiative of our little father the Tsar (knout, deportation, hanging) the billionaire has had constructed, in The Hague, a kind of Pasteur Institute of Peace.[65] Diplomats, reinforced by men of science, instead of making hol-

---

[65] Tsar Nicholas II was the instigator of the first Hague Peace Conference of 1899, as a result of which moves were made to found a "Peace Palace" there, for which the industrialist and philanthropist Andrew Carnegie was persuaded to provide the finance ($1,500,000) in 1903. (It is now the location of the International Court of Justice, where one of the authors of the most recent Balkan bloodbath is currently in the meshes of a procedural system that would probably have astonished Pierre Labrique almost as much as e-harmony would have astonished clients of the Milner Institute.)

low speeches, are seeking, in superbly-equipped laboratories, to isolate the various microbes of war and prepare a serum of peace. Thus, we are entitled to hope that in the near future, the work of these scientists will have delivered us forever from the scourge that has decimated humankind for so long.

May Carnegie and the Tsar, those two truly good men, be praised!

I said "has had constructed." Indeed, when one is American and possesses billions, one passed from plan to execution with a rapidity of which we have no idea. Scarcely had the great benefactor Carnegie manifested the desire for that pacific foundation than, in the calm meadows of Holland, between two canals in which tranquil water lies perpetually dormant, a palace had arisen as if by magic! A modern-style palace of tomorrow, whose soft and pleasantly concave lines seem to give flexibility to marble and a rubbery compliance to iron. In the immense rooms the light flows in waves. A rival of Puvis[66] has decorated its walls with frescos symbolizing the joys of peace: smiling and serene, processions of maidens advance among the flowers of the fields beneath a sky of unparalleled purity. Olive branches serve as a motif for the ornamentation of the woodwork as well as the wallpaper; and, in an evenly-conditioned atmosphere, a mysterious orchestra sends forth perfect harmonies.

The scientists, who do not wear the carnivalesque costume of our diplomats, circulate placidly, their hands in their coat pockets and pipes in their mouths, and their discussion hall is, quite naturally, a concert hall.

From the center of the palace rises a communications tower, in which the semaphoric, telegraphic and telephonic services of the entire world are brought together. Clerks are specially commissioned to scan the political horizon at every minute of the day and night. As soon as a black spot is sig-

---

[66] Pierre Puvis de Chavannes (1824-1898) painted several famous murals, including one in the Sorbonne and one in the Panthéon.

naled, the watchman notifies the chief of practical works. The latter takes a specimen of the black spot into his laboratory, examines it, studies it, grinds it into a powder, extracts the morbid germs and sows them in various culture media.

Recently, the peace laboratories have been overflowing with work. Apart from the Moroccan conflict, and extremely black spot has been detected in the direction of the Orient. Out there, the belliferous microbe known as balkanic constitutes a permanent nucleus of infection. The debris of twenty races, the detritus of a hundred peoples, the residues of countless sects are agglomerated behind the Gate in that antechamber of Europe; that confused mass, which has been compared, not unjustly, to a legume salad seasoned *à la turque*, is in perpetual fermentation. For centuries, people have striven to remedy that condition; the most highly-reputed physicians of peoples have exhausted the resources of their art there in vain.

It was up to the Nicholas II-Carnegie Institute to bring a modern solution to that hair-raising oriental question.

The laboratory assistants had no need to arm themselves with powerful microscopes to assure themselves that the frightful microbe of war was proliferating in the aforementioned black spot. They recognized no less easily that it belonged to the most dangerous variety of the species called fanatic—and everyone knows that microbes of that species multiply with an incredible rapidity in media warmed by nationalistic and religious rivalries, subsequently to acquire an exceptional virulence.

Macedonia, since it is necessary to call it by its name, must, in consequence, be their natural habitat. Every inhabitant of the country, in fact, claims that his race or his beliefs set him against those of his neighbors; and until now, to prevent these conflicts from taking on too bellicose a form, no better means has been found than confiding to the Turks the duty of carrying out, among the disparate populations, frequent and vigorous blood-letting.

The supervisor of the experimental sociology laboratory, charged with presenting a report to the International Committee of Pacifiers, became quite perplexed.

"Damn it, damn it!" he murmured, while stuffing his pipe. "This is very serious, very serious! These want to remain Turks or Tartars, those want to be ruled by the Greeks, others prefer the Bulgars, the Serbs, the Wallachians—what do I know? It's marvelous—everyone in the country is a foreigner!"

"And a nationalist, of course," put in a laboratory assistant.

No one has any more right than anyone else to the territory," the supervisor continued, "any more than anyone has to any point on the globe whatsoever, since the land remains and they disappear. It's therefore necessary to give it to all of them. Here's an admirable opportunity to form, with these heterogeneous elements, united by the same idea of independence and emancipation, a new people! Can you imagine new notions of association and solidarity injected in profusion into the country; individual liberty developing its activity and initiative there; and rivalries transforming themselves into praiseworthy competition, by virtue of the cooperation of all in the common endeavor, and the mutual aid that they'll render in making the disinherited of today into the happy people of tomorrow?"

"It would be a big step toward pacification," observed the assistant respectfully, "but I fear, Master, that you can't destroy the frightful microbe in that way. That the practice of free existence can cause nationalities of origin to be forgotten we see every say among the immigrants to the United States, but you're not taking into account the religions that incessantly foment hostility between Muslims, Jews and Roman, Greek, Russian and Syrian Catholics, etc., etc..."

"You're absolutely right, my friend. I intend to stipulate in my report that it's also appropriate to inject emancipated thought. All previous religions having successfully failed to keep their promises, it's best that a new people don't adhere to any of them. It can easily be demonstrated to them that the mysteries of their respective religions are a veritable hoax, and that supernatural intervention, about which the talk incessantly, is a trick. They'll forget those beautiful legends as the tales of olden days are forgotten, and will be united by the same respect for natural morality, the principles of which are within the grasp of the simplest minds.

The atheist serum was therefore prepared, in accordance with these ultra-modern givens, and presented to the International Committee for Peace, in solemn session, as the only one capable of combating the balkanic microbe efficaciously.

When its composition had been explained to them, the delegates of the European powers, assembled in the great hall inundated with light, where the smiling maidens of the frescos symbolized the joys of peace, were momentarily struck with amazement. The mysterious orchestra stopped playing; then the murmurs rose up. Certainly, everyone ardently desired peace, but they all desired, even more ardently, a part of Macedonia. Russia, which supported the Bulgarian claims, was the first to become indignant and declared that it would be delivering the country to the worst anarchy. Austria, which cherished Bosnia, declared that, on the contrary, a strong authority like its own was necessary to hold these cosmopolites in respect. England, which supported Greece, protested against the inconvenience of the method, and Italy, which coveted Albania, smiled pityingly. As for the representative of Germany, whose sovereign marches hand in hand with the Great Turk, he recalled that his Emperor had just solemnly declared that one could not govern without God, and that religion was necessary for children and peoples. The well-known spiritualism of the French delegate gave him a duty to oppose the employment of any such serum.

However, the pacifiers of the Hague agreed that they ought to do something for Macedonia, and, after a long discussion, they fell into accord with regard to requesting the Gate to substitute for its Muslim police Protestant police recruited in Switzerland.

246

The impious laboratory supervisor was replaced by a puritan—and that is why, in spite of the liberality of the billionaire Carnegie and the scientific research of the Institute in the Hague, the balkanic microbe will continue its ravages for a long time.

XI. The Philosopher

I could not neglect, in order to bring my investigation to a satisfactory conclusion, a visit to Baltimore to see John Wilfrid Theobald Portius Barnett, director of the Immortality Co. Ltd. That company is not, as one might initially suppose, a life insurance company; no, it is a society formed with the objective of winning a prize founded by a group of billionaires.

The rich Yankees in question are, in fact, haunted by an obsessive idea—that of immortality. Artists, writers, scientists and captains—people not worth five dollars—pass on to posterity, while they, in spite of their colossal enterprises, their humanitarian foundations, their regal gifts and their ruinous eccentricities, are not certain of arriving there. If they were only certain, quite certain that a part of themselves would survive—a soul, mental fluid or wave—but unfortunately, philosophy, whether supported by religion or science, only gives them rather risky assurances on that score. The idea that they, the men of gold, will one day only have the value of a few shovelfuls of ashes, is particularly unbearable to them; oblivion scares those omnipotent masters of the marketplace, and the problem of our destiny, which, since human beings became human, has tormented their pride, poses itself to these practical calculators in all its mathematical precision. They are no longer content with fables, revelations and dreams, theses, hypotheses and other philosophical speculations; they require certainty.

That is why a certain number of them have come together and decided to offer a prize of a hundred million dollars—which, as you can see, is not exactly a bagatelle—to the person who brings them precise and scientific information regarding what happens after death.

Immediately, centralizing all the research carried out and to be carried out, the Immortality Co. Ltd. was formed, under the direction of John Wilfrid Theobald Portius Barnett, and, in going to its establishments in Baltimore, I really was, this time, making a voyage to the other world—no longer merely the world that is on the far side of the Atlantic, or the one that will exist tomorrow, but the beyond whose mysterious existence has always tormented humankind.

In spite of my letters of recommendation and the personal intervention of one of the billionaire shareholders, I was categorically and rather impolitely refused entry to the severe building enclosed by high walls, the citadel of sorts in which, in solitude and silence, the philosopher Barnett works. It is not admissible that a door may be closed to the reporter of the *Universal Informer*, and since I was not to be allowed in with a good grace, I decided to trick my way inside.

I could, strictly speaking, have introduced myself using the classic method of borrowing a supplier's costume, but in a house so well guarded, the comings and goings of suppliers and service staff had to be rigorously channeled, and I would not have seen anything. Bribe a junior employee? That would not do me much good. It was, before anything else, necessary to inform myself as extensively as possible about the interior workings, in order that, once I got in, I could find my own way around and see what it would be interesting to discover.

The few indications that I was able to obtain from laboratory assistants or cleverly prepared aides were utterly contradictory. Some talked about spiritualism, occultism and magic, others about hypnotism and magnetism, yet others of biological and physiological research, of dissections and vivisections; some even suggested that experiments were being conducted on living human beings! Whatever was going on there, the somber building had a detestable reputation in the vicinity. People looked at it fearfully, as a redoubtable place in which, under the cover of science, the blackest crimes were being perpetrated.

What lent credence to these suppositions as that a large number of sick people had been seen entering the company's hospital who, it was said, never came out. From these narrations, true or false, I concluded that the experimental philosopher must indeed be operating on living subjects, and I immediately resolved to present myself in that capacity.

In consequence, I made contact with a black beggar who had solicited admission, and, for a rather large sum, he consented to let me have his turn. One evening, therefore, he told me that it was fixed for that night. He dressed me in his rags; I blackened my face and hands as best I could and presented myself at the entrance and the late hour he had indicated to me. This time, the door opened and I slipped in. I was inside!

Taken to the administrative office, which resembled any office in any company, I found myself in the presence of two individuals: a tall blond fellow and a short dark-haired one, evidently supervisors. They asked me a host of questions, to which I thought it prudent only to offer stupid and nonsensical answers.

On examining me more closely they realized that the swarthiness of my face only gave me the appearance of a black man, and that dishonesty, combined with my idiocy, motivated the short dark-haired man to make a charming reflection to the tall blond one: "How can you expect to find anything immortal in a specimen like this?"

To which the other replied: "This very abjection proves the existence within the creature of a superior essence; for, if it did not exist, it could not be diminished."

"I'll wait for you to prove that by other means than words."

"In the meantime," the tall blond went on, "what shall we do with the individual? We can't make use of him for psychic studies, nor in the physiological laboratories."

"He might be useful in the dissection department," said the short one.

"Let's send him to the amphitheater, then."

Then, just like that, without further ado, they didn't give me time to breathe or to say what I thought; they weren't going to hang about: I was to be taken apart as soon as I had arrived. I am certainly very fond of my profession, but my passion for reportage did not extent as far as risking being dissected in order to furnish copy to the *Universal Informer*. The prospect of feeling scalpels cutting into my skin sent a rather disagreeable shiver down my spine, and I almost cried out, making a fuss by demanding my ambassador and humanity. Fortunately, I reflected that by so doing, I would lose the benefit of all my efforts, that I would still have time to make my identity known, and that, finally, people did not cut other people's throats as unceremoniously in a civilized country.

Thus, without saying a word, I followed the black man—a genuine one—that I had been given as my guide, seeking by the flickering light of the lantern he held in his hand to take the best possible account of the layout of the place.

Having passed through a studio of typewriters and calculators, still at work, and along a corridor on to which opened a vast library and study-rooms, we arrived in a moonlit courtyard planted with trees, which seemed to me to have giant proportions. So far as I could tell, there was no symmetry in the order of the buildings that surrounded it, nor architectural uniformity in the constructions of the same group. To the right, my black man identified a black mass with feebly-lit windows as the Physiology Department. It looked much like a hospital to me, with wards of invalids, an operating theater and laboratories. To the left, I noticed the bizarre silhouette of an edifice reminiscent of a temple or a necropolis; he told me that it contained the Evocation Rooms. Further on, a small workshop working at full tilt was the Fluid Factory. Finally, beneath a terrace, a low windowless building with a glazed roof appeared, with pale walls on which the conical shadows of a row of cypresses were projected: the amphitheater!

The interior was even less reassuring. I vaguely distinguished human forms lying on stone tables, and further away, anatomical specimens of shelves; then, in special rooms, instruments that reminded me of those used in olden times to question bandits, and kill them, if necessary. We followed—in a deathly silence, it must be said—a long damp corridor beset by corpse-like odors. At the far end, my guide opened a door and I found myself in the lodgings intended for me: a camp-bed, a shelf, a toilet and a stool: the furniture of a condemned cell.

"Goodnight," said the black man, and left.

The few reflections that came to mind at that moment were rather morose. I told myself that I might protest all I liked, but if it pleased these gentlemen to experiment on my person until the point at which the soul survived the body, it would be quite impossible for me to prevent them from so doing. Should I await their pleasure and let myself be bled like a chicken? Certainly not. As nothing worse could happen to me than being dissected, I swapped my rags for an orderly's smock, swiftly cleaned myself up, and set out to explore.

I intended to go back along the dark corridor, lighting my way with a few matches, go through the rooms and out into the moonlight. This time, the corridor seemed interminable; I used almost all my matches without seeing the end of it. I had evidently gone astray; without realizing it, I must have gone into a subterranean passage opening into the corridor. Fortunately, I noticed the double rail of a service tramway embedded in the floor, and, as a railway always goes somewhere, I followed it.

A wall soon blocked my route, however. I raised my eyes, and saw a circle of light far above my head, as if I were at the bottom of a well. I recognized the cage of an elevator, climbed up on to the platform, pressed a button, and, a few seconds later, arrived soundlessly in a small glazed courtyard adjacent, if I were not mistaken, to the Physiology Department. I had taken the route followed by the cadavers that passed from the hospital to the amphitheater in reverse.

There was a door in front of me; I opened it. Menial workers were hurrying past; I joined them, and thus entered a room where a tall old man was standing in the midst of young men, whom the personnel surrounded respectfully. I soon understood that an important experiment was being carried out at that very moment by John Wilfrid Theobald Portius Barnett, aided by his collaborators, and that all of them were so sharply focused on the philosopher's words that no one was paying any attention to me.

"Yes, gentlemen," he was saying, "in a few minutes, perhaps we shall be in possession of a truth that humans have sought in vain every since they obtained consciousness of themselves. Tomorrow, there might be no more unknown!"

"We shall have isolated the immortal essence of human being!" proclaimed the tall blond fellow I had seen when I came in.

"The reign of ponderable matter will be over; that of the imponderable will begin," declare the short dark-haired one. Then, slyly, he said to his colleague: "It's the end of spiritomania."

"Rather say that it's the annihilation of radiomania!" the other replied.

"Serenity, gentlemen," said the philosopher, "while destiny is accomplished."

Only then, by hoisting myself up on a stool, did I perceive a patient lying on a low table. He was enveloped in a sort of network of exceedingly thin wires and helmeted with recording apparatus, some of which indicated the form of his pulse and the heartbeat, other the intensity of respiration, the variation of his temperature, muscular strength, nervous tension, the energy of his will and thought, etc. Aides were nothing down the various modifications from time to time. A physician was lavishing the cares of his art upon him, a magnetizer was hypnotizing him, and other attentive operators seemed to be ready to seize the soul on the wing, so to speak, at the point of its exhalation.

From the conversations of my neighbors, I learned that they had been waiting a long time for such a favorable opportunity to cut through the great question conclusively. That very night, a company electrician had been accidentally electrocuted, and the numerous trials that had already given appreciable results with the anemic and cachetic patients dying in the hospital, carried out on this healthy and robust subject, could not fail to be definitive.

In the vast white, bare and well-lit room the group of men leaning over a moribund individual, with the anxious expressions on all their faces contracted by the feverish anticipation of the unobserved phenomenon, took on a grandiose and impressive solemnity. The conversations ceased. All the motionless witnesses held their breath. I was gripped by an insurmountable anguish.

In the midst of that nervous silence, only disturbed by the dry clicking of instruments…a bell rang!

The heart had stopped beating.

The tall blond fellow, followed by his aides, ran to the evocation chamber in order to catch the soul off the dead man therein; the short dark-haired one precipitated himself toward the switches and the physician began rhythmic tractions. Portius Barnett remain motionless, his chin in his hand, his eyes fixed on the cadaver, waiting for the results obtained by his collaborators.

At that moment, it was as if the body lying on the table became phosphorescent; that, it appeared was due to the influence of W- and Y-rays on the vital waves. And the short dark-haired man cried: "You see, the waves emanating from our body while it is alive, and which explain quite simply all the phenomena of suggestion, telepathy, magic, second sight, and the influences of will, sympathy and love, don't cease immediately after death, and are prolonged, dispersing like any fluids in the great reservoir of the world."

"You're talking about the vital force," said the philosopher Barnett, "but the vital force isn't consciousness."

"Consciousness," the short man replied, "is nothing but a fugitive reflex; that man lost consciousness long before losing his life, and I don't admit that consciousness can exist without the phenomena that produce it."

253

"Master! Master!" said the tall blond man, coming in precipitately. "We've isolated the conscious fluid; the spirit of that unfortunate is fixed in our receiving apparatus; you shall have the honor of being the first to interrogate it!"

In the previously mute room there was an eruption of "hurrahs," a tempest of "bravos" and the stamping of feet. People congratulated one another warmly. There was now no more doubt; the proof had been obtained mathematically; the spirit survived the body and he company was about to bank the hundred million dollars. The theory of spirits had crushed by its superiority all the rival theories: the physicists with their electricity, their magnetism, their radiations and their waves crushed; the psychologists with their research into the secretion of thought and the localization of the soul, crushed. For two pins they would immediately have sacked the fluid factory, the hospital and the amphitheater.

As everyone, after that explosion of joy—including me, of course—headed for the exit in order to go and find the electrician's soul in the evocation room, a long-drawn-out yawn was heard. I turned round; the other did likewise; and we saw our subject, on the table where we had forgotten him, stretch his arms, while the needles of the recorders flickered over the graph-paper on the cylinders.

A frisson of mystic terror ran through the audience, as if they had just seen a ghost or a phantom loom up before them. It was an apparition all the more fantastic because the body's soul was next door, in the evocation room, and it had lost its vital radiation!

In the midst of the general alarm, the physician uttered a satanic snigger. He had recognized a systolic pause of the heart, but had not breathed a word about it, letting the others proclaim their victory and infer more and more.

"Where am I?" murmured the patient, blinking. "Who are you?"

Fear gave way to amazement. The man was thinking; therefore he existed! If he existed, his soul could not be simultaneously found in him and in the receivers. Its presence had, however, been clearly observed. It was, therefore, necessary to admit that, by virtue of an as-yet-unexplained phenomenon, the man had come back to life after being dead.

John Wilfrid Theobald Portius Barnett advanced solemnly.

"Gentlemen, you have often observed sick people recover from a fainting fit or unconsciousness, emerge from lethargy or a coma, but since Lazarus of Biblical memory, it has not been given to us to see a man rendered to life after real death. I have no need to tell you how important this event is, and what precious information we might obtain therefrom for the future of our company."

Then turning to the electrician, he said to him in an entirely reassuring tone: "You are, my friend, in the premises of the Immortality Co. Ltd., of which I, Barnett, and the director and you are an employee, attached to the electrical department."

"Yes," said the man. "Yes, I remember...once, a long time ago. But it seems, at present, that I've come back from a long way away?"

"Exactly. You were dead, and you've come back from the other world."

"You think so?"

"I'm sure of it—ask these gentlemen. Now, as your impressions are still fresh, tells, I beg you, what you felt."

The bewildered unfortunate raked his brains for some time. "It seemed to me that I was at the bottom of the sea...then I heard the water buzzing louder and louder in my ears. I rose up...rose up...finally, I reached the surface. I opened my eyes...and found myself here."

"Good—but don't you remember anything before? You touched a cable that shocked you..."

"Yes, I touched a cable."

"And afterwards?"

"Afterwards...afterwards... but there was nothing... nothing!"

"Most certainly!" cried the short brown-haired man. "There was nothing! And Lazarus, when he recounted his impressions of his voyage in the other world must have said the same thing: there was nothing. For, if he had seen anything else, he would have said so, and we would know about it."

"Philosophy, however, offers us irrefutable proof of the survival of our personality, with the attributes that characterize it: self-consciousness and the memory of the past."

"Then our subject wasn't dead, and your spiritualists, believing that they had isolated his soul, had caught nothing in their receivers but the emanation of their own imagination!"

Taking advantage of the silence that followed this declaration, the physician had his patient carried triumphantly away to a hospital room, and the disappointed service personnel stole away silently, disappearing like bats into their holes. Only the chiefs remained, grouped around the director, all just as perplexed and frustrated.

"In my opinion," the tall blond man repeated, "the experiment cannot have been other than a success."

"Undoubtedly," replied his adversary, "since it succeeded even though the subject wasn't dead."

"As to whether his death was apparent or real, one could argue for a long time, but give me another subject as healthy as that one, and you'll see."

"You're saying that because you know, I can't."

"The repeated requests that I've made to the government to send us those condemned to death," said Portius Barnett, "were refused indignantly."

"Can we not come to an arrangement," a young man suggested, "with a gentleman who wishes to commit suicide, and would be glad, in disposing of a futile life, to serve our experiments by means of his death."

"Suicide is a crime, and we could be deemed his accomplices."

"There are black men so miserable and backward that it really isn't a crime, but a service rendered, to deprive them of their life."

"Hang on," said the tall blond fellow. "A creature presented himself this very evening so dirty and degraded that we took him for an idiot. He was a white man, but one of rare stupidity. Not knowing what to do with him, we sent him to the amphitheater to help the attendants. Well, I ask you, what crime would there be in experimenting on an individual like that?"

This little discussion had the effect of reminding me of the reality of the situation. While those gentlemen were asking one another, with an utterly philosophical serenity, whether they could dispatch me from life to death, I was there, a few paces away from them, alone, sitting on a chair. Thus far, they had not paid any attention to me, taking me for an orderly, but if they succeeded in perceiving that I was the fake black man, that the fake black man was the reporter from the *Universal Informer*, and that, furthermore, I had witnessed their failed experiment and heard all their discussions, would they not give me a hard time and might I not, whether I liked it or not, become the subject of a vengeful experiment? Would they not think that it would be even less of a crime to get rid of a dangerous reporter than a inoffensive imbecile?

These pioneers of the unknown, haunted by their obsession, seemed to me to have singularly lost sight of common morality. The sinister rumors circulating in their regard no longer seemed to me to be exaggerated; these men might already have more than one murder on their elastic conscience! Would it be it the first time, in any case, that scientific researchers had rendered themselves guilty of frightful crimes in order to discover a truth?

I saw myself lying on the low table, helmeted with apparatus and succumbing to the effluvia of chloroform or the like.

The gentlemen were, in fact, discussing at that very moment what kind of death it would be best to employ, and they were all rallying around a narcotic, in a dose calculated to lad to slow death, without cries, protests, pain or the patient even perceiving it.

One young man had a pious scruple: those condemned to death were notified, in order that they could put their conscience in order with respect to religion; should the unfortunate not be warned? Since they believed in immortality, in order to be reconciled with themselves, they ought to let the soul prepare itself.

To that, the philosopher replied that in war, one does not alert those who are about to fall, and that furthermore, given that thousands upon thousands of men were sacrificed for a piece of land, a crown, an unhealthy ambition, an insult or even a misunderstanding, he did not see why one should worry overmuch about sending a miserable human wreck *ad patres*.

That argument won the day. It was now no longer a matter of deciding when to operate. Some suggested waiting until a more scrupulous examination of the subject had been carried out; others contested its usefulness—and since all the instruments were ready, they wanted the experiment to take place right away. They supported this proposal with the argument that no one, or almost no one, had seen the man come in and no one would worry about his disappearance. Their comings and goings would not astonish the staff that night; after the shock they had had, it was only to be expected that the chiefs would need to exchange opinions and come to some agreement. Finally, once they were all reassembled, they would be able to operate tranquilly in the calm of the night, without the aid of the service staff, whose presence a little while ago had been something of a hindrance.

"Shh!" said one of them, nudging the speaker with his elbow and pointing at me, at the back of the room.

All gazes turned toward me.

"It's only an amphitheater orderly," said the short dark-haired man, deceived by my costume. "Those fellows don't hang about with the others and are absolutely discreet. On the contrary, he might be useful to us."

"Well, gentlemen," concluded, "since we're all in agreement to get it over with as quickly as possible and emerge from the doubt in which we've already been flounder-

258

ing for too long, all right!" Then, addressing me, he said: "Get a lantern and take us to the amphitheater through the underground tunnel."

Without hesitation, I unhooked a lantern from the corridor and headed for the elevator, which I took down, once all the gentleman had gathered on the platform. Then, at their head, I advanced into the tunnel, wondering anxiously whether I needed to turn right or left. Frankly, the situation was becoming comical; I was serving as guide to the men who wanted to murder me! And I rejoiced, secretly, in thinking about the disagreeable surprise that awaited them when they found that I was no longer there, and that they could not apply the chloroform mask that one of the aides was carrying to my face.

Having arrived in the corridor, I was fortunate enough to find my way and recognize the door of my home, which I opened quietly, as I had been instructed to do.

There was a man lying on the bed!

I had a moment of strange folly. Troubled by all those ideas of evocation, isolating and duplication of the personality, I wondered where my true self was. If I was the person lying on the bed, who was holding the lantern? What if, while my primary self was asleep, another self had fled, had witnessed the resurrection of the electrician and brought the experimenters to the amphitheater?

Suddenly, the idea struck me that, as in many fantastic stories I had read, I was prey to a frightful nightmare—and without pausing to think about all the absurdities of that supposition, without seeing the illogicality of the action it suggested to me, I hurried to the bed to wake the sleeper, who had to be me. I gripped that second self by the arm so roughly that he sat up on the bed.

It was my black beggar, who, even though I had paid him a considerable sum, had wanted to obtain the benefits of his admission, and had slipped in behind me without being seen, with the cunning of a Redskin.

I believe that John Wilfrid Theobald Portius Barnett uttered a terrible oath. The assistants and aides turned toward me threateningly. But the attitudes of the tall blond man, the short dark-haired man and the man holding the choloroform mask displayed such pitiful disappointment that, in spite of the horror of the situation, I started giggling; and that nervous giggle, after the apprehension I had just endured, was prolonged into uncontrollable crazy laughter.

"He's lost his mind!" cried the philosopher.

"He's a lunatic, escaped from the Experimental Psychology Department," declared the physician. "I don't recognize him as one of our amphitheater orderlies."

"I recognize him," said the short dark-haired man, looking up at me from under my nose. "It's the filthy idiot that we admitted last night, and on whom we were thinking..."

"But in that case," retorted the tall blond, "where did the chap who was lying here, and who's now gesticulating like a man possessed, come from?"

"We're the victims of abominable machination," declared Portius Barnett, "and this man has been hired by our enemies!"

"No, no," I hastened to say. "I'm simply a reporter from the *Universal Informer*. I what was happening in the mysterious establishments of your company. Thanks to this man's ticket of admission, I was able to get this far—and now I know."

This declaration, instead of calming things down, one provoked a rumble of fury that was followed by a violent explosion of wrath. I thought that they were about to fall upon me and that, in spite of everything, my final hour had well and truly arrived. Those men, however, who had decided only a short while before, to execute a poor defenseless idiot in cold blood, hesitated before attacking me, and I took advantage of that brief moment to shout that I was a French citizen, that the consul and my ambassador had been notified of my presence in the headquarters of the Immortality Co. Ltd., and that if they touched a single hair on my head it would be so much the worse for them, and for the Republic of the United States.

Portius Barnett stopped his collaborators with a gesture and turned toward me, quivering.

"I take exception in the strongest terms to your behavior. You have entered here like a malefactor to steal our secrets. Whether you're French or Iroquois, no legislation can tolerate such a violation of a domicile, but that hardly matters. There is something much more serious for us: you have seen experiments whose true significance escapes you; you have heard things said that you have certainly misinterpreted; you must not, after leaving his house, bring discredit, scorn and shame upon our company. You must not! I won't stand for it! Come with me."

The philosopher dragged me into the corridor, holding me by the arm, and began to plead his case with a strange vehemence.

"We're all men of science. The promised hundred million dollars are less tempting to us than the glory of being the first to penetrate the unknown of death. Our clinicians, the most famous in the Union, are making a special study of mental maladies, and when, alas, a death occurs, my anatomists search here for the relationships that might exist between thought and anomalies of the brain. They have already made considerable discoveries in that direction."

As we came out of the main door and climbed back up to the esplanade, he went on: "But research into the substance of our organism only constitutes a tiny part of our program. Our physicists complete the work of our psychologists by studying the products of the reactions of life: fluids, radiations and waves corresponding to thought, will, the sentiments, the imagination, etc., etc.

"The results obtained with respect to that order of phenomena are surprising. From fluids, we have been led to occupy ourselves with spirits. What underlies magic and spiritualism? We have made appeals to the most authentic mages, the most renowned mediums and magnetizers, and I am forced to confess that they have achieved entirely convincing stabilizations of spirits, and isolations of souls. It only remains for us now to interpret scientifically the prodigies of their empiricism, to inaugurate the wireless telephone that will link our world to the other. We have the goal in sight; I might almost say that in my soul and consciousness, it has been attained!"

Portius Barnett stopped, as if in ecstasy, intoxicated by the emphatic speech he had just made. After a pause, I hazarded an observation timidly.

"The experiment that I was able to witness did not, it seemed to me, produce the result that you expected. Then again, I thought I remarked between your section heads a certain...I won't say hostility, but rivalry, which makes it difficult for you to reconcile their different ways of seeing. Who can ever bring into agreement spritualists, radiationists and materialists, those who believe in immortality, limited survival or annihilation?"

"Me," he replied in the tone of a man who has just made a strong resolution.

We then found ourselves near the buildings of the Physiological Department. Portius Barnett summoned his collaborators and told us to go into the experimental laboratory—the same one I which, scarcely an hour earlier, the electrician had been resuscitated. He switched all the lights on, went to the operating table, and, speaking this time with a solemn and impressive calm, said:

"Gentlemen and dear collaborators, like me you're awaiting with tortuous anxiety the definitive experiment that will unite all our efforts in a bundle of proofs affirming a unique verity. Like you, I thought that tomorrow would not dawn without your having seen the coronation of your efforts; hazard had procured us an exceptional subject; providence did not want to abandon us. Drawn in pursuit of the truth with all the ardor of our convictions, we would not have hesitated to sacrifice a life that we thought futile and miserable, in order to endow humankind with the greatest gift that it would have received since the creation of the world. An event that I cannot qualify has reminded us that we did not have the right to dispose of that life.

"Tomorrow, the man that was about to be your subject will go abroad, proclaiming that we wanted to murder him, that the establishments of our company are a lair of murderers and torturers, that our invalids are our victims, that we carry out on them, as has already been insinuated, mortal vivisections. You know, however, that I have always opposed similar research, in spite of the keen desire we all had, knowing that it was the only means by which we could resolve the formidable problem. In any case, tomorrow, opinion aroused against us will put the entire apparatus of justice in motion; your sanctuary will be violated, your laboratories sacked, your instruments put under seal; you will be put in prison, and your work—our work—will be irredeemably lost!"

A shiver ran through the audience. Once again I began to tremble for my life. It was no longer a matter of death by surprise or vengeance, but death by necessity. My disappearance had become indispensable to the smooth functioning of the Immortality Co. Ltd., and obligatory for the security of the director and his aides.

I was wondering whether, in order to abridge my suffering, I should submit to the mercy of those gentlemen's anesthetic, when the philosopher went on forcefully:

"Well, my dear collaborators, that shall not be; your hope will not be disappointed, your efforts will receive the coronation that they merit. The decisive experiment will be carried out; it will take place right now!"

A formidable cheer welcomed these words. I was surrounded. Seized by the arms, the torso and the legs, I felt myself lifted up like a feather and carried to the operating table.

With an abrupt movement, Portius Barnett had undressed and he was already lying down, holding the chloroform mask, ready to apply it to his face. I was dropped to the ground, in order that they might interrupt their master's gesture—but he pushed away those who wanted to prevent him from committing suicide.

"Leave me be—soon I shall speak to you in the evocation chamber; go to the receivers." And as they persisted, he added, very calmly: "Don't deprive me of the joy of being the first to enter into communication with you."

The disciples hesitated, and I saw that they were about to let him accomplish that act of sublime folly—but I, whose life the man had, after all, just saved twice over, leapt forward and tore the murderous mask from his hands.

"I can't," I cried, involuntarily, "be the cause of your death. I believe in the honesty and the integrity of your research! I promise you that I will only speak of it eulogistically, to destroy to the extent that I can the absurd legends that are circulating with regard to your company. I hope that an opportunity will soon arise for you to confirm your audacious hypotheses by experiment; and on that day, it is necessary that you shall be in the midst of our collaborators to receive the felicitations and thanks of all humankind!"

The philosopher John Wilfrid Theobald Portius Barnett shook my hand, without saying a word, stood up and allowed his aides to put his clothes on again. Then he asked them to provide me with a snack, took amiability as far as to offer me an overcoat and hat, and only parted from me at the door.

"Say clearly," he repeated, one last time, "that we have it: certainty!"

And the tall bond fellow added, in my right ear: "Immortality!"

While the short dark-haired men murmured to my left: "Oblivion!"

XII. Epilogue

In different parts of the Union, more discoveries were indicated to me, some more interesting than others—for instance, thinking automata, individuals provided with new senses, children obtained artificially, that of an astronomer who had succeeded in modifying universal gravity, etc., etc. Finding myself well-documented with regard to the world of the future, I thought it prudent to suspend my investigation. I therefore announced my return to the editor to the *Universal Informer*, and a few days later, I was in his office.

I experience a genuine embarrassment in reporting here the amiable words with which my boss greeted me. He wanted to thank me for my professional zeal and congratulate me on the conscientious fashion in which I had accomplished my mission. My colleagues in reportage, he affirmed, had only seen the United States superficially thus far; I had penetrated the utmost depths of the American soul, had discovered the New World for a second time, and he was on the brink of comparing me to Christopher Columbus.

My editor then handed me an enormous bundle of letters, which, not knowing my address, he had been unable to forward to me. Unknown correspondents were demanding detailed information regarding the discoveries that I made and identified, and had even attached return postage—which gave me a rather nice collection of postage stamps. The first two I opened were conceived as follows:

Brussels, 13 March 19**
Monsieur Jean Jullien,
Man of Letters,
Paris

Some time ago, I read an article signed by you in the Universal Informer regarding the Psuquet House. That article interested me greatly. I made mention of it in a paper that I recently presented to a philanthropic association. Now I have been asked to develop, *next Thursday*, the idea of the Psuquet House, which has been deemed most interesting. I am greatly embarrassed, for I only know about it what you have written. Perhaps you have taken your article from American works that deal with the subject?

I would be very grateful to you, Monsieur, if you could enlighten me by indicating the source of your information, or lending me for a few hours the publication that inspired you.

I am entirely at your disposal, Monsieur, in case I may be of some use to you; I beg you to accept my thanks in advance and to believe in my perfect consideration.

L.C.

Le C. par B., canton de Vaud,
5 April 19**
Monsieur,

As you say very clearly, there is only the New World for eminently practical inventions able to contribute to the wellbeing of the human species. The Milner Institute appears to me to hold the record among so many philanthropic works, the creation of which we witness every day. The picture of it that you have painted has awakened a keen interest in several female persons of my acquaintance, not to mention myself. You will easily understand why, Monsieur, when you know that I have five daughters to marry.

A slight doubt still subsists in my mind, however—can such an endeavor really exist? After you have made our mouths water, Monsieur, it is your duty to tell us the truth: is the Milner Institute a myth or a beneficial reality?

You will, I hope, Monsieur, want to satisfy the curiosity of a vigilant mother, and accept, along my thanks for the horizons you have opened up, the expression of my distinguished sentiments.

Madame Th. D.

After reading these letters I was stunned. I went pale and red by turns; an uncontrollable tremor had take possession of me, and I felt that I was about to faint. My editor reached out toward the button of an electric bell in order to summon help; I stopped him.

"It's nothing," I said. "You merely see me consternated to have surprised the credulity of so many good people, for, I can now confess to you, there is nothing authentic in my investigation but the two letters I have just read."

The boss burst out laughing. "Ha ha! Did you believe that I was ever taken in by your investigation?"

The compliments that he had addressed to me on arrival had permitted no doubts as to his sincerity, but he was a very clever individual, who never let himself be caught in a ridiculous situation.

"I published your articles," he concluded, "because my public prefers the implausible to the true, and, in sum, because today's utopia is tomorrow's verity."

Pierre-Simon Ballanche: *Hebal's Vision*

(1834)

The Story

A Scotsman[67] endowed with second sight had had very poor and distressing health in his youth. Sharp and continual pain had filled the entire first part of his life. Nervous accidents of a most extraordinary kind had produced the most singular phenomena of somnambulism and catalepsy. It seemed to him that the atmosphere was the general organ of his own sensations, and that all the disturbances it experienced, he experienced himself, as if they were, in some sense, passing through the sphere of his being.

More than once he had hallucinations that reconstituted momentarily the form and existence of people whose death was mourned, or which rendered present those whose absence was regretted. He saw and heard the heroes of all the ages, both those whose names were consecrated by history and those whose only reality was in fiction or poetry. The distant sound of a bell transported him swiftly into the midst of the most intimate scenes of life, sometimes in order for him to experience the gentle emotion of a gracious epithalamium which promised a happy destiny to young newlyweds, sometimes to make him shiver as if he had heard the funeral knell of an old man sated with days.

Atmospheric manifestations had a thousand things to tell him about the most distant countries. All beings and objects had a voice. It was, so to speak, the soul of Creation conversing with his own soul. He believed that he had traveled, without the intermediary of his senses, in regions of pure intelli-

---

[67] The protagonist is represented a Scotsman—or, as the original subtitle has it, "the chief of a Scottish clan"—even though Ballanche is clearly talking about himself, because "Clan Hebal" is an anagram of Ballanche.

gence. That solitary exaltation of all the physiological and psychological faculties, which was the object of so much study in the ancient mysteries and is so discredited in our day, had been produced in him by the extreme susceptibility of his painful organization. Nevertheless, that state, independent of the normal state, which constituted a different individuality, had the fortunate aspect that the illness only afflicted him without his being aware of it.

Then, no longer being contained by the bonds of subordination of creatures between themselves, and the servitude of creatures to the objects of Creation, his mind wandered freely among the worlds and among the laws governing the worlds. Like Job, it dared to ask God to account for his works, and God deigned to reply to the human thought. Then it conceived notions of time and space that it could conceive only in those moments; and then, for that thought, thus enfranchised, the ideal life was real life; and then, it was not astonished by the asceticism of India that goes as far as the most complete absorption of a human being in his cause; and then, the memory of personal facts was replaced by the memory of universal facts, and moving time became immobile eternity.

The thaumaturges who had appeared in the great epochs of transformation for the human race, the sibyls of the Romans and the druidesses of Gaul, were perhaps in contact with that mysterious chain of human destinies, all of whose rings are contained one within another. Hebal had some reason to believe in such prerogatives.

He sometimes sensed that he was in an anterior life, which mingled with the origins of the universe, and his soul marveled at the marvels of the unfathomable work of Creation.

Thus, he thought of himself as having a real existence in the past; he felt that he was assimilated to anterior humankind; eventually, he felt that he had become the general initiate of the mysteries , the universal man, living an infinite life, cosmogonically, mythically and historically.

A soul escapes the hands of God. Its astonishment in the midst of the ensemble of things, when it rejoices among incorporeal intelligence; its even greater astonishment when it is imprisoned in organs; and finally, its astonishment when it is liberated from the prison of its organs: Hebal experienced these three astonishments more than once.

His mortal life was distinct from his immortal life.

During his mortal life he woke and he slept.

And his mortal life, the symbol of his immortal life, marched in parallel with the life of the human species.

And he was conscious of the analogy between his own time with the time of the human species; and his own time, like that of humankind, was divided into cosmogonic, mythic, historic and apocalyptic times.

He went around the globe; he flew from sphere to sphere.

Everywhere at the same time, in every place, before the phenomenal manifestation of the universe and after that manifestation, he knew that he always retained the same identity, as he knew that humankind, the human species, always retained the same identity.

The ontological principle of human being is a cosmological principle, and that cosmological principle rests in the dogma of the fall and the rehabilitation.

From that emerges the analogy of epochs brought together by the mind, and which, in such states of mental exaltation, seem to be brought together in time—which enabled him to understand that everything is contemporary for a person who can conceive the notion of eternity.

Furthermore, so complete is the assimilation of the totality of human destinies with a single individual destiny that it renders everyone capable of reading them within themselves, by intuition in the past, and by the same intuition in the future.

In fact, if everyone, by virtue of an intellectual faculty developed without limit, could grasp that magnetic chain of universal, continuous human destiny, would they not have at the same instant the sentiment of that entire destiny, in the past and in the future, reflected in its entirety in the indivisible lightning-flash of the present?

Pythagoras had the instinct of a powerful assimilation such as had produced the pantheism of India, and which served to explain it. The old Italian philosophy only lacked the revelation of the ontological principle of human being, exposed in the psychological story of Moses, admirable summarized in the Genesiac history of the human species in relation to Creation.

Human beings arrived at their final hour, who, at that moment, have a kind of concentrated impression of their entire life, will also have the sentiment of their anterior life, abysmed in infinity, of their life individualized in time and the presentiment of their future life, still in possession of the consciousness acquired by the proof of the capacity for good and evil; those human beings present an image of the intelligent faculty in contact with the general chain of human destinies.

Hebal had found himself in that extraordinary situation several times. Perhaps it is the one that follows death, apparent to everyone. Perhaps it was given to him, before dying, to have visions similar to those that death itself gives.

Hebal, therefore, had an idea that he dreaded not being able to express before dying: one idea, the most difficult of all human thoughts. Often, for that reason, he employed his strength of will to resist death.

Toward the age of twenty-one, his health was restored; that state of suffering ceased, and with it that alternation of his ordinary sensations with his accidental sensations—an alternation that had previously modified all his perceptions. For several years, nothing remained to him but a nervous instability and a sensibility very easy to disturb. The notions that he had formed of time and space persisted; his meditations on collective humankind had the same consequences and the same intensity. He had retained a certain habit of isolation, which followed him even into society. He made himself a solitude in the midst of society. He was thought to be distracted when he was occupied in scaling the heights of thought or descending into the abysms of origins.

Reading poets and philosophers transported him more easily than others along all the routes traced by the imagination and science, but more often, he marked out new ones. No hypothesis regarding the successive states of the globe, the ancient o=monuments of humankind or humans and their society, was unknown to him; and according to a series of facts of which he had a profound sentiment and a sympathetic conviction, he composed his own history of the human species, one and many, evolving and identical.

One day, therefore, Hebal was absorbed in his vague contemplations of humans seeking humankind, of individual consciousness assimilating general consciousness—in sum, of human being in relation to the universes of sensation and intelligence. His eyes were glued to a clock on which time was measured by three hands, and he was attentively considering the relative progress of the three hands. He compared that little man-made clock to the great clock of the universe, whose phases are in irrefutable harmony, established by the eternal Geometer, lofty problems with which human science is ardent to measure itself.

At that moment, as was his habit, he did not hesitate to apply the notions of time and space that he had formed to his own life and to universal life—in sum, to the ensemble of human destinies contained between two infinities.

It was late summer; the dusk of evening was extending its veil of silence, of meditation, of long reverie on the subject of nature. The vision of the countryside, illuminated by the last gleam of daylight, floated before his eyes like the commencement of a dream. Indecisive and monotonous sounds came to undulate faintly on the edge of his hearing.

At every hour, the clock played a tune that was adapted to the words of the *Ave Maria*, and the tune in question was very sweet.

The little click preceding the tune was heard; the second hand precipitated itself toward the number sixteen; the hour hand was touching the ninth.

Hebal did not go to sleep, but the interior world seemed to disappear for him; his thoughts, disengaged from everything that might constrain it or mark their flight, no longer found any limit either in time or in space. A remembrance of a new kind presented itself to his mind; it was the remembrance of all the magnetic apparitions with which the first part of his life had so often be filled. The apparitions that made a point stand out from the totality of things grouped themselves together, acquiring a unity, while classifying themselves with the rapidity cleaving a cloud. There suddenly resulted from that a magnificent ideal epic, both successive and spontaneous.

And that epic took on a dithyrambic form. The strophe, as in primitive lyrical poetry, represented the sky of fixed things, the antistrophe the sky of mobile things, time and eternity, the finite and the infinite; the epode summarized the harmony of the two movements. Like Pythagoras, he saw a noble siren playing the lyre at the extremity of every circle of the celestial spheres, and the majestic cadence of the sphere combined with the cadence of all the others, and the seven fundamental numerical notes produced an endless concert, an eternal dance.

Thus, all of Hebal's visions were summarized in a single vision, and he no longer felt any desire to resist death.

I

Strophe

The centuries collapsed into an indivisible instant. The great astronomical periods disappeared like the shadow of a sundial's gnomon. The palingenetic revolutions, firstly those of the globe, then those that preceded history, and finally those that are accomplished in the presence of history and are enclosed in a chronological frame, glided like and immense and marvelous mirage. And the future succeeded the past, in order to become one with it; and dogma and myth appeared at the beginning and the end; and the first and last ages of the world died away in equally obscure horizons.

Then Hebal understood even more clearly than someone who succeeds in conceiving of eternity. He understood even more clearly that there is no succession for God; he finally understood that the divine word gives birth to all things.

It was thus that the great epic unfolded before his mind; but he read it as one expresses a single thought, a divine thought; he contemplated it with a sight that embraced all times, places, people and things simultaneously, for it was an epic in action, living the powerful and instantaneous life of evocation.

Antistrophe

Nevertheless, before the unfolding of the great epic, a light entered into Hebal's mind; and his enlightened mind had seen and felt what no language could express, for that was the authority of things.

A power existed: a power with no name, no symbol, and no image.

It was absolute, unconditional existence, abstract of any form and any limit, sufficient to itself: a spectacle impossible to describe, for it was the idea considering the idea.

And yet Hebal sensed; he sensed infinity.

And yet Hebal saw; he saw the space in which all phenomena would be.

And a hymn uncadenced by sound formed a harmony that hearing could not comprehend; and that hymn spoke the universe, which was one of God's thoughts, not yet a word.

And a light that had nothing material about it illuminated objects in the gaze of unexpressed ideas.

And time had no astronomical periods; time was undetached from eternity.

God had not put time into eternity, nor worlds in space.

God rested in his immensity, in his ineffable solitude, in his faculty of containing everything before he had produced any substance.

God was thus prior to all things, and all things emanated from him; and creation was potential prior to being enacted.

Did God have any needed to radiate outside himself, to manifest himself in things and existences? Did he need to be contemplated, worshiped, loved? Did he need to make sure of his power of realization? Was he not sufficient to himself?

Who could demand that he account for the rationale of his works?

And who could have caused him to emerge from his rest?

But he decided to emerge from his rest; he emerged therefrom without effort, without ceasing to contemplate himself.

Epode

God, before anything existed; God, then intelligent substances.

And among these intelligent substances, some were errant, and a place was necessary in order to invest them with form—the form that would serve to regenerate them by way of proof.

First, matter, with the plastic faculty.

And form became the condition of existence.

275

And God alone had no form.

And Hebal saw with an intellectual sight the globes, the spheres, the beings, and the laws of the globes, of the spheres, of the beings; and it was all nothing but the divine thought.

And he was moved by the objects that were that thought.

And it was then that the human idea, pure of all form, distraught in the divine idea, understood the form that was not, the thought that would be speech.

And it was then that, confounded in the divine idea, the human idea began to contemplate the work of creation in potential, and already the human idea, assimilated to the divine idea, found that everything was good.

Hebal, therefore, before the manifestation of things and beings by creation, had seen and felt them, dormant in the thought of God, as human thoughts are in human thought before their actual expression, with the difference that actual human thought in enslaved by perishable organs, restricted by the narrow bounds of creation, condemned never to pass over the threshold of abstraction.

Thus, eternal geometry had its laws before the worlds came to be submissive to them.

It was the same with chemical affinities, before bodies came to test them.

Thus, vegetability and animality existed before there were vegetables and animals.

Now the universe can be born; matter may emerge from nothing, and appear in various forms; organization and life may be manifest.

II

Strophe

Our paltry planet, cast into infinite space, with its laws of gravitation and projection, takes its place in the universal harmony. The word of the Creator is the mold that gives it a spherical form by virtue of those primitive laws whose effect lasts forever. An external crust hides its incandescent entrails. Great cracks break its scoriated surface. Mountains are produced with such effort that, if the earth had not been contained in the powerful mode of the word, it would have split apart, and nothing would have rolled in its desolate ellipse but sterile debris. The beds of seas are hollowed out with a similar effort. The continents take shape like vast slashes. Vegetables full of creative sap cover them, in order to elaborate a brutal atmosphere.

That atmosphere, elaborated by the plants that are the garment of the earth, which serve neither as shelter or nourishment, are to be successively appropriate to animal life in its various degrees of organization. The air and the waters are populated by various species. Plains, hills, valleys, lakes and springs reflect the light, and the clouds pour out fertile inundations. The animals that fill these astonishing solitudes fly, swim, crawl and walk, unable to encounter any masters. They devour and are devoured. They live, and breathe without admiration and love. A creation without a goal! A spectacle without spectators! A world without prayer and worship! No voice that expresses a sentiment or a thought! Confused noises! Sounds that say nothing!

Hebal's heart is gripped by fear.

But that atmosphere, rendered appropriate to animal life, needs to be, if it is permissible to put it thus, profoundly animalized, in order to be put in contact with the more delicate organs of those who will be spectators and monarchs, who will be able to know and worship, with faces turned toward the heavens. For them, the exhalations of the earth would be fatal if they arrived too soon. Climate and seasons are dormant in the chaos of a nature in search of its laws.

It required many centuries to prepare the habitation of human beings, and those silent centuries will only subsist in bleak and sad geological imprints.

Hebal thus had the impression of centuries anterior to humankind, a keen and rapid impression akin to a poignant sensation that that would kill if it endured.

He knew the science that would be the labor of human intelligence. Celestial globes traced curves that would be calculated. Other globes escaped calculation. There is one which describes a parabolic line whose term is infinite. Every globe has its name, known to God, and its laws, which he has made. Their number is equal to that of atoms without weight, measure or dimension.

Hebal sees the strata superimposed on the earth, which indicate cycles—an immensity of cycles—in the formation of the earth.

Thus, everything bears the imprint of a universal contemporaneity, which reposes in infinity. Thus, our naked and arid globe, before being organized, only knowing the eternal geometrical laws, orbits in space, with the porphyries, the granites, and the silicas that would be the beds of its seas and the escarpments of its mountains, and the humus that would be its vegetal earth. And while the earth only presents a sterile mass, and while great vegetables prepare the atmosphere thereafter, around them, for animals and humans, it travels the signs of the zodiac unwittingly, balancing on an axis that is sometimes equatorial, sometimes polar. And while the great reptiles come thereafter to slither in liberty amid those frightful wildernesses, and while, later, terrible quadrupeds reign unopposed, while light arrives in eyes devoid of intelligence, while air is respired by organs that do not know how to make sounds imprinted with thought, where is humankind? Where is the essence of humanity?

Human beings do not exist. The essence of humanity is in the thought of God.

Antistrophe

Now the divine thought decides to produce humankind. Here, bewildered human thought is refracted in a dogma like light in a prism, and yet the dogma must reflect the intimate and transcendental nature of humankind. The ideal epic affirms a mysterious fact, whose realization is ideal and mysterious. No chronology can express the time for an epoch in which the human essence is not in rapport with the external phenomena of Creation.

Hebal understands that when that essence was detached from the universal intelligent substance in order to be itself it received the gift of responsibility—which is to say, the capacity for good and evil.

And it has only received consciousness of itself in order to be a free creature, acting upon the world to complete it; its intention will be a destiny, its strength a power.

Hebal has the sentiment of an utterly marvelous physiology, a psychology more marvelous still, reposing in the bosom of a divine ontology.

From the beginning, however, human will gives birth to a destiny that Providence must break; human strength attempts a power beyond that which is attributed to it, and which, in consequence, encounters an invincible obstacle.

The laws of Providence are irrefutable; Providence reestablishes the harmony of its laws at the very moment when that harmony is threatened,

A long cry of pain escapes all the corners of the immense universe and learns that the new intelligence has succumbed to the ordeal.

Immediately, the Creator has come to the aid of his creature, and the decree of condemnation has been a decree of forbearance and mercy.

Hebal feels simultaneously the fallen being and the rehabilitated being, forming but one sole being, one identical being, reconstructing itself, condemned to march henceforth on the path of progress in order to reconquer what it has lost, the flair of its primitive ontological principle—for the principle, which alone constitutes identity, has not perished.

Epode

Fallen from their high sphere, human beings are imprisoned in organs. Labor—which is to say, a succession for further ordeals—is imposed upon them in order to replace the unknown ordeal to which they have succumbed.

And human beings, having arrived on the earth, which is given to them as a heritage, but a temporary heritage, immediately set about appropriating the earth's surface, by the labors that must change its surface. And they cover it entirely with their first generations, in order to struggle everywhere, with a unanimous effort, against all the exuberant vegetative powers, against all the animal powers that flee before them, or which they learn to subjugate to the yoke of domesticity, against the elements that they must bend and tame. And it is said that humans complete the earth; and it is said, too, that by analogy, that it is given to them to contribute to the creation of the earth. Such is the continuing labor that is far from being complete.

The globe of the earth is thus delivered to human beings, in order that they might modify it by cultivation; in order that they should go around it; in order that they should study its general and particular laws; in order that they should exercise upon it the intellectual magism that tends to spiritualize matter; in order that they should study their relationship with the phenomena of the world, with the marvelous mysteries of the world of pure intelligences; in order that they should search for the place occupied by the poor planet, their place of exile, among the celestial bodies, objects of an endless contemplation.

And human beings are divided into two sexes, and the division of sexes is a cosmogonic law from which they would have escaped, but which also becomes their law: unity broken produces succession. Evil is dispersed in the generation of being, in order to attenuate its intensity.

Humans are bound to reconstruct themselves; for them, time will reconstitute eternity.

What subsists after the fall is free will exercising itself in variety before arriving at unity; it is the power of the return to unity by expiation. And when the return is accomplished, it will become the work of rehabilitated humankind.

And the division of the sexes will be the emblem of the division of castes and classes in primitive human institutions.

Thus, therefore, the division of human faculties between the individuals that must be born of the breakage of unity is the fundamental idea of the division of castes and classes.

And all the institutors of peoples will have the sentiment of that division, which is that of the active principle and the passive principle.

From that cosmogonic event, the fall and the rehabilitation, a dogma so profoundly buried in the mystery of origins, results the separation of the sexes, the attribution of castes and classes, and the distinct characteristics of races.

The passive sex will doubtless achieve equality with the active sex, since it belongs to the same original essence. That equality cannot be perfect, since the physiological difference with continue to exist.

Thus the emblem of castes and classes will survive castes and classes, which ought to be abolished by the virtue of Mediation.

And human identity attests its Genesiac unity, and prophecies its definitive unity.

All these notions, Hebal had intuitively, and he knew again the succession of cosmogonic time, mythic time and historic time. Nevertheless, an immobile thought of eternity came to mingle with the mobile thought of time, that all those times issued from one another would be perpetually reproduced, since the human species is always identical and what it was in the past it will be throughout the future.

Hebal's contemplation is uninterrupted.

III

Strophe

Before the commencement of historic times, therefore, humans covered the entire earth. There were incessantly occupied in solidifying ground that crumbled beneath their steps, directing rivers, clearing forests, limiting the domain of animals and making fire and iron obedient.

And universal traditions speak of six cosmogonic days, which are six great revolutions brought about by frightful cataclysms.

And God was said to have rested on the seventh day—which is to say, to be confined to the irrefutable laws that he had imposed upon all things. And it was by virtue of condescension for a being become successive that the names of parts of phenomenal time were given to his divine actions.

And humans were said to have a facial resemblance to God, for it was given to them to comprehend the laws imposed on things.

And the divine breath had produced primitive human speech, a fugitive image of immortal thought.

And humans named things and beings; they named God. They did not know the intimacy of things, but the relationships of things to themselves, and their knowledge was thus restricted because they had succumbed to the ordeal of the capacity for good and evil. They had to achieve it one day because rehabilitation placed them on the path of progress.

In order to arrive at the intimacy of things and beings, however, it is necessary for humans to begin with self-knowledge, for it is a key that opens the treasures of Creation.

Furthermore, to arrive at a knowledge of God, it is necessary for humans to study in themselves their resemblance to God.

Now God has no need of a sign to know himself; the subjective faculty and the objective faculty are not separate in absolute existence.

Humans, being successive, need a sign in order to take account of their own intelligence. In them, the subjective faculty and the objective faculty are not simultaneous.

Hence, for them, the necessity of speech.

Antistrophe

Such were human beings; such are they still.

And they shivered and they labored.

And woman, who had emerged from the flesh of man during a magnetic sleep, and who was given to him as a companion, gave birth in pain.

And the evil was dispersed and subdivided, in order that it might lost its intensity.

And human beings had only been separated into two sexes in order to be subjected, by succession, to the sole ordeal by which their faculties were troubled.

And woman was said to have led man into temptation, because woman is the volitional expression of humankind.

And the ancient anathema weighed upon human beings because they were unable to master, in their volitional faculty, the capacity for good and evil—without which, however they would not have be able to accomplish God's plan for them.

And reason was subjugated and enslaved for not having been able to tame the will.

And women, in all cosmogonies, were said to have introduced evil to the earth.

And the Redeemer was promised to humans at the very moment of their fall; and the Redeemer was to emerge from the volitional faculty of humans—which is to say, from women.

And men were the active sex, and women the passive sex, and their souls are equal, for men and women are of the same essence.

And prayer and Redemption unite in order to bring human back to the lost unity, and the unity remains in potential, and, veiled, produces solidarity and charity.

283

Epode

Hebal only had intelligence of these marvels at the moment when the curtain of historic times was lifted for him.

Nevertheless, historic times were still far off; Hebal could only see them in the future, but that future was beginning to be sketched out in the distance.

Universal traditions relate that the earth was accursed because of human beings, and yet beings had populated it before them.

The revelation was not given to present humans of what it is good for them to know or to discover, in order that they might be subjected to the ordeal of mystery.

Hebal could not go any further, for he had not passed through the palingenesis of death.

And all the principles that constitute the diversity of human beings are manifest in the generations that precede the cataclysm attested by the memory of the entire human species.

A first victim and a first murderer, and it is the first murderer who founds the first city; and the first city is a shelter, and the first legislator is a fratricide: a terrible symbol!

And the institutors of religion, and the inventors of arts, and those who are called giants, and those who receive the title of the children of God, and Lamech, the other murderer, and Enoch rise up to the heavens: who will attempt to explain all of that antediluvian cosmogony?

And the earth is threatened with a return to ancient chaos—but God would not want to abolish the ordeal inflicted upon the human species.

Noah collects, under the eyes of the Creator, the seeds and principles of all things, of all organization, of all life; he collects them seven times.

And the mysterious ark floats on the great waters.

And human beings, emerging from the ark, are required to remake the earth and the climates of the earth.

And human generations disperse over the entire earth.

284

They divide up the earth and the climates of the earth.

The human language is broken and divided; the human races share out among themselves the debris of the human tongue.

The human races are characterized by the blessings and curses of the forefathers of the human races.

Now the aurora of historical times is beginning to shine.

And historic times will unfold in turn before Hebal, and be explained by intelligence of original and Genesiac facts, for the human species is identical to itself.

And it was proved to Hebal that human essence had cosmogonic time as well as the globe.

And he was able to focus his attention on historic facts.

And historic facts are posed with a sad majesty, like a single fact, a continuous fact that finds the cause of its developments within itself.

And ordeal and initiation, redoubtable testimony of primitive dogma, were but a tissue of long, interminable calamities; without the history that precedes any chronology, how could Hebal know the reason for so many scourges, so many misfortunes, for war, slavery, the division of classes and castes, for anguish, for death?

What! So close to the cradle of the human race, and already there are great empires, powerful peoples, vast metropolises! And already seeds are falling on the threshing-floor, and the threshing floor has been swept more than once by the terrible harvester! It is because centuries have passed without Hebal perceiving them, because they have scarcely left a trace in human memory. And those unknown founders, and those nameless conquerors, and those events which were not sung by any poet: all that is dust. Behold, an old world has disappeared; but human beings survive; they survive with their traditions, their castes, their social forms.

And all the forefathers of the human race, dispersed over the entire earth, have been named by primitive tradition, which is a general tradition; and their names express the faculties that characterized them, the secrets of which they were the custodians, the missions that the peoples issued from them have accomplished.

In addition to the cosmogonic time of the entire human race there are the cosmogonic times of individual races, of individual countries, of every individual of the human race.

And at every step the great problem poses itself: where is the cradle of the human race? Where is the cradle of each individual race? Where is the cradle of each individual human?

But everywhere human thought is being imprinted on monuments, impregnating the soil, like the resemblance of God on the human face.

Hebal is plunged into religious admiration. The universal mystery does not astonish him, because it has been given to him suddenly to penetrate the ontological and cosmological principle of human being; because he knows, by virtue of a sudden and spontaneous illumination, what human essence is in the harmony of the worlds; because, at that moment, all the traditions spread over the surface of the earth make him hear a unanimous cry of assent; and because, finally, contact with the chain of universal destinies has stirred within him all the power of conviction, all the sympathy of identity.

Then he understands the mystery of language, which is articulate sound, sound magnetized in every vocal apparatus by every human being, by every human faculty, by the thought that God had revealed to his sleep.

Then an inspired analysis enables him to decompose the great synthesis that rests in all human languages.

Then he finds in the roots of words the permanent expression of revelation and spontaneity; in grammatical form the varied expression of human reason, the issue of divine reason; in trope and rhythm the expression of the imagination in relation to the spectacle of the earth and the heavens, with nature and beings; in all that marvelous ensemble, the symbol, the inspiration, the music, the poetry, the prophetic faculty exercising itself on the past and the future, a spontaneous, free, progressive psychology of humanity.

IV

Strophe

The mission of the Hebrew people is revealed to Hebal. He recognizes the patriarchs, depositories of the ancient promise.

With Moses he visits the sanctuaries of Egypt, and with him, he extracts his people from the house of servitude to lead them through the desert to the promised land.

The Ark of the Covenant, the stations in the desert, the wandering tribes, the troubles, the battles, the returns to idolatry, everything is symbolic. It is the type and image of the initiation of the human species.

Hebal had recognized Abraham, the pontiff king, that priest of Salem, that king of justice, Melchisedech, of whom the generation before and after have remained unknown, and who was dressed in eternal sacerdocy.

He sight had been dazzled on Sinai.

He had heard Isaac, Ezekiel and Jeremiah.

Daniel had recounted the potential events that occur in heaven before passing into action on earth.

And the people had wearied of the government of God, and Samuel had decreed all the prerogatives of royalty. Kings had sat, first on the throne of Judea, then on the thrones of Israel and Judea; and all the laws that rule dynasties and people had been known.

How beautiful were the days of Esdra and Nehemiah!

How beautiful were the days when the Jews, raising the walls of Jerusalem, held a trowel in one hand and a sword in the other, as they had once celebrated the Passover without setting down the traveler's staff.

And the glorious family of Maccabees excited an immense admiration.

And the time of the accomplishment of the promise approached; and the promise resounded increasingly in the world; and the promise took on several diverse forms among the nations.

One glance sufficed to embrace seventy times seven years.

And around these great events, which are the axle of the marvelous wheel of human destiny, grate occasional distant rumors: they are empires that rise and fall; they are obscure and dazzling dynasties that perish enveloped in the same darkness; they are peoples who disappear as if they had never existed. How many times, in different places, have terrible anathemas been pronounced, fatal words written by an inflexible hand on the walls of the banqueting hall where a pitiless dominator is rejoicing! But Egypt, the empire founded by Nimrod, Phoenicia, Tyre and Sidon, the memories of which remain solely in the prophecies that condemned great metropolises to perish! Where are Sesostris and Alexander? Has the eye time to follow a flash of lightning through the cloud? And yet, something remains of Alexander: he transported the Orient into Egypt. And yet, something remains of Egypt: an immense realization of death, all human science becoming a vast mute hieroglyph.

Antistrophe

The Pelasges have marked the first transition of the Orient to the Occident; the Hellenes have created fantasy. The heroic centuries are but a memory.

Moses, Orpheus and Buddha have divided the empire of human intelligence between themselves.

The expedition of the Argonauts, the war of the Epigones and the ruin of Troy form a poetic beacon on the far historical horizon, where one still perceives the personifications of races and the migrations that will be illustrious Greece.

Seven cities have disputed the birth of Homer, but Hebal has searched in vain for the marvelous old man.

Those songs which acquire a name, which put on a face, which become a poet, show Hebal how each people strives to make it epic, how each race strives to make its own, how all these successive epics must end up producing the general epic of the human race, how the thought of that definitive epic, one in its magnificent diversity, is nothing other than the very thought of the universal religion.

The gigantic conceptions of the Orient have come to be founded in Greek anthropomorphism.

The heroic races have disappeared from the soil that they fashioned with their strong hands, and they have let monuments that will cause subsequent ages to say: how powerful were those who preceded us on the earth!

Hebal's attention is scarcely attracted to the murmurs in the public square of Athens. It is entirely focused on the struggle between the Dorian and Ionian principles that is manifest in the Peloponnesian war; he sees therein the antagonism between destiny and the human will; if Sparta tries in vain to stereotype heroic civilization, it is also in vain that Athens exaggerates human emancipation.

But although the death of three hundred Spartans at Thermopylae was futile for Greece, it is still useful to the world, for noble actions are the solace of minds.

Socrates drinks the hemlock; the tearful genius of Greece turns away, knowing that a people that kills its prophets is doomed.

The tragic muse and the comic muse have caused their accents to resound. The lyric muse can no longer excite masculine courage. Eloquence has lost its power; the reign of the sophists has begun.

The mysteries of Eleusis are staged.

The sibyl of Delphi is no longer the expression of national amphictyony.

The Greeks are no more now than the soldiers of Philip and Alexander; and Greece will end up as a Roman province.

Aristotle and Plato hasten to bequeath to the future, one the world of fact and science, the other the world of ideas and art.

Such is the brilliant episode of Greece.

The movement of Greece was aborted; Hebal knew why; it is because human will, on its own, is inadequate to achieve its initiation.

Nevertheless, Greece has saved the progressive and plebeian principle of which it was the custodian.

The democrat of Athens, who have committed so many errors in Sicily, on the shores of Great Greece, who were so stupid and improvident, who let Socrates drink the hemlock, who lulled themselves with the harmonious satires of Aristophanes, were nevertheless well worthy of the Occident. They vanquished the great king at Salamis. The victory of Salamis still reigns over the world.

That is not all; they created art, and art is the noble crown of plebeian genius.

Epode

All the empires of the Orient are static.

The progressive destinies of the Occident date from the era of the Olympiads, but their development is considerably anterior.

The events are distinct; nevertheless, they appear together before thought, which embraces them all simultaneously.

Thus Hebal sees at the same time a domination born that will succeed all others, the one that will one day give birth to the modern world.

Old Evander and blind Thamyris, amid the hill of future Rome, talk about an unknown future.

A cloud that passes over the Pelasges and the Sicules prevents their perception.

Here again Hebal was astonished to see that the beginning of human affairs is never the beginning of human destinies, and that history is always obliged to sink into the horizon of myth.

V

Strophe

Where, then, is the cradle of the Roman people? Is it from the lair of a she-wolf or a nest of brigands that the people will emerge who will subjugate the world? And will not the world one day be the Roman world? A first king, who is a fratricide, founds the eternal city, establishes marriage by abduction—and no one knows how Romulus died, because he vanished in a storm.

A second king provides a religion, but science searches in vain for the rites of the religion provided by Numa. Hebal, however, sees the ruminal fig-tree, the goat's marsh, and the wood and spring of Egeria. He sees the field where the three brothers of Rome battled the three brothers of Alba.

Another king plants in Roman soil the legal branch that will become the great plebeian tree.

Hebal turns his gaze to the rascal path—and shields fall from the sky! And the Tarquins! And Lake Regilla! And Horatius Cocles! And Porsena! And Mutius Scevola! And Junius Brutus! And Lucretius! And Tarquin dying in exile!

Hebal turns his gaze again, but Brutus does not turn his own. And each king is a personification of a social entity; and these marvelous personifications complete the powerful number seven, which is a cosmogonic and planetary number. All these symbolic royalties succeed one another in a dubious twilight, which is no longer night but not yet day. And every origin goes back to exposed children and fratricides: a primitive emblem of the violence of the social condition. Ordeal! Initiation!

And the law of the Twelve Tables, the august debris of an anterior law! It governed before being; it will govern after having been.

And the new people is obliged to battle incessantly to conquer its own territory.

And in the midst of the various events of that continuous war, three fats stand out like three luminous points. They are the plebeian secessions. The first, in the Aventine, produces conscience; the second, on the Crustumerian Mount, produced marriage; the third produces dignity. Thus the plebeian is the human making itself. And Hebal follows all the phases of that antagonism of the stationary principle and the progressive principle, an antagonism that it a law of the fallen and reha-bilitated human species, which is the hidden spring of Roman history, and of all history.

Antistrophe

Rome and Carthage dispute the empire of the world.

Hannibal and Scipio acquire immortal glory.

The Gauls believe that they have stifled the Roman giant, but it has too great a destiny to accomplish.

The Gracchi show their imposing and noble face, bright with the flame of Prometheus, which will consume them. And Marius and Sulla, and Caesar and Pompey share out the bloody shreds; civil war—a single civil war—covers the world. Pharsalia and Actium decide the possession of the world.

And the tribunal, born obscurely of the first plebeian se-cession, after having grown in discord and in war, is personi-fied, and becomes an emperor. And Octavian, in the name of Augustus, reins without division. The imperial purple hides his crimes; all the perfumes of an imitative poetry burn at his feet. Horace and Virgil charm the world for a long time.

Epode

The world is at peace. Peoples rest in a universal truce, which does not last long. The oracles of the Romans fall silent. The sibyls, having become foreign to an old world that will perish, can no longer do anything but promise nations the Desideratum; the nations are expectant.

And various voices are heard.

"I shall summon, the Orient, which is my servant."

"Where is the Desideratum of the eternal hills? Let him appear?"

"Heavens! Pour your dew from on high, and let the clouds weep Justice!"

"How beautiful are the feet of the one who brings the great redemption!"

And the Etruscans told the Romans that the Peacemaker would be born of a virgin.

A woman would encompass a man, and that woman would be *the* woman, and that man would be *the* man.

And that man would have the name Emanuel, God with is.

And the sibyls speak like Isaiah and David.

The prophets that bring word of the Mediator form but a single word, and that word expresses all of human destiny throughout the extent of time, time posed upon eternity, and that word, again, which is simultaneously cosmogonic and apocalyptic, which unites the marvel of heaven, earth and the universe with the marvels of the one and identical humanity, escapes from all the depths of Creation.

Hebal knew the perpetual and endless sacrifice, which is a peaceful sacrifice, not bloody.

Nevertheless, there would be flesh and blood at the moment of the manifestation of the sacrifice for the human race, fallen and regenerated.

And a great frisson ran through all of Hebal's organs, and the frisson was that of all Creation gripped by a dolorous sympathy for the future that will be the present.

VI

Strophe

And the volitional faculty of humans, concentrated in a weak woman, who is purity itself, receives the spirit of God; the Creator identifies with his creature; the Redemption promised to human beings at the very moment of their fall is born of a virgin. He has been conceived without the collaboration of a man, and he is called the Son of Man. Bethlehem, an obscure but predicted place, is the royal city. A stable is the palace of the Child's promised to the nations. Oriental Magi and poor shepherds surround his cradle. Angels bring him the adoration of the heavens.

Hebal is sunk deep in a divine ecstasy. His prayer is of love. The universal mystery does not astonish him because it has been given to him to penetrate the ontological principle of human being, because he knows what humankind is in the harmony of worlds, because all the traditions spread over the surface of the earth cause him to hear a unanimous cry of assent, because contact with the chain of human destinies has stirred within him all the power of conviction, and because he has been inundated by the glory of the heavens.

The divine Child grows up in wisdom and all kinds of perfection. His mother searches for him, and finds him among the doctors.

Christ is baptized in the waters of the Jordan by the holy precursor, and a voice from heaven proclaims him the Son of God.

The spirit of temptation shows him, from the tower of the temple, the kingdoms of the earth, and he disdains the kingdoms of the earth. Hebal also feels pity for the splendors of the dust, for he has just glimpsed the splendors of heaven.

The spirit of temptation transports into the desert the one who will animate the desert, and the spirit of temptation flees the Desideratum of the nations.

The Savior cures the sick, resuscitates the dead, converts the fishermen, calms the tempests.

And the crowd follows in the Savior's footsteps.

And his immense forbearance confounds the accusers of the adulterous woman.

And he promises the Samarian that spring of fresh water that staunches thirst eternally. The time comes, and has already come, when people will no longer worship here or there, but in mind and in truth.

And he is with Martha and Mary, and with the sister of Lazarus.

And he allows a woman to wash his feet with perfumes.

And he takes his pleasure with the children of humankind, bearing their burdens, loving them until death. He weeps with them; with them he eats the bread that is their customary nourishment; with them he drinks the wine that is their joy and their strength.

And he does not disdain the publicans; and every soul is dear to him.

And he explains to Nicodemus the great mystery of rebirth in spirit, the mystery of the new humankind, but Nicodemus cannot understand it yet.

The Messiah is transfigured on the Tabor; the glare of his garments dazzles Hebal's eyes.

Here he is entering Jerusalem in triumph; the mount of the triumphant pacifier is a donkey. And he weeps in Jerusalem, for the day has come.

And he celebrates the last Passover with his disciples. He institutes the Last Supper by pronouncing the word that, throughout the ages, will make of his body and blood a perpetual and endless sacrifice.

Antistrophe

And Hebal remembers the mystic lamb immolated at the commencement of the world; and he understands that the mystery of regeneration is an ever-present cosmogonic mystery.

And he remembers too that bread and wine are very powerful emblems among all peoples. And he tells himself that the word Eucharist expresses grace and love.

And while Christ institutes the universal religious marriage, he leans on the shoulder of his beloved disciple. And the Savior of humankind sympathizes with the one who will betray him.

Sweat and blood run over his face in the Garden of Olives, because he is appropriating all pain and all sin to himself.

He keeps vigil and he prays, and his disciples succumb to sleep, for fatigue overwhelms the children of humankind.

Soldiers come to arrest him, and the prince of the apostles tries to defend his Master, but the Master orders him to sheath his sword.

And the price of the treason has been thirty deniers. And the one who has received the price of the treason does not want to keep them, and the priests buy the potter's field with them—and an ancient prophecy is fulfilled.

And the prince of the apostles denies his Master three times.

Now the prince of the apostles was a poor fisherman.

And the Son of the Virgin appears before the human judge.

And he is crowned with thorns. A reed scepter is placed in his hands. A scarlet cloak covers his bruised shoulders. He is delivered to outrages and mockery. And it is said to him: Behold the man.

And a murderer is preferred to him.

And an entire people demands his blood, and an entire people cries out, to call upon itself and its children the blood of the innocent.

And he walks to Calvary bearing his cross, and tells the women who follow him not to weep for him.

And only one man helps him to bear his cross, who is not one of his disciples.

And a woman wipes the bloody sweat from his beautiful face.

And he is nailed to the tree of opprobrium, with this inscription: Jesus of Nazareth, King of the Jews.

And he is placed between two malefactors.

And he promised to one of the two the kingdom of heaven.

And thirst devours him, but a soldier only offers him gall and vinegar to drink.

Another soldier opens his side with the iron of a spear.

He complains of being abandoned by his celestial Father.

And men say to him. mockingly, that since he can work miracles, he ought to make use of one in order to descend from the cross.

He commends his mother to his beloved disciple.

He utters a loud cry, and then, lowering his head, he says that all is consummated.

And when the Human-God renders the last sight on Golgotha, a groan is heard similar to that which burst forth at the moment of the fall; and that groan immediately becomes a canticle of love and gratitude.

And the gods of the nations flee, and the oracles of the Romans fall silent.

Epode

The unfathomable mystery of the expiation is accomplished.

The veil of the temple is torn away. Darkness covers the earth. The stones of sepulchers stir.

The heavens open, and Hebal hears the repercussion of the endless hymn, the hymn of reconciliation, the hymn of the lamb immolated at the commencement of the world.

The earth is in view of all the celestial spheres.

And voices among the people say: He was truly the Just.

And he is taken down from the cross. And lots are cast for his garments, in order to recall the last of the ancient prophecies related to him.

And he is laid in a new sepulcher.

A stone is placed on his sepulcher, and soldiers watch in order that the body should not be removed.

But if the mystery of rehabilitation has been accomplished on earth for living men, and for those yet to be born, it has not been accomplished for the generations that sleep in the tomb.

Christ goes to Hell to undo the ancient anathema of the generations that have lived on the earth, and the virtue of expiation frees the past.

Destiny is vanquished in that which is most irrevocable; it is vanquished in death.

And the human species, from the commencement of time until the end, participates in the rehabilitation.

And great joy bursts forth in heaven.

And on the third day, Christ is resuscitated among the dead.

And the soldiers will have guarded the sepulcher in vain, which will remain empty until the consummation of the centuries.

And the Resurrected reappears among his disciples, and grants them the gift of tongues, and tells then to go and name his name among all the peoples.

And he rises up again into the glory of his Father.

And all of human destiny, in the past and in the future, in time and outside time, is summarized and transfigured in the life of the one who wanted to be the sin in order to be the salvation, to be the fault in order to be the forgiveness, the one who was made in our image in order that we might become his.

Hebal has the true intelligence of human being, of the universal religion of humanity.

VII

Strophe

The disciples of the Crucified cover the earth in order to spread the accomplishment of the promise, as the forefathers of the human race covered the earth in order to populate it at the commencement of the race.

And they will have, like them, the gift of tongues.

And the ancient traditions remain identical to the traditions of the promise.

Stephen, the first martyr, sees the heavens open while he is stoned by the people; a fanatic keeps his garments.

And the first martyr is the type of all those who bear witness.

And the one who keeps the garments of the first martyr will be the apostle of the nations.

And he fisherman of Judea who had denied his Master three times comes, with a traveler's staff, to shake the dust of his feet over the gods of the nations, and the gods of the nations fall.

And the persecutor who was vanquished by the spirit of God on the road to Damascus goes to preach the unknown God in the city of Plato, which has become the city of sophists.

And Saint John, on the Isle of Patmos, has the revelation that would show him the entire series of human destinies.

Jerusalem hosts the first Council.

Seven churches in Asia Minor will found Christian initiation for the Orient.

It was founded in the catacombs of Rome for the Occident.

And the fisherman of Judea sealed with his blood the faith that would govern the world.

And the persecutor who became the apostle of the nations sealed with his blood a religion still devoid of rites.

And Hebal sensed then the great work of regeneration operating simultaneously throughout a world grown old.

And the world grown old will renew itself under the name of Christendom.

And the new humankind has seen what Nicodemus was unable to comprehend, seen in solitude and in the family, in private and public life; unknown virtues will come to astonish the sages of the era.

And misfortune will no longer be an opprobrium.

Antistrophe

Nevertheless, at the edge of the world, which was still the Roman world, in the Northern seas, unknown seas, there is an island conquered by Caesar's arms; and at the edge of that petty universe, there remains a rock on which the Roman eagle has never been raised. As long as liberty finds a foothold, as long as it can take flight from the smallest eyrie, in order to extend its flight from there over a thousand countries, in order to make its powerful voice resound there and awaken peoples bent beneath the yoke of slavery, it is permissible to hope.

Three terrible cries resound from the banks of the Tiber to the lakes of Caledonia. The first is to declare the world submissive. The second cry announces that a rock has remained inaccessible to the arms of the masters of the world; and the masters of the world are indignant, and the peoples make vows. And generous sympathies are also a power. Roman grandeur began by means of a refuge; the genius of liberation can commence by means of a refuge. Rome assembles all the energy of its destiny to vanquish a rock. The force that has subjugated the world breaks momentarily against the rock like a vast sea against a grain of and. But the grain of sand disappears at the third cry. Liberty no longer has anywhere to place its foot. Thus, Caledonia was for the entire world what Thermopylae had been for Greece. Sonorous Harp of the Bard, fall silent in the presence of universal despotism.

Epode

Undoubtedly, Hebal had his eyes fixed from afar on the mountains of Erin, when he saw such a resurrection of such a glorious past.

But he is tranquil, for he knows that liberty does not inhabit a rock, and that a new generation has it in its heart.

Political liberty, one day, will give birth to the liberty that gives birth to regeneration.

The fatality resulting from the fall will be abolished.

Thus, firstly, the struggle of humankind against the forces of nature.

Then, the struggle of human liberty against Destiny.

Then, the accord of Providence and human liberty.

Then, finally, charity substituted for solidarity.

And the universal religious marriage, symbol of symbols, perpetual and endless immolation, peaceful sacrifice that summarizes, completes and annuls all sacrifices, is the great expression of the religion of humanity.

VIII

Strophe

The vanquishers of the masters of the world are hidden in the catacombs of Rome itself.

And the Tarpeian Rock, which was for so long the Caucasus of the Occident, sees the irons that keep the emancipator captive quietly eroded.

Three bloody persecutions attest the grandeur of Christian initiation. And the blood of martyrs spilled immeasurably is an immeasurable seeding. And all the martyrs resemble Stephen.

And Jerusalem falls, as if into a gulf of blood and fire.

And Palmyra, built by Solomon, disappears into desert.

And Zenobia has passed through the three great initiations of the human species.

Other events are scarcely noticed by Hebal.

While Mithridates opposed to the Romans the last resistance of cunning and a will of iron, Odin, followed by his brave companions, launched forth from the shore of the Black Sea to the shores of the Baltic, and created a religion that would be the bloody religion of Scandinavia.

And the Barbarians who were to renew the face of the Roman Empire increase in ignored climates.

And Roman corruption is equal to is grandeur.

Antistrophe

Hebal finds an immense distraction in the Museum of Alexandria; there he witnesses the entire evocation of a past that is not destined to perish. And all the theurgical philosophies that have stirred human intelligence from Empedocles to Apollonius of Tyana appear to be eclipsed by Christian philosophy.

And all religions appear to affirm the universal religion of the human species.

It is at this moment that Hebal sees rising before him a world that he had previously misunderstood.

It is at this moment that the Orient and the Occident recount their mutual adventures, adventures that are the whole of human destiny.

The Himalayas, Sinai, the Caucasus, the Taurus and the Tarpeian Rock form the horizon of the old world simultaneously evoked by all the sibyls, all the prophets, all the philosophers and all the beliefs that die and are born, by all the sacerdotes who finish and commence.

What! The Indian Trimurthi in the Himalayas!

What! The Thracians of Samothrace fleeing the transparent seas of Greece and coming to settle amid the chaos of ice and fire that is scarcely distinguished in the misty sea of Iceland.

What! Prometheus lying chained to the steep summits of the Caucasus!

What! All fables taking on reality! And myth, in the distances of humanity, projecting great shadows equal to dogma!

"Woe betide him who scandalizes!" says a voice.

But the Himalayas, the Caucasus, the Taurus and the Tarpeian Rock fade away in the thunder and lightning of Sinai.

Sinai itself fades away in the ravishing splendors of Tabor,

Hebal knew the perpetual prophecy of the Hebrew tongue.

He knew the absolute existence revealed with the name of Jehovah.

He knew the identity of the human species in all eras, manifest by the intimate sentiment of the Mediator.

He knew the Old and the New Testament.

He knew the accord of the Persians with the Hebrews, the Egyptians and the Greeks with the Syrians.

He saw that Alexander had wanted to reconstruct Syrianism and Hellenism.

He understood that had Socrates died for the logos.

Finally, he knew where the insufficiency of various epicisms lay: those of schools founded by human wisdom, those which reposed in ancient sanctuaries and those of which the priesthoods of the gentility were custodians

And Constantine caused the Christian religion to pass from the status of a secret religion to that of public religion. He enunciated a fact that fallen Roman grandeur had hidden, for he was the one who write the lat regulations of the auguries.

Hebal sought the *labarum* in the air; but the cross of the Savior of men projected a divine light from the heights of Golgotha, which illuminated the entire horizon of the human world.

And Julian wanted to go backwards and attempted a labor beyond human strength. And a fine genius and a noble character fell into opprobrium and absurdity.

Epode

Hebal had followed the long struggle between Christianity and Paganism, and that struggle was over; but another was about to begin.

Humans were in possession of a subjectivity assimilated to their consciousness; they would battle for the forms of the objective.

Such is the reason for the heresies that divide the empire of mind.

And the Barbarians come to disperse the debris of the old societies.

And Mohammed suddenly appears in the world.

And Africa is erased from the map of civilization.

And Europe will find itself squeezed between the already-pallid religion of Odin and that of Mohammed, bursting with youth.

And the religion of Mohamed rolls its waves as far as the fields of Touraine. There it encounters a hero who causes it to retreat, as, much later, the battle of Lepanto will conclude its action in Europe.

Hebal hears again the splintering of empires, and the entire mythology of the Middle Ages is grouped around Charlemagne, and shines alone in the darkness.

And while Hebal collects so many things in his mind, the empire of Charlemagne crumbles in the bosom of that same darkness.

And Pépin, the mayor of the palace—which is to say, the tutor of kings and military leader—and Abbé of Paris, comes to the throne.

And the successors of the fisherman of Judea protect the people against the strong feudal hierarchy, working at the same time to create a universal monarchy.

Then was manifest the principle of two powers. Hildebrand, by the ascendancy of faith, wanted to bind the temporal principle to the spiritual principle.

And the temporal principle resisted; and interminable struggle was engaged for centuries.

What a task, incessantly suspended and resumed, was that of developing the great French unity, preparing for the government of peoples by means of mores and opinions!

And the crusades posed the barrier, within the shelter of which Europe was able to constitute itself.

And St. Louis founded modern civilization.

And Christian principles reigned briefly in Jerusalem.

And Constantinople fell to the power of the Turks.

And the modern world, which already had a spontaneous literature, received from fugitive Greeks the movement of a literature of imitation.

French unity would have been stifled by implacable divisions if the principle of that unity, necessary to the direction of the new destinies of Europe, had not been marvelously identified by a magnanimous virgin, a providential sibyl, who triumphed and died on a pyre.

America is discovered; Galileo founds experimental philosophy; two worlds open up, one of commerce, the other of science.

And pious humanity veils its face before the calamities of a world increased in size by an entire hemisphere.

And China and Japan, visited by missionary scholars, provide human facts that serve to complicate and clarify the immense question of origins.

The Iberian peninsula disengages itself from Moorish domination and extends its own over the old and new hemispheres.

Hebal saw all those things simultaneously, and heard all the discourses at the same time.

IX

Strophe

And Luther's schism arrives to alarm beliefs already shaken by mores.

The shadows of those who preceded that powerful heresiarch seem to wake up in their tombs to say: "It was in vain, then, that we have been murdered and mutilated by iron and fire! It was in vain that Gothicism has been downed in the blood of the Albigenses! One can kill entire nations but one cannot kill ideas!"

And the Jesuits begin a great empire, which has its provinces all over the world.

And humanity and religion veil their face, for the earth is inundated anew with blood in the name of all that is holiest upon the earth. And still: one can kill people, but one cannot kill ideas.

And the long reign of Louis XIV shines at first with great brightness, and then fades away in sad misery.

Kings of Europe, how did you witness without emotion the scaffold of Mary Stuart? Now see Charles I climbing in his turn on to the same scaffold.

Have Oliver Cromwell and Milton taught you nothing?

Do you know what Peter I is doing in the construction yards of Amsterdam? Terrible among the terrors of an unknown north, he is about to reveal an empire that will one day menace many empires.

It is in Constantinople that the keys to Europe and Asia are deposited. The stupid Turk is keeping them for whoever will be able to take them.

And Descartes and Bacon give birth to the eighteenth century.

And the French Revolution comes to complete the mission of the eighteenth century.

And the cup of misfortunes is poured out over France, and the intoxication of glory is no consolation.

And a great victim has fallen.

And a man of old launches himself upon the world stage.

He reconstructs Charlemagne's empire, and he wants to take ideas backwards as he has taken the idea of power backwards.

And the battles he fights are battles of giants.

And the spirit of the French nation retreats to resemble the one that Julian desired.

And twice he loses the empire, and twice his fall shakes the world.

He dies on a rock lost in the immense seas of the Atlantic, a tomb worthy of a Titan.

And the exile has brought back liberation by expiation.

And the volitional principle and the fatal principal recommence the struggle that had been suspended by the captive of St. Helena, when he reigned over peoples and kings.

And the Restoration, unwittingly, has been the age of the emancipation of thought.

And the Restoration has been completely misunderstood by those who ought to be protecting it.

And the dynasty was considered as a cause and not as an instrument.

And the rebellious instrument was broken by a sudden and spontaneous effort.

And lightning would not have been as prompt. And a multitude acted as one man, like a single intelligence.

House of France, you have tried to conserve the ancient fatality from which Providence had resolved to free you, because it had resolved to free the world.

A silence follows: the silence of admiration.

And the peoples recount in the distance the victory of a great multitude, which was but one man, a wise and powerful man.

And the old kings have retired into exile, and have excited profound pity, for it has been understood that they were devoid of intelligence and misunderstood their mission.

Nevertheless, in these days of crisis in which an entire people expresses itself by a sudden and unpremeditated movement, it is a mystery that will challenged minds until it has emerged from its solemn obscurity. Human societies advance incessantly; incessantly, a past is destroyed, and a future forms. Successive manifestations constitute palingenetic epochs. At these epochs, human societies are bound to divine a double enigma, the general enigma of humankind, and the enigma of the present ordeal: it is at that price alone that they are assured of progress.

Thus the spontaneous Sphinx of the barricades has flown from the Louvre to the Tuileries, and from the Tuileries to the Hôtel-de-Ville.

Who will have the sentiment of the social transformation, perhaps accomplished prematurely? In whom will the thought of all be assimilated? Who will declare the right resulting from the unexpected event? Who will force the accidental concrete to produce the normal abstract?

Hebal is not mistaken in this respect. Two stages of initiation have been overtaken simultaneously. The law of successive development intends that humans should atone for a step taken without a preparatory ordeal. Hebal foresees great disturbances. But the law of progress is so powerful that it will finish up reestablishing harmony.

And the struggle of the volitional principle and the fatal principle will recommence between France and Europe.

An entirely new Europe must emerge from the former Europe, still clad in worn-out institutions as in an old cloak.

An apparent incredulity threatens to abolish all belief; but the religion of the human species will be reborn, more brilliant and more beautiful.

It will be reborn at the moment when the Middle Ages will have yielded their last sigh in their death throes; resurrection is the daughter of death.

Has it not been said: "I shall engrave my law in their entrails, and I shall write in their hearts."

And has Christ not said: "I have other ewes that are not of this flock."

All the expressions of intimate beliefs tend to summarize themselves in a symbol that is formed in silence, in the midst of terrible agitations of human society; and a few sounds of that future symbol are already beginning to mingle with the funeral knell of the dying Middle Ages.

Hebal does not seek out these theurgies, these magical and superstitious sciences, which, at the end of a religious cycle, attempt to substitute themselves for faith.

He knows very well that the human species is not giving birth to a new religion, because he knows that everything is in Christianity, that Christianity has said everything.

All the Christian communions are gravitating toward a Catholic unity; the time has come when all heresies will confess their insufficiency.

It is in vain that, in the metropolis of civilization, the sign of the promise has been outraged; the civilizing cross will reign over the world.

Greece, Belgium and Poland have demanded the liberty promised to the children of the faith—and look at the miracles that have been produced! Will their renown be immortal palms for as many heroes?

A voice, the ardent prayer of a entire people demanding baptism in blood, rises toward the heights of heaven, toward the mother of Christ.

"Let Poland, which calls you her Queen, which has so often been the firmest support of Christianity, flourish again under the protection of the Holy Gospel, and also be the aegis of the liberty of peoples. Holy Virgin, if the All-Powerful has decided, in his profound wisdom, that our entire Christian fatherland must suffer a martyr's death, like your Son, let it glory be part of the eternal glory of the world!"

Hebal sees once again Sagonte and Saragossa, Thermopylae and Missolonghi, and the rock of Caledonia, and the bloody division of Poland, the sad conclusion to a beautiful history that is beginning again.

Let civilization be saved once more!

Will Italy not conquer its independence, and will the Iberian peninsula not enter into the law of progress?

The eternal city knows that a new reign is promised for it; the Roman pontificate will declare the traditions of which it is the custodian.

The peoples will no longer be penned up according to the caprice of conquests or politics. Three limits will be recognized to mark the diversity of nations: mores, languages and geographical basins. And the natural lines will not harm the great unity of the human species, expressed by the universal religion.

All general sympathies and all the sympathies of races are manifest again as in primitive times; it is the certain sign of an immense regeneration.

And Russia will cease to be a European power.

A mission will be accorded to it to stir up Asia.

How many more times will Austria be camped on the banks of the Brenta and the Po?

England will rip apart the last teguments of the powerful chrysalis.

In the same way that France and Europe want to act as one person, the entire world, in its turn, will want to do so.

Another curtain is torn away, another seal is broken.

And the past recounts the future.

And a voice makes itself heard: Who will tell the future?

Europe, then, reconstitutes itself.

And a general frisson is felt throughout Creation.

The blood that was shed on Golgotha finally proclaims the abolition of the death penalty, and declares the impiety of war. And solidarity become charity.

The law is founded on the identity of human essence.

Christianity achieves its evolution; it reigns over the world, but it is a peaceful reign.

And Christianity, identical to itself, accomplishes its promises in all its traditions, which are the general traditions of the human race.

Perfectibility emerges from rehabilitation.

The successive ordeals have led to emancipation.

The Occident triumphs. Now the Orient is shaken up and loses consciousness of its immobility.

Islam succumbs in the struggle.

Even China become progressive.

The Ganges is crossed.

Everywhere, the glare of dogma extinguishes the uncertain gleams of myth; traditions are resplendent above and beyond the condescension of symbols.

And at the remotest point of the future, at the limit of the final horizon of humankind, human beings complete the creation of the earth. By means of a new magism they spiritualize nature.

The animals disappear, for all life has become, by assimilation, human life.

Thus are all the successive animalities that have preceded humankind summarize one another successively; everything has ended up being subsumed in humankind, the final term of Creation for the globe of the earth.

Antistrophe

Hebal believes that he is witnessing the death-throes of the immense universe.

The laws that made its harmony seem to have ceased.

And yet the celestial bodies continue to follow their ellipses, traced since the origin of things, in silence. But the earth, the earth alone, no longer knows where its equator is or where its poles are. It totters on its axis. Its atmosphere has become fatal again. All life is perishing, as in the days of the Deluge. Hebal feels himself dying in the bosom of that universal anguish. His soul, detached from his mortal envelope,

312

floats over that vast ruination; it prepares to contemplate a new act of supreme power. The earth, an extinct globe devoid of life, vegetable or animal, is hurled into another corner of space.

At a sign from the supreme power the entire human race awakes from death.

Humans emerge from the bowels of the earth, from places that were mountains, valleys or deep sea-beds. They raise themselves upright, and do not recognize either the earth or the heavens, for everything has changed. Hebal puts on for the last time the garment of dust that he had just quit. He finds himself in the midst of the multitude that is the entire human race.

And the beasts were roaring in the last limits of the Creation that no longer was. And the domestic animals, and the mute fish, and the birds, were quivering as if touched by a galvanic rod. But for the animal races it was only an apparent resurrection, for humans alone were really resuscitated. But the immaterial was not to be annihilated, and all life had taken refuge in human life.

What a spectacle!

The human species, the only subsisting form, awaking from death, and setting out, as Job once did, to interrogate the Creator, the Creator whose work is about to perish! So many generations speaking with a unanimous cry, having become an articulate voice, a single voice, the voice of universal humankind; and that voice is a groan, which contains the image and the memory of all human calamities from the beginning to the end.

And that groaning voice of anguish and death, says:

"Behold the earth that was given to me as a heritage!

"Behold the earth that I watered with my sweat, that I bathed with my blood, that I have kneaded with my tears!

"Behold the earth as it has been made by deluges, tempests, volcanoes, scourges, cataclysms and the unfruitful labor of humans!

"I have struggled against the forces of nature; I have struggled against the elements; I have made the soil and the climates! The forces of nature have tamed me; the elements have vanquished me; the soil and the climates have risen up against me!

"I was dust and I have become dust again!

"And my life has been nothing but a battle, and anguish.

"Why so many calamities, so many crimes, so many dolors?

"Why war, devastations, slavery, castes and classes? Why human sacrifices, superstitions, infamies? Why have innocent young women and chaste spouses been profaned?"

And all of that cry of universal humankind seemed to be summarized in the cry that escaped the Mediator on Golgotha: "Why have you forsaken me?"

But God does not debate as once he had debated with Job, his servant. An immense intellectual clarity descends upon the human race.

Hebal's consciousness, assimilated to the universal consciousness, has understood without any speech resounding in the expiring world.

Epode

And the earth, instead of the splendors that were inherent in the sight of mountains, waters, forests and the play of light in the clouds, is enveloped by a real light.

A clap of thunder devours or globe, which is lost in space like a diamond in the chemist's crucible.

The form that veiled matter in assimilating it disappears; matter is returned to nothingness; thus, matter and the form of matter have disappeared. Sensation is no more; the world no longer has an external vestment to appear to organs. Beings have retreated into their essences.

The dust, all the atoms of which have been mingled with animal or vegetal life, all the atoms of which were the support of sounds, odors, light and physical properties, having become

314

gaseous and ethereal, is lost in the bosom of incommensurable space, and then has no longer been.

In the realms of eternity, sight sees and is not mistaken. That which is, is not an appearance. Form is a reality; it is not transitory.

Calm of the eternal abode: analogy of that which was before Creation with that which is after Creation has disappeared.

Once again, idea contemplates idea.

The soul no longer has location.

Humankind has completed the successive ordeal that was inflicted to take the place of the ancient ordeal.

The capacity for good and evil has produced liberty in good.

The human essence has sanctified its terrestrial organs.

Humankind has accomplished the law of its being.

It knows the goal of creation.

It knows itself.

It knows God.

It identifies with the Mediator.

It no longer inhabits either the entrails of woman nor the darkness of the tomb.

It will no longer emerge from the dust in order to return to the dust.

The resemblance of God will no longer be engraved on its fugitive features.

Jesus transfigured on Tabor: such is cosmogonic humankind; such is humankind at the end of time.

And humankind was an intellectual flower growing on a terrestrial stem, an immortal flower whose foot was buried in a soil destined to perish.

Human intelligence before, intelligence afterwards.

The earth, the futile theater of human action, when phenomenal humankind is no more.

The laws of the world are troubled by the liberty of intelligent beings; the harmony of intelligent wills with the ultimate will is reestablished.

But other events have taken place before the ultimate event. The Mediator has judged the living and the dead.

Centuries have been heaped up on centuries, and it has not been granted to Hebal to see the last.

And it is only on the last day of the last century that the Sin of Man has appeared as on Tabor. And, no longer an ironic speech, the word of truth has said: "Behold the man!"

The Story

That strange contemplation ended for Hebal and he heard nine o'clock chime.

His voyage, which had embraced the entire duration of the ages from the beginning to the end, had been accomplished in the time that it took the clock to play the tune of the *Ave Maria*.

Thus, his magnetic reverie, composed of all the dreams of a life magnetic itself, of a life that, for several years, had so often been a kind of habitual dreams, that last reverie, which was an active epic, the plastic intuition of human destinies in their magnificent unity, had commenced with the tune of the *Ave Maria* and finished with it.

And he experienced a great fatigue. He did not have the time to recount what had happened to him, and no one around him suspected it.

And he had not been able to recount all that he had seen, and he had not been able to describe al that he had felt, for successive speech is impotent with regard to such an instantaneity.

And he was not even certain of the exactitude of his language; he had passed too abruptly from the region of the mind to the region of form.

And he rendered the last sigh in pronouncing the word *eternity*.

He had sensed that every human life is the summary of all of human destiny, and that a human life can only summarize itself at the palingenetic moment of death.

At that moment, undoubtedly, all the curtains have been raised for him, all the seals have been broken, and he has had the true sentiment of things of which he had previously had an obscure sentiment.

The inspiration marked a visible trace on his visage, but that definitive inspiration was unable to produce any other external expression than a fugitive trace on his features, soon extinguished.

317

Now the tune of *Ave Maria*, which had lulled his ear during his rapid voyage in the regions of the mind, seemed to rest again upon his face; for it is the amicable sign of Mediation, and Mediation is the key to the enigma of humanity.

Heroic Poland, you do well to invoke the mother of the Savior of humankind! And the virgin *par excellence* is human will absorbed in the divine will.

The Church has fixed for 25 March the celebration of that great mystery, the mystery of the assimilation of the human will to the divine will; that is the feast it names the feast of the Annunciation; and it is the day of that festival that Poland entire has said, like a single human being prostrate at the foot of the holy altar, the admirable prayer whose words Hebal heard rising toward the heavens.

To give an idea of the manner in which Hebal considered time and space, here is a passage from a letter he wrote to one of his friends:

God encloses infinity within a molecule of matter. He encloses the perception of eternity in an indivisible instant. Let us represent by means of thought the tiniest insect in Creation. Our eyes cannot perceive it; the most powerful microscope can scarcely show it to us. And yet there is a life there, an action, a locomotive faculty. That insect has been tinier still, since it has been born, since it has developed. That is not all. A movement of circulation maintains within it that organic life so obscure for us. Some kind of fluid comes and goes throughout the apparatus of channels that only analogy demonstrates; for our eyes, aided by the most powerful instrument, stop at the external form of such an animal. It is, however, true that the fiber of that being has a location in space, and that every movement of circulation that operates within it has a location in time. If it has eyes itself, and that is incontestable, how can the extreme tenuousness of the organ be conceived? How can an idea be formed of the molecule of light that can awaken the sense of sight within it? How can the objects that it sees be

318

imagined, which it attempts to reach, the circle of which forms the entire sphere in which it stirs imperceptibly? Its most extensive horizon is doubtless circumscribed within a space that, in a sense, does not exist for us; but for it, as for us, light travels at sixty-six thousand leagues a second before reaching its eye coloring the objects that limit its narrow horizon. But again, every molecule of light that penetrates such an eye, has a location in space, and every span traveled by it must be traveled in a time that needs to be repeated a hundred and sixty-five million times to make up a second.

Now suppose a human intelligence with the faulty of arriving at that appreciation of time and space. Penetrate further into the hypothesis: suppose a human intelligence capable of a rapidity of conception analogous to the rapidity of sensations that is required to appreciate such measurements of time and space. It follows that the intelligence in question would have, within a second, a succession of thoughts equal to all those that human intelligence in general could produce, in a state of wakefulness lasting at least four months; a minute would then be equivalent to twenty years of a life spent in wakefulness and meditation—a continuous and uninterrupted meditation. Furthermore, I believe that I am timid in my calculation. Thus, all historical times, whatever limit you care to assign to hem, could be encompassed within a few hours.

It is easy to see that the hypothesis is not exhausted.

In another letter, he wrote:

The miracle of Joshua is a theosophical miracle.

"And the sun stood still, and the moon stayed, until the people had avenged themselves upon their enemies. Is not this written in the book of Jasher?" (Joshua 10:13)

I do not want to go into the theory of miracles in general.

I only want to say that the examination of Joshua's, recounted according to tradition, as the words of the Bible itself indicate well enough, could give rise to a philosophical thesis on objective and phenomenal time, and subjective an intellectual time.

Here something happened to a multitude that ordinarily happens to a single person, albeit in very rarely circumstances. In fact, it is the very rare event of an action being accomplished simultaneously with the thought. Then the movement of the external world seems to stop.

The judges of Galileo, and Galileo himself, would have been most embarrassed by it.

Thus the miracle of Joshua also gives rise to an examination of the power of an individual acting on other individuals and on things.

Joshua is a powerful will forcing other wills to condense successive actions into a single action, an instantaneous action.

The inspiration that makes him command the sun to stop is authority pushed to its highest energy; it transforms an army into an exterminating whirlwind.

The laws of God are eternal. The laws of nature established by God are immutable.

Miracles are neither a suspension of those laws or an exception to them.

If a miracle is a Providential coup d'état, it is a coup d'état that results from those same laws, as dictatorship is contained in the ancient Roman constitution.

The theosophical miracle of Joshua is not an isolated fact in the history of the human mind.

Indian books offer us several examples of that condensation of events into a very limited time, which gives to certain times the prerogatives of eternity.

A terrible battle between the Kurus and the Pandus was to decide the fate of all India. The two armies confronted one another. Already arrows were flying through the air to begin the battle.

At that moment, Krishna, who is the Divinity in a human form, and Arjun, his cherished disciple, both mounted on chariots, emerged from the ranks of the armies, one on each side, and met in the space that remained free before the hand-to-hand engagement.

Such is the famous episode in the Mahabharata.

That episode, known by the name of Bhaghavad Gita, is, I believe, the most complete of the ancient doctrine of the Hindus on religion and morality. Krishna instructs his disciple in that which it is most important for him to know: the nature of the soul, human destiny, the duties that he must fulfill toward his fellows, and toward the Divinity; in sum, the route that he must follow to achieve eternal happiness.

It is evident that, in the mind of the poet, that astonishing dialogue is a contemplation without any appreciable duration of time, for an entire ay would scarcely have been sufficient, in solitude and with total liberty of mind for such a conversation to have taken place between the two interlocutors—which is to say, between God and the valiant archer.

SF & FANTASY

Henri Allorge. *The Great Cataclysm*
Guy d'Armen. *Doc Ardan: The City of Gold and Lepers*
G.-J. Arnaud. *The Ice Company*
Charles Asselineau. *The Double Life*
Cyprien Bérard. *The Vampire Lord Ruthwen*
Aloysius Bertrand. *Gaspard de la Nuit*
Richard Bessière. *The Gardens of the Apocalypse*
Albert Bleunard. *Ever Smaller*
Félix Bodin. *The Novel of the Future*
Alphonse Brown. *City of Glass*
André Caroff. *The Terror of Madame Atomos; Miss Atomos; The Return of Madame Atomos; The Mistake of Madame Atomos; The Monsters of Madame Atomos*
Félicien Champsaur. *The Human Arrow*
Didier de Chousy. *Ignis*
Captain Danrit. *Undersea Odyssey*
C. I. Defontenay. *Star (Psi Cassiopeia)*
Charles Derennes. *The People of the Pole*
Georges Dodds (anthologist). *The Missing Link*
Harry Dickson. *The Heir of Dracula*
Jules Dornay. *Lord Ruthven Begins*
Alfred Driou. *The Adventures of a Parisian Aeronaut*
Sâr Dubnotal *vs. Jack the Ripper*
Alexandre Dumas. *The Return of Lord Ruthven*
Renée Dunan. *Baal*
J.-C. Dunyach. *The Night Orchid; The Thieves of Silence*
Henri Duvernois. *The Man Who Found Himself*
Achille Eyraud. *Voyage to Venus*
Henri Falk. *The Age of Lead*
Paul Féval. *Anne of the Isles; Knightshade; Revenants; Vampire City; The Vampire Countess; The Wandering Jew's Daughter*
Paul Féval, *fils. Felifax, the Tiger-Man*
Charles de Fieux. *Lamékis*
Arnould Galopin. *Doctor Omega; Doctor Omega & The Shadowmen*
G.L. Gick. *Harry Dickson and the Werewolf of Rutherford Grange*
Edmond Haraucourt. *Illusions of Immortality*
Nathalie Henneberg. *The Green Gods*
V. Hugo, P. Foucher & P. Meurice. *The Hunchback of Notre-Dame*
Michel Jeury. *Chronolysis*

Gustave Kahn. *The Tale of Gold and Silence*
Gérard Klein. *The Mote in Time's Eye*
Jean de La Hire. *Enter the Nyctalope; The Nyctalope on Mars; The Nyctalope vs. Lucifer; The Nyctalope Steps In; Night of the Nyctalope*
Etienne-Léon de Lamothe-Langon. *The Virgin Vampire*
André Laurie. *Spiridon*
Gabriel de Lautrec. *The Vengeance of the Oval Portrait*
Georges Le Faure & Henri de Graffigny. *The Extraordinary Adventures of a Russian Scientist Across the Solar System* (2 vols.)
Gustave Le Rouge. *The Vampires of Mars The Dominion of the World* (w/Gustave Guitton) (4 vols.)
Jules Lermina. *Mysteryville; Panic in Paris; To-Ho and the Gold Destroyers; The Secret of Zippelius*
Jean-Marc & Randy Lofficier. *Edgar Allan Poe on Mars; The Katrina Protocol; Pacifica; Robonocchio; Tales of the Shadowmen 1-8*
Xavier Mauméjean. *The League of Heroes*
Joseph Méry. *The Tower of Destiny*
Hippolyte Mettais. *The Year 5865*
José Moselli. *Illa's End*
John-Antoine Nau. *Enemy Force*
Marie Nizet. *Captain Vampire*
C. Nodier, A. Beraud & Toussaint-Merle. *Frankenstein*
Henri de Parville. *An Inhabitant of the Planet Mars*
Gaston de Pawlowski. *Journey to the Land of the 4th Dimension*
Georges Pellerin. *The World in 2000 Years*
Pierre Pelot. *The Child Who Walked on the Sky*
J. Polidori, C. Nodier, E. Scribe. *Lord Ruthven the Vampire*
P.-A. Ponson du Terrail. *The Vampire and the Devil's Son*
Henri de Régnier. *A Surfeit of Mirrors*
Maurice Renard. *The Blue Peril; Doctor Lerne; The Doctored Man; A Man Among the Microbes; The Master of Light*
Jean Richepin. *The Wing*
Albert Robida. *The Adventures of Saturnin Farandoul; The Clock of the Centuries; Chalet in the Sky*
J.-H. Rosny Aîné. *Helgvor of the Blue River; The Givreuse Enigma; The Mysterious Force; The Navigators of Space; Vamireh; The World of the Variants; The Young Vampire*
Marcel Rouff. *Journey to the Inverted World*
Han Ryner. *The Superhumans*
Brian Stableford. *The New Faust at the Tragicomique; The Empire of the Necromancers (The Shadow of Frankenstein; Frankenstein and*

the Vampire Countess; Frankenstein in London); Sherlock Holmes &
The Vampires of Eternity; The Stones of Camelot; The Wayward
Muse. (anthologist) *The Germans on Venus; News from the Moon;*
The Supreme Progress; The World Above the World; Nemoville;
Investigations of the Future
Jacques Spitz. *The Eye of Purgatory*
Kurt Steiner. *Ortog*
Eugène Thébault. *Radio-Terror*
C.-F. Tiphaigne de La Roche. *Amilec*
Théo Varlet. *The Xenobiotic Invasion; Timeslip Troopers* (w/André
Blandin); *The Martian Epic* (w/Octave Joncquel)
Paul Vibert. *The Mysterious Fluid*
Villiers de l'Isle-Adam. *The Scaffold; The Vampire Soul*
Philippe Ward. *Artahe*
Philippe Ward & Sylvie Miller. *The Song of Montségur*

MYSTERIES & THRILLERS

M. Allain & P. Souvestre. *The Daughter of Fantômas*
A. Anicet-Bourgeois, Lucien Dabril. *Rocambole*
A. Bernède. *Judex* (w/Louis Feuillade)
A. Bisson & G. Livet. *Nick Carter vs. Fantômas*
V. Darlay & H. de Gorsse. *Lupin vs. Holmes: The Stage Play*
Paul Féval. *Gentlemen of the Night; John Devil; The Black Coats*
('Salem Street; The Invisible Weapon; The Parisian Jungle; The
Companions of the Treasure; Heart of Steel; The Cadet Gang; The
Sword-Swallower)
Emile Gaboriau. *Monsieur Lecoq*
Steve Leadley. *Sherlock Holmes: The Circle of Blood*
Maurice Leblanc. *Arsène Lupin vs. Countess Cagliostro; Lupin vs.*
Holmes (The Blonde Phantom; The Hollow Needle); The Many Faces
of Arsène Lupin
Gaston Leroux. *Chéri-Bibi; The Phantom of the Opera; Rouletabille*
& the Mystery of the Yellow Room
Richard Marsh. *The Complete Adventures of Judith Lee*
William Patrick Maynard. *The Terror of Fu Manchu; The Destiny of*
Fu Manchu
Frank J. Morlock. *Sherlock Holmes: The Grand Horizontals; Sher-*
lock Holmes vs Jack the Ripper
Antonin Reschal. *The Adventures of Miss Boston*
P. de Wattyne & Y. Walter. *Sherlock Holmes vs. Fantômas*

David White. *Fantômas in America*

SCREENPLAYS

Mike Baron. *The Iron Triangle*
Emma Bull & Will Shetterly. *Nightspeeder; War for the Oaks*
Gerry Conway & Roy Thomas. *Doc Dynamo*
Steve Englehart. *Majorca*
James Hudnall. *The Devastator*
Jean-Marc & Randy Lofficier. *Royal Flush*
J.-M. & R. Lofficier & Marc Agapit. *Despair*
J.-M. & R. Lofficier & Joël Houssin. *City*
Andrew Paquette. *Peripheral Vision*
R. Thomas, J. Hendler & L. Sprague de Camp. *Rivers of Time*

NON-FICTION

Stephen R. Bissette. *Blur 1-5. Green Mountain Cinema 1; Teen Angels*
Win Scott Eckert. *Crossovers* (2 vols.)
Jean-Marc & Randy Lofficier. *Shadowmen* (2 vols.)
Randy Lofficier. *Over Here*

HEXAGON COMICS

Franco Frescura & Luciano Bernasconi. *Wampus*
Franco Frescura & Giorgio Trevisan. *CLASH*
L. Bernasconi, J.-M. Lofficier & Juan Roncagliolo Berger. *Phenix*
Claude Legrand, J.-M. Lofficier & L. Bernasconi. *Kabur*
Franco Oneta. *Zembla*
L. Buffolente, Lofficier & J.-J. Dzialowski. *Strangers: Homicron*
Danilo Grossi. *Strangers: Jaydee*
Claude Legrand & Luciano Bernasconi. *Strangers: Starlock*

ART BOOKS

Jean-Pierre Normand. *Science Fiction Illustrations*
Raven Okeefe. *Raven's L'il Critters*
Randy Lofficier & Raven OKeefe. *If Your Possum Go Daylight...*
Daniele Serra. *Illusions*

www.ingramcontent.com/pod-product-compliance
Lightning Source LLC
Chambersburg PA
CBHW022221010726

47493CB00002B/543